THE THREE
CROWNS

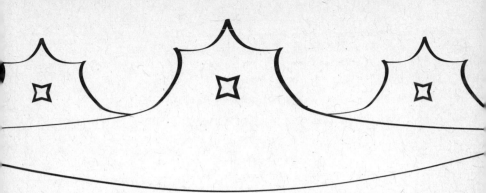

THE THREE CROWNS

The Story of William and Mary

JEAN PLAIDY

THREE RIVERS PRESS
NEW YORK

Copyright © 1965 by Jean Plaidy

Excerpt from *Royal Sisters* copyright © 1966 by Jean Plaidy, copyright
renewed 1994 by Mark Hamilton

Published in the United States by Three Rivers Press, an imprint of the
Crown Publishing Group, a division of Random House, Inc., New York.

www.crownpublishing.com

Three Rivers Press and the Tugboat design are registered trademarks of
Random House, Inc.

Originally published in hardcover in Great Britain by Robert Hale
Limited, London, in 1965, and in hardcover in the United States by G.P.
Putnam's Sons, New York, in 1977.

This book contains an excerpt from the forthcoming Three Rivers Press
reprint of *Royal Sisters* by Jean Plaidy, which was originally published
as *The Haunted Sisters* by Robert Hale Limited, London, in 1966. This
excerpt has been set for this edition only and may not reflect the final
content of the forthcoming edition.

Library of Congress Cataloging-in-Publication Data
Plaidy, Jean, 1906–1993.
The three crowns: the story of William and Mary/by Jean Plaidy —
1st trade pbk. ed.
p. cm.
1. William III, King of England, 1650-1702—Fiction. 2. Mary II,
Queen of England, 1662-1694—Fiction. 3. Great Britain—Kings and
rulers—Fiction. 4. Queens—Great Britain—Fiction. I. Title.
PR6015.I3T457 2010
823'.914—dc22
2010010945

ISBN 978-0-307-34624-7

Printed in the United States of America

Design by Maria Elias

10 9 8 7 6 5 4 3 2 1

First Three Rivers Press Edition

Contents

THE BIRTH OF MARY
1

THE FAMILY OF YORK
8

FAITH AND DEATH
38

THE BRIDE FROM MODENA
69

THE PASSIONATE FRIENDSHIP
110

THE THREE CROWNS
147

YOUNG WILLIAM
151

THE ORANGE BRIDEGROOM
181

THE RELUCTANT BRIDE
198

AT THE ORANGE COURT
232

THE UNFAITHFUL HUSBAND
257

THE ZUYLESTEIN SCANDAL
274

ROMANCE AT THE HAGUE
287

THE WIFE AND THE MISTRESS
309

THE VITAL QUESTION
332

THE CONFLICT OF LOYALTIES
346

KING WILLIAM AND
QUEEN MARY
355

THE THREE CROWNS

THE BIRTH OF MARY

*T*hroughout the day the sounds of rejoicing had echoed in St. James's Palace. All the bells in London were ringing to welcome the new Queen; and by night the light from a hundred bonfires was reflected in the April sky.

The King continued to sup with Lady Castlemaine each night, a fact which made many shake their heads and ask themselves what wedded happiness there could be for the Princess from Portugal, in spite of the fact that her bridegroom was reckoned to be the most charming Prince in the world, having inherited the gaiety, wit, tolerance, kindliness and, alas, the sensuality of his grandfather, the great Henri Quatre of France, these many years since murdered by the knife of François Ravaillac.

The feastings, the ceremonies and pageants delighted the people of London—always ready to admire a King who had made England merry after years of puritan rule. They had jeered as the effigies of past heroes were hanged and insulted, while they cheered when the merry, ugly, fascinating King moved among them, with his band of hilarious-mannered, elegantly attired, rakish courtiers who attempted to become as notorious as Charles himself. And there were the ladies. Always the ladies! "Who will entertain him to supper tonight—and after?" asked his subjects indulgently. Stories of his escapades never failed to amuse. He was amorously insatiable, approachable, charming—all that a nation could ask of a King returned to his kingdom after being forced, by a dreary Parliament, to live in exile. And now there was a bride from Portugal.

At least one woman in St. James's Palace was not concerned with the festivities. Anne Hyde paced up and down her apartment, her hands on her heavy body, and all her thoughts were for the child who would soon be born. She hoped fervently for a son—Anne Hyde's son, who could, in time, be King of England. Not that it was likely, especially now that the King had a bride and several illegitimate children already to prove his virility. There was young Monmouth for one, a lusty fellow whom many—Charles included, so it was said—wished was legitimate. But Anne's child would be in the line of succession, and until Charles and his bride produced a child, might be considered a possible heir to the throne.

She walked to a mirror which hung on the wall; it was so long that she could see her reflection from head to feet. She grimaced at the ungainly sight. She had never been a beauty at her best. All the more reason to be congratulated on having succeeded in making a marriage with James, Duke of York and brother to the King.

One of her women came into the apartment.

"Your Grace . . ." she began anxiously.

Anne shook her head. "Leave me. I will call you when I need you."

"But . . ."

Anne waved her hand. "I shall know in good time. Everything is going as it should. I wish you could shut out some of the noise from the streets."

"Ah, Your Grace, there is so much noise. The people are mad with excitement. The crowds in the Mall are so great that there is danger of being trodden underfoot. I saw His Majesty." The woman smiled. "He bowed and smiled at me . . ."

Anne's lips turned up at the corners sardonically. The King had a way of looking at a woman—any woman—and forever after that woman believed that he had been as excited by the encounter as she was. Charles was never too pressed to bestow those smiles on any female subject. He was a natural exuberant lover of women, and although James lacked that overwhelming charm, he was enough like his brother to make a wife watchful.

"I've no doubt he did," answered Anne abruptly.

"And my lord Duke rode with him . . . a fine figure of a man, Your Grace. And getting more and more like His Majesty every day."

"I trust not in every way," retorted Anne.

"Oh, Your Grace!" The slight titter, the shine of the eyes, and the parted lips, meant that she was thinking of an occasional encounter with one of the royal brothers. Charles might have kissed her. Had James? "The Duke is such a devoted husband. As for His Majesty, his time has come. Although they say the Portuguese Princess . . ."

"Is not worthy of him?" interrupted Anne. "I'll swear that's what they say."

"Doubtless she will look magnificent in her jewels, Your Grace, but who would not?"

Anne shrugged her shoulders. "I will call you when the pains begin in earnest."

The woman bowed and retired. They were talking about Catherine of Braganza as once they had talked of Anne Hyde. So Catherine was plain. Strange that these two men—the King of England and his brother the Duke of York, both noted for their susceptibilities where women were concerned—should have plain wives. Not so strange that Charles should, for his was a marriage of diplomacy, uniting England with Portugal, and Catherine had brought a desirable dowry. But the Duke had married for love—secretly and in great haste—Anne Hyde, who had been at the time of the marriage so far gone in pregnancy that it had been necessary to hurry on the ceremony.

That had happened almost two years ago and the child who had made the hasty marriage necessary was now dead. But James did not regret his marriage, she was sure. His fidelity was doubtful but she, Anne Hyde, was certain that although he might find women at his brother's Court more beautiful, he would never find one who meant to him what Anne Hyde did; not for any other would he have faced the wrath of his family as he had for her; and as long as she did not put too tight a rein on his extramarital adventures he was hers to command. She knew well enough that it was folly to expect fidelity from the grandsons of Henri Quatre.

Now, while he rode with his brother and acknowledged the cheers of the people—for his successes at sea had won him fame and popularity second only to that of the King—he would be thinking of her, praying for a boy as she was; anxiously thinking of her travail. He was as good a husband as she could hope him to be.

The pains were more definite now and she wondered whether to call her women, who were waiting with the midwife in the anteroom; this was rare privacy; and she owed it to what was happening outside; how many of those who must remain in the palace wished they were in the streets joining in the revels?

She began to think of her first encounter with James. He had been about twenty-two at the time, she about nineteen and in the service of James's sister, the Princess of Orange. That had been before the Restoration when Charles and James had been two penniless princes wandering about Europe looking for friends who would help them regain their kingdom. James and his mother had arranged to meet the Princess of Orange in Paris and when she, Anne Hyde, had traveled there with the Princess from Breda, the Duke had noticed her. But he noticed all young women; and it was only later when he came to Breda to see his sister that the irresistible passion flared up between them.

"I'll marry you," James had said; and she had believed him, but she knew that the daughter of Edward Hyde, one of the King's most trusted ministers, now Earl of Clarendon, was obviously no match for the heir presumptive to the British Crown; and when she had learned that soon there would be an end of Puritan rule in Britain, that royal Charles would be welcomed back as King and that James would go with him, her hopes of marriage were slight. She had believed then that a Princess would have been found for James and that his lightly given promise of marriage should be broken.

She shivered even now, remembering May 1660, the return of Charles to England, and herself ready to give birth in five months' time! She believed she would love James to the end of her life for the attitude he took at that time. He declared he would brave his brother, her father, his formidable mother, and all the world for her sake and that of their child; and he had meant it. He had his small share of Stuart charm, and although he did not make promises as readily as his elder brother, he tried to keep those he made; and on a September night—six weeks before her son was born, Dr. Joseph Crowther had married them in her father's house in the Strand.

But that had not been the end of danger. The Queen-Mother had raged against the match—so had Anne's ex-mistress, the Princess of Orange; as for Anne's father, he had been as incensed as any, declaring that she deserved to be taken to the Tower and sentenced to death. How unnatural a father, to fear so much for his own safety, that he was ready to sacrifice his daughter!

There had been one who had taken the situation more lightly, and it was fortunate for her that he was the most powerful of them all. The marriage was made, said Charles, with a shrug; his sister-in-law was an intelligent woman; James wanted her for his wife. Let the matter rest there.

He was ready to embrace her and welcome her into the family.

She smiled now, thinking of him, with his clever, swarthy face, ready to light up with appreciation for a handsome woman, or to give a kind and careless smile to any who wanted it.

It was small wonder that Anne's thoughts went back to that time of terror now that she was to bear another child. She remembered lying in her sickbed after her confinement when the news had been brought to her that her husband was in a state of frenzy because he had heard a rumor that the child was not his. Sir Charles Berkeley, the Captain of her husband's guard, had declared that he was the father, that he was ready to claim it and make Anne his wife.

How she had hated the lying Berkeley! He had desired her and because she had refused his attentions, this was his revenge. So distressed had she been that her attendants had feared for her life; and in her despair she had begged the Bishop of Winchester to come to her, and before him and the Duchess of Ormonde she had taken a solemn vow swearing that Berkeley had never been her lover and that the father of her child was James, Duke of York. She might have died then; she would always believe that she had been near to death; but into her bedchamber had come the King, his smile kind, his eyes troubled and she knew that he was thinking: "God's fish, what does my brother see in this woman!" But with what gratitude did she kiss the long white fingers which were held out to her.

"Never fear, sister. You have been wronged, but we'll put the scandalizers to shame." And because he had stood beside her, events had turned in her favor. "Get well," he commanded, "and join us for the Christmas festivities."

She had wondered what her reception would be. Because the King had shown her kindness, the Court would—publicly; but that virago, Henrietta-Maria, had insisted that she would not receive her, nor would the Princess of Orange; and they would have their followers. Moreover, James, beset by fears and suspicions, did not come near her, and that was the worst blow of all. She had often since wondered what would have happened if the Princess of Orange had not been struck down with the smallpox. She had died in December, just as the Christmas festivities were beginning; but on her deathbed she made a confession that she had slandered Anne Hyde; and Berkeley, fearing that she had betrayed his duplicity, had presented himself to James and confessed that he had lied.

Berkeley was subtle enough to make a good case for himself. "Your Highness," he had pleaded, "I was anxious to serve you, and greatly fearing the effects of this marriage on your future, hastened to break it. I would have married the lady Anne and cared for the child for your sake. And it is because I see how heart-wounded you are that I make my confession."

James was so delighted by this confession of devotion that, with typical Stuart good nature instead of taking revenge on Berkeley, he remembered how they had always stood together in battle and how firm their

friendship had always been. He came rejoicing to Anne, begged her forgiveness forever doubting her; and all was well.

And now that child was dead, but she was about to bring another into
the world.

But this child would arrive with little notoriety, for the King had a
wife and all believed that in a year the marriage would be fruitful; and the
child Anne Hyde was bearing on this April day would merely be the cousin
of a King.

Now she must retire to her bed for the pains were beginning in earnest.

On the last day of April a daughter was born to the Duke and Duchess
of York; she was christened Mary after her Aunt Mary of Orange and her
ancestress, Mary Queen of Scots.

In the streets the bonfires burned and the people rejoiced; but it was
not the birth of the little girl that the people were celebrating; it was the
coming of a new Queen to England—a wife for their merry King, who,
they believed, would soon give them the boy who would be heir to the
throne.

It seemed in that light that little Mary's birth was of no great significance to any but her loving parents.

THE FAMILY OF YORK

*I*n the nursery of their grandfather's Twickenham mansion the two little girls of the Duke and Duchess of York played contentedly together. Three-year-old Mary and one-year-old Anne were completely ignorant of the reason why they had been sent to Twickenham; they did not know that the capital of their uncle's kingdom was becoming more and more deserted every day, that the shops of the merchants were gradually closing, that people walked hastily through the narrow streets, their mouths covered that they might not breathe the pestilential air, their eyes averted from those tragic doors on which red crosses were marked. They did not know that the King and the Court had left the capital and by night the death cart patrolled the streets to the cry of "Bring out your dead."

They were, Mary told Anne, in Grandpapa Clarendon's house because it was in the country which was better than being in the town.

Anne listened, smiling placidly, not caring where she was as long as there was plenty to eat.

Mary watched her cramming the sweetmeats into her little round mouth, her fat fingers searching for the next before the last was finished.

"Greedy little sister," said Mary affectionately.

Mary had felt conscious of being the elder sister ever since she had stood sponsor for Anne at the latter's baptism. That occasion had been the most important of her life so far and remained her most vivid experience. Her father had impressed upon her the significance of her role and she had stood very solemnly beside her fellow sponsor, the young wife of the Duke of Monmouth, determined then that she would always look after Anne.

Looking after Anne was easy, for there was nothing Anne liked so much as being looked after. Everything Mary possessed she wanted to share with Anne. She had told her sister that she might hold her little black rabbit, stroke its fur, even call it *her* rabbit if she wished. Anne smiled her placid smile; but in fact she would rather have a share of Mary's sweetmeats than her toys and pets.

Mary thought Anne the prettiest little girl in the kingdom, with her light brown hair falling about her bright pink face, and her round mouth and plump little hands. She herself was darker, less plump and more serious. Having to look after Anne had made her so.

Two of the nursery women stood in a corner watching them.

"Where would you find a prettier pair in the whole of England?" one demanded of the other.

"It's small wonder that their parents dote on them."

"Mary is the Duke's favorite."

"And Anne the Duchess's."

"Often I've seen my lady Duchess take the pretty creature on to her lap and feed her with chocolates. It's easy to see from where the little lady Anne gets *her* sweet tooth."

The two women put their heads closer together. "My lady Duchess is become so fat. If she does not take care . . ."

The other nodded. "The Duke will look elsewhere? He does that already, but never seriously. She leads him by the nose."

"She's clever, I'll admit that. It surprises me that she gives way to her love of eating. Did you see the new traveling costumes they were wearing when they left London? The Queen looked well enough in hers . . . but you should have seen my lady Castlemaine. She was magnificent! Velvet coat and cap . . . like a man's . . . and yet unlike and somehow being more like a woman's garb for being so like a man's. Most becoming. But our Duchess! I heard some of them sniggering behind their hands. More like a barrel than a Duchess they were saying."

The other said: "I wonder when the Court will return to London?"

They were both sober.

"I hear it grows worse. They say that now grass grows between the cobbles."

They looked at each other and shivered.

Then one said solemnly: "We are fortunate to be here in the country."

"It's a little too near London to please me, for they say it is spreading."

"Where will it end? Do you believe it is because God is angry with the King's way of life?"

"Hush your mouth. It won't do to say such things."

"Well, married three years and no sign of an heir and now this terrible plague. Why if our Duke and Duchess were to have a boy, do you realize he could be King of England? Imagine us. In the nursery of the King of England."

"And if they shouldn't and the King not either . . . well, then, our little Lady Mary would be Queen."

They stared at the children with fresh respect.

The one grimaced. "That's if we all survive this terrible plague."

"Oh, we're safe enough in Twickenham."

A third woman joined them. It was obvious from her expression that she brought news which she knew was of the greatest importance.

"Haven't you heard. Yesterday one of the stewards complained of pains. He'd been to the City."

"No! How is he now?"

"I heard that he was most unwell."

The two women looked at each other in dismay; the shadow of the plague had come to pleasant Twickenham.

That night the steward died, and the next day two more of the Earl of Clarendon's servants fell sick. Within a few days they too were dead. Twickenham was no longer a refuge. The plague had discovered it.

When the Duke and Duchess came in haste to Twickenham there was a tremor of excitement all through the house. The Duke went straight into the nursery and picking up Mary kissed her tenderly before looking earnestly into her face.

"My little daughter is well?" he asked anxiously. "Quite well?"

"Your Grace," said her nurse, "the Lady Mary is in excellent health."

"And her sister?"

"The Lady Anne also."

"Begin preparations without delay. I wish to leave within the hour."

The Duchess was fondling Anne, feeling in the pockets of her gown for a sweetmeat to pop into that ever ready mouth.

"Well, there is no time to be lost," said the Duke.

He looked at the Duchess who had sat down heavily with Anne on her knee. She held out her arms for Mary who ran to her and was embraced while her Mother asked questions about her daughter's lessons. But Mary sensed that she was not really listening to the answers.

The Duke watched his wife and their two daughters, and in spite of his anxiety and the need to hurry he had time to remind himself that he was pleased with his marriage. Not that he was a faithful husband. Charles was furious with him at the moment, because he had tried to seduce Miss Frances Stuart whom Charles's roving eyes had selected for his own. There was not much luck in that direction, either for himself or Charles, he feared. Arabella Churchill was more amenable, so was Margaret Denham. Ah, Margaret! She was an enchanting creature. Eighteen years old and recently married to Sir John Denham who must have been over fifty and looked seventy. Denham was furious on account of this liaison, but what could he expect? The King had set the tone at Court, so no one expected his brother to live the monogamous life of a virtuous married man.

Anne objected of course, but mildly. Anne was clever; her only folly seemed to be her over-indulgence at the table. Nor was her desire to gratify a perpetual hunger obvious at the table only. In her apartments there were boxes of sweets in most drawers and on tables so that she found them at her elbow wherever she happened to be.

He had not been so unwise after all when he married Clarendon's daughter, although Clarendon was fast falling out of favor. Poor old man! He had suffered real terror at the time of the marriage and now declared that his fortunes had begun to sink ever since his headstrong daughter had married the heir presumptive to the throne.

Anne had been upbraiding him for blatantly indulging in his affair with Margaret Denham when news had reached them of the outbreak of plague in Twickenham. That had sobered them both. Of what importance was her obesity, greed, and dominating ways, or his unfaithfulness compared with the safety of their children!

Perhaps more than anything in the world, he mused, he loved his elder daughter.

"Mary," he said, "come here, my child."

He noticed with pleasure how eagerly she came to him.

"My darling," he said, "you are a big girl now, old enough to understand a great many things."

He lifted her on to his knee. She was delighted by the satin of his coat, the lace ruffles at his neck and sleeve, his long dark curls which seemed all the more wonderful because they could be taken off and put on a stand.

"We are going away, Mary."

"Now?"

"We are leaving in an hour. You will like to be with me . . . and your mother?"

"Anne is coming?"

"Certainly. You do not think we would leave Anne behind?"

She laughed with happiness; and he put his lips to the smooth cheeks. He told himself that he would rather anything happened to him than that that delicate cheek should be raged by plague spots, and a sense of urgency seized him. Every moment might be important. He would not rest until they were far away.

"Where are we going, Papa?"

"To York, my dearest, they are preparing for our departure now." He called to the nurse: "Is the baggage ready? Then begin to prepare the children. It is a long journey to York."

"But Papa," said Mary, "*you* are York."

He patted her head; even in his haste marveling at her. What Charles would give for a child like this! he thought. Even though she is a girl.

"My love, York is also a city . . . our city. And from there I shall be near the fleet and we will watch out for the wicked Dutchmen and keep them from our shores."

"Tell me about the Dutchmen, Papa."

"Later," he said. "When there is time. Now we are leaving at once. See, your nurse is waiting to dress you for the journey. Why, my little one, you and I will have many a talk in the days to come. I want you to know about what is happening to our country. You must never forget that you are my daughter and His Majesty's niece."

Mary remembered and believed herself to be the luckiest little girl in England. Her father was the best man in the world; her mother was the best mother; and in addition, she had for an uncle the one to whom everyone must bow and, she was certain although she believed it might be a secret between them, to her he was not a great King at all, only Uncle Charles, who could make her laugh and all the time wished she were his daughter instead of her father's.

It was a happy family that stayed at York during those months which followed the retreat from Twickenham.

There was reconciliation between the Duke and the Duchess, for the Duke was not near enough to his mistresses to pay court to them, which was a matter of great satisfaction to the Duchess, and since the Duke was ready to concede to her in everything but his affairs with women, the household was harmonious.

They both agreed that it was like returning to those first weeks of marriage when it had seemed the whole world was against them and they had determined to stand together whatever the consequences.

Together now they supervised the education of Mary, who, they believed, was very intelligent. The Duke liked to have her with him when he received officials from the Navy and he would often call attention to her.

"I tell you this," he said one day to Samuel Pepys, who had come to see him with some Navy estimates, "the Lady Mary of York understands much of what you are saying."

It was an exaggeration, but Mary always listened attentively, for her greatest joy was in pleasing her father.

She worked hard at her lessons so that she could have his approbation and looked forward to those hours when he came to the nursery to be with her. Often when Anne was with her mother, Mary and her father would be together, and the Duke's servants said that their master loved his daughter Mary beyond everything in the world.

One day he came to her a little sadly, and lifting her on to his knee and putting his cheek against her hair, told her that he would have to leave her. "But only for a little while," he consoled.

"Oh, Papa," she answered blankly and he wept as he kissed her.

"Listen, my little one" he went on, "Uncle Charles is in Oxford and I have to join him there because that is where the Parliament is. There is much work to do when you are a King and the brother of a King. Do you understand?"

She nodded, lacing her fingers in his and gripping them as though to indicate that she would not let him go without a struggle.

"That is good because you will have to understand the duties of kingship. Why, my love, it could so come about that you might one day be a Queen of England . . . a Queen in your own right, sweetheart. Think of that."

"And Anne?"

"Oh, Anne is your little sister. You are before her. But Uncle Charles has no son."

She was puzzled thinking of handsome Jemmy, whom she loved so much and who was known as Monmouth. She had thought he was Uncle Charles's son.

"No, he has no sons who could inherit the throne," went on her father, "so therefore if Uncle Charles died I should be King. And if I were to die . . ." She looked alarmed and he kissed her tenderly. "I shall not for years and years . . . but one day I shall be a poor old man and you will be a woman with husband and children of your own. Then, my love, if Uncle Charles had no children at all and you did not have a little brother, you could be Queen of England."

It was all very complicated to her, but he was glad he had told her; it was as well to learn as early as possible what part one might have to play in the country's affairs.

Then he changed the subject abruptly; he told her wonderful stories of how he had been a soldier in Europe and he and Uncle Charles had been two wandering exiles because the wicked Oliver Cromwell had driven them from England. He had many exciting adventures to relate; but what Mary liked best was the story of how the people decided that they wanted no more of the puritan rule and sent to Europe for the Princes. She liked to hear how he and Uncle Charles came back to England, how the bells rang out and the people strewed their way with flowers while they danced in the streets and laughed and embraced each other because England had ceased to be a somber place.

"They knew Uncle Charles would make them laugh again," said Mary.

Her father nodded. She was right. Charles had made them laugh at his witticisms, at his careless good nature, at his never ending adventures with women.

When James left soon for Oxford, Mary missed him sadly, discovering that she loved him better than anyone in the world—better than her mother, better than cousin Jemmy, better even than Anne.

Each day Mary hoped to hear that her father would be with them; she worked hard at her lessons, wishing to surprise him, and her mother was proud of her, but Mary knew that secretly she loved Anne best, although the child never made any effort to win affection; she smiled placidly at everybody, and grew fatter every day.

There were occasions when the Duke paid a visit to York and they were the happiest days for Mary. She would be at his side all through the day; and even when important people came to see him she was not dismissed. He would hold her on his knee while he talked; and she listened because she knew that was what he wanted her to do. Thus she learned a little about the wicked Dutchmen who were threatening England on the high seas; she also heard news of the terrible plague.

One day her mother sent for the little girls and taking Anne on her lap and drawing Mary into the crook of her arm, she said: "How would you like to go back home?"

Home? But this was home. Home was where her mother was, where her father came when he could escape from his duties.

"You are going to have a very happy time," explained the Duchess, popping a sweet into Anne's mouth. "You are going to live in Richmond Palace, where a nursery is being prepared for you, and you will have a lady governess and other little girls to be your companions."

Mary was a little puzzled; but her mother was smiling while Anne contentedly crunched, and later when she heard the servants talking about it and understood how happy they were to be going, as they said, "home," she was happy too.

Lady Frances Villiers, the youngest daughter of the Earl of Suffolk who had married Colonel Edward Villiers and given him a family, was congratulating herself on her appointment.

"For," she told her husband, "it seems clear that the King will never have an heir; and in that case the most important children in the country will be under my care."

The Colonel agreed that the position looked promising for the future.

"Edward and Henry are well placed at Court," went on Lady Frances, "and the girls will now have their opportunity. They will be close companions of the Lady Mary and the Lady Anne, and I shall impress upon them the importance of making that friendship firm."

"I am sure you will, my dear," her husband answered.

"In fact," went on Lady Frances, "I shall speak to Elizabeth without delay."

She sent one of her maids to find her eldest daughter and when Elizabeth stood before her she surveyed her with a certain uneasiness. Elizabeth was disquieting. Although only ten years old, she seemed already wise; she would be the eldest in the royal nursery and for that reason, as well as because of her character, would attempt to take charge.

"Elizabeth," said her mother somewhat peevishly. "Stand up straight. Don't slouch."

Elizabeth obeyed. She was graceful, but there was a cast in her eyes which gave her a sharp yet sly look.

"The Lady Mary and the Lady Anne will soon be arriving. I trust you realize the honor which the Duke and Duchess are bestowing on you by allowing you to be their companion."

"Is it an honor?" asked Elizabeth.

Yes, she was sharp, alert, and a little insolent.

"You are foolish. It is a great honor as you know well. You know the position of the Lady Mary."

"She is only a little girl . . . years younger than I."

"Now you are indeed talking like a child. The King is without heirs; the Lady Mary is the Duke's eldest daughter and he has no son. If the King has no children and the Duke no son, the Lady Mary could be Queen."

"But the King has sons, and they say . . ."

"Have done," said Lady Frances sharply. "You must remember that you are in the royal service."

"But I do not understand. *We* are the Villiers."

"Then you are more foolish than I thought. Even a child of your age should know that every family however important must take second place to royalty."

"Yet they say that my cousin Barbara Villiers is more important than Queen Catherine."

She was indeed sly? And how old? Not eleven yet. Lady Frances thought that a whipping might be good for Miss Elizabeth. She would see.

"You may go now," she said. "But remember what I have said. I should like you and the Lady Mary to be friends. Friendships made in childhood can last a lifetime. It is a good thing to remember."

"I will remember it," Elizabeth assured her.

Lady Frances, her daughters ranged about her, greeted the Princesses as they entered the Palace.

She knelt and put her arms about them. "Let us forget ceremony for this occasion," she cried. "Welcome, my Lady Mary and my Lady Anne. I think we are going to be very happy together as one big family."

Mary thought they would be a very large family. There were six daughters of Lady Frances: Elizabeth, Katherine, Barbara, Anne, Henrietta, and Mary. Barbara Villiers was a name Mary had often heard whispered; but she did not believe that this little girl was that Barbara whose name could make people lower their voices and smile secretively.

Lady Frances took her by the hand and showed her her apartments. Anne's she was relieved to find were next to her own. Lady Frances seemed kind but Mary wanted to be back in York with her own mother and the possibility of her father's coming any day; she was disturbed because she sensed change, and she did not like it. Anne was not in the least worried; she believed that she would be petted and pampered in Richmond as she had been in York.

Mary was not so sure. She was constantly aware of Elizabeth Villiers, who was so much older than she was, seemed so much wiser, and was continually watching her, she was sure, in a critical manner.

Those days became faintly uneasy; and it was mainly due to Elizabeth Villiers.

Supper was being prepared in the King's apartments. Barbara Villiers, Lady Castlemaine, would be his chief guest; Rochester, Sedley, and the rest would be present; and it would be one of those occasions on which the King could indulge his wit, and afterward they would all leave except Barbara with whom he would spend the night. A pleasant prospect, particularly for a man who had known exile.

It had been said that "Uneasy lies the head that wears a crown," he ruminated, which was true enough. Not that he was a man to worry unduly. He had had enough of cares and intended to enjoy life, but there was one anxiety which haunted him; he had made a declaration never, if he could help it, to go a-wandering again, and there had been more determination and sincerity behind that declaration than there often was in his utterances.

He could laugh at himself—seeing in the King of England a sinful man. I should be a good King, he thought, if women were not so important to me. But his need of them had been born in him, as it was in James. James would be a contented and happy man, if it were not for women.

We are as we are because we must be, mused Charles. And he tried to remember the stories he had heard of his maternal grandfather, who it had been said was the greatest King the French had ever known; yet he too had had this failing.

It was well enough to love a woman—even if she were not one's wife. Another French King, Henri Deux, had proved that in a most sober relationship with Diane de Poitiers. But this was different. This was not a woman; it was women. And while he was entertaining Barbara he was thinking of Frances Stuart and the pretty little actresses of Drury Lane— and others. He was thinking too of his poor sad little wife Catherine who had had the misfortune to fall in love with him before she had given herself time to discover the kind of man her husband was.

The trouble was that he was so fond of them all; he hated hurting them or displeasing them; he would promise anything to make them smile, unfortunately promises should be redeemed. Perhaps one of the reasons why he clung to Barbara was that she was ready to rage and scream rather than weep and plead.

These were frivolous thoughts at such a time. His reign had been far from peaceful; what if the people decided that kings brought a country no better luck than parliaments? There was war with the Dutch and it was but a short time ago that his capital city had been devastated by the great plague, when death had stalked the streets of London, putting an end to that commerce on which he had relied to bring prosperity to the land. It had been one of the greatest disasters the country had known; and the following year another—almost as terrible: the great fire.

He knew the people asked themselves: "Is this a warning from heaven because of the profligate life led by the King and his Court?" In the beginning they had loved the pageants, the play, and the magnificence of gallants and ladies. They had said: "Away dull care! Away prim puritans! Now we have a King who knows how to live and if he makes love to many women that is the new fashion." What amorous squire, what voluptuous lady, was not amused and delighted by such a fashion? "Take your lovers! It is no crime. Look at the King and his Court. It is the fashionable way of life."

But no one had laughed at the plague and fire and these disasters had revived the puritan spirit. There were still many puritans in England.

But when they had seen the King and the Duke of York working together during the great fire—going among the people, giving orders, they had loved them. It was comforting to contemplate that one only had to appear to win the people's cheers. In secret they might deplore his way of life but when he was there with his smiles, his wit and, most of all, his cameraderie, he was theirs. To the men he implied: "I am the King, but I am only a man and you are a man also." To the women: "I am the King, but always ready to do homage to beauty in the humblest." They adored him, and it was due to that quality known as the Stuart charm.

Poor James, he had missed it. James was too serious. In some ways a pale shadow of brother Charles; in others quite different. James lacked the light touch.

He was relieved that James would not be with him tonight, for James had no place at these amusing little supper parties.

"I would to God Catherine would get a son," thought the King. "For if she does not then it is brother James who will wear the crown after me and I wonder whether the people are going to love him as they should."

A smile touched his lips as his thoughts immediately went to Jemmy— beautiful Jemmy, who was wild as all young men must be, and who was ambitious, which was natural too. It was a pleasure to see that young man in the dance—leaping higher than the others—always seeking his father's attention as though he wanted proof of his affection at every moment of the day. As if he needed it. It was his and he should know it.

"Though, would he be so eager for that affection if I were plain Master Charles Stuart?" There was no need to answer that question. He appealed to women almost as much as they appealed to him; but how many of his easy conquests did he owe to his crown? Most of them, he thought with a wry smile. Young Charles Stuart, the exile wandering through Europe looking for men, money, and arms, had not been so successful as the middle-aged King; and the answer: The Crown! The irresistible Crown!

As the King sat brooding he heard a commotion outside his apartments.

"Let me in!" cried a voice. "I demand to see the King. For the sake of his soul . . . let me in."

Charles raised his eyebrows. Surely not another fanatic come to warn him of the fires of hell. He hesitated; then as the voice continued to shout he left his apartment. On the staircase an elderly man was struggling in the arms of his guards. There could not be much to fear from such a creature, he was sure. He said: "Release the fellow. Then perhaps he will tell us what his business is."

"I come to warn Your Majesty."

"A familiar occupation of my subjects," murmured Charles lightly, wondering where he had seen that face before; if the features had not been distorted in madness, he believed he would have recognized him.

"I am the Holy Ghost come down from Heaven."

"Then I should say I am pleased to make your acquaintance and accept the fact that since you are holy and I am merely royal you are entitled to disturb my peace."

"I am the Holy Ghost!" cried the man, beating his chest.

"Poor fellow," said Charles. "He is indeed distressed."

"Mad, Your Majesty."

"What has brought you to this state?" asked Charles gently.

"My wife," said the man. "She is young . . . scarce eighteen."

"I see that like myself it is long since you were that age."

The King's tone seemed to calm the man for he nodded soberly.

"And she is unfaithful."

"A common failing and to be expected, when eighteen mates with . . ."
The King came closer and peered into the man's face.

One of the guards asked His Majesty's pleasure with regard to this
disturber of his peace.

"Treat him gently," said the King. "He is much distressed."

"It's the royalty. It bemuses them," murmured the madman.

Charles was puzzled; he knew the background of all his present mistresses and did not believe one of them could possibly be this man's wife.

"Pray tell me your name," he said.

"I am the Holy Ghost."

"Where do you live?"

"In my house in Scotland Yard."

"Scarcely a fitting domicile," murmured Charles.

"He comes quite openly. The whole household knows. They laugh
behind my back."

"An embarrassing situation for a celestial being." Charles signed to the
guards. "Take him away. Take him to his home and let me know who he is.
Perhaps I will speak to his pretty young wife."

One of the guards said: "Your Majesty, he is Sir John Denham."

"John Denham of a surety. Now I remember. Our Irish poet. He was
loyal to our cause. And now he has come to this through marrying a young
wife. Well it is a folly many commit and suffer for. Take him quietly to his
home."

Now it was clear to Charles. As he returned to his apartments he
remembered that the royal lover was his brother James whom everyone
knew had taken Margaret Denham, this man's young wife, to be his mistress. The whole Court would now be talking of how the liaison between
Margaret Denham and the Duke of York had driven poor John Denham
mad. How like James to involve himself in such a scandal.

There was something ineffectual about James. He was a good fellow—
affectionate, sentimental, and doomed to attract trouble because he simply
did not know how to live. He mismanaged his life. Why had James not

come to see him earlier when he was summoned? Charles had wanted to settle the unfortunate affair of Clarendon and who could explain what had to be explained more tactfully than the old man's son-in-law. There again James was a fool. His marriage was one of love, he had declared; he would have no one but Clarendon's daughter and she, of course, was very eager to have him—not only because of his royal blood and the fact that he was heir presumptive to the throne, but at the time of that trouble she had been growing bigger every week. Clarendon's daughter and a commoner! James would always be in trouble.

And now the husband of his mistress was going about declaring he was the Holy Ghost and the reason was that James had made him a cuckold.

Charles was feeling exasperated with James when a message was brought to him that his brother was asking for an audience.

Charles commanded that he be brought immediately.

"Well, brother?" he said.

James bowed stiffly; then his manner relaxed. He was not unlike Charles, not so tall but even so more than medium height; and he had a natural dignity. His features were similar; the difference was in their manner. The King was natural, at ease, lazily charming; James was reserved; he was considerably more handsome than Charles, but completely lacked his brother's charm. Charles was nonchalant; James was very serious; Charles succeeded in winning his subjects' affection without trying. James tried hard and did not often succeed. He had been popular when he had resounding successes at sea, but that popularity waned with failure, whereas Charles never lost the acclaim of the people in spite of his scandalous behavior. The Duke of Buckingham had said of them: "Charles could if he would, and James would if he could!" A remark which many believed summed up succinctly the differences between the brothers.

"I believe Your Majesty wishes to discuss the vexatious matter of my father-in-law," said James.

"Ah," retorted Charles, "what a family you have married into!"

James retorted: "And what a Chancellor Your Majesty has got yourself."

"Methinks he will be Chancellor little longer, for the truth is his behavior and humor have grown insupportable, and I can no longer endure it, finding it impossible to live with."

"Yet," said James, "he is a man who has done good service."

"And he is your father-in-law."

James snapped his fingers.

"Your wife will not be pleased." Charles smiled. "But then there are other matters in which you displease her, so I believe."

"What can Your Majesty expect? I am your brother."

Charles smiled lazily at James. "I should expect you to give a good account of yourself to your little friends," he said. "I would not have it otherwise. Wives alas can be demanding."

"I think the Duchess and I understand each other."

"Then you are indeed a fortunate man, for a wife who understands and smiles at her husband's peccadilloes is beyond rubies. But the lady's father?"

"This is the end, is it not?"

"There is no other way, brother. He has been a good minister in the past . . . and that I remember. But he has become overbearing. He works against me and the Parliament. Many are calling for his blood. I shall try to save him from his enemies . . . if that is possible. But I want him to go, James. Tell him that I want no more of him. Persuade him to go quietly and his reward shall be to live in peace."

"I shall speak to him."

"Speak gently, for he is an old man. But tell him to go . . . while he can."

"I shall do my best."

"And there is one other matter. The husband of a friend of yours called on me this day. The Holy Ghost. Have you the honor of his acquaintance?"

James looked puzzled.

"Investigations proved my visitor to be come not from the celestial regions but from Scotland Yard. His name is Denham. Can you enlighten me?"

"Denham?" said James. "Margaret's husband."

"An Irish poet who has been a good friend to our father and ourselves. We should remember our friends, brother."

"I have naught against him. I scarce know the fellow."

"It is understandable since you know his wife very well. A strong friendship with a lady often means one of slightly less warmth with her husband."

"She is but eighteen . . ."

"A delectable age!"

"And he is fifty and looks seventy. What can he expect marrying one so young?"

Charles smiled cynically at his brother.

"Alas," he said, "the people expect *you* to conduct your affairs with discretion."

"Your Majesty's affairs are . . ,"

"Not always discreet. The King's prerogative, brother. Remember you are not yet King."

"And you are asking me . . ."

"Only to have a little care. I liked not the look of our friend Denham. He was a sick man with a purpose in his eyes. I am warning you to be discreet. That is all."

"I will go along to Scotland Yard. I will discover what this means."

"Then I pray you go quietly, for the sake of your Duchess. I trust the lady is well. And the children?"

James's face lightened up at the thought of his daughters. They were well, he told Charles; and he began to enlarge on the cleverness of Mary, to which Charles listened indulgently. He was fond of his nieces, particularly Mary, and his was too generous a nature for envy. Although he earnestly wished for legitimate heirs he did not grudge James his.

"I begin to despair of sharing your good fortune," he said ruefully. "The Queen cannot get children. So James, you should prepare yourself to take on my burden in due course."

"Not before I am an old man myself, I trust."

"Do you, James? Have you no desire to wear the crown?"

"I would leifer see Your Majesty with a healthy son."

"Would to God Jemmy were legitimate."

He was still hankering after making Monmouth legitimate, thought James. One of the grudges Charles had against Clarendon was that the old man had stood out against Monmouth's legitimization.

"Doubtless Jemmy shares your feelings on that score," added James.

Charles grimaced. "Forget not what I have told you. Speak to your father-in-law. Show him the wisdom of graceful retirement. It is so much more dignified to step into obscurity than to be forced into it . . . or worse."

"I will do my best."

"My good brother, I know you will. Now I would have you leave me for the hour grows late and my guests will arrive and you, I know, have your own friends awaiting you."

As James left his brother, he was thinking of what he would say to his father-in-law. Poor old man, his was a familiar fate. He had too much power and believed himself invincible. He had angered Monmouth by standing against his legitimization; he had made an enemy of Lady Castlemaine by trying to turn the King from his immoral way of life. A man could not afford to make powerful enemies; and his self righteousness and sanctimonious manners had in time antagonized the King. So with his ministers baying for Clarendon's blood on one side, and his beloved bastard and his demanding mistress on the other, it was inevitable that Clarendon's end should be in sight.

He would try to persuade him to go quietly which was the best course open to him—and although it would anger his enemies, the King would be pleased. Whatever else Charles was, he was kind; he never wanted revenge; he had loathed the act of taking the bodies of the Roundhead leaders from their graves and submitting them to insults. He had never wanted revenge on his enemies. "Enough," he would cry. "Have done." But if he were kind he was also lazy. He would give Clarendon the chance to save himself from his enemies and if the old man obstinately refused to, then that would be his affair.

Tonight, of course, he would forget Clarendon's imminent fall and all unpleasantness in the company of Lady Castlemaine. He remained enamored of that virago although it was difficult to see why. And he had still made no progress with Frances Stuart, for which James was thankful, although he himself was in the same position with regard to this most beautiful and aloof young lady at his brother's Court.

He was going straight to Scotland Yard. He must see Margaret. He must discover what this account of her husband's calling himself the Holy Ghost was all about. Was Denham going mad? And were his enemies going to blame him for this? Were they going to say that the scandalous behavior of the Duke of York with Denham's wife had unbalanced the old fellow? In that case almost every husband at Court should be unbalanced. It was absurd.

Margaret would reassure him; she always did. She was so young and gay and she made him feel so. His affair with her was common knowledge and he had not cared except that he would have preferred to keep it secret from his wife. But Anne had learned by now that she must accept his infidelities; it was inconceivable that the Duke of York, brother to that greatest of libertines, King Charles II, should not have a mistress or two.

Arriving at Scotland Yard, he made his way to the house of Sir John Denham, where he was conducted to his mistress's apartments. When they had embraced she told him that Sir John had been strange lately, that he had sworn vengeance on her and her lover and that appearing before the King as the Holy Ghost seemed to be his idea of discomfiting them.

James found the youthful charms of his mistress so delightful that in her company it seemed of little importance what her husband did.

Sir John Denham appeared quickly to recover from his brief aberration. He begged the King's pardon which was readily given; and the Duke of York continued his visits to Scotland Yard, a situation to which Sir John seemed to have become reconciled.

James felt triumphant. He conducted his affairs, he believed, as successfully as his brother. Barbara Villiers created scandal enough and so did the playgirls, but he at least had chosen his mistresses from a higher social scale than the latter.

His Duchess was angry, but that was natural. He would give way to her in some ways and she must perforce give way to him in others. For one thing, she was reading books, constantly talking with priests, and was arousing suspicions that she was leaning very close to Catholicism. That would scarcely bring her popularity and was a more serious matter than taking a mistress or two.

James's visits to Scotland Yard were growing more and more frequent. He was deeply involved with Margaret and now that her husband had, as he said, overcome his folly and accepted this truly natural state of affairs, there was no need for them even to be discreet. Lady Denham was the Duke's mistress and that was an end of the matter.

But one day when he made his way to the Denhams' residence he was met by one of Sir John's servants who attempted to bar his way.

James was astounded; then it occurred to him that the fellow did not recognize him.

But he did, for he stammered: "Your Grace . . . you should not go up there . . ."

Should not mount the stairs to his mistress's room when she was expecting him, when he had been there a hundred times!

"Stand aside, fellow," he began; then he noticed that the servant was trembling and trying to tell him something.

"Your Grace . . . a terrible tragedy . . ."

"Lady Denham?"

"Your Grace . . . Lady Denham is . . . dead."

"Dead! It's not possible. I saw her yesterday. How can it be?"

"They say, Your Grace, that it was chocolate. A poisoned cup of chocolate."

The Duke pushed the man aside. He ran to his mistress's room and throwing open the door stood aghast, staring at the bed.

Several people, who were in the room, stood aside as he slowly advanced and stood looking down at his murdered mistress.

The great topic of conversation at Court and in the streets was the Denham affair. Rumor ran wild. Sir John Denham had poisoned his wife because she was unfaithful to him with the Duke of York. The Countess of Rochester, another of the Duke's mistresses, had poisoned her because of jealousy on account of the Duke of York. No matter what the rumor, the name of the Duke of York was always mentioned and because of this there was greater interest in the affair than there would otherwise have been.

A few puritans condemned the Duke of York and the manners of the Court, but those who were in favor of the new freedom—and these were the majority—turned suddenly against Sir John Denham, who had married a young woman and murdered her, her only sin being that she was in the fashion.

As a result, crowds gathered outside Sir John's house brandishing sticks and knifes.

"Come out, John Denham," they chanted. "Let's see how you like the same medicine that you gave to your wife."

When Sir John's life was in danger as if by magic all signs of his madness disappeared. He had the rumor circulated that if he lived long enough he would give his wife a magnificent funeral at St. Margaret's Westminster at which burned wine would be distributed to all who cared to partake of it.

Public feeling toward Sir John immediately changed. He now became a generous man, a wronged husband. The Duke of York was the real villain of the story—he and Sir John's slut of a wife. Those who had previously waved threatening weapons, now drank his burned wine and commiserated with him. But there had to be a culprit, for someone, the crowd was certain, had put poison into Lady Denham's chocolate. There had been rumors of the Duchess's jealousy, so what more natural than that a jealous woman should seek to rid herself of her rival? This was the best story so far. An erring husband; a jealous wife.

The people were eager to believe they had discovered the murderess. It should be the Duchess of York.

The elder Villiers girls were whispering together, every now and then glancing at Mary who sat with her sister Anne trying to interest her in writing her name. Anne was smiling as Mary guided her hand. She did not greatly care for the task, but she loved to be with Mary and tried to do all she could to please her and their heads were close together as they bent over the table.

"There were such crowds," whispered Elizabeth. "They were going to kill him. And they would have . . . if he had not promised them wine at the funeral."

"It would have served him right," put in Katherine.

"Oh no, it wouldn't. It wasn't his fault. He was just angry."

"But if he poisoned her . . ."

"Don't talk so loudly." Significant glances were sent toward the Princesses at the table. Anne did not hear them; the tip of her tongue slightly protruded from the corner of her mouth showed that she was trying hard to do what was expected of her. Mary was listening intently, because she knew by the tone of Elizabeth's voice that she was talking of something which was unpleasant and which in some obscure way, concerned her, Mary. "Our mother would punish you if she knew you talked of such matters . . . especially . . ." A quick look in the direction of the two at the table.

So it is before us, that she must not speak of this, thought Mary.

"If a wife takes a lover," went on Elizabeth speaking very distinctly, "her husband has a right to poison her, even if . . ."

"But the people are angry that he poisoned her?"

"Don't interrupt. Even if her lover was . . . someone in a high position."

"But if . . ."

"Katherine! You know you must not speak of it . . . *here*."

Mary leaned over her sister so that Anne's soft hair caressed her cheek. How happy she would be, she thought then, if there was no one in her nursery but her dear sister. They could have been happy together—perhaps Barbara might stay with them. Barbara was the Villiers girl she liked best, and was more gentle than the others.

"No, Anne," she said, "that is not good. Just look at that second 'n'."

Anne put her head on one side and smiled adoringly at her sister.

"You do it, Mary. You do it so beautifully."

Mary wrote "Anne" firmly in the script of which she was rather proud.

"It's a much nicer name when you write it," commented Anne, snuggling close to her sister. "I don't think I should learn to write it when you do it so well."

"Oh, Anne, you *are* lazy!"

The Villiers girls were still whispering together; but Mary wanted to go on laughing with Anne; she wanted to shut her ears for fear she heard so much of what they were saying that she understood. She was sure it was unpleasant.

The Duchess of York was a proud woman. The passion which had inspired the Duke to shut his eyes to all obstacles when he married her, had perhaps made her expect too much from their marriage. She had certainly gained a great deal for, as wife to the heir presumptive, she was a powerful woman and as it was said that she led the Duke by the nose in all things but his codpiece, her significance was accepted by all.

But her pride was deeply wounded by his constant love affairs. She was a fool to expect fidelity perhaps; but he might have used a little discretion. Of all his mistresses there was one who stood most firmly in his affections; and it was this very firmness which infuriated Anne. Arabella Churchill was a woman to be reckoned with. She was ambitious, Anne was sure; and the fact that she was no real beauty, made her all the more to be feared.

Lady Southesk, Anne had forgiven him. The woman had, as Anne had remarked cuttingly to her husband, "passed through the hands of so many gentlemen that she must be slightly soiled by now." Anne would not demean herself by showing jealousy of such a creature whose powers to amuse must surely be short-lived.

Frances Jennings had succeeded in giving Anne a few anxious moments when the slut deliberately dropped the Duke's love letters to her at the feet of the Duchess. There was Elizabeth Hamilton and of course Margaret Denham who had come to an end which was unfortunate for her; but none of these worried the Duchess as the Churchill woman did. She was ambitious that one; already she had induced James to look after her family. George Churchill had been found a place in the navy and John in the army.

She might rail against James; he would listen patiently, perhaps promise to mend his ways; but of course he had no intention of keeping that promise for more than a few hours.

If she had the time and inclination for such an adventure she would take a lover. She almost had a few years ago. Henry Sidney was one of the most handsome men in the Court; he had been Groom of the Bedchamber and when he had become her Master of Horse Anne had been thrown constantly into his company. How wounded she had been at that time, knowing that her husband was turning more and more to his mistresses and understanding that she would never be able to divert his attention from them! It had been more difficult in those days to accept humiliation.

And how furious James had been when he suspected Sidney of being her lover! How he had ranted and raged—which was so unlike him. His jealousy had been gratifying but he refused to agree that what was acceptable in a husband should be in a wife; and Sidney's handsome face had not appeared at Court for a long time. The plague had followed quickly on that affair, but Anne was sure that Henry Sidney remained in the Duke's mind, as memorable a disaster as the great sickness.

She was thinking of this as she sat alone in her bedchamber, asking herself whether the recent Denham tragedy would make James a little more careful in his choice of mistresses when she noticed a paper which had evidently been thrust under her door.

Going to it and, bending carefully as she must on account of her weight, she picked it up, and taking it to the window read it. As she did so the color came into her white flabby face. It was a verse . . . a lampoon directed against her, telling of her jealousy, of the Duke's preference for another woman which had caused her to have a dose of poison put into that woman's chocolate.

This was too much. To endure his infidelities was one thing. To be accused of poisoning his mistresses was another. If it had been Arabella Churchill there might have been some reason in it. But to dare to accuse her of murdering the insignificant Margaret Denham was beyond endurance.

Grasping the paper in her hand she went along to her husband's apartment. Mary was with him, but she scarcely saw the child.

"Look at this," she said, thrusting the paper into his hands.

James read it; and before he spoke he caressed his daughter's head.

"Go now, my dear," he said, giving her a little push toward an antechamber.

When Mary had disappeared Anne said: "This is more than I will endure."

James lifted his shoulders. "There are always these lampoons."

"They would not be if your conduct did not give the writers what they are looking for."

"They would always find something."

"I suspect Rochester to be the author of this."

"That man! I would my brother would dismiss him from the Court."

"Dismiss his boon companion. He would rather see you gone, James . . . you with your scandals and your follies."

"I doubt I'll ever make a scandal as great as my brother's."

"He is the King. He can keep twenty mistresses at a time and the people will applaud him. You, my dear Duke, do not enjoy the people's indulgence to that extent. And when your mistresses are murdered—well, that is a serious matter. Charles has not been involved in that sort of scandal."

"You are shouting," said James. "You will be heard."

"Those who listen will only hear what they already know."

"I forbid you to talk in this way."

Anne laughed. "*You* forbid *me*. It is no use trying to cover up your indiscretions by playing the great duke and stern master. It will not do. I shall not endure these humiliations."

"You have not always been so virtuous yourself, if I remember rightly. What of Henry Sidney?"

"Henry Sidney. He was merely my Master of Horse."

"And of you it seems."

"A fabrication which existed in your mind. It was so convenient to delude yourself that your wife was unfaithful—since you had deceived her with . . . how many? Or would it be impossible to count?"

"You are overwrought."

"I have just been accused of murder. What are you going to do about that?"

"I tell you, there will always be lampoons. They are written daily about Charles and Barbara Castlemaine."

"I do not think they have been accused of murder."

"Oh, come, that suggestion is not serious."

"Adultery. Lechery. They are to be expected in this Court. In fact, if one is not a lecher or an adulterer one is considered old-fashioned, behind the times. But murder has not yet been judged a virtue."

"Anne, be calm."

"I do not feel calm."

"We cannot talk with ease until you do."

"And you would rather leave me until I am calm? That is a good excuse. You would rather be off with that sly-eyed Churchill woman. Very well, go to her. I'll warrant she has thought up some new request to ask of you in exchange for her favors."

"Is that what Sidney did? What did you have to grant him for his?"

"You are insulting."

"And are you not?"

"I have reason to be. Oh, you make a great show of being an irate husband. Banishing poor Sidney from the Court. It was such a shocking thing he did. Smiled at your wife. Showed her some pity because she must continually suffer the degradation of her husband's infidelities paraded daily before the Court under her very nose with little regard for *her* feelings . . ."

In the anteroom Mary listened. She did not want to listen; but her father had forgotten that the door through which she had gone led only to the anteroom and once there, there was no escape.

She wished they would not talk so loudly. As she listened she kept seeing Elizabeth Villiers's sly face. Elizabeth was right then. There was a shocking scandal about her father and her mother.

It was so hard to believe. A short while ago he had been laughing with her; she had sat on his knee and he had been telling her stories of his adventures as he loved to. Now he was quite different. She could not believe that the kind and gentle man was the same one who was shouting at her mother. To discover that people could change so quickly was alarming; it made the world seem an insecure place.

She did not want to hear their quarrels; she did not want to know of them; she wanted to live in a world where there were only herself and her sister Anne, where everything was pleasant and comfortable, and there were no grown up people with their sly furtive secrets which she only half understood.

She was afraid that one of them would come into the anteroom and find her there. She would not be blamed because they rarely blamed her, they were always kind to her; it seemed that it was only to each other that they were unkind. But she knew instinctively that they would be upset if they knew she had overheard their conversation, and that was why she remained.

After a long time they seemed to tire of the quarrel. She heard the door open and shut, and she wondered whether her father was now alone.

She opened the door of the anteroom cautiously and looked out. With great relief, seeing that the apartment was empty, she tiptoed away.

A postmortem showed that there was no poison in Margaret Denham's body but the rumors still persisted and many were certain that the Duchess of York had murdered her for jealousy.

Sir John Denham continued to write his pieces which gave pleasure to certain members of the Court. It was beginning to be said that the affairs of the Duke of York were as notorious, though not nearly so skillfully managed, as those of his brother.

FAITH AND DEATH

*I*t was the thirtieth of January, a very solemn day for members of the royal family and therefore throughout England.

Mary knelt on the window seat watching the snowflakes falling down. Every now and then the bells could be heard. All over the country they were tolling for Charles the Martyr.

Mary did not know why her grandfather was a martyr; she only knew that she had to be very solemn when she spoke of him. Her father's eyes grew very bright when he mentioned Charles the Martyr; and she did not like to ask questions because it saddened him to talk of the subject. She had heard whisperings about the Dreadful Day. In Whitehall she averted her eyes at a certain place because that was where *it* had happened. *It* was a dreadful shadow which hung over the family, and which must never be mentioned all the year, only on that cold and dismal day which was the thirtieth of January.

Mary breathed on the glass and rubbed a hole in the mist. It was very cold outside. Perhaps one day she would ask her father to explain. It would be when he was in a merry mood. Then perhaps he would tell her quickly and it could be forgotten.

She started suddenly because someone was standing behind her, and turning she saw Elizabeth Villiers, smiling her secret sly smile.

"How long have you been standing there?" demanded Mary.

"Does it matter?"

"I asked you a question."

"I know, and I asked you one."

"It is not good manners to answer a question with a question."

Elizabeth laughed; she had a habit of laughing at ordinary remarks as though they were foolish in some way which Mary was too young to understand.

"When I was riding this morning I saw the King with my cousin, Barbara Villiers," volunteered Elizabeth.

Mary sighed. Elizabeth brought her cousin Barbara Villiers into the conversation whenever possible. When she called her sister Barbara she always called her Barbara Villiers, although the others were merely Katherine, Anne, or whatever the case might be. Mary herself had never seen Barbara Villiers, Lady Castlemaine, but she was constantly hearing of her; and she was a little tired of the woman.

"My cousin Barbara is more important than the Queen." "My cousin Barbara only has to say what she wants and it is hers." "The King loves my cousin Barbara more than anyone on earth." "My cousin Barbara is really Queen, not that dull old Catherine."

Mary did not believe that. She loved her Aunt Catherine who was always kind to her; and she loved Uncle Charles; and when she saw them together they always seemed to be fond of each other and no one ever suggested—certainly not Charles—that Catherine was not the Queen.

"You are always talking of your cousin Barbara Villiers," said Mary, turning back to the window.

"Well, would you rather talk of Margaret Denham who was killed because of your father?"

"I don't know what you're talking about."

"You are a baby. You don't know anything. You don't really know why everyone is so glum today. All you know is that it's because it's the thirtieth. It's silly anyway to pretend to be sad. It was all a long, long time ago. Before *I* was born."

"What was?"

"The execution. That's what they're supposed to be remembering. But they are only really pretending to be sad."

"When was it?"

"Don't you know?" This was one of Elizabeth's favorite remarks. She could never tell anything without prefacing her revelation with an incredulous observation on one's ignorance. On this occasion Mary was too curious to pretend.

"No, I don't know," she said.

"They took him to the banquetting hall and chopped off his head."

"Who?"

"Charles the First. Your grandfather, of course."

"Who did?"

"The Parliament, of course."

"They didn't."

"They did." Elizabeth smiled knowledgeably. "It's what they do to Kings and Queens when they don't like them," she said maliciously.

Elizabeth knew when to make an exit. She retired, leaving a very uneasy little girl kneeling at the window seat. There was no pleasure now in looking out of the windows and trying to count the snowflakes. Every time a bell tolled she shivered. The world had become very insecure. Mary's imagination was showing her her grandfather, who looked like her father or her Uncle Charles, only much older; his head was not on his shoulders. It rolled in the snow making it red instead of white. She pictured the crowds watching and they were whispering about her grandfather and her father. Margaret Denham had died because of her father—her good kind father who would never hurt anyone. What did it mean? There was so much in the world that she could not understand and Elizabeth was telling her that the world could be a frightening place.

A terrible place indeed where the people cut off the heads of Kings. Elizabeth's voice kept coming back to her.

"It's what they do to Kings and Queens—if they don't like them."

James Scott, who had been known as Fitzroy and Crofts and was now the Duke of Monmouth and Buccleuch, rode from Whitehall to Richmond on his way to visit his uncle the Duke of York, whom he would always loathe because he believed that but for him the King might have been persuaded to legitimize him.

The King had said: "Now, Jemmy, ride over to Richmond where your uncle James is with his family. Make yourself pleasant. I like not quarrels in families."

Monmouth had scowled; he knew his father was very indulgent toward him and he exploited this; but there were occasions when Charles reminded him that he was the King and then Monmouth knew it was wiser to obey.

So here he was, riding over to Richmond, in order to make himself pleasant to his uncle and his fat wife.

There was one burning passion in Monmouth's life and that was to be King of England. It seemed so cruel to him that merely because his father had omitted to marry his mother he should be set aside. Why should James's children—those two girls and the sickly boys, whom everyone said would never reach maturity—come before him, simply because their father had married their mother. That marriage might so easily not have taken place, but Anne Hyde had been more fortunate than Lucy Walters.

There were some who whispered to him that there had actually been a marriage—those he called his friends. Yet his father had not denied it but considering how at one time he had longed to make him legitimate, would he not have been delighted to admit he had married Lucy Walters if this had been the case?

Monmouth believed he would have made a perfect Prince of Wales. The King doted on him, forgave him his misdeeds, had bestowed on him titles and a rich heiress. In fact, Charles had given him everything except the one thing he wanted: to be heir to the crown.

People bowed to him as he passed. He was such a handsome fellow, so charming, so personable. The gay son of a gay king. His spirits rose for he was certain that the people wished he was Prince of Wales too. The Duke of York was not popular—or at least not as his father was; and who would better follow his father than his father's son?

Of course life in every other respect was good. He was eighteen, rich, honored wherever he went, the companion of the King, flattered, attractive to women; and although he was not clever or witty like the King and his friends, they excused that on account of his youth. He was clearly the King's son; tall, dark, yet he had inherited his mother's beauty; what he had taken from his father was a love of racing and women; he was no coward; he was generous. No one could doubt he was the son of his father.

And now to Richmond. On what excuse? He was not going to let James think that he had come over to curry favor. What did he care for James? James was not very popular at the moment. The Denham affair was still remembered and whenever it was talked of James's name was always mentioned.

He would talk of the ballet he was planning for the King's pleasure and tell them he hoped the Duke and the Duchess would take part, slyly suggesting the part of some sylph for the Duchess. That would be a good joke against her. As for James he should have the part of a libertine with sly references to his prowess which *he* would not see but the clever Court wits would soon understand.

When he reached Richmond Palace he did not ask to be conducted to the Duke of York's presence. It occurred to him that James might refuse

to see him, or even make him wait. The Duke of Monmouth would accept
no such insult from the Duke of York. Therefore he waved aside the Duke's
servants and said he was in no hurry. Thus, left to himself, he came to
the children's apartments and wandering in found Mary and Anne were
with the Villiers girls. It appeared that the eldest of these girls was in
charge. The Duke was not attracted by her; she was too plain, and there
was a slight squint in her eyes. But his cousins were charming, particularly
Mary, who rose at the sight of him and flushing a little came forward. It
irritated him that her rank should be considered higher than his when she
was merely the daughter of the Duke of York, and he was the son of the
King. Yet because her father had married her mother.... It was the old
complaint which made him almost sick with anger.

"It is my cousin!" cried Mary, her dark almond-shaped eyes betraying
her pleasure. She was an enchanting child and Monmouth, who always
found beauty irresistible, knelt, and taking her hand kissed it.

"Come here, Anne," commanded Mary, and her sister waddled over
to him. She was remarkably plump and even as she greeted her cousin she
was sucking a sweet.

"I trust I see you well," he said.

"We are well thank you, cousin," answered Mary gravely. "And we
trust you are also."

Elizabeth Villiers was pushing forward. A pox on her! thought Monmouth. These Villiers give themselves too many airs.

"I was passing," he said pointedly, "and I thought it would be pleasant
to call on my cousins."

Elizabeth looked angry, her sisters watched her, ready to take their
cue from her. Mary was not one to harbor grudges, but since Elizabeth
had worried her with references to her father and grandfather she was glad
to be relieved of her company; and she could not resist a glance over her
shoulder as Monmouth took her hand and that of Anne and led them to
a window seat.

Monmouth, ever conscious of his birth, was ready on every occasion to assert his royalty and now implied that he regarded the Villiers girls merely as attendants on the King's nieces. It was an insult for which Elizabeth would never forgive him.

As Mary sat on the window seat with Anne, their cousin between them, she noticed that the Villiers girls had disappeared.

"When are you coming to Court?" asked Monmouth.

Mary said that neither her father nor her mother had told her.

"Do they have plenty to eat at Court?" asked Anne, and Monmouth described the Whitehall banquets for Anne's delight.

Then he turned to Mary. "But you would rather dance, I'll swear."

Mary admitted it.

"Then you must come to Court and we will dance together. I will tell them to devise a ballet in which you shall join."

"Oh my lord Monmouth," cried Mary, "that would be wonderful."

"I'm your cousin," he replied. "You should call me Jemmy, as my father does."

"Cousin Jemmy," repeated Mary looking happily into his face, which she thought was the most beautiful she had ever seen. He was grown up, yet not old. His skin was fresh and smooth, his eyes flashing and deeply set. He was kind, too.

"Always at your service," he said, standing up and bowing. Then he took her hand and made her dance a few steps.

"You would be a good dancer," he told her. "You must ask your father to have you taught."

"We are to be soon."

He whispered: "Before your sister grows too fat."

"I am always telling her she eats too much," Mary whispered back.

They laughed together; it was so pleasant sharing a joke with Cousin Jemmy.

He showed her how to dance as they did in the ballet while Anne remained on the window seat; she was not interested in dancing; nor was she so taken with Cousin Jemmy who had brought her no sweetmeats when all the visitors who wished to please her brought them for her.

As for Mary she clearly adored her cousin and he was delighted with her. She was a pretty creature, so innocent and unaware of her rank. He was certain that if he told her she took precedence over him she would not know to what he referred, and when he explained, assure him that he was certainly more important than she was. She soothed his mood, and to his surprise he found that his visit to the Duke of York's house in Richmond was more pleasant than he had believed it could be.

As they danced and smiled at each other Mary suddenly grew serious. He asked her if anything troubled her and after a moment's hesitation she said: "Cousin Jemmy, could you tell me about my grandfather?"

He looked at her in some astonishment. Then he said: "Oh, he lives in France now. He felt it was best to leave England for a while."

"I don't mean Grandfather Clarendon but Grandfather Charles the Martyr. They cut off his head didn't they . . . because they didn't like him?"

"Some didn't like him. It was the wicked Parliament men. They cut off his head and afterward were made to wish they hadn't."

"They were very wicked, were they?"

"Very wicked."

"Cousin Jemmy, no one will cut off Uncle Charles's head . . . or my father's?"

Cousin Jemmy laughed, not as Elizabeth laughed, but to show that what she suggested was not possible. She felt very relieved.

"Lady Denham died because of my father . . ." she began.

"Why," said Jemmy, "you have been listening to the scandalmongers. There are always plenty of them about. The thing to do is to let what they say go into one ear and out of the other." As he said this he was laughing; and somehow only to look at Cousin Jemmy's kind face—which must also be the most handsome in the world—was a comfort.

Mary found that it didn't matter what Elizabeth said about kings or her father; Elizabeth was not important now that Cousin Jemmy was her friend, and that made her very happy. Whenever she was frightened or bewildered she would remember Jemmy; perhaps she could tell him what puzzled her and she was sure he would always be able to explain it.

Jemmy took her hands and twirled her round; she was laughing and a little breathless but so happy.

She was thinking how different everything seemed since he had come; as for Monmouth, he was asking himself why they had not married him to Mary. If Charles had no legitimate heirs and James's sickly boys died, this girl could one day be Queen. If he had been her husband would they have been ready to waive his illegitimacy?

This thought made him warm toward the enchanting little creature who so adored him.

When James, Duke of York, entered the apartment, he saw the Duke of Monmouth dancing with his daughter, and Mary so evidently enjoying the boy's company. There was nothing which could have endeared him more to his nephew than this friendliness toward his favorite daughter.

Monmouth felt that visit to Richmond was well worthwhile. Effortlessly he had made peace with James; and it was pleasant to be adored by the Lady Mary of York who could, in certain circumstances, become the Queen of England.

The Duchess of York lay on her bed, where she now spent a good deal of her time. Many thought her indolent physically, although mentally alert. She was growing more and more unwieldy and she knew that she would continue so unless she cut down the consumption of sweet things. A cup of chocolate! How soothing to the nerves! How comforting the hot sweet drink which helped to divert the thoughts from the dull nagging pain which she was feeling more and more frequently in her left breast.

She was afraid of that pain; it had been slight at first—just a twinge which she had felt for the first time during a Court Levee; she had forgotten it until a month or so later when she had felt it again. Now scarcely a day passed when she was not given a twinge to remind her that all was not well.

When one was young it was natural to believe that one would live forever. Death seemed so far away as to be an event which overtook others; but recurring pain brought death nearer, and to contemplate death meant that one grew more and more concerned with the hereafter. She was beginning to believe that the Catholic Faith was the true one.

For this reason she often slipped out of the Palace of Whitehall or Richmond or wherever she should happen to be to visit Father Hunt, a Franciscan who talked with her, gently and persuasively and after each meeting with the friar she felt closer to Catholicism.

It was dangerous. The people of England were firmly Protestant. The memory of the Smithfield fires was too recent; and some old men had heard their fathers talk of those days when the island had been under the shadow of an attack from Spain, when it had been feared that the ships of the Armada, which were being assembled to attack England, came not only with guns and weapons of war but the rack and all the Inquisition's instruments of torture. "Never shall the Inquisition come to these shores!" said the English; "The Church of England for us. No popery!" The Sovereign of England was head of the English Church and the English wanted no direction from Rome.

It was a dangerous matter therefore when the wife of the man who might well be the King of England should become a Catholic. Yet, if one believed one had discovered the truth, what was to be done? Worship in secret was the answer—as thousands were doubtless doing at this time.

A difficult problem, but at least one which turned her mind from the nagging pain in her breast.

She wanted to talk with James of her religious feelings and wanted to share this new experience with him, for she believed that he, like herself, would find much to attract him in Rome. But she was uncertain and this was a dangerous matter.

Her women came in to help her to bed. Indolently she allowed them to disrobe her and put on her night clothes. She lay lazily on her bed when they had left her, thinking of the meeting with Father Hunt tomorrow, and the points she would raise with him; and at the same time hoping that the pain would not begin for she fancied it was growing more acute.

She slept and dreamed that a woman had come into her room, a shadowy form which glided to the bed and looked down at her. In the woman's hand was a cup of chocolate.

Anne rose on her elbows and cried: "You are Margaret Denham risen from the grave."

With that the figure disappeared and Anne was staring into the darkness not sure whether she had been dreaming this or whether the apparition had actually been in the room. It was so vivid that she made up her mind that she had actually been visited by Margaret Denham's ghost.

She felt the heat on her chin and putting her fingers to it found they were wet.

She began calling for candles and in a short time several of her women were hurrying into the room. They gasped when they saw the blood on her face.

"Your Grace, what has happened?" cried one.

"Margaret Denham has been in this room," answered Anne.

"She . . . has harmed Your Grace?"

Seeing that there was blood on her sheets Anne recoiled from it in dismay.

By this time the commotion had awakened the Duke in the nearby chamber and he came hurrying in and when he saw the blood on the Duchess's face he cried out in dismay and taking her in his arms demanded to know what had happened.

"Margaret Denham came to me. This is the result."

The Duke called for more candles, and saw that the blood was coming from the Duchess's mouth. When closer examination proved that she had bitten her tongue, there was great relief in the apartments.

"It was the fright, Your Grace," said one of her women.

"Her Grace has had a bad dream," said the Duke. "Awaken one of the physicians and send him here."

When the doctor came he was able to assure the Duke and Duchess that no harm was done; she had bitten her tongue, which would be a little sore, particularly when hot food was taken, but it would quickly heal.

The blood had been washed from the Duchess's face and hands; the sheets had been changed and she lay back while the Duke sat by her bed watching her.

"I fear," said James, "that you have had this evil dream because Margaret Denham has been much on your mind."

"She will not be forgotten it seems."

"Nonsense. In a few months no one will remember her name."

"Oh, James, make sure that there are no more Margaret Denhams."

"My dear, how could I know that she would die in such circumstances?"

"It would have been of no account how she died if you had been a faithful husband to me."

James sighed. "That is a matter we have discussed many times before, Anne. Let us have done with it."

"It was as though she were here . . . in this room, James. As though she upbraided *me.*"

"You are not well. I have noticed that you have been looking tired of late."

"There is nothing wrong with me." Her hand imperceptibly touched her breast.

He leaned over and kissed her. "Oh, Anne," he said, "if you were a humble merchant's wife and I that merchant, it would have been different."

"Being humble would not have changed your nature, James. There is a wildness in you . . . a need for women which is paramount to all else. You inherited it from your grandfather who, I have heard, had more mistresses than any King of France. What more could be said?"

"Yet," said James, "there is no other that can claim my heart but you."

"Spoken like a Stuart." She laughed. "I'll swear Charles is saying the same at this moment to one of his ladies."

"But *I* mean it, Anne."

"Stuarts always mean what they say . . . when they say it." She lay against him. "It is good to have you with me, James. There is much of which I would speak to you."

He kissed her and she was aware of the passion which was so ready to be aroused. Perhaps it was not for fat Anne Hyde, the mother of his children (two only of whom were strong and healthy and they girls), no, not for that Anne Hyde, but for the young girl whom he had met and loved at Breda, the girl whom he had seduced, making marriage a necessary but still a greatly desired event.

This was how it should have been for all the years of marriage—James forgot his mistresses; Anne forgot the recurring pain in her breast, the secret visits to the priest. Though fleetingly she assured herself that soon she would discuss her views with James, for she wanted to share her faith with him as she had shared her life.

But for that night they were merely lovers as they had been in the days at Breda.

After that night the Duke and Duchess of York were more often in each other's company than previously. The Duchess's influence over her husband appeared to have increased and although James visited his mistresses occasionally, he was devoted to his wife. As for Anne, she was more interested in discussing religion than any other subject and it was remarked that in conversation she seemed inclined to veer toward Rome.

James's great interest was, as it always had been, the navy; he had won great honors at sea but when de Ruyter, the Dutch commander, sailed into the Medway and destroyed several of the King's ships, including the Royal Charles, and then had the temerity to sail up the Thames as far as Gravesend, the efficiency of the Duke of York began to be doubted.

Clarendon, who had once seemed all powerful, was in exile; and now the Duke of York, whose wife was suspected of being a Catholic, was showing signs of following her lead.

In the midst of rumors and suspicions James had a slight attack of smallpox and as soon as he was ill his virtues were remembered rather than his faults; the Duchess who was expecting a child in three months' time was constantly with him; and they both prayed for a son because Charles was hinting once more that he would like to legitimatize Monmouth.

Monmouth was the darling of the King and the Court. He often visited Richmond, to the delight of Mary; but what he was most interested in was the health of the Duchess. She had been looking strained and tired of late; her skin was growing sallow, and some of her attendants had reported that she was suffering occasional pain.

If the child was stillborn, reasoned Monmouth, his father might well prevail on his ministers to have him, Monmouth, legitimatized.

"And that," he repeated to himself again and again, "would be the greatest day of my life."

He could never see the Crown and the ceremonial robes without picturing himself wearing them and thinking how well he would become them! If only James had no children! The little Prince was sick and it was hardly likely that he would live. The girls were so healthy though—particularly Mary. Anne of course was such a little glutton that she might burst one day through overeating; she was like a ball as it was. And the Duchess did not look like a healthy mother-to-be. There was great hope in Monmouth's heart that summer.

He was looking about him for friends who would help him to what he so passionately desired, men such as George Villiers, Duke of Buckingham—a wit, a rake, but a shrewd man, and one of the King's favorite companions. He was a man fond of intrigue and had recently hoped to make Frances Stuart the King's mistress and govern through her. No plan was too wild to interest him. He had just left the Tower whither he had been sent for fighting with the Marquis of Dorchester—an ungainly scuffle, with Buckingham taking possession of Dorchester's wig and Dorchester pulling out some of Buckingham's hair in retaliation. Later he had again been sent to the Tower for, it was said, dabbling with soothsayers concerning the King's horoscope. But Charles could always find reasons for forgiving those who amused him, and he did not like such as Buckingham to leave him for too long at a time.

Buckingham was no friend of James, Duke of York. Could it be that he might be a friend of Monmouth's?

He must find powerful friends. Clearly if the King had no male heir and James neither, it would be to his benefit; and when the King died and it was James's turn? Well, would the people of England accept a Catholic King? Monmouth was certain they would not. Therefore he would show them that he was staunchly Protestant. He would begin now, laying his plans, forming friendships with men such as Buckingham who would be of use to him, letting the people know that if they did not want a Catholic King there was a good Protestant waiting to serve them—the only reason why he was not proclaimed the heir, being the fact that his father had failed to marry his mother—and some said that this was a falsehood.

All through those summer months Monmouth waited for news of the Duchess's accouchement. It was a sad day for him when he heard that she had been brought to bed of a boy.

The Duchess of York was on her knees in the small antechamber and with her was Father Hunt. They prayed together for a while and when she rose the priest said to her: "I thank God that you are now rid of doubt."

"I thank Him too," she answered. "I will never now falter. Coming to understanding has given me great comfort."

"You will find greater comfort."

"Father, this is something I have told no one yet. I fear I have not long to live." She touched her breast. "I have a pain which grows more agonizing with the passing of the weeks. I have known others who have had such a pain. It increases and in time kills."

"Then, Your Grace, it is good that you have come to understanding in time."

She bowed her head in assent. "Father, I have talked to my husband of the doctrines of our Church and I know him to be interested. Before I die I should like to bring him to the truth. There are also my children."

"Your Grace, this is a matter for great delicacy. Speak to your husband, but use caution. Your children, it would be said, belong to the state and as this state is not yet ready to come to the light, it is necessary to exercise great caution."

"Rest assured I shall do so," replied the Duchess.

She left the priest and went to her apartments; and later when the Duke came to her she told him that she wanted to speak to him very seriously.

"James," she said, "I have become a Catholic."

He was not surprised; she had betrayed her leanings to him many times. In fact, the Catholic religion appealed to him; he liked its richness, its pomps and mysteries. He had often thought how comforting it would be to confess his sins and receive absolution; and when one sinned again to know that one had but to repent and do penance to wipe out the sin. The less colorful Protestant church was not so appealing. His mother had been French and a Catholic; his grandfather had been a Huguenot, it was true, but he had changed his religion when it was expedient to do so with the remark which had never been forgotten that Paris was worth a Mass. Charles was like that. He would change his religion for the sake of peace. But James was different. He was idealistic and a man who could not see danger when it was right under his nose. Perhaps he even found a thrill in courting danger. Perhaps the very fact that he knew the disquiet which would arise through the country if one so near the throne became a professed Catholic, made the proposition the more irresistible.

He took her hands and they talked long and earnestly.

"I will instruct you in the doctrines, James," said Anne. "I am sure you will want to be converted as I have been."

It was a new bond between them. Since his attack of smallpox they had become closer, and when they had lost their newly-born son their grief had been great, but it was a shared sorrow and his amorous adventures outside the marriage bed had never been fewer.

"We must be careful," he said. "This must be a secret between us. You will have to be cautious when you are with the priest. The people would be against us if they knew."

"You in particular, James. For myself I do not believe I am long for this world. I have not told you before, but I think you should know now. I have a recurring pain in my breast and I know it is serious."

He was horrified. "But the doctors . . ."

"They can do nothing. I know something of what this means. I did not want to tell you, but now you will understand my urgent desire to prepare myself. And I do not want to leave you, James, knowing that I did not share with you all that I have come to understand."

They wept together, he deeply regretful of all the anxiety he had caused her, she sorry for her nagging sarcasm.

"We have been like two children lost in a wood," she said. "But now we see a light."

He demanded to know more of her illness and would not accept her pessimistic view.

He cares for me in very truth, she thought; and somehow the knowledge made her the more sorrowful.

"The light is the Holy Catholic Faith, James. Do not ignore it," she entreated.

He told her that he loved her; that he had never regretted the decision he had made when all his family were against him. They would be together now . . . for the time that was left to them.

"Together in mind and body, James?" she asked.

"In all things," he answered.

The Duchess and Duke came frequently to Richmond. They wanted, they said, to be together with their children.

Mary was horrified to find that her feelings had changed toward them. She could no longer relax happily in her father's arms. When he took her on to his knee she could not help thinking of Margaret Denham who had died because of him. It was complicated and difficult to understand, but it was repellent. Her mother had changed. She had become grotesquely fat; her face was the color of uncooked pastry; and with her bloodshot eyes she was not an attractive sight. Mary could not help comparing her with some of the beautiful women she saw frequently.

Sometimes her father would declare that they were all going to be happy together. He would tell her, Anne and poor little Edgar, who was growing more weak every day, stories of his past; but somehow they no longer fascinated as they once had. Mary was beset by doubts that they were only true in part; that if one could look into them with the farsighted eyes of an adult one would discover something unpleasant.

One day the Duchess sent for Mary, and when she went to her apartments the little girl found her mother lying on her bed. Her face was sallow and the sight of her propped up on pillows with her hair falling loose about her shoulders made Mary want to glance away.

She took Mary's hand and bade her sit on the bed so that they could be close.

"You are the eldest of the family," she said. "Always remember that."

"Yes, mother."

"There is one thing I want you always to do for me. Look after Anne."

"But . . ."

"I know you are thinking that you are only a little girl and that you have your father and me, but I am thinking of the future when we may not be here."

Mary's face puckered. "You are going away?"

"No, my dearest child, not now. I am thinking of the time ahead when perhaps it will be necessary for you to be a mother to your little sister and brother. You will, won't you?"

"Yes, mother."

"Come and kiss me. It will seal our bargain."

Mary hid her repulsion and solemnly kissed her mother.

Elizabeth Villiers saw Mary leaving her mother's apartment. She looked at her slyly as though to suggest that she knew what had taken place. How could she? Mary asked herself. But she was beginning to believe that Elizabeth Villiers knew a great deal.

When they were alone together Elizabeth whispered: "Are you going to be one?"

Mary did not understand.

"It won't be allowed," Elizabeth went on virtuously. "We won't let you . . . even if you want to."

"I don't understand you?"

Elizabeth put her lips close to Mary's ear. "Your mother's one. They are all saying so. They're wicked. They all go to hell. That's where your mother's going."

Mary was horrified. Had her mother not suggested that she was going away?

"Yes," said Elizabeth, "they frizzle like a sheep on the spit. The good angels turn them round to make sure they get thoroughly brown on all sides. That's what happens in hell and *they* all go there."

"You're . . . hateful."

"Because I tell you the truth?"

"I don't know what you're talking about."

"Don't you know anything?"

"Yes," said Mary, "I know I hate you."

"You mustn't hate. You go to hell for hating." Elizabeth made the movement of turning a sheep on a spit and there was an ecstatic light in her eyes.

"Stop it," said Mary.

"That doesn't stop. It goes on for eternity, and you know that means forever and ever . . . amen."

Mary turned to go but Elizabeth caught her arm. "We won't have Catholics here," she said. "Your mother's one. She tries to hide it but everybody . . . except you . . . knows it."

Mary wrenched her arm free of her tormentor, and as she ran from her, heard Elizabeth's taunting laughter.

She was puzzled and uneasy.

The King had heard the rumors of his sister-in-law's conversion and guessed that James was following her lead; he himself favored the Catholic faith and would have proclaimed this fact but for the memory of those early wanderings of his. He was more realistic than James and understood the temper of the people better than his brother. James was a sentimentalist; Charles was never that.

Charles hated intolerance and he would have liked to bring some relief to his Catholic subjects. It would give him a great deal of pleasure to reunite England with Rome—providing of course the changeover would not bring about trouble, which was the last thing he wanted. But he was a King and a Stuart and in spite of his good nature and love of peace there was in him an innate belief in the Divine Right of Kings. Why be a King if one must be governed by a Parliament? How tedious constantly to be told that he could not have this or that grant of money! And he was a man who always had a demanding mistress at his elbow.

Every Stuart would be haunted throughout his life by the martyred King Charles I. They would always remember how, being in conflict with his Parliament, he had lost his head. No Stuart should ever run afoul of his Parliament, and yet how could he but help it?

The nation was behind him, and he was convinced that the people would never allow the head of the second Charles to roll, for his father— with all his nobility and virtuous ways—had never appealed to his subjects as his merry son had done.

Could he take a chance?

How many chances had he taken during the days of exile—and after? It was second nature to take chances.

He needed money—desperately; and the Parliament would not grant it to him, so his eyes were on France. His sister—his beloved Minette, the favorite of all his sisters, who was married to the brother of Louis XIV— had been in secret correspondence with him. Minette had assured him of Louis's good will toward him; she had made him see that a French alliance was imperative. Imperative to the King or to the country?

"The King *is* the country," said Charles to himself with a cynical smile.

Sir William Temple had formed an alliance with Sweden; but negotiations were going on with Spain at the same time—and of course France.

Colbert de Croissy, the French ambassador, had proposals to put before him; he brought letters from Minette; Louis was ready to pay the King of England handsomely for his cooperation, but it was an alliance which, for the time being, must be kept secret even from the King's ministers.

What Louis wanted was alliance with England, and he would feel happier if this alliance were with a Catholic England. The King of England was half French; his mother had been a Catholic and it was natural that he should lean toward her religion. The King would be willing enough; but England was a Protestant country and the people would not easily be led to the Church of Rome. Still, a King could do much.

Charles knew that Louis wanted England to join forces with him for an invasion of Holland, and Charles to make public his conversion to the Roman Catholic Faith; he wanted the Church of England abolished and

England to return to Rome. For these concessions he was ready to make Charles his pensioner, and was ready to supply men and arms should the English reject the Catholic faith.

Minette would soon arrive in England to persuade her brother, for Louis knew that Charles found it difficult to refuse the women he loved what they asked; and without doubt he loved his sister, perhaps more deeply—certainly more permanently—than any other woman.

So much desperately needed money, mused Charles, and all for a Mass.

He sent for James, for this was a point wherein they would be in sympathy, and as his brother came into his apartment Charles was struck by his pallor.

"You are not looking well, brother," he said. "I trust naught ails you?"

"I was never the same since I threw off the pox, and since the boy went . . ."

Charles nodded. "And I hear sad news of my good sister Anne."

"She spends most of her time at Richmond with the children now."

"And on her knees, I hear."

James looked at his brother sharply.

"Ah," went on Charles, "it is unlikely that I should not be informed on such a matter. So the Duchess has now completely gone over to Rome?"

"She has not openly confessed to doing so."

"Our lives are an open secret, brother. And you? You are still toying with the faith, I hear. Nay, do not look startled. I myself am in like case."

James's eyes shone with hope. "Then I am right pleased," he said.

"You should more reasonably be disturbed. What think you the people of this realm will say to Catholic monarchs?"

"This is the true faith. We must stand by what is right."

Charles raised his black eyebrows and smiled sardonically at his brother. "Nay, James," he said. "This is a matter we take with caution. You should tread more warily. I am warning you. The Duchess goes her way; but is it for you, the heir presumptive to the Crown, lightly to follow?"

"It is not a matter of following," cried James hotly. "It is a matter of seeing the truth."

"The truth, brother, could be that, when your turn came, the people would have none of you."

"Then . . . for the sake of what I believe to be the truth . . ."

"You would cast aside the Crown? It is not always so easy, brother. Men and women do not take this matter of worship lightly. They do not say I will do it this way and you that. No, they say my way must be your way."

"The Catholic faith I am convinced is the true way."

"Others have been convinced before you, James. And where has it led? Look back over the past. Weigh the blood which has been shed in the name of religion. You could not. It is too vast, brother, and there are no measures great enough. I should not care to see bloodshed in this country, and two brothers sent on their travels again."

"What then, Charles?"

"I am warning you. Do what you must do in secret, 'tis better so . . . as yet. And warn the Duchess."

"She is ill, Charles; to her the most important thing in this life is her leaving of it."

"Brother, it may well be that before long I shall confess myself to be of our mother's faith. It may be that under my rule England will return to Rome."

James's eyes were shining. "A glorious day for England!"

"So say you? And who else James, who else? How many of my now loyal subjects would, on that day, rise up against me. The English are a lazy people, James. They shrug aside what would make a civil war elsewhere; but when their rights are touched on, when they make up their minds to take a stand, they stand firmly . . . more firmly than any other people in the world. That is what we have to remember—unless we are prepared to gamble."

"You were always a gambler."

"But like all good gamblers I don't take a risk until I see the chances of a win to be in my favor."

"And so . . ."

"This is a secret, James. Our sister will shortly be coming to England. My sweet Minette, how I long to see her! It is so long since I have done so.

She will be Louis's ambassadress. Even my closest ministers will not know what the treaty contains."

"And you will sign this treaty?"

"I shall think on it, James."

"You need to turn to the truth, Charles . . . you need this fervently."

"I need money even more," answered Charles lightly.

Charles and James were more friendly than they had been for a long time. The plans which the King was considering and which were known to his brother brought them close together; but the fact of their sympathies in religion was an even closer bond.

James was reconciled to his brother's flippancy, Charles to James's sentimentality. They were bound together in a common endeavor: to bring Catholicism back to England and—though James did not feel as strongly about this as Charles—never to go wandering again.

They were together on a hunting expedition in the New Forest when a messenger from France presented himself to Charles.

It was clear from his attitude that he brought bad news; and when they heard it it stunned them.

Their mother, Henrietta-Maria, was dead.

They thought of her—the dynamic little woman, whom many people said had in a large measure helped Charles I to his end. James remembered her raging against his marriage, refusing to receive Anne, doing everything she could to make their lives wretched. Yet, she had been his mother and she had suffered deeply.

Charles thought of her as she had been in the days of his childhood. "Mam," who had imperiously guided her children, and sought to rule their lives. He had never been her favorite, and on his restoration she had wanted to rule England through him. They had had their differences; but she was his mother. Then he thought of Henriette—his Minette—who had been the Queen's favorite child. Poor Minette, what must she be suffering now! And his grief was more for his sister than for his mother.

The brothers returned to Hampton and the Court went into mourning.

There was mourning at Richmond too, where the Duchess remained with her little son and daughters.

Charles came to see them there; he told Mary how her grandmother had had to leave England and how her Aunt Henriette, who he hoped would shortly come to visit him in England, had escaped to France with her governess, Lady Dalkeith, dressed in tattered clothes, and how she had been called Peter by her governess during this perilous journey because she was too young to understand and referred to herself as Princess, which on her baby tongue might be mistaken for Peter.

Mary never tired of hearing stories of her family's adventures; and indeed she believed that no other family could ever have experienced such stirring events.

Whenever Uncle Charles came, the occasion seemed a gay one, even when it was a time of mourning.

The Duchess was pleased to see the King's interest in her eldest daughter. James loved the children too; they would have two powerful people to look after their interests, she thought.

And when she retired that night she said to herself: "Death is in the air."

She was right. The following May Charles met his sister Henriette at Dover. There he secretly signed the treaty with Louis XIV, pledging himself to join France in an invasion of Holland and to confess his conversion to Rome. There was one clause which had decided Charles to sign. He could declare his conversion at a time of his choosing. That was what he clung to, for who was to say when was a good time to make such a declaration. It might well be that there would never be a good time.

But Louis would pay his pension all the same.

He was distressed that he could not spend longer with his beloved sister; but her husband the jealous Philippe, would not allow her to tarry even on the business of his brother, Louis XIV.

So Charles must content himself with this brief glimpse of his beloved sister; and even while he mourned to lose her, his eyes alighted on one of her beautiful maids of honor. Her name he learned was Louise de Kéroualle and she was a Breton; he begged his sister to leave her in England, but this Henriette told him she could not do because she was responsible to the girl's parents.

However, Louise and Charles exchanged looks and he knew that when he sent for her she would come to him.

So Henriette left in triumph, having received the signature for which she had come, to return to the King of France whom she loved and to her husband whom she hated; and she was a little sad to be leaving the brother whom she loved, for she knew that for the sake of the King of France she had persuaded him to do a reckless thing.

Charles was gallantly gay, knowing that he would not suffer because he was determined not to. He would receive Louis's money and keep his side of the bargain—in the words of the treaty—"when he considered the time had come to do so."

It was not such a bad arrangement, to let the King of France finance him for the sake of a vague promise. The only risk was that what he had promised should become known to his subjects. But he doubted not that he would know how to deal with an emergency should it arise.

Henriette returned to France and almost immediately news came that she was dead. Poisoned, said the rumors, through drinking iced chicory water.

When Charles heard the news he went to his apartments and stayed there. Never had the Court seen the King so stricken, and there was an air of melancholy everywhere.

The Duchess of York murmured: "Another death in the family. Oh, yes, indeed, death is in the air."

The Duke and the Duchess were reading letters which had been brought to them at Richmond, where they now spent the greater part of their time. The Duchess found it difficult to conceal her illness and kept to her apartments for days at a time. When the pain threatened she took sedatives containing opium and thus kept it at bay. But she knew that she was coming near to her end. For this reason her main preoccupation was with the future life. She was reading a letter from her father—a sad man in exile—for she had thought it necessary to tell him that she had become a Catholic.

He was disturbed. She knew that he believed the source of his troubles had been her union with the Duke of York, but she was convinced that this was not so. His overbearing manner, his criticism of the King's way of life had become unsupportable to Charles; moreover it was natural that the King should want younger ministers, men such as Buckingham, more like himself.

She was a foolish woman, wrote Clarendon. She should take great care. In every way was the Church of England superior to that of Rome. He knew her obstinacy, however, and he could understand from the mood of her confession that she was convinced and would stand firm. Therefore he was giving her a word of advice. If she wanted to keep her children at her side, then she must keep also her secret. Once she confessed that she was a Catholic, the King would be forced by the will of the people to take them from her.

These words made her ponder, for she knew there was much truth in them.

In his apartments James was also receiving disturbing news. This had been carried to him by a Jesuit, Symond, who had brought it from Pope Clement IX.

James had wanted to know whether the Pope would give him a dispensation if he, a Catholic, kept his religion secret and worshipped openly in the Church of England.

The answer was No. As a true Catholic he must proclaim himself as such, no matter what worldly advantages were lost to him.

Neither the Duke nor the Duchess were enjoying reading their letters.

James had been ill and was now convalescing at Richmond and it gave him great pleasure when Mary sat in his bedchamber and read or talked to him. She wished that she could have been happier in his company; she could not understand why she did not feel—as she could only express it—comfortable. She had listened to conversations in the nursery and whenever she was with her father she remembered these; she had a vague and unpleasant idea of his activities, and inwardly she shrank from him because she could never rid herself of images which came into her mind.

Then there was her mother who seemed daily to grow more ugly. Mary promised herself that she would never eat to excess, for she believed that her mother's bloated and unhealthy appearance was entirely due to the enormous amount of food she consumed. Anne, who had inherited her mother's appetite, should be warned.

It was the earnest wish of the Duke and Duchess to live these weeks as a happy family, to prove to themselves that their efforts to marry had been well worthwhile. The Duke remained at Richmond, faithful to his wife; the Duchess had grown gentle and uncritical, in fact she was often too exhausted to be anything else.

But with the children—Mary, Anne, and little Edgar—she attempted at times to be gay; and sometimes they would play games together; but there was an unnatural gaiety about those games which Mary detected; and those weeks which should have been so happy were overshadowed for her by a lack of ease. A sense of doom hung over her family and because she did not understand why it was there, who had caused it to be there, and what it was, she was all the more fearful.

There was a hush throughout the Palace. Mary, Anne, and little Edgar were in the nursery with Lady Frances and the Villiers girls. Even Elizabeth was subdued.

The Duchess of York had given birth to a daughter who had been named Catherine after the Queen. The infant was weak, though still living, but the Duchess was sinking and there was little hope of recovery.

The gentle Portuguese Queen Catherine had come to her bedside and was with her now. The Duke was there too and there had been much mysterious comings and goings.

Mary with Anne and Edgar waited in silence to hear what was happening; all day long they waited and no one came to tell them.

The Duke knelt by her bedside, remembering moments from the past which now seemed to him to have contained complete happiness. Never again would she upbraid him for his infidelity; never would they talk together of the mysteries of faiths. His eyes were wet with tears. He wanted her to live, for he could not imagine life without her.

His recent illness had weakened him and he wept easily. He thought of the children in the nursery, Mary, Anne, Edgar, and the new baby who, like Edgar, already had the mark of death on her.

"James," whispered Anne.

"My dearest?"

"Stay with me till the end."

"I could not bear to leave you."

"You must, James, soon, for the end is near."

"Do not speak of it."

"So you cared for me in very truth? Do not weep then, but rejoice. Soon I shall be past all pain."

"You are content to go, my love?"

"The pain has been great, James, but I die in the true faith. Do not let anyone come to my bedside and attempt to dissuade me. I know the way I am going. It is the chosen way."

"Have no fear," said James.

"And you believe as I believe?"

"I do."

"Then I am content."

When a messenger had entered the room to say that Bishop Blandford was outside, James left the sickroom and went to him.

"Your Grace," said Blandford, "I trust I am in time."

"The Duchess cannot see you," James replied. "She is a Roman Catholic and does not wish to be disturbed now with attempts to bring her back to the Church of England."

"Your Grace, allow me to see her. I will not attempt to dissuade her. I will speak to her as to a Christian of either Church."

"If you will swear to do this you may see her. I will not have her disturbed."

The Bishop promised and went to the Duchess's bedside.

When he had left, having kept his promise, James sent for Father Hunt and certain people whom he knew to be of the Catholic faith. The last rites were performed and when this was done the Duchess asked her husband to come near to her.

He was holding her in his arms, the tears streaming down his cheeks, when she died.

James asked that Mary be brought to him; he wanted to see his favorite child alone.

As soon as she entered the room Mary knew what had happened for he stood looking so lonely and desolate; and when he saw her he held out his arms.

"My dearest daughter, we are alone now. She has gone."

He picked her up and rocked her in his arms as though she were a baby.

"I have my children," he said. "Thank God she has left me them." He began to talk about her mother, telling of her virtues and how they had loved each other with a rare devotion; he trusted that when Mary married she would make as happy a marriage as that of her parents.

As happy a marriage as that of her parents? But what of the rumors? What of Margaret Denham . . . and others? What of the quarrels she had overheard? Had he forgotten? Could it be that he was not truthful?

He talked of when she married. She knew in that moment that she never wished to marry. She would like to live forever with her dear sister Anne.

"I don't want to marry, Father," she said.

He smiled and stroked her hair.

"So you will stay with your old father and comfort him, eh?"

It was not what she had meant, but the thought seemed to please him so she said nothing.

The Duchess was buried in Henry VII chapel at Westminster, and it was noticed that the Duke of York looked more and more to his elder daughter for consolation.

THE BRIDE FROM MODENA

oon after the death of the Duchess of York two new girls were introduced to the household at Richmond—Anne Trelawny and Sarah Jennings; and with the coming of these two the power of the Villiers was undermined, Anne Trelawny becoming Mary's great friend and Sarah Jennings, Anne's. Elizabeth Villiers was furious but there was nothing she could do about it; and she was beginning to realize that she had not been very clever because now that Mary was growing up she was becoming more important and the attitude of those around her was changing.

Mary herself was aware of this. "When I have my own household," she confided to Anne Trelawny, "I shall dismiss Elizabeth Villiers."

As yet she was far from that happy state.

Young Edgar died very soon after his mother, to be followed almost immediately by the new baby Catherine. The Duke was very sad and declared that he could only find comfort in the company of his daughters.

"Why does death always happen to us?" Mary asked him.

He held her tightly and put his cheek against hers. "It is happening all over the world," he explained. "It is a sad fact that many are born not to reach manhood or womanhood. But we must be good to each other, my little daughter, for you and Anne are all I have to love now."

She looked steadfastly into his face and thought of the rumors she had heard. "The Duke of York, like his brother, is a great lover of all women." Whispers. Laughter. There were many women, according to what she had heard. Then how could she and Anne be the only ones he had to love?

"You have been hearing talk of me," he said, and she felt the blood hot in her cheeks. Now he was going to tell her something shameful, something that she believed she would rather not hear.

"You have heard that I have been ill. It's true I believe that I was going into a decline; but my health has improved, dearest Mary. I shall be with you for a long time yet."

Her relief was evident. So he was referring to his ill health not that vaguely mysterious shameful life. He saw it and misconstrued the feeling which prompted it; his eyes became very tender.

"My dear little one," he said, "it is your love which makes life bearable for me." He stroked her hair. Then he said: "Mary, have you thought what Edgar's death means?"

"That we shall never see him again."

"Something besides. If the King has no children and when he and I are dead, it will be your turn."

She looked alarmed and he said: "Oh, that is for the years ahead, but your uncle and I will not live forever. And then, Mary, you could be Queen of England, for I shall never marry again."

She was very grave and he kissed her gently and said: "Do not be unhappy, dear child. We will not talk of the far, far distant future. Here is the present. We have lost dear ones, but let us remember that we have each other."

Elizabeth Villiers came into the schoolroom to find Mary there alone. Mary picked up a book and prepared to leave.

Elizabeth was defiant. She had been foolish but she was not going to admit it, for she knew Mary would always consider her an enemy.

"I suppose," said Elizabeth, "that you are thinking now Edgar is dead you will be Queen of England. That will never be."

"You seem to know so much. Does His Majesty ask you to share his counsels?"

"You never will be Queen. Your father will marry again."

"He will never marry again."

Elizabeth laughed and Mary turned away. But Elizabeth's words stayed in her mind.

Charles was well content. He had a new mistress whom he adored in Louise de Kéroualle, the girl who had come to England to comfort him after the loss of his sister; she it was whom he had seen in Minette's suite and coveted; he guessed of course that Louis had sent her to spy on him, but she was so desirable and the very fact that she was probably working for Louis added a piquancy to her charm. Charles was sure of his ability to look after himself as far as both Louis and Louise were concerned. There had as yet been no occasion to proclaim his faith to his country and he told himself sardonically that there might well never be—and he was receiving the installments of his pension from the King of France. A very satisfactory state of affairs.

A year had passed since the death of the Duchess of York and James was beginning to feel the need of domesticity. Often he thought tenderly of his late wife, recalling all the joys of the conjugal life and forgetting its restrictions. He was, he decided, not a man to live alone. Those days at Richmond, when he had believed himself to be going into a decline, and had lived quietly with his sick wife, their children about them, had been the happiest of his life. He forgot his infidelities, Anne's jealousy, the scandals and trials. Looking back he saw them all about a great open fireplace playing games such as "I love my love with an A." How proud he had been of Mary's quickness, how indulgent of young Anne's inability to find the right word! How he had prompted little Edgar! Oh, happy days! But how could he enjoy more like them without a wife?

He had soon deceived himself into the belief that his had been the happiest marriage in the world. And the reason? He had married for love. Those early struggles against his family and Anne's—how well worthwhile they had been.

If I married again, he told himself, it would be for love.

He did not at first recognize the charms of Susanna Armine, Lady Bellasis. She was neither very young nor very handsome. But one day something in her manner reminded him of his dead wife and the more he saw of her the more pronounced this likeness seemed to become and he began to picture her seated at a fireside with children around her.

From that moment he started to fall in love and his resolutions not to marry again were swept away.

He courted Susanna. At first the Court paid little heed, except to murmur that James had chosen a hard task because Susanna was known to be the most virtuous matron at Court. Charles looked on cynically. How like James, he thought; he would always make difficulties for himself. And why did he always select the least beautiful women!

Susanna appeared at first to regard the Duke of York merely as a friend and because of the nature of his attachment James was content for a while that this should be so. He would talk to her of the loss he had sustained and she confided in him her own troubles.

Her marriage had not been a happy one on account of her late husband's fondness for drink.

James condoled with her. "I, who was extremely happy in *my* marriage, can perhaps sympathize more deeply with those who had to make do with so much less."

"I thought I should never live through the disgrace," sighed Susanna, "when they came home and told me he was dead. Killed in a duel—in itself a criminal act. He had taken too much to drink and . . . his opponent killed him."

James put his hand over hers. There were tears in his eyes.

"How you must have suffered!"

"Moreover my husband was a Catholic; and my son is being brought up in the same religion."

James was ardently enthusiastic. He did not think she should regard that with any misgivings; he would talk to her of his opinions which, she would understand, in view of his position must be kept as secret as possible. "But I feel none the less seriously for that," he assured her.

She was a member of the Church of England, she told him, and nothing would change her, because she was convinced there was one true faith and that was the one she would always follow.

James was determined to convert her; she was determined to convert him; but far from making a rift between them, this drew them more closely together. She was his dear theologian, he told her; not even the Archbishops could put up such a case for the Church of England as she did, but he was going to demolish her arguments . . . one by one.

In this he failed and he was almost glad to fail, for it seemed to him that never had he heard such brilliant discourse. He pictured hours at the domestic hearth when they would talk to each other of their feelings for religion and perhaps between them, come closer to the truth than any had ever come before, because he had to admit he was moved by her arguments. She was brilliant; she was sound; she was even beginning to shake his absolute faith.

And that, he told himself, is what I need. Before I become a Catholic,

I must be sure that I am entirely one. There are too many risks to be run for me to take this lightly. What a joy therefore to discuss with Susanna. He called her his confessor, his guide and comfort.

This idyllic state of affairs could not go on.

One day Susanna said to him: "I have heard rumors which distress me. Your Grace's visits to me have been noted and I believe that we have become the subject of one of the Court lampoons. Doubtless my Lord Rochester is behind this for it is what one would expect of him."

James could not bear to see her distressed. "I will find out who did this and have him punished."

Susanna shook her head. "That will not stop the rumors. More likely will it strengthen them. Nay, you must not come here so frequently; and when you do come we must not be alone."

James was aghast. Not see Susanna! Not talk of what he called "their secret matter"! He could not endure such a state of affairs. But he agreed that it was intolerable that Susanna should be compared with those women of light morals who had been his mistresses.

He made a decision. His first marriage had been for love. Why not his second?

"Susanna," he said, "will you marry me?"

She was astonished. Marry the King's brother who was heir presumptive to the throne? It was impossible. The King and the Parliament would never allow it. When James married it must be to some foreign princess, and the marriage would be for state reasons.

"My dear," murmured Susanna, "that which you suggest could not be."

"It shall be," retorted James. "I married for love once and I shall do so again."

"It will never be permitted. I shall never forget the great honor Your Grace has done me, but I fear this is the end of our friendship. It breaks my heart and I know it saddens you. But the fact is without marriage we cannot be together as we wish; and I greatly fear that the King himself would forbid such a union."

"I was told this before, but I married as I wished. I swear to you I will do so again."

He kissed her tenderly, stemming his passion. He went to his apartments and wrote a promise of marriage which he sent to her without delay; and he made no secret of the fact that he had written it. He wanted the scandalmongering Court to know that Susanna Armine was not his mistress; nor ever should be, although he loved her so tenderly, because she was going to be his wife.

The King sighed deeply when he heard the news. He sent for his brother.

"James, James," he cried, "what new folly is this? Do you seriously believe that a man in your position can marry the widow woman?"

"If you are referring to Lady Bellasis . . ."

The King raised his eyebrows. "To whom else should I refer? Don't tell me you have given more promises of marriage to more widows?"

"She is the only one I can ever marry."

Charles sighed with affected relief. "At least there is only one! No, James, this is out of the question."

"I have heard that tale before."

"Alas, so have we, and it grows a little more wearisome the second time than the first. You cannot make a fool of yourself again—not at your age, brother."

"I do not consider . . ."

"Alas, you never do. A little more consideration, James, and you would be a better politician, a better future King, and perhaps a better sailor."

"I am in love with Susanna."

"I see you are indeed a lovesick boy. Now I pray you oblige me by going to your lady. Tell her that you will give her a house and land, a resounding title perhaps in time; but there will be no marriage. I am sure she will understand."

"She could not understand such a proposition. It is marriage or nothing."

"Alas, poor James, that it should be nothing as far as this good lady is concerned. Do not fret though. There are many fair ladies in the Court; some are very happy to accept a house and land . . . they will not ask for the ultimate sacrifice."

"Charles . . . I beg of you . . ."

"Pray do not beg. I never could abide beggars. Leave me now and think on what I have said."

When James had gone Charles summoned certain ministers to his chamber. When they were assembled he said: "The Duke of York grows restive. It is time he married. Find a suitable bride for him, and we will get the matter settled as soon as possible."

When Susanna understood that if James married her against the wishes of the King and the country he might be rejected by them, she herself decided to break off their friendship.

There was one last interview between them before James went off to join the Navy, for war with the Dutch had broken out again.

"I see," said Susanna, "that I can never be happy again. For if I married you I should continually reproach myself for the harm I had done you; and since I cannot, I shall think of you with longing all my life."

"Do not despair," cried James. "Once I have beaten the Dutch I will fight for our happiness."

She smiled sadly, for she knew that he would not.

She begged though to be allowed to keep his promise of marriage. It would be a little souvenir of the esteem in which he had held her and show the world that theirs had been an honorable relationship.

He declared he would come back to her. They embraced affectionately. Then James went off to win the battle of Solebay and restore to the Navy some of its lost prestige.

Meanwhile in London plans went ahead to marry the King's brother with as little delay as possible.

James, Duke of York, being the only living brother of the King and heir presumptive to the British throne, was one of the most desirable matches in Europe, but the negotiations for his marriage to a suitable lady were again and again frustrated.

The first choice—favored by the French—was Madame de Guise, but James would not have her, complaining that she was short, ungainly, and did not enjoy good health so would be unlikely to bear him children. The second, Mademoiselle de Rais, he also declined for similar reasons. The Archduchess of Inspruck seemed an ideal choice as far as he was concerned, for she was a Catholic; and he sent off Henry Mordaunt, Earl of Peterborough, who was not only a servant but a friend, to make the necessary arrangements with all speed. Unhappily before the marriage could be completed the mother of the Archduchess died and she decided to choose her own husband. She chose the Emperor Leopold I.

There were three other ladies who were considered suitable: these were the Princess Mary Anne of Wirtemburg, the Princess of Newburgh, and Mary Beatrice, Princess of Modena. These three were charming girls, but the most delightful of all was Mary Beatrice who was only fourteen years old.

Peterborough first visited the Duke of Newburgh with the object of reporting to his master on his daughter. He found her charming, but a little fat—and since she was so now, he asked himself what she would be in ten or fifteen years' time. He did not believe her worthy of his master, and as his object was known and he went away without completing arrangements for a marriage, this was never forgiven the Duke of York but remembered against him by the young lady for the rest of her life.

A picture Peterborough acquired of Mary Beatrice enchanted him for it showed him a young girl of dark and startling beauty, but since she was not yet fifteen it had been decided that negotiations should go ahead for bringing the Princess of Wirtemburg to London.

Mary Anne of Wirtemburg was living in a convent in Paris and hither Peterborough hastened, where he asked for an interview with the Princess and told her that her hand was being sought by James, Duke of York, heir presumptive to the British crown. Mary Anne, a gay young girl who found convent life irksome, was delighted, and being inexperienced unable to hide this fact. Peterborough was relieved, although he thought often of that lovely young girl who was by far the most beautiful of all the candidates.

These negotiations however were destined to fail, for suddenly Peterborough had an urgent message to stop them.

Having already informed Mary Anne that she was to marry the Duke, he was horrified by these instructions. It appeared that the King's mistress, Louise de Kéroualle, who was now the Duchess of Portsmouth, had selected a candidate—the daughter of the Duc d'Elbœuf; and although the King guessed that his mistress's plan was to bring her fellow-countrywoman into a position of influence that they might work together, so besotted was he that he allowed the negotiations already begun by Peterborough to be withdrawn.

It was typical of Charles that while he listened to his mistress and made promises to give her what she asked, he should find an adequate excuse for not doing so.

Mademoiselle d'Elbœuf he decided was too young for marriage to the Duke of York, being not yet thirteen; and James, being of more sober years, needed a woman who could be a wife to him without delay. So

Louise de Kéroualle did not have her way as she had hoped; but at the same time it was impossible to reopen negotiations with Mary Anne of Wirtemburg.

The Duke of York must be married. There was one candidate left. It was therefore decided that plans to marry James to Mary Beatrice of Modena should go forward without delay.

When James saw the picture of Mary Beatrice he was completely captivated and felt faintly relieved—although he would not admit this— that Susanna had rejected him.

When he showed it to Charles the King agreed that there was indeed a little beauty.

"She reminds me of Hortense Mancini," said Charles, nostalgically, "one of the most beautiful women I ever saw. You're in luck, brother."

James believed that he was. "Why," he said, "she cannot be much older than my daughter Mary."

"I can see you are all eagerness to have her in your bed."

James sighed: "I have a desire for domestic happiness. I want to see her at my fireside. I want her and Mary and Anne to be good friends."

Charles raised his eyebrows. "Spoken like a good bridegroom," he said. "One thing has occurred to me. The Parliament will do all in its power to stop this marriage. Your little lady is a Catholic and they will not care for that."

"We must make sure that the matter is settled before Parliament meets," said James.

"I had thought of that," Charles told him slyly.

He wanted to ask: And how is Susanna at this time? But he did not. He was kind at heart; and he was relieved that James had come out of that madness so easily.

Henry Mordaunt, Earl of Peterborough, Groom of the Stole to the Duke of York, had a task to his liking. He was going to Italy to bring home Mary Beatrice Anne Margaret Isobel, Princess of Modena, and although his previous missions of this nature had ended in failure, he was determined this should not; he was secretly delighted because as soon as he had seen the portrait of this Princess he had made up his mind that she was the ideal choice for his master.

Peterborough was devoted to the Duke of York; he was one of the few who preferred him to his brother; and since Mary of Modena was quite the loveliest girl—if her picture did not lie—that he had ever seen, he wanted to bring her to England as the new Duchess of York.

James had pointed out to him the necessity for haste. "Because," James had declared, "unless the marriage has been performed before the next session of Parliament, depend upon it they will make an issue of the fact that she is a Catholic and forbid it to take place."

Peterborough had therefore left England in secrecy; he was, he let it be thought, a private gentleman traveling abroad for his own business.

When he reached Lyons after several days, and rested there for a night before proceeding, he was received with the attention bestowed on wealthy English travelers, but without that special interest and extra care which a messenger from the Duke of York to the Court of Modena would have received. He planned to be off early next morning that very soon he might be in Italy.

While he was resting in his room a servant came to tell him that a messenger was below and would speak with him. Peterborough asked that the man be brought to his room, thinking that a dispatch had followed him from England. To his surprise it was an Italian who entered.

"I come, my lord," he said, "with a letter from Modena."

Peterborough was aghast. How did the writer of the letter know he was on his way to the Court. Who had betrayed his mission?

He took the letter and the messenger retired while he read it, but the words seemed meaningless until he had done so several times.

"The Duchess of Modena has heard of your intention to come here to negotiate a marriage for her daughter Mary Beatrice Anne Margaret Isobel, and wishes to warn you that her daughter has no inclination toward marriage, and that she has resolved to enter a convent and lead a religious life. I thought I must give you this warning, that you may convey to your Master His Majesty King Charles the Second and His Royal Highness the Duke of York, that while the house of Esté is very much aware of the honor done it, this marriage could never be." This was signed "Nardi," Secretary of State to the Duchess of Modena.

Peterborough was bewildered. His secret mission known! And moreover the Duchess already declining the hand of the Duke of York for her daughter!

And these messengers, what did they know of the contents of the letters? Was the project being discussed in Modena and throughout the countryside? Was this going to be yet another plan that failed?

Peterborough was determined that this should not be.

He asked that the messenger be sent to him and found that there were three of them. He offered them refreshment in his room.

While they drank together, he said: "It is strange that the Duchess of Modena should think it necessary to write to me. I am only a traveler who is curious to see Italy."

But of course they did not believe him; and as soon as they had left him he sat down to write to Charles and James, to tell them of this incident.

All the same, he lost no time in continuing with his journey, and in due course arrived at the town of Placentia, where he found Nardi, the writer of the letter, awaiting him.

"I have come," said Nardi, "to deliver to you a letter from the Duchess of Modena in which she herself will confirm all I wrote to you. Her object is, that such a great country as yours should not openly ask for that which cannot be granted. There are other Princesses in the family who might interest the Duke of York."

Peterborough replied, thanking the Duchess for her concern for him, but he was a private person.

All the same he fancied that the Duchess, while telling him that Mary Beatrice was not available, was very eager for him to choose another member of her family. And why not? Alliance with Britain was a great honor done to the House of Esté, petty Dukes of a small territory. Peterborough did not believe in all this reluctance; and the more he thought about the matter, the more determined he became to bring back Mary Beatrice for his master.

The reason for the Duchess's attitude was the young girl herself, her fourteen-year-old daughter.

The Duchess loved her daughter dearly. Her children, Mary Beatrice and Francisco, who was his sister's junior by two years, had been left in her care when her husband Alphonso d'Esté had died. Laura Martinozzi, Duchess of Modena, was not of royal birth, although she belonged to a noble Roman family, but she had sufficient energy and wit to rule her little kingdom. She was a strong woman, determined to guard her children; and when Alphonso died—he had suffered from the gout for many years—she was determined to be both father and mother to them.

She loved them with the force of a strong nature, but this love rarely showed itself in tenderness because she was determined to prepare them to face the world and for this reason she decreed that they should be most sternly brought up.

Mary Beatrice loved her mother too, because it quickly became apparent to her that all the whippings and penances which were imposed on erring children were for their own good. If she could not repeat her Benedicite correctly she would receive a blow from her mother's hand which sent her reeling across the room; when on fast days it was necessary to eat *soupe maigre*, a dish which revolted Mary Beatrice and made her feel absolutely sick, she was forced to eat it, because her mother explained, it was a religious duty. The little chimney sweeps with their black faces had frightened Mary Beatrice when she was very young for she thought they were wicked goblins come to carry her away; and the Duchess, hearing of this, forced her little daughter to go into a room where several little chimney sweeps had had orders to wait for her. There she was to talk to them, in order to learn that fears must be boldly faced. Little Francisco's health suffered from bending too closely over his books and the doctors thought that he needed more exercise out of doors. "I would rather not have a son than have one who was a fool without learning," was the Duchess's answer.

She was the sternest of parents, but in spite of this had so aroused her children's respect and admiration that they loved her. No sentiment was allowed to show; there was only sternness; but each day the Duchess spent much time with her children; she supervised their lessons and was present at meals, and they could not imagine their lives without her. She was the all-powerful, benevolent, stern but strict guardian of their lives.

When Mary Beatrice was nine years old her mother decided that she should go into a convent where she would be educated by the nuns. Here in this convent she found an aunt, some fifteen years older than herself, in whose charge she was put, and life flowered suddenly for Mary Beatrice. The affection of her aunt astonished and delighted her, because she had never been allowed to feel important to anyone before; she still admired her mother more than anyone in the world, but she loved her aunt; the nuns were kind too, kinder than her mother had been. If she made a little error there was no resounding box on the ears; and since she was not forced to eat *soupe maigre*, life in the convent was so delightful by comparison with that of the ducal palace that Mary Beatrice decided that she would become a nun and spend the rest of her days there.

This was the state of affairs when she was recalled from the convent to the ducal palace.

Her mother received her with more warmth than was usual and Mary Beatrice knew that she was secretly pleased.

"Sit down, my daughter," said the Duchess. "I have news for you, which I think you will agree with me is excellent."

"Yes, Mother."

"The Duke of York will most certainly be the next King of England." The Duchess paused. "You do not seem to understand."

"I am sorry, Madame, but I have never heard of the Duke of York nor of England."

"Your education is being neglected. What do you do in your convent?"

"We pray, Madame. We meditate. We . . ."

The Duchess waved an impatient hand. Religion was an important part of life, but it was necessary to learn something of the outside world. Never heard of England! What did this girl know of the politics of the world? Had it been a mistake to send her to a convent? Should she have been brought up in a more worldly manner? There was nothing to complain of in her religious education, but . . .

"England is one of the most important countries in the world," said the Duchess sharply. "I will see that you are instructed in its history— and its importance to Europe and ourselves—without delay. The King of England has no son or daughter who would inherit his crown; but he has a brother who is heir presumptive to the throne. This is the Duke of York; and he is asking for your hand in marriage."

The girl turned pale. "Marriage, Madame? That is impossible. I am to be a bride of Christ."

"I was not aware that I have been consulted, daughter."

"Madame, my life is in the convent. I belong in the convent."

"You are too young to make decisions affecting your future. You are not yet fifteen and—naturally—you will do as I say."

"Madame . . . the idea of marriage is repugnant to me."

"You know nothing of it. I shall decide."

The girl was suddenly rebellious. "I shall not marry," she cried. "I shall not!" And she fell into such a passionate storm of weeping that even the Duchess could do nothing to restrain her.

She looked at her daughter, that rippling jet black hair, that delicate skin, the dark firmly marked eyebrows, the heavy lashes, the perfect oval face and thought she was so beautiful that she must be one of the loveliest girls in the world.

The Duchess imagined her daughter—fourteen years old, married to the Duke of York, twenty-five years older than herself, already a father; and his reputation, although not quite as bad as that of his brother, the King of England, was decidedly tarnished.

Imagine this delicate—and surprisingly passionate—creature in his hands!

For the first time in her life the Duchess wavered. The honor of union with England should not be missed, but for Mary Beatrice, no. It was too much.

Perhaps the attention of the Duke of York could be diverted to one of the other princesses of Modena, someone older, more knowledgeable in the ways of the World.

The Duchess would try it before she forced her innocent young daughter into the arms of the over-amorous and, by reputation, even lascivious Duke of York.

During the next days Mary Beatrice grew so pale and despairing that her uncle Rinaldo d'Esté conferred with the Duchess concerning the proposed marriage, and when they called in the Duchess's confessor, Father Garimbert, they all agreed that, while the immensely influential union could not be abandoned, they must try to find another bride for the Duke of York.

"Twenty-five years her senior," mused Rinaldo, shaking his head.

"That will be less noticeable as she grows older," put in the Duchess, "and he is more likely to cherish a young girl than an ageing woman."

"The Princess should never be allowed to mate outside her religion," added Garimbert.

"Nor would she," was the Duchess's answer, "for the Duke of York is known to be a Catholic."

"A secret Catholic. I like that not," replied Garimbert, whose views always carried great weight with the Duchess. The outcome of these interviews was that the Earl of Peterborough should be invited to the Court; that he should be asked to suggest another Princess of Modena to his master; and that failing that Mary Beatrice might be persuaded to change her mind.

Immediately Secretary of State Nardi was dispatched to the lodgings of the Earl of Peterborough to invite him to the Court.

The Earl of Peterborough was delighted to receive an invitation from the Duchess and confidently set out for the Modena Palace. When he arrived he was taken at once to the presence of the Duchess who greeted him with warmth and respect, although it was obvious that she was a little uneasy.

"My lord Earl," she told him after the formal greeting, and when she had bade him sit down at his ease, "while being deeply conscious of the honor your great country does mine, I have to tell you that my daughter's wish is to become a nun and that she has no desire for the married state."

"Your Highness, the Princess is young as yet. She can have little knowledge of the happiness this marriage could bring her. Nor, if I may say so, can she understand all that is entailed in the life of a recluse."

"You speak truth, my lord. But she is of a delicate constitution and I do not know how she would fare in a colder climate than that in which she has lived her life."

"Our climate is temperate, Your Highness; and although we do not enjoy great warmth neither do we suffer from excessive cold. It would be the desire of the Duke of York to give his wife every comfort."

"Of that I am sure. But then shall we say that the main objection to this marriage is the fact that although I am told the Duke of York is a Catholic, he has not openly declared his faith. Before this marriage could take place it would be necessary to procure a dispensation from the Pope."

"And, Your Highness, if this dispensation were procured, there would be no further obstacles to the marriage?"

The Duchess hesitated. "As I told you, my daughter is very young. There are other members of my family who might be more suitable for His Grace of York."

"Madame, the Duke of York has set his heart on marriage with your daughter. This is the alliance which is acceptable to him."

The two regarded each other in silence for a few seconds; and during them the Duchess weighed up all that this alliance would mean to Modena; she knew also that it would be an alliance with Mary Beatrice or none at all.

"Yes," she said decisively, "if there is a dispensation, then I am of the opinion that the affair could be happily concluded."

"I should esteem it a favor if I might meet the Princess."

The Duchess bowed her head in assent.

When the Duchess led her daughter to the Earl, he could scarcely hide the effect her beauty had upon him. She was startlingly lovely—even more than her picture had led him to believe, and in that moment he had decided that, however difficult this task, he was going to succeed and take this strikingly beautiful girl home to his master. Her jet black hair fell about her shoulders, simply dressed as was becoming to one so young; but her lovely dark eyes were deeply troubled and he wanted very much to reassure her that she would have nothing to fear from his master who was the kindest man he had ever met.

The girl eyed him warily and it was clear that she, knowing his mission, was not very pleased to see him.

"My lady Princess," said the old Earl, when he had bowed over her hand, "I ask you to forgive me if I have in any way disturbed your tranquillity, but I have come to ask your hand for the Prince who is my master and to assure you that if you will consent to be his wife you will be one of the happiest women in the world, for he is a Prince of such geniality and kindness that you cannot fail to love him."

Mary Beatrice did not look at her mother as she began to speak quickly. "I am obliged to the King of England and his brother for this great honor, but I wonder why they chose me when there are so many Princesses more worthy than I . . ."

"There could be none more worthy."

She silenced him with an imperious wave of the hand. "If I am forced to accept this proposal when I have vowed myself to another sort of life, I do not see how I can ever be happy."

"Your Highness is mistaken. I who well know my master can assure you of that."

"You know him well and mayhap have influence with him. Then if you would be of service to me, I beg of you dissuade him from this marriage and beg him to look elsewhere."

The Earl was exasperated. Glancing at the girl's mother and seeing the sadness in her stern face, he felt depressed. The girl had too much spirit. If he were not careful this attempt to bring her home to James was going to fail. And having seen her, having written to his master of her incomparable beauty, how was James going to content himself with any other?

The interview was unsatisfactorily ended and the Earl continued in his despondency.

Mary Beatrice was exultant when she heard the Pope had refused to grant the dispensation. She embraced her seventeen-year-old friend and attendant Senorina Molza, and declared herself happier than she had been since this horrible proposition was made to her.

Senorina Molza, a little older and more experienced than the Princess, was more moderate in her joy. She had seen the comings and goings to the Duchess's apartments and guessed that the matter would not be allowed to end there.

The Duchess was being told how foolish she would be to pass over this chance of alliance with a great and powerful country. It would be pointed out to her that her daughter might well one day be the Queen of that country. All knew the value of these alliances.

"They can do nothing...nothing since the Pope refuses," declared Mary Beatrice. "Why are you so glum?"

"I am just praying that they will heed His Holiness," answered her friend.

"But of course they will. My mother is a good Catholic. How could she possibly go against the Pope's wishes?"

"How could she indeed?" murmured the Senorina Molza.

"Then cheer up. I should like to sing. I feel in the mood for singing."

But Mary Beatrice's joy did not last. The Cardinal Barberini, the Duchess's most trusted adviser, was at that moment closeted with her, explaining to her that to lose this great opportunity would be a folly which she would never cease to regret, and if the marriage took place, it would not be difficult to obtain papal forgiveness. The Duke of York was at heart a Catholic, and it was possible that His Holiness would come to regard the marriage as good for the Catholic world. It might well be that Mary Beatrice would influence her husband to become a declared Catholic and if it happened that James should one day take the throne, it would be almost a certainty that he would bring Britain back to Rome.

The Duchess was persuaded. Even without the dispensation, the marriage should take place.

When the news was brought to Mary Beatrice she was stunned; her women, the little Molza and Anna Montecuculi tended her; they bathed her tear-stained cheeks; they knelt beside her and told her that perhaps she would come to love England and her husband; they tried to make pictures of the glories of Court life in England. But poor Mary Beatrice could not be comforted. She declared that her heart was broken and that the only state she could pray for was death.

On a bright September day the Earl of Peterborough, who was to stand proxy for his master, was taken from his lodgings by young Francisco, Duke of Modena, and the Prince Rinaldo, to a chapel in the Ducal palace, and there he was married in the name of the Duke of York to Mary Beatrice of Modena.

An obscure priest married them, because no other would agree to do so, since the marriage was taking place without the dispensation from His Holiness. The bride's eyes were swollen with weeping and she walked like one in a dream. Her ladies stood about her ready to support her should she faint, which they expected, for she had taken very little food since she had known this marriage was to take place.

There could never have been a more reluctant bride.

The Earl was angry. This was he believed the greatest honor that had ever come to Modena and the girl was receiving it as though she were a beast being taken to the slaughterhouse. The Duchess was uneasy; as for the proxy bridegroom, he was afraid that something was going to prevent the marriage at the last moment.

But nothing did, and the ceremony proceeded. The Duke of York was married by proxy to Mary Beatrice and not until the diamond ring, the outward symbol of union was put on to that white and reluctant finger, was the Earl's relief apparent. Now he could prepare to take home to his master the one whom he believed to be the most beautiful girl in the world.

When James in London heard the news he was delighted. A wife, at last! And, if Peterborough could be believed, a beauty.

His eyes grew misty at the thought. He saw the years ahead, the children they would have—lots of them, girls as well as boys. He would spend much time with them. He remembered that period when he and Anne had lived with their children in Richmond Palace ... those months when they had both been ill and had believed themselves to be not long for the world. Anne had been right regarding herself; but he, by the blessing of the Virgin, had recovered his strength. They had been wonderful years—lived in the shadow of death it was true; but he would find even greater happiness when the sense of urgency was removed! With this young girl from Modena he would recover conjugal happiness. She and their children all about them. What greater joy could there be on earth?

They would have sons. He would have liked to see his dear Mary Queen of England, because of all his children she would always be his favorite; but it was better to have a boy. Mary would understand that. Yet never, he was sure, would he love a child as he loved Mary.

He wanted to share this joy with his beloved daughters. He could scarcely wait to tell them, so he went with all speed to the schoolroom, where he was delighted to find Mary alone with her sister Anne. His heart was full of love for them as he watched them for a second or so before they saw him. Purposely he had come unannounced because he wished this to be a very private meeting.

They were bending over a table drawing together and Mary was pointing out to Anne some fault in her work. What a pretty pair! Anne so placid
with her rosy cheeks and light brown hair; Mary so dark and graceful, so
serious—his darling best-beloved.

"My dearest daughters."

They looked up and in that moment he felt he was the happiest of
men. A lovely young girl for a bride . . . a girl not much older than this
delightful daughter. Oh, the future was going to be good indeed.

They had both risen, but he would have no ceremony on such an
occasion; he strode to them and putting one arm about each held them
against him.

"My dearest girls!" he murmured.

"You are very happy," said Mary, the perceptive one. "Something has
happened to please you, Father."

"It is something I am longing to tell you. I am providing you with a
playfellow."

Mary's long dark eyes were clouded. Another girl, she thought, to
invade the nursery, perhaps to be a friend rather to Elizabeth Villiers than
to her. Was this a matter for such rejoicing?

"You will be so delighted with her," went on James. "You too, Anne."

Anne smiled a little vaguely, and her father went on: "My daughters,
you will have more than a playfellow. You will have a mother."

"But our mother is dead . . ." began Mary.

"Alas, alas! We have never been happy since then, have we? So I
thought I should provide you with another. I have been married to a
charming young girl—only a few years older than you are, Mary. Are you
not pleased?"

"You said a playfellow," said Mary slowly. "This is a stepmother."

"She will be your friend, playfellow, *and* mother. My children, I see
happy days ahead for us all."

Mary smiled, only half convinced. She had already come to suspect
change.

$\mathcal{N}ow\ that\ the$ marriage by proxy had been completed, Charles and James waited for the storms to rise.

They were not long in coming. The Earl of Shaftesbury asked for an audience with the King.

Charles studied his minister sardonically and as he asked his business was well aware that he had come to protest and what about.

"Your Majesty," began Shaftesbury, "it is with great regret and misgiving that I hear of the plan to marry the Duke of York to the Princess of Modena. I beg Your Majesty not to proceed with this plan which I am convinced would not please the people."

"Your request comes a little late, my lord. The alliance is completed and the Duke already married to the lady."

Shaftesbury turned pale. "Your Majesty, then there is but one thing to be done. The marriage must never be consummated."

"You cannot be asking me to deprive these two people of so much anticipated pleasure—and one my own brother!"

"Your Majesty, I fear the reaction of the people."

"You must not be so fearful, my lord. This is a matter for the Duke. He is pleased with his marriage and a man of his kind needs a wife. Let him enjoy her."

"A popish marriage will not please the people, Your Majesty," insisted Shaftesbury. "But since it is an accomplished fact, should not the Duke of York retire from Court to live as a country gentleman?"

"I do not think this would be gracious welcome to his bride. I am also of the opinion that to ask the Duke of York to retire to the country would be an insult to the King's brother."

There was a gleam of rare anger in the King's eyes which caused Shaftesbury to retire hastily.

The mist hung on the trees in the gardens of Richmond Palace. It seeped into the apartments where Mary bent over her needlework. Very soon all the children would assemble in one of the gardens to see the burning of the effigy of Guy Fawkes, and the Pope, because this was the Fifth of November—the anniversary of that day when Mary's great-grandfather and his Parliament might so easily have become victims of the Great Gunpowder Plot. It was celebrated each year, more some said because the people liked displays than because they felt any great regret for King James I.

Anne Trelawny was sitting close to Mary and as usual the Princess Anne was in a corner whispering to Sarah Jennings. Anne's needlework was always neglected; she hated work of any sort and always made the excuse that she could not see, and because of this affliction of the eyes she was generally humored.

Elizabeth Villiers was primly stitching. She was smiling secretly as though she were well pleased.

"It'll be fun when the bonfire starts," she said. "This is a special Guy Fawkes day."

"Why?" asked Anne Trelawny.

"Don't you know?" Elizabeth was supercilious; she was looking at Mary.

"I don't see why there should be anything special about it," said Anne Trelawny.

"You don't know much! It's because the Lady Mary and the Lady Anne have a new stepmother."

"Yes," said Mary, turning to Anne Trelawny. "She is not much older than I and my father said she will be like a playfellow."

"A stepmother," said Elizabeth with a grimace, "*I* shouldn't like a stepmother."

"She won't be like an ordinary stepmother," suggested Anne Trelawny. "She's so young. Perhaps she will be with us."

Elizabeth looked scornful. "No matter how old she is, she's a step-mother. And the people don't like it. That's why they are going to make this a special Gunpowder Plot day. I heard them in the streets this morning. They were shouting: 'No popery.' And you know what that means."

Mary looked from one to the other, but Anne Trelawny tried to change the subject. "Last Fifth of November, one boy was burned to death in the palace bonfire."

"There'll be more burned to death tonight," gloated Elizabeth. "They'll all be shouting 'No popery' and letting everyone know they don't like this popish wedding."

"What nonsense you talk," said Mary loftily.

Anne Trelawny smiled at her in agreement. Elizabeth bent over her needlework; it was pleasant, reflected Mary, to have Anne Trelawny as her ally.

The young bride did not land at Dover until the twenty-first of November although the proxy marriage had taken place on the thirtieth of September. Desolate and frightened she had done everything she could to delay it. She was married, her mother had told her, and nothing could alter that; therefore she must reconcile herself to going to England and being a worthy Duchess of York. Mary Beatrice wept and pined; she ate so little and wept so often that her health began to suffer, and to reconcile her a little her mother agreed to go with her to England. This pacified her a little and when she knew that Signorina Molza, Signora de Montecuculi and Anna, and Signorina Turenie were to act as her personal attendants at the English Court she was even more cheered. But there were occasions when she considered what all this change in her life was going to mean to her; she was being torn from her home to live in a strange country; she would have to say good-bye to her brother who had been her friend all her life; she would have, eventually, to lose her mother, for although the Duchess would accompany her to England, naturally she would not stay there; and most terrifying of all, she must be a wife—and to an old man, yet one who had had many mistresses as well as a previous wife. The thought of physical contact with such a man horrified her.

She was in such a state of despair that she prayed every day for some calamity to occur—she believed she would have welcomed anything which would have prevented her arriving in England.

Preparations continued and at length the day fixed for her departure drew near, and with her mother, her friends and attendants she began the long journey through France. So desperate had she become that one morning when Anna Montecuculi came to waken her she found her delirious and suffering from a fever. This was the beginning of an illness which gave great alarm to everyone, for so distressed in mind was she that they feared for her reason. Her mother was at her bedside throughout the day and night; and as she sat there the Duchess wished that she had not been persuaded to agree to this marriage. However, it was done now; her daughter was married—albeit by proxy—to the Duke of York and nothing short of her death could prevent her going to England. It was two weeks before Mary Beatrice recovered and then Louis XIV invited her to rest awhile at his Court until she regained her strength. This put heart into Mary Beatrice because it was certainly going to mean some delay.

When Louis met her he was delighted with her beauty and charm, and she was fêted and honored by him and his Court; he told her that he would be delighted to have her with him forever. These were empty compliments, she was well aware, and now that she realized the inevitability of her fate she had accepted it, but her lovely face was marked with melancholy and those who loved her were very sad on her account.

She would never forget her despair as she saw the coast of France receding; she prayed for a storm which would destroy the vessel and then immediately thought of all the others who would suffer with her. That must not be, she knew. She wanted a storm in which she and she alone would lose her life.

A tragic way for a bride to come to her bridegroom.

A strong wind arose, but that seemed only to mock her, for it carried her vessel to Dover with greater speed than, said the sailors, could have been hoped for.

On the sands she found waiting for her—her husband. He was old—very old, she thought—and there were wrinkles about his eyes; and because she had imagined him to be an ogre he seemed to her like one. He took her hands and then embraced her, and assured her he was very happy to see her. She tried to smile but could not do so; and when he drew back to look at her, he said: "But you are beautiful . . . even more beautiful than they told me you were."

His eyes, his warm and passionate eyes, took in each detail of her lovely face.

"Why, my little wife," he went on, "you are going to be happy. We are going to be the happiest family in the world."

She was aware of her husband's attendants standing by; her mother was beside her, so was the Earl of Peterborough, whom she regarded as her enemy because she believed that if he had been less determined the marriage might never have taken place.

There was no turning back now. The quiet of the convent would never be hers. She was aware of her husband's desire for her; she knew that he was longing for that second marriage, in which there would be no proxy for the bridegroom, with an intensity which matched that of her dread.

Her hand was in his; he held it firmly as though to say she should never escape him. She was shivering, believing that this consummation of which she knew so little but which she dreaded, would be even more alarming, even more shocking than she had feared.

He whispered to her: "You are happy to be here?"

She was too young to hide her feelings. "No, no," she answered.

He was taken aback, but the desire in his eyes was touched by a certain tenderness. "You are so young. There will be nothing to fear. I will do everything in my power to make you happy."

"Then perhaps you will send me home."

Those about them had heard her words. Her mother was frowning, and Mary Beatrice knew she would be scolded but she did not care. She had always been brought up to believe it was wrong to lie. Well, she would tell the truth now.

James smiled whimsically as he broke the horrified silence. "My little bride," he said kindly, "it is natural that you should be homesick . . . just at first. Soon you will understand that this is your home."

The next day the marriage was solemnized in accordance with the rites of the Church of England and Mary Beatrice then wore, as well as the diamond ring which had been put on her finger at the proxy marriage, a gold ring adorned with a single ruby which James gave her during this ceremony.

James had done all he could to pacify her; he sat beside her at the banquet which followed; he expressed concern at her poor appetite; he coaxed her and endeavored to persuade her that she had nothing to fear from him. She wept bitterly and made him understand that no matter how kind and considerate he was, he had torn her away from the life she had chosen and now she would be forced to live in a manner repugnant to her.

James was a practised lover, his experiences in that field being vast, and he used all his powers to lessen the ordeal which he understood faced this young wife of his.

He explained to her the need for them to have sons; their son, he told her, might well be King of England; it was for this reason that marriages were arranged. He was sure she would wish to do her duty.

Mary Beatrice lay shuddering in the marriage bed. She prayed, while she thought he slept, that something would happen to prevent the events of that night ever being repeated. She did not know that James lay wakeful beside her, thinking of the passion he had shared with Anne Hyde before their marriage, asking himself what happiness there was going to be for him and this girl who was nothing but a child, nearer to his daughters than to him.

The bride must surely be one of the most beautiful girls in the world. Anne Hyde was far from that. Yet what a travesty of his first marriage was this. He believed that she dreaded his touch, loathed him for the loss of her virginity; she had made him feel ashamed, a raper of the innocent.

This was not the union for which he had longed.

The wedding party did not stay long in Dover, but were soon on their way to London. All along the route people came from their houses to see the Italian bride. She was viewed with curiosity, admiration, and suspicion. She was after all a Catholic and the Duke was suspected of being one; and although her youth and beauty enchanted all who beheld her, there were murmurs of "No popery."

The Duke rode beside his bride and in spite of his misgivings he could not disguise his pride in her, and as he watched her acknowledging the acclaim of the people with grace and dignity in such contrast to the frankness in which she had shown her dislike of him, his spirits lifted a little. She was after all a Princess, and would know what was expected of her.

He began to think with pleasure of his latest mistress. How differently she would welcome him! A man could not make continual love to a woman who was repelled by the act. But Mary Beatrice would change—and when it had ceased to become a matter of duty, when she could respond with ardor, then would be the time to build up that idealistic relationship for which he, being a sentimental man, longed.

They slept at Canterbury the first night where the citizens welcomed them with affection. Pageantry was always a delight in Restoration England; the people had been too starved of it during puritan rule, not to find pleasure in it, whatever the cause; but Mary Beatrice could find none in the beauty of the Cathedral City; she felt bruised and bewildered and there was nothing for her but the thought of past horror and the dread of more to come. And the second night in Rochester her mood had not changed.

And so they came to London and at Gravesend, amid the applause of the spectators, the Duke of York took his Duchess aboard his barge, which, decorated with evergreen leaves, was waiting for him.

James had successfully hidden his disappointment in his marriage and appeared to be quite delighted with his bride. As they stepped aboard, to the accompaniment of sweet music which was being played by the barge musicians, he told her that somewhere on the river they would meet the royal barge and he was sure that his brother would be on board.

"The King will wish to greet you in person at the earliest moment," he told her, and when he saw the look of fear cross her face, he smiled grimly. The reputation of Charles had in all likelihood reached her, as his own no doubt had, and she was going to be as repulsed by the King as by the Duke. He hoped she would not be as frank with Charles as she had with him; but he ruefully accepted the fact that Charles would doubtless know how to deal gracefully with the situation whatever it should be.

"You will have nothing to fear from the King," he told her. "He has a reputation for kindness and he will be kind to you."

Her expression was stony; he thought ruefully she would be almost unbelievably beautiful if she would smile and be happy.

Down the river sailed the barge; the bells were ringing, and sounds of revelry came from the banks; there were cheers, and shouts for the bride and groom to show themselves. This they did, waving to the people as they sailed along. James was once more pleased to notice that his wife did her duty in this respect. How different it might have been, sailing down the river on this November day, if he had had a happy young girl beside him who was prepared to love him as he was her.

At length they met the royal barge, and a messenger boarded the

Duke's with a command from the King. His Majesty was eager to greet his brother's bride and he wished the Duke to bring her to him without delay.

James smilingly reassured her, saw the fear in her face, and thought it was a pity she, being so young, was unable to hide her feelings. He was dreading that moment when she came face to face with her brother-in-law—the rake of rakes, the man whose reputation was known throughout the whole of Europe—Charles, King of England, whose mistresses ruled him and the only comfort in that situation was that they were so numerous.

Poor little Mary Beatrice! They should never have made such a little nun of her.

Charles was waiting on deck, and taking his wife's hand James led her forward. He saw the lovely eyes lifted to that dark humorous face, already marked with debauchery yet losing none of the charm which had been there when Charles was a young man of twenty. Perhaps there was a deeper kindliness in the lazy, yet shrewd eyes, perhaps the charm increased with the years which was nature's special concession to one who loved life—as he loved his mistresses—passionately while he refused to take it seriously.

Mary Beatrice bowed low but Charles took one look at her lovely face, her graceful body, and with an exclamation of delight lifted her in his arms.

No one could dispense with ceremony more naturally and gracefully than Charles and whatever he did, he had the gift of making the action seem acceptable and charming.

"So I have a sister!" he cried. "And what a delightful one! I trust my subjects have been giving a good account of themselves." He glanced quickly at James and his eyes said: You fortunate devil! Would I were in your place.

Mary Beatrice was surprised at the complete revolution of her feelings. She had come on board prepared to hate this man; she had been fighting her feeling that she might not betray the aversion she felt for him. Instead, she was smiling, glad to put her hand in his, finding it a pleasure to be led to the rail to be seen standing side by side with him by the watchers on the bank.

"Why, my dear," he said in that soft tender voice he invariably used for attractive women, "you are very young, and you have come a long way from home. It is a trying ordeal, I understand full well, for I remember when I was young I was forced to leave my home . . . under very different circumstances than those in which you have left yours. The homesickness . . . the yearning . . . my dear sister, they have to be lived through to be understood. But remember this, that although you suffer from leaving your home, you bring great pleasure to us because you have come to live among us. Now you shall sit beside me and tell me what you have left. I have a fondness for your mother, of which I shall tell her soon. I remember how desolate she was when you lost your father and how she brought up you two children. A bit stern eh? *Soupe maigre?* Ah, I have heard of that! Rest assured, little sister, we shall not force you to eat *soupe maigre* while you are with us."

Mary Beatrice was smiling, and James looked on in astonishment. What power was this in his brother to charm? How could he, in his careless way, in a few short moments put at ease this girl whom he himself had tried so hard to please.

He could not answer that question. All he knew was that from the moment Mary Beatrice met the King she became a little less unhappy, a little more reconciled to her marriage.

When the party arrived at Whitehall the bride was conducted into the palace and there the King presented her to his Queen.

Mary Beatrice was greeted by the quiet Catherine with affection, while the King and the Duke looked on benignly. Mary Beatrice's mother had told her that the Queen of England would be her friend because, like herself, she was a Catholic living in a country where the recognized religion was that of the Reformed Church.

"We will have much in common," Catherine told her; the Queen's voice was a little sad, for she was wondering how this young and clearly spirited girl would deal with her husband's infidelities. She, Catherine, had been bewildered, humiliated, and deeply wounded by those of the King. She hoped that Mary Beatrice would not have to suffer as intensely as she had. "I trust," went on Catherine, "that we shall be friends and that we shall have informal hours together."

Mary Beatrice thanked her and then turned her attention to the two young girls who were being brought forward.

These were her stepdaughters—the Princess Mary and the Princess Anne. She studied them eagerly for the elder was not so many years younger than herself. Mary was about eleven years old—tall, graceful, with long dark eyes and dark hair. Her manner was serious and because Mary Beatrice guessed she was as apprehensive as she was herself, she felt a longing to show her friendship for this girl, and for the second time her spirits were lifted and the prospect of her new life seemed a little less grim.

It was possible to have a little informal conversation with her stepdaughters and then she realized that neither of them resented her and were anxious to be friendly.

"My father tells me that you will be as a sister to us . . . just at first," Mary told her. "But you are in truth our new mother."

"I will do my best to be all that you wish of me," answered Mary Beatrice.

She looked at Anne who gave her her placid smile; and she knew at once that they would help her to bear her new life.

Charles smiled knowledgeably at his brother.

"I trust you are taking advantage of your new state, brother?" he asked lightly.

James frowned. "She is beautiful, but very young."

"It is rare that men complain of the youth of their mistresses or wives."

"She is but a child and they have brought her up with a craving to be a vestal virgin."

"I trust for the honor of our house she can no longer aspire to such folly."

James was moodily silent and the King went on: "Some of your enemies are suggesting that, having made this Catholic marriage, you should for the sake of peace retire from Court. It was hinted to me only the other day. How would you like, James, to leave Court and take your little beauty into the country?"

"My place is at Court."

"So think I," said Charles. "But methinks also, brother, that if you were as successful at courting your wife as you are at courting trouble you would by now have persuaded her that the life of a vestal virgin is not nearly so exciting as that of Duchess of York."

"I do not propose to leave Court."

"Nor do I propose that you should. I have already said so. But the people are not pleased with you, James. You stand for popery and the people in these islands do not like it."

"What am I to do?"

Charles lifted his shoulders. He too secretly stood for the Catholic Faith; he had even made a bargain with Louis to bring his country back to Catholicism—yet he dealt with these matters shrewdly, graciously, and secretly. Why could not James do the same?

"Act with caution, brother. Stand firm. Remain at Court. Honor your little bride. Let every man know that you realize he envies you the possession of such an exquisite young creature, which I am sure he does. Do your duty. Let the Court and the people know that while she be young and so beautiful and a Catholic she is also fertile. Do this, James, and do it boldly. And, would you like a further word of advice? Then get rid of the mother."

"But my wife's great consolation is her mother."

Charles smiled shrewdly. "It is a fact, brother, that when a Princess comes to a strange land and is a little . . . recalcitrant, she changes when she is no longer surrounded by relations. The old lady reminds her daughter by her very presence of all that she has missed in her dreary convent. Get rid of the mother, and you will find the daughter becoming more and more reconciled to our merry ways. There is little room for vestal virgins and their dragons here at Whitehall."

James was silent. Charles who had charmed Mary Beatrice, who conducted his affairs with skill, who was a Catholic at heart and kept the matter secret for the sake of expediency, who had dared make a treaty with France which could have cost him his throne, whose wife was as Catholic and as foreign to Whitehall as Mary Beatrice and yet was in love with him—must understand what was the best way to act.

It was six weeks since Mary Beatrice had arrived in England. Christmas was over and she was astonished at the extravagance with which it had been celebrated. She had discovered that her charming brother-in-law scarcely ever spent his nights with the Queen; that fidelity and chastity in this island were qualities which, among the King's circle, were regarded with incredulous pity; she was surprised that Queen Catherine longed for her husband's company almost as intensely as Mary Beatrice prayed she would not have to endure hers; this Court was gay and careless; it was immoral and irreligious. It was all that she had feared it would be and yet she was a little fascinated, if not by it, by certain personalities. The chief of these of course was the King. He was making her fascinated by his Court as she was a little by himself.

When, during the Christmas festivities, she heard her mother was to leave England, she wept bitterly.

Duchess Laura comforted her, pointing out that she could not leave Modena and her son, the young Duke, forever. She had done an unprecedented thing when she had come to England with her young daughter, but now Mary Beatrice was old enough to be left.

"I shall die of sorrow," declared Mary Beatrice.

"You will do no such thing. You have your friends, and your husband is kind to you."

Mary Beatrice shivered. Kind he was; but she wished there were no nights. If it were always daytime she could have endured him.

"When you leave me," she told her mother, "my heart will be completely broken."

"Extravagant talk," said the Duchess, but she was worried.

When by the end of December the Duchess had left for Modena, James discovered his wife to be in such a state of melancholy that he wondered whether he should leave her to her Italian women attendants for a few days. It was disconcerting to know that he was almost as great a cause of her wretchedness as her mother's departure.

A few nights after the Duchess had left, Mary Beatrice said to her husband: "When I am with child as I must soon be, then you need not share my bed."

James looked at her sadly.

"Then," he said slowly, "it shall be as you wish."

Her ladies had prepared her for bed. She shivered as she did every night. Soon he would be there. She anticipated it with horror: his arrival, the departure of the attendants, the dousing of the candles.

He was late. They were chattering away, not noticing, but she did. She must be thankful, she told herself, if the dreaded moments were delayed even for a short while.

They talked on and on—and still he did not come.

"His Grace is late," said Anna.

"Perhaps we should leave you," suggested one of the others.

Mary Beatrice nodded. "Yes, leave me. He will be here soon."

So they left her and she lay shivering in the darkness waiting for the sounds of his arrival.

They did not come.

For an hour she lay, expectant; and finally she slept. When she awakened in the morning, she knew that he had not shared her bed all night.

She sat up, stretched her arms above her head, smiled and hugged herself.

If all nights were as the last one would she enjoy living at her brother-in-law's Court? The gowns one wore were exciting; so was the dancing; she did not greatly care for the card playing but she need not indulge in that too much. She was one of the most important ladies of the Court and the King made sure that everyone realized this.

How strange this was! Her mother had left her; she was alone in a foreign land; yet, when she was free of the need to do her duty as a wife, she was less unhappy than she had believed possible.

The next night she waited and he did not come; and during the following day she knew why.

It was Anna who told her, Anna who loved her so much that she shared her unhappiness to a great degree and knew her mistress's mind as few others did.

"He spends his nights with his mistress. I do not think you will often be worried by him. This woman was his mistress before the marriage and I have heard that he is devoted to her."

"His mistress!" cried Mary Beatrice. "But he has a wife now."

"But the marriage was for state reasons. He will continue with his mistresses. He is like his brother."

"I see," said Mary Beatrice blankly.

"I do not think you will be greatly troubled with him in future."

"I shall tell him that it does not please me that he should continue with this woman."

Anna opened her eyes wide. "But do you not see? While he is with her, you are free of him."

"Yes, yes," said Mary Beatrice. "That is a matter for which I must be grateful."

"Well, if you want to be rid of him, who better to take him from your bed than a mistress?"

"You are right, of course," replied the young Duchess.

Night, and her attendants had left her. She was waiting for him, expectantly, angrily. It was five nights since he had been to her.

She did not believe she was pregnant. He had no reason to think so either. Yet he continued to spend his nights with his mistress.

It was humiliating. She, a Princess, to be left alone because he preferred another woman! She was his wife. He had pretended to be so pleased because she had crossed the seas to come to him; the Earl of Peterborough had wooed her urgently and tenaciously on his behalf in spite of her protests.

Now here she was—neglected on account of a mistress!

Was that his step outside the door? He was coming after all. She sat up in bed, clasped her arms about herself, apprehensive, terrified.

But it was not his step. She stared about her darkened room, and knew she was to be alone again.

She thought of him with that woman. What was the woman like? Beautiful she supposed. All mistresses were beautiful. Men went to them not for the sake of duty; it was all desire where a mistress was concerned. For the sake of such women, they left their wives . . . lonely.

Lonely. She was lonely!

She lay down and began to weep silently. Perhaps he would come and find her weeping. He would say: Do not be afraid. I'll go away because that is what you wish.

He would be pleased to go because he preferred to be with his mistress than to do his duty with his wife. So it was duty?

Mary Beatrice's eyes flashed angrily and she dealt her pillow a blow with a clenched fist.

Then suddenly she put her face on her pillow and gave way to her sobs.

A realization which bewildered her had come into her mind.

She wanted James.

THE PASSIONATE

FRIENDSHIP

The girls made a pleasant picture walking in Richmond Park; four of them were arm in arm—the special friends: the Princesses Mary and Anne with Anne Trelawny and Sarah Jennings. Sarah was such good company and the Princess Anne kept screaming with laughter at her comments.

Behind were two of the Villiers sisters—Elizabeth and Katherine—outside the magic circle of friendship. Mary pressed Anne Trelawny's arm to her side in a sudden gesture of happiness. It was pleasant to have such a friend; she felt completely at home with Anne Trelawny; and since she had always been devoted to her sister, she was now in the company she loved best. Sarah Jennings was a little overbearing, but Anne thought her so wonderful that Mary accepted her as a member of the quartette.

Princess Anne peered shortsightedly ahead and said: "Let's go toward that tree over there."

Following the direction in which she was pointing, Mary could see no tree; but there was a man standing on the grass.

"It's not a tree, Anne," said Mary. "It's a man."

"Oh no, sister, it's a tree."

"It's a man," insisted Mary.

Anne turned away and replied: "I'm sure it is a tree."

"Well, we'll go and see. I am determined to show you that you are wrong."

Anne shrugged her shoulders in her lazy way. "Oh, I'm sure it's a tree. I don't want to go that way now. Let us go back to the Palace."

Mary looked reproachfully at her sister. Anne must be taught a lesson, and Mary was going to teach her that she must not make observations and insist that they were true before proving them.

Releasing Anne Trelawny's arm and taking her sister's she led her across the grass. As they came near to the object of dispute, it began to walk.

"There," cried Mary triumphantly. "You cannot doubt now what it is?"

Anne had turned her head and was smiling blandly in the opposite direction. "No, sister," she said, "I still think it is a tree."

Exasperated, Mary said: "Oh, Anne, there is no reasoning with you. Let us go back to the Palace."

As they came within sight of the Palace she forgot to worry about this unfortunate aspect of her sister's character because she saw the Duke of Monmouth giving his horse to one of the grooms.

A call from Jemmy was always a pleasure.

Monmouth had called on the sisters whom he knew were always pleased to see him. He had thought of a new idea for bringing himself to his father's notice; not that that was necessary for Charles was always very much aware of him; but Monmouth longed to show how he excelled in all courtly attainments, how much more popular he was than his Uncle James, how much more the people esteemed him than they did his uncle. When

Monmouth had first heard that James was to have a young wife he had been angry and depressed. A young wife would probably mean sons, and once a son was born to James, Monmouth's hopes of being legitimized would completely disappear. It was only while there would be no one to follow James but his two daughters that there was a chance that Parliament would agree to make a male heir by this legitimization; and once the Parliament wished that, Charles, Monmouth was sure, would be very ready—or at least could be easily persuaded—to agree.

Unfortunately James was now married—and to a young and beautiful girl. It was almost certain that there would be issue. Then the bell would toll, signifying the burial of Monmouth's hopes.

But Jemmy was by nature optimistic and exuberant. He never accepted defeat for long. The marriage was one of the biggest blows to his hopes that could have been given him; and yet almost immediately he began to see a glint of brightness.

The celebrations of the last Fifth of November had been an inspiration to him. Whenever he heard the shout of "No popery" in the streets he rejoiced. James might produce legitimate sons but he was a Catholic and the people showed clearly on every possible occasion that they did not want a Catholic on the throne.

The young Duke of Monmouth had, in the last weeks, become a man deeply interested in matters of religion. He was seen at his devotions frequently; although he continued to live as gaily as anyone at the Court, his conversation was spattered with theological observations. He was ostentatiously Protestant; and already the Protestants were beginning to look on him with great favor.

The seed was being sown. It might not bring forth a good harvest but that was a chance he had to take. Against the Catholic Duke of York, the legitimate successor to the throne of England, there was the Protestant Duke of Monmouth—a bastard it was true, but a little stroke of the pen could alter that.

Perhaps, then, he mused as he made his way to Richmond Palace to ingratiate himself with the Duke's young daughters, the marriage was not altogether a bad thing. If the young Duchess failed to produce the heir—and he prayed that she would fail to do this—if it were a plain contest between York and Monmouth . . . well, who could say what the outcome would be? But he must hope there would be no offspring; these young children had a way of worming themselves into the hearts of the people, were they Catholic or Protestant.

He had heard talk too that Charles was thinking of taking the education of Mary and Anne out of their father's hands since the Catholic marriage. All to the good. Let the people understand that the King was aware of the dangerous influence of Catholicism which had tainted the York branch of the family. It would help them to think more kindly of Protestant Jemmy.

"Hail, cousins," cried Monmouth, as the sisters hurried to him to be embraced.

"Great news. Can you dance? Can you sing?"

Anne smiled and nodded but Mary replied: "We are not very good, I am afraid, cousin Jemmy."

"Well, we will soon remedy that. Now listen. I am arranging for a ballet to be performed before His Majesty. How would you like to play parts in it?"

Anne said: "It will be wonderful, Jemmy."

"But we are not clever enough to perform before His Majesty," added Mary.

"My father is lenient toward those he loves." Jemmy, Mary noticed, always referred to the King as "my father," as though he were afraid people were going to forget the relationship.

"But he does not care to be wearied," put in Mary sagely. "And I fear that we might do that."

Monmouth put his head on one side and studied the girls shrewdly. Mary was wise for her age; and there was truth in what she said.

"Suppose," he suggested, "you danced and recited for me now. Then I could judge whether you were good enough to perform before my father."

Anne was willing enough. It never occurred to her to worry what people thought of her. If they did not like what she did, she would shrug her shoulders and forget. Mary was different; she hated not to be able to please.

Anne performed carelessly and badly; Mary made too much effort and was equally bad.

"I have an idea," said Monmouth, "you shall have lessons. Then I think you will be very proficient. I've set my heart on your dancing with me before the King. In fact, this has been written with parts for you in mind. So it has to be."

"Shall we need many lessons, Jemmy?" asked Mary.

"Very many and with the best teachers. Leave this to me."

It was wonderful, Mary told Anne afterward, to be part of Jemmy's ballet. Jemmy said that they would be at Court and that it was time they were there.

"I've always wanted to go to Court," Anne answered. "Sarah says we should be there. Sarah would enjoy it . . . and of course if we were there so would she be."

"We must do our best to improve our dancing," said Mary.

"So that we may be invited to go often to Court?" murmured Anne.

"So that we do not disappoint Jemmy," added Mary.

As a result of Monmouth's plan, Mrs. Betterton, the principal actress at the King's Theater, arrived at Richmond in order to instruct Mary, Anne, and their friends on how to speak on a stage, how to walk on to one, how to conduct themselves with grace, charm, and utter naturalness.

James had readily given his consent to her appointment because he knew how much Charles enjoyed theatrical performances and he thought it a good idea that his daughters should shine before their uncle.

The girls enjoyed their lessons and adored Mrs. Betterton who seemed so gay and amusing to them and made their lessons more of a game than a task.

Mary was happy. Her new stepmother had proved to be a gentle creature who seemed to want to please her as much as she, Mary, wanted to please her stepmother. The grim creature Elizabeth Villiers had tried to conjure up had no likeness to her at all; and it was good to prove Elizabeth wrong. The days when she practised dancing with Jemmy were for her touched with a kind of bliss. Every night when she said her prayers she mentioned Jemmy; she told herself that next to her sister Anne she loved Jemmy; but she was not sure whether, in her secret heart, she did not love him best of all.

He whispered to her that he was going to command John Crowne, the poet, to write a play with a ballet and the principal part should be for her. The part he had chosen for her was that of Calista, a nymph of Diana.

John Crowne was in despair.

He went to the Duke of Monmouth to remonstrate with him.

"My lord, how can I write Calista for the Princess Mary. Have you forgotten that Calista is raped by Jupiter?"

Monmouth laughed. "It will do me good to watch the effect of that on His Grace of York. His dear little daughter raped!"

"Nay, my lord. I would not wish to place myself in jeopardy. The King would not be pleased."

"You can trust me to put my father in a good mood."

"Indeed yes, my lord. We know how he dotes on you, but I fear this would not be suitable for a young girl. May I suggest that the rape does not take place, and that Calista succeeds in escaping from Jupiter in time." He hurried on before Monmouth could protest. "And I could write in a part for the Princess Anne, for I know how the Princess Mary loves her sister to do everything with her. For the younger Princess there will be the part of Calista's younger sister Nyphe. And for Jupiter . . ."

Monmouth said sharply: "I have the girl for Jupiter. She will play the part well."

"Your lordship . . ."

"Lady Henrietta Wentworth," said Monmouth smiling. "She will be perfect."

The proposed play and ballet was being discussed throughout the Court and the King himself had expressed his interest. Jemmy was in charge and Jemmy was probably the best dancer at Court; moreover, Charles was pleased that he was interesting himself in Mary and Anne, who now that they were growing up, would have to take more and more part in Court life. Calista, Charles decided, should provide the Princesses' introduction to Court.

In Queen Catherine's apartments, Margaret Blagge, one of the Queen's maids of honor, was on her knees praying that she might be spared the need to play in Calista. Monmouth had seen her and selected her for the part of Diana the goddess of Chastity. She feared that he was considering the possibility of making an onslaught on her virtue and because he had seen in her one of the few chaste women at his father's court he would not be satisfied with anyone else to play Diana.

Margaret had been maid of honor to the Duchess of York before her death and after that event had joined the Queen's household. The laxity of morals practised by those about her made her long to escape from Court. It was not that she wished for life in a convent; she could visualize a future with a husband and children—but away from Court, far, far away.

This revulsion had caused her to find great comfort in seclusion. And now to have been chosen to appear to dance and act before the King—something which she considered immoral in itself—horrified her.

But it was no use protesting. Monmouth insisted. She had refused him what he desired; well, now he would refuse her.

Lady Henrietta Wentworth burst into the apartment—a lovely creature, some years younger than Margaret.

"Why, Margaret, what are you doing? Not on your knees again? And what are you weeping about?"

Margaret stood up. "I am to be Diana in Calista."

Henrietta smiled. "I can see no reason for mourning. I am to be Jupiter—the bold lover. Do you know I almost rape the Princess Mary. According to Ovid I did, but John Crowne fears the wrath of the Duke of York if aught ill befalls his daughter, so she is going to be allowed to escape me."

"I would that I could be released from this."

"Released! My dear Margaret, how many girls do you think would not give all they possessed for your opportunity."

"Opportunity . . . to sin!"

"Margaret. What sin is there in dancing?"

"I see it as a sin."

"You should have been born years ago. You would have enjoyed living under Oliver Cromwell. This Court life is not for you."

"Then why should I have to take part in it?"

"Because, my dear, in spite of your seriousness, you are very pretty. And the part of chaste Diana was made for you."

"I have told the Duke that I do not wish to take the part."

"And what said he?"

"He waved my reluctance aside. He would have none of it."

"The Duke of Monmouth," said Henrietta slowly, while a smile touched her lips, "is a man who will always have his way."

"Not always," insisted Margaret. "And I cannot play this role. The players are to be most sumptuously clad and covered in jewels. My lord Monmouth must realize that I am not rich. I have no jewels. So therefore he must find someone else to play Diana. I think that will be the answer, don't you?"

She looked at Henrietta, who did not answer. She was staring into space smiling—her thoughts far away.

Charles summoned his brother and when he arrived told him that he was distressed to have been obliged to come to a certain decision but he believed James would see at once that it was inevitable.

"Since your marriage to your little Catholic, the people have not been pleased with you, James. We may as well face it. You have shown yourself to be too good a Catholic. Even though you don't profess your Catholicism publicly, all know that you are devout enough in secret. They are complaining that your girls are being brought up to be little Catholics too."

"But this is not true."

"Maybe not. But we don't have to consider what is true but what is being whispered. Whispering can be as damning as the truth. You'll have to pass over the girls' education to my jurisdiction, James. There's no help for it."

"But they are *my* daughters."

"And if neither of us get a son Mary could be Queen and Anne could follow her. It's for this reason that the people want to see them taken from the care of a Catholic and given a good Reformed preceptor. There's no help for it, brother. Grin and submit with a good grace. You will see them constantly. It will merely be that I shall put someone in charge of their education."

"And whom have you in mind?"

"Compton, Bishop of London."

"Compton. I hate the fellow."

"A pillar of the Reformed Church, brother; and for that reason I select him. The people will find pleasure in my choice."

"The people?"

"Yes, brother, they by whom we retain our crown; and unless you have a taste for the wandering life, never let us underestimate their importance."

James was sad and angry; but there was no help for it. The care of his children was taken from him and given to a man whom he neither liked nor admired.

Elizabeth Villiers was furious because she had not been given a part in Calista although that pushing Sarah Jennings had.

"Why do you think John Crowne has written that part for you?" she asked Mary.

"Jemmy says it is because I should be at Court and this is an introduction."

Elizabeth blew between her lips. "He wrote the part because until your father has a son you are second in the line of succession and he wants to be sure of your patronage if ever you are Queen. It is as simple as that."

"What nonsense!" said Anne Trelawny. "Parts are often written for people. Why shouldn't the Lady Mary have a part written for her?"

"One doesn't have to be royal to have a part written for one." That was Sarah Jennings executing a difficult step. It was obvious that she believed the company would be enchanted by her performance and sooner or later someone would be writing a ballet especially for Sarah Jennings.

One had to smile at Sarah, who clearly believed herself to be the most important person in the schoolroom, for all that she was the most humbly born. The Princess Anne, her constant crony, was beginning to agree with her; and her outrageous conceit baffled Elizabeth Villiers.

The Princess Anne, taking the part of Nyphe, sister to Calista, practised indolently, and looked, Mary thought, very pretty in her costume which set off her round fresh-colored face and chestnut brown hair.

Unfortunately the eye complaint which had been troubling her for a long time had had the effect of contracting her lids and this gave her a look of vagueness; but even this was not unattractive because it made her seem helpless, which was appealing. Mary, with her dark hair, long, almond-shaped eyes, and lovely skin was very attractive; no one could doubt that she was a Stuart.

There was great excitement in the Palace when the Princesses and their suite were preparing to leave for Whitehall. Sarah Jennings said that it was the beginning of change; and even Elizabeth Villiers, a little subdued since the coming of Sarah, accepted this. Lady Frances spoke seriously to her daughters. They might not be appearing in the ballet, she reminded them, but any change in the fortunes of the Princesses was a change for them.

Elizabeth Villiers, who was now quite a young woman, was beginning to realize that she had been rather foolish. Sarah Jennings had taught her a lesson. Sarah had chosen the docile Princess Anne for her friend and although she dominated Anne, at the same time made herself so pleasant that the Princess never wanted Sarah to leave her side. Thus Sarah Jennings was becoming more prominent in the circle than any of the others—largely due to her forceful character. It was too late now to ingratiate herself with Mary, for Mary already disliked her heartily; and in any case Mary had chosen Anne Trelawny for her friend.

Elizabeth Villiers therefore decided that she must be more cautious now; because once Mary was in command of her own household she would certainly dismiss those whom she had no reason to love. But although Elizabeth grew more pleasant, her hatred had not diminished at all, and secretly she greatly enjoyed seeing Mary discomfited.

Riding to Whitehall from Richmond was in itself an adventure. The people came out to cheer the little cavalcade because they already knew that the King had taken the girls' education under his care and that the Protestant Bishop of London was in charge of them. That the Bishop was no scholar was unimportant; he was a Protestant and in view of their father's unfortunate leanings those poor children were in need of protection.

Moreover, the fact that Charles was having the girls brought up in the

Protestant religion could mean that the evil rumors concerning his own convictions were false. This conjecture gave pleasure to the people.

Arriving at Court, the Princesses were warmly welcomed by all. And what a gay and colorful scene it was! Everyone wanted to do honor to the girls and sought ways of pleasing them—their father and stepmother, the gentle kindly Queen, Jemmy, and their benign and witty Uncle, Charles, the King himself.

Mary in the shimmering dress in which she was to play Calista was both nervous and exalted. She was so anxious to please her father, who wanted her to be a success at Court, but feared that she might disappoint him. When she confided these fears to Jemmy, he laughed at her.

"Why, cousin," he said, "you look so beautiful that my father and his Court would forgive you however badly you danced. But you won't dance badly. You'll enchant them all."

Jemmy kissed her lightly on the forehead; and she thought earnestly: I must not fail. I must not disappoint Jemmy.

Anne suffered no such qualms. She would do her part and if she was a failure, well then, it would soon be forgotten. Sarah had said so and Sarah was invariably right. All the same Sarah was determined to make a success of Mercury; and Sarah knew she would.

When they were preparing to go on to the stage they were joined by Margaret Blagge and Henrietta Wentworth, the latter radiant in contrast to her companion.

Mary attempted to comfort Margaret.

"Why," she said, "you look very beautiful. I am sure everyone will say you are a perfect Diana. Your dress is so lovely. What brilliant stones."

Margaret said: "They terrify me. I had no diamonds to wear and the Duke induced the Countess of Suffolk to lend me these."

"They become her well do they not?" asked Henrietta.

"So well," said Mary, "that everyone's eyes will be upon her."

Margaret shivered.

"Oh, come," said Henrietta impatiently, "there is no harm in dancing."

"I prefer not to," replied Margaret.

"Is she not foolish, my lady Mary?" asked Henrietta. "Here she has a chance to look beautiful in all those diamonds, to dance before the King and she is ungrateful."

"I am sorry," said Mary earnestly.

"You are very good."

"Nonsense," cried Henrietta. "This is meant to make everyone happy and surely that is good. You must smile as a compliment to the lady Mary. This is her ballet."

"You alarm me," murmured Mary. "I feel everything depends on me."

"There is no need to fear," Henrietta soothed her. "Jemmy will be supporting you. He will look after you and see that all is well."

"I am so grateful to dear Jemmy."

"As we all are," added Henrietta.

They turned, for a girl had come into the room.

"I wondered," she said, "if I could be of help."

"We can do with help, Frances," replied Henrietta.

Frances Apsley, maid of honor to Queen Catherine, seeing the Princess, made a deep curtsy. Mary felt a sudden excitement for she had never seen anyone so beautiful and wanted to keep looking at her; the lovely dark eyes were serene; the beautifully shaped head so gracefully bowed, the smooth dark hair so shining; the expression kindly and intelligent.

"My lady," said Henrietta, "this is Frances Apsley."

Mary said: "I am pleased to make your acquaintance."

"It would be an honor to serve you," answered Frances.

They stood smiling, each completely conscious of the other's charm.

"Margaret is never satisfied," Henrietta was saying. "She is complaining that she has one of the best parts in the ballet and is laden with diamonds."

Margaret was speaking in response to Henrietta's taunts, but neither Mary nor Frances Apsley were listening.

How frightened Mary was when she stood before them all. They applauded her kindly; she saw her father looking anxious on her behalf, seated near her uncle. He was kind and she wished that she could love him as he loved her. There were times when she did love him dearly as now; but she could never forget the rumors she had heard of him. She did not fully understand his relationship with those women who had caused her mother so much anxiety; but she imagined what took place between them; it was vague and horrible and she tried to shut her mind to it; but there were occasions when pictures crept in unbidden.

Then she noticed Frances Apsley watching her intently. Their eyes met and Frances smiled.

"She wants me to succeed," thought Mary. "She will be unhappy if I do not."

Mary was determined then to dance as she never had before.

The music had begun and her legs felt heavy; but there was Jemmy smiling and whispering: "Come on. It's only a game after all."

And then because of Jemmy, Frances Apsley, and her father, it became the fun it had been when they had practised at Richmond and she danced as well as she ever had.

She was delighted to see Margaret Blagge's success. She looked so beautiful in her shimmering dress—the perfect Diana. Surely, thought Mary, she must be enjoying the approval of the spectators.

Sarah Jennings tried to get nearer to the audience that she might be noticed; as for Anne, she performed with a carelessness which everyone seemed to find amusing.

Dryden's epilogue was read and they all knew that the ballet had been a success. The King was delighted—particularly with his nieces; he saw this for an excellent beginning of Court life for them.

James was almost in tears; nothing could have given him greater pleasure than the success of his daughters. The King declared that such shimmering talents must not be hidden when he congratulated John Crowne, Mr. Dryden, his nieces, Jemmy, and all the dancers.

In the dressing room where the company had prepared themselves, Mary found Margaret Blagge in great distress.

"I was wearing it about my neck when the ballet began. I cannot understand it. How could I have lost it?"

Mary asked to know what and when Margaret replied that it was Lady Suffolk's diamond, she was horrified.

"But it must be on the stage."

"I have searched everywhere. Oh, my lady Mary, what shall I do? It is worth eighty pounds. I cannot replace it. I don't possess eighty pounds. What shall I do? No one will ever trust me again. And to think I tried so hard *not* to borrow it. This is a judgement. I knew it was sinful."

To see the lovely maid of honor so distressed, upset Mary. It seemed to her a terrible calamity to have borrowed a valuable diamond against one's will and then to have lost it.

"No one will ever trust me again," sobbed Margaret.

"We must look everywhere you have been."

"They have already done so. My maids have looked. I have looked. There is no sign of it. I daren't tell Lady Suffolk."

"Are you sure you've looked everywhere?" asked Mary.

"I . . . I think so."

"I will look. I am rather good at finding things. It is big enough and it sparkles so, it ought not to be difficult to find."

"That's why I greatly fear that someone has found it and kept it."

"Oh, poor Margaret. I will look and if I can't find it perhaps I could ask my father what is the best thing to do."

"Lady Suffolk will never forgive me, I know. I shall have to replace it and I don't see how I can."

Mary went off purposefully; she would search in every place where they had been.

She made her way to the stage, passing the anterooms on the way; she wondered whether Margaret had gone into any of these and forgotten. Mary would search every one because she could not bear to see lovely Margaret so unhappy.

She searched the first of these without success, and went to another. There was no light in this room except that which came through the window, but there was a full moon. She hesitated. Would it be possible to find the diamond in this light? It was big and sparkled, so perhaps it would be visible. She would take a good look and then perhaps call for candles. She heard a sound and knew at once that she was not alone. Someone else had come to this room.

She was about to say that she was looking for a lost diamond when, her eyes having become accustomed to the light, she saw them, and recognition was instantaneous. It was Jemmy and Henrietta Wentworth, and she knew what they were doing.

She stood for a few seconds and then ran from the room.

Jemmy and Henrietta! But Jemmy was married.

She was shocked and horrified: and there was some new emotion too which she had not experienced before. She was not sure what it was; she only knew that she had been fond of Jemmy, and was horrified that he could so betray his wife.

She ran out of the room and on to the stage. How foolish of her, for the hall was crowded and she would be seen.

"Is anything wrong?"

Mary turned round; she was looking into the lovely face of Frances Apsley.

"So . . . it is you," stammered Mary.

"You seem distressed, my lady."

"Yes . . . yes . . . I believe I am."

"If I could help you . . ."

"I do not know."

"If you feel that you could confide in me . . ."

"Yes, perhaps I could."

Frances Apsley took Mary's hand and led her into an anteroom, similar to that in which Mary had seen Jemmy and Henrietta Wentworth, but this one was lighted.

"There, let us sit down."

They sat in one of the window seats and Mary leaned against Frances and felt comforted.

"I don't think I can tell you," she said. "It was . . . disgusting. It was someone I know."

"I think I understand."

"Do you? But that is clever of you."

Frances smiled. "I am a good deal older than you."

"I am eleven," said Mary.

"That makes me nine years older than you."

"You are very wise and beautiful."

Frances laughed. "I think you may not be very discriminating."

"I only know," said Mary, "that when I saw you I knew that I had never seen anyone so beautiful."

"When you come to Court you will meet many beautiful people."

"Perhaps," said Mary. "But when I see perfection I know it. I am so honored that you spoke to me. Do you know, *that* does not seem important any more."

"I am glad. I am sure it was not of any great importance."

"No. It is only when things like that happen to people of whom one is very fond . . . And I was fond of . . ."

Frances laid a hand over that of the Princess. "Don't think of it. It is best forgotten."

"Meeting you has made it seem unimportant. Your name is Frances. I think it is a lovely name—but not lovely enough for you, of course. I want to go on talking to forget *that*. Do you understand?"

"Yes," said Frances, "I understand. Let us talk of the ballet. You danced beautifully, and of course you were the center of the play. Diana was charming."

"Oh, that reminds me. She is so distressed. I was looking for it when . . ." Mary turned to Frances. "You are so wise. Perhaps you can help me comfort her. Margaret Blagge has lost a diamond which belonged to Lady Suffolk, and she is terrified because she is afraid she will have to replace it and she is not rich."

"It will likely be found."

"Yes, Frances, but if it is not? Poor Margaret is almost ill with grief. You see she did not want to dance in the ballet because she thinks dancing sinful, and she did not want to borrow the diamonds. It is very sad."

Mary's long dark eyes were expectant as she lifted them to the face of her new friend.

"Have you told your father?" asked Frances. "He might be able to help."

"Do you think he would?"

"I am sure that if you asked him he would want to do it . . . just to please you."

"You are right, Frances. Oh how clever you are. Let us go to him at once."

"You wish me to come?"

"Yes, I want to show him that I have a new friend. He will be so delighted that I have found you."

Frances laughed. "I do not think so," she said.

"But you are wrong. He wants me to be happy. He loves me very much and I . . ."

She frowned. She did love him; if only she did not have to imagine . . . what she had seen this night with Jemmy!

She hated it. It was degrading and humiliating. But she would not think of her father and Jemmy. She had a new friend—Frances Apsley— and *their* relationship would never be sullied by degrading actions.

"Let us find my father," she said. "I will ask him, because I cannot bear that Margaret should be so unhappy."

The Duke of York was in the company of a handsome woman but when he saw his daughter coming toward him he turned from her.

"Something is wrong, my dearest?" he said.

"Father, I wish to speak to you. Frances thinks you may be able to help us."

James smiled at the young maid of honor whom he knew slightly, she curtsied and he led them out of the hall.

"Now, tell me what is wrong," he said, when he had shut a door and they were in that anteroom which Frances and Mary had just left, and Mary explained how Margaret had been forced to act against her conscience and not only dance but borrow diamonds, one of which she had lost.

"And what sort of a diamond is this?" asked James.

"It is worth eighty pounds."

James touched his daughter's cheeks lightly with the tips of his fingers. "Well, sweetheart, that does not seem such a mighty sum. What if I promise to find a diamond to replace this one—that's if it cannot be found."

"You mean that you will give it to Margaret so that it need not be known that she has lost one?"

"If that would please you."

"It pleases me very much."

"Then so shall it be."

Mary smiled shyly from her father to Frances Apsley. "This is a very happy night," she said.

"That night," **wrote** Mary to her new friend, "was the most important in my life because in it I met you."

Everything had changed. Not only were she and her sister frequently at Court, not only were they present at Court functions, but Mary was soon deep in a new and exciting friendship.

Frances filled her thoughts; when she was with Frances that seemed to her the greatest happiness in the world. She adored Frances—the way she walked, talked, looked. Life was suddenly full of pleasure for she had a friend such as she had never had before; and the love she felt for her sister Anne was a mild affection compared with the passionate devotion Frances inspired.

Everyone at Court was ready to be charming to the Princess Mary. The King had no legitimate heirs and until the Duke of York produced a son, Mary could well be the future Queen: it was known that the King had a special interest in his nieces and that meant that all those who were ambitious should share this.

The girls remained at Richmond Palace under the care of Lady Frances Villiers, but Henry Compton, whom the King had appointed as Governor of their studies, did not greatly care whether they studied or not. Mary, who since the days when she had wished to please her father had developed an interest in knowledge, continued to work hard, but Anne rarely looked at her books.

"My head aches," she would say. "And my eyes are watering."

Anne's eyes were her excuse to be lazy. But she was so good tempered that no one minded; and she continued to use her affliction whenever she wanted to escape from something which bored her. The new life suited her admirably. To be petted, to be continually given presents of sweetmeats (for her weakness was now becoming well known) to be often at Court, to spend her evenings with the cards, a dish of sweets beside her, to be constantly in the company of her dear friend Sarah and sister Mary, what more could she ask from life?

Mary might study French with Pierre de Laine until she became proficient. Anne would listen to her sister reading in that language and clap her plump hands.

"My darling sister, you are so clever. It does me good to hear you. I wish I were more like you."

"You could learn as easily."

Anne laughed. "Oh, it would strain my eyes. And I could never be as clever as you, my dearest."

"You are lazy," Mary would say in the indulgent voice she had used to her sister when they were children; and Anne would merely laugh.

"One clever daughter is enough for Papa."

Sometimes Anne would attempt to draw, for she had a certain talent. The Princess's drawing teacher, Mr. Gibson, who was a dwarf, did all he could to encourage her; and often she would sit with her sister lightly sketching. Mrs. Gibson helped her husband in teaching art for she too was an artist; and together these little people were one of the wonders of the Court for they had produced nine ordinary sized children. Gibson had belonged to Queen Henrietta-Maria before his marriage and was a specially privileged person in the household.

A pleasant life, made wonderful for Mary by this deep friendship. When she was at Richmond she constantly longed to be at St. James's because Frances lived there with her parents Sir Allen and Lady Apsley. Their friendship was unusual, Frances had said, because she was so much older than the Princess; and this gave it a piquant flavor. Yet the difference in their ages seemed unimportant for Frances was as attracted by Mary as Mary was by Frances.

There was always so much to talk about; and to sit close beside Frances, holding her hand, seemed to Mary complete happiness. Mary realized that this was how she had wanted to love her father and perhaps Jemmy; but she never could because between them was the shadow of some shame, not quite understood but ever present. Lampoons had been written about them; they were untrustworthy because of this; they were in a sense shameful and could never enjoy a relationship of idealistic love such as that which existed between Frances and Mary.

"Frances," said Mary on one occasion, "I shall never marry. I could not bear to marry. I shall call you my husband and I shall be your wife, and perhaps one day we can leave the Court and have a little house together."

Frances laughed and said it was because Mary was young that she talked in this way; but Mary shook her head, and when she next wrote to Frances she called her her husband and signed herself her loving wife.

She was sitting with her sister one day drawing with the Gibsons when Lady Frances came into the room. She was carrying a letter in her hand, and Mary started up in dismay for she recognized it as one which she had written to Frances Apsley.

Lady Frances dismissed the dwarfs and Princess Anne and when they had gone she put the letter on the table.

"My lady," she said, "this is your handwriting?"

Mary admitted that it was.

"It is addressed to 'my dear husband' and signed 'your wife Mary'."

Mary did not answer.

"And addressed to Frances Apsley. What does it mean?"

"It means," said Mary, "that she is my dear friend and . . . I wrote to her."

"You seem very fond of her."

"She is the dearest person in the world."

"H'm," said Lady Frances. She picked up the letter and tapped the table with it. "I do not think you are wise to write so extravagantly to this young woman."

"But I say nothing that I do not mean."

Lady Frances was faintly worried.

As soon as Lady Frances had disappeared the Princess Anne came quietly to her sister who was sitting thoughtfully at the table—the letter which she had taken from Lady Frances still in her hand.

"What was wrong?" demanded Anne.

"I am accused of writing extravagantly to a friend."

"What friend?"

"A very great friend."

"Please tell me," wheedled Anne, sidling up to her sister.

Mary wanted to talk of Frances Apsley and having begun found it difficult to stop. Frances was perfect, she explained, so good and unsullied, there was no one in the world as beautiful or as good as Frances and Mary loved her passionately.

Anne was interested.

"I have seen her," she said. "I want to be her friend too."

"You always wanted to copy me, Anne."

"Not always," her sister corrected her. "You eat like a little bird."

"And you like a lion. Yes, that's true."

"But all the same," said Anne, "if you have a dear friend, I must have one too."

Mary Beatrice was no longer the serious girl who had wanted to be a vestal virgin. She found great pleasure in the entertainments which were the fashion at her brother-in-law's Court. No one had been more thrilled to see the pageant which had featured her husband against the Duke of Monmouth when they had reconstructed the siege of Maestricht for the amusement of the Court. How thrilled she had been to see James in action as a general, building trenches and giving orders and showing what a brilliant strategist he was. The King looked on with great amusement and many witty asides to his friends. Charles realized as fully as anyone present that there was more than play in the rivalry between his brother and his natural son. James wanted to show the Court that he was a better general than Jemmy could ever be, while Jemmy was burning with zeal to show them that youth, energy, and boldness were a better choice than age and experience.

Such a situation was bound to amuse Charles and his friends, but it was impossible to know whose side Charles was on. He doted on Jemmy, but he was never a fool where his affections were concerned and saw the loved one's faults as clearly as the virtues. In any case, Charles was not a man to love for virtue. He knew that his handsome brash Jemmy was so fond of his father largely because of what he hoped to attain through him, and that his exasperating brother was a man of honor. He never forgot that James was the legitimate heir of England and that although the people deplored his religious views they would always remember that he was the legitimate son of a King.

So the siege of Maestricht played out on a stage was more than a pleasing pageant.

Mary Beatrice, watching it, was deeply conscious of her husband. She would not have believed it possible when she first came to England that she could have such strong feelings for that man. He was twenty-five years her senior; he was a sensual man; he made demands on her which she had never thought it would be a pleasure to fulfill; but how wrong she had been. Mary Beatrice, once longing for the virgin's life, had now become a woman passionately in love with her husband.

It was a marvel to her that she who had once lain in the nuptial bed shivering at the prospect of his approach, now lay waiting for him, her only fear being that he would not come but decide to stay with one of his mistresses instead. She was passionately jealous of his mistresses; she had remonstrated with him about them, but although he was always kind, and implied to her that they were not as important in his life as she was, he would not give them up.

She had discovered a great deal about her husband's first marriage— for she never tired of hearing about it and asked numerous questions. She knew that he had loved Anne Hyde his first wife so much that he had defied his formidable mother, his brother, and all his family for her sake. They had made life unpleasant for poor Anne Hyde, except the King who, when he saw that everyone was against her, sought to be kind to her.

She could well believe that. Had he not been kind to her? Looking back now she believed the change in her had begun when she had met the King.

Now she watched her husband and she prayed that he would triumph over Monmouth, because she knew that Monmouth hated James; but she believed James to be too kindly to hate his nephew.

She was pregnant and as she put her hands on her body which was beginning to swell, she was filled with love and tenderness for the child who would be born in five months' time. Her child and James's. She longed to have the child; she wanted to protect it from all the misfortunes which could beset a royal infant.

And when she looked at James, there in the mock battle against the King's bastard, she wanted to protect him too.

The Princess Anne must follow her sister whenever possible, so as soon as she saw Frances Apsley she became violently attracted by her.

Mary was not altogether displeased; she was delighted whenever anyone admired Frances, and as she loved her sister dearly she found it hard to be angry with her. But she was tortured that Frances might prefer Anne to herself, which she thought might be possible. Anne, with her easygoing nature, was popular; people understood Anne more readily than they did Mary; so it seemed to the elder sister that Frances might very well find the younger more attractive.

Mary had given Frances the name of Aurelia—a character from a Dryden comedy—the Aurelia of the play being a delightful creature, whose company was greatly in demand. Mary herself was Clorine, a shepherdess from one of the Beaumont and Fletcher works—a faithful character who was constantly misunderstood.

When Mary could not see Frances her only consolation was in writing letters to her. To her beloved Aurelia she told of her undying devotion, imploring her always to love her exclusively and to remember that she was the loving husband to her Mary-Clorine.

As Lady Frances Villiers did not approve of this correspondence and Mary was in constant dread that something would be done to stop it, the letters had to be smuggled out of Richmond Palace to St. James's. The dwarfs, Mr. and Mrs. Gibson, who loved their mistress and wished to please her, conveniently obliged and did the carrying. So a pleasant atmosphere of intrigue had been created and when Mary looked back to those dull days before she had known Frances Apsley, she wondered how she had endured them.

Anne refused to be left out. She even bestirred herself to write to Frances, although writing was an occupation which held little charm for her.

One day Mary found her bent over a letter and looking over her shoulder saw that she was writing to her beloved Semandra.

Anne put her hands over the letter, pretending to hide it.

"Who is Semandra?" asked Mary.

"Well, if she is Aurelia to you she cannot be to me."

"Semandra! That is one of the characters in Mithridate."

Anne nodded. "Mrs. Betterton wants me to act in it. And Ziphares is in it too. So while Frances is Semandra I shall be Ziphares."

"Anne, why do you always have to copy me? Can't you think of anything for yourself?"

Anne looked astonished. "But why should I, when I have my dear clever Mary to think of everything?"

Mary wanted to feel angry and exasperated; but how could she? She loved Anne and could not imagine ever being without her.

She thought then that she would like to spend the rest of her life in a little house—far from the Court. She and Frances together. They would have cows and she would do the milking; and she would cook like a country woman. Anne should visit them . . . often, very often.

She was smiling at her sister. "Really, Anne, you ought to try and do something of your own."

Mary Beatrice was longing for a son. The people expected it of her; if she had a boy he would be the heir to the throne; it was no wonder that everyone watched her with apprehension during those waiting months.

When she was indisposed her health was the main topic of conversation. Every night she prayed for a son.

Poor barren Queen Catherine spent much time with her and they became good friends, for it seemed that since Catherine could not provide the heir to the throne she was content for her sister-in-law to do so.

It was a great responsibility.

She guarded her health with the greatest care all during the cold dark autumn days, and early in January she went to St. James's Palace to await the birth.

On the ninth of that month she knew her time was near; and with relief and apprehension waited for the beginning of her ordeal.

Outside the snow had begun to fall and the bitter wind blew along the river. Her women were bustling round her.

This was the most important birth in the kingdom.

She awoke on a dark Sunday knowing that her time had come; she called to her women.

It seemed to Mary Beatrice that all the world was waiting breathlessly for the child she would have.

She was aware of voices as she emerged from unconsciousness. The room was lighted by many candles and her pains were over.

Someone was bending over her.

"James," she said.

"My dear."

"The child?"

"The child is well and healthy. And you must rest now."

"But I want to see ..."

He said: "Bring the child. ..."

The child? Why did he continue to say the child? She knew of course. Had it been a boy he would not have said the child.

They brought the little bundle; they laid it in her arms.

"Our little daughter," said James tenderly.

"A daughter!"

But when she held the child in her arms she ceased to care that it was not a boy.

It was her child. She was a mother. She laughed scornfully at that foolish girl who had believed that the ultimate contentment could only be found within the walls of a convent.

She lay in her bed, drowsily content. My daughter, she thought. There would be others. Next time a son. But she was entirely content that this one should be a daughter.

She thought of the future of the child. Should she be brought up with her half-sisters? But they were much too old. Moreover they were in the care of the Protestant Bishop of London. The Protestant Bishop! Why should her child be brought up as a Protestant? She was a Catholic, James was a Catholic; even though he was not publicly known as one. Why should they not be allowed to bring up their children as they wished?

When James came to see her she told him that she wanted the child baptized as a Catholic.

"My dear," said James, "that is not possible."

"But why? I am a Catholic and so are you."

"Our little daughter is in the line of succession to the throne. The people of England will not accept a Catholic baptism."

"This is my daughter," said Mary Beatrice obstinately.

"Alas, my dear, we are servants of the state."

He did not discuss the matter further, but Mary Beatrice lying back on her pillows continued to brood. Why, because she was young, should she be continually told what she must do? She had been married against her will and nothing could alter that, even though she was now glad that she had been. She was not going to allow anyone to dictate to her where her child was concerned.

She sent for her confessor and when he came she said: "Father Gallis, I want you to make ready to baptize my daughter."

Father Gallis raised his eyebrows, but she went on: "I want no interference. Indeed I will have no interference. My daughter shall be baptized in accordance with the rights of *my* Church. I care not what anyone says. That is what I have decided."

Father Gallis, secretly pleased, obeyed his mistress and the little girl was christened on her mother's bed, according to Rome.

Charles came to call on his sister-in-law.

He sat by the bed smiling at her.

"I have come to welcome my new subject," he said genially.

The baby was brought to show him.

"She is charming," he said, and he smiled from James, who had accompanied him, to the beautiful mother.

"You are very proud of your achievement," he went on, "and rightly so. Have you decided on her names?"

"Yes, Your Majesty," answered Mary Beatrice, "she is to be Catherine after Her Majesty."

"A pretty compliment," murmured Charles, "and one which will satisfy the Queen."

"And Laura after my mother."

"Who, rest assured, will be equally gratified. Now, let us talk about the arrangements for this blessed infant's baptism."

Mary Beatrice's heart began to beat fast. It was one thing to talk defiance to her confessor; another to do so to the King's face.

"Your Majesty," she said slowly and she hoped firmly, "my daughter has already been baptized in accordance with my Church."

Charles was silent for a few seconds then he smiled. "Catherine Laura," he said. "What charming names!"

Mary Beatrice lay back on her pillows. She had won. She should have known that the easygoing King would let her have her own way.

The Queen came to visit her.

"I am so touched that the baby is to be named after me," she said.

"I should perhaps have asked Your Majesty's gracious permission."

Catherine laughed. "It would have been readily given as you knew. And the King has asked me to discuss the baby's baptism with you."

"But . . ."

"It is His Majesty's wish that it should take place in the chapel royal where the bishop will perform the ceremony."

"In accordance with the Church of England?"

"But of course."

"When did His Majesty request you to come to see me?"

"Only half an hour before I arrived."

Mary Beatrice lay back on her pillows. He had shown no signs of anger. But then he rarely did. He had merely smiled and then made plans to have it done the way he wished it.

She was afraid then that some punishment would fall on Father Gallis for what he had done, and as soon as the Queen had left she sent for him and told him what had happened.

He said they could only wait for the King's vengeance.

They waited. Nothing happened. And then the baby was baptized according to the King's desire and the rites of the Church of England. Her sponsors were the Duke of Monmouth and the baby's half-sisters, Anne and Mary.

The King did not refer to the matter again. He hated unpleasantness, Mary Beatrice was to learn; but at the same time he liked to have his way with as little fuss as possible.

Mary was in despair. The family of her dear Aurelia were moving from St. James's Palace to St. James's Square.

"What will this mean to us?" she demanded. "How can we meet when you are not at the Palace?"

"My dearest," answered Aurelia, "we must content ourselves with letters when we are apart; my family will often be at St. James's or Whitehall and you must contrive to be there when I am."

Mary was a little comforted.

"I shall give you a cornelian ring so that when you look at it you will always remember me," said Aurelia.

"It will comfort me," answered Mary.

When she returned to Richmond she was pensive. Frances in St. James's Square was no longer easily accessible but they would meet and there would be letters; it was a warning that life did not go on indefinitely in the same pleasant pattern.

Change came.

Daily she waited for Gibson to bring her the cornelian ring. Anne, who had wept with Mary when she had heard that Frances was moving

from the Palace, declared that she too must have a ring for remembrance; and when the cornelian did not arrive Mary believed that Frances had sent it to Anne instead.

She poured out her jealous anguish in a letter.

"Not but that I think my sister do deserve your love more than I, but you have loved me once and now I do not doubt that my sister has the cornelian ring. Unkind Aurelia, I hope you will not go too soon, for I should be robbed of seeing you, unkind husband, as well as of your love, but she that has it will have your heart too and your letters, and oh, thrice happy she. She is happier than I ever was for she has triumphed over a rival that once was happy in your love, till she with her alluring charms removed unhappy Clorine from your heart . . ."

But Anne did not have the cornelian ring; and all in good time it came to Mary.

A happy day, which almost made her forget that communication would be more difficult now that Frances was going to St. James's Square.

In spite of her love for Frances, which was all absorbing, Mary still had an affection for her cousin Monmouth; and now that she was growing up and was a great deal at Court she had many friends among the maids of honor. She was mildly fond of a number of them, but her passion for Frances meant that she had little room in her heart for others.

Eleanor Needham, a beautiful young girl, was a friend of both Mary and Frances; so that when Eleanor was in trouble and she had to confide in someone, she chose the Princess Mary.

But this did not happen until the interfering Sarah Jennings had made it necessary.

Sarah dominated whatever household she found herself in; her passion for management was irresistible to her. She had quarrelled with most of the maids of honor and was continually trying to call attention to herself. She had made the Princess Anne her special charge, but since Mary had become so attached to Frances (and Anne must follow her sister in everything) Anne had become less friendly with Sarah.

Sarah was alert; there was little she missed; and she it was who warned the Duchess of Monmouth to watch her husband and Eleanor Needham, for she was certain something was going on there.

The Duchess told Sarah to mind her own business, to which Sarah retorted that if she could not take a warning she was welcome to the consequences of her blindness. The Duchess accused her husband, mentioning Sarah, at which Monmouth called on Sarah and told her that if she did not keep her sharp nose out of his affairs she might not be in a position to much longer, for that same nose would not reach the Court from the place to which he would have her banished.

Sarah was furious; but then Sarah often was furious. All the same she was aware of the power of the King's favorite son; and although she might talk of upstart bastards out of his hearing, she was a little afraid of what he might do. Sarah knew that it was most essential for her to keep her place at Court if she were going to make the marriage that was necessary to establish her social position.

So before Eleanor came to Mary she had had an idea of what was happening and now that she was so knowledgeable of how people at Court conducted themselves, she was not surprised at the outcome.

"My lady," said Eleanor, "I am with child and I must leave the Court very soon."

"Is it Jemmy's?" whispered Mary.

Eleanor nodded.

"Poor Eleanor. But what will you do?"

"Go right away from here and no one shall ever hear of me again."

"But where will you go?"

"Do not ask me."

"But Eleanor, can you look after yourself?"

"I shall be all right."

"But I must help you."

"My dear lady Mary, you are so kind and good. I knew you would be. That is why I had to say good-bye to you. But I shall know how to look after myself."

"You should stay at Court. No one takes much account of these things here."

"No, I shall go. But I wanted to say good-bye."

Mary embraced her friend.

"Promise me that if you need help you will come to me?"

"My good sweet lady Mary, I promise."

Mary told Anne what had happened, and how sorry she was for poor Eleanor.

"Sometimes," said Mary, "I think I hate men. There is Jemmy who is as gay as ever while poor Eleanor is so unhappy she has to go right away. How different is my love for Aurelia."

Anne nodded, and taking a sweet from the pocket of her gown, munched it thoughtfully.

Mary went into her closet and sitting at her table wrote that she was taking up her new crow quill to write to her dearest Aurelia.

She told her about the quarrel between that busybody Sarah Jennings and the Duke and Duchess of Monmouth, which was on account of Eleanor Needham. It was sad, wrote Mary, that a woman should be so ill-used. They had both been fond of Eleanor, and now she had left the Court to go, as she said, where no one would hear of her. How Mary longed to escape from the Court where such intrigues were commonplace.

"As for myself, I could live and be content with a cottage in the country and a cow, and a stiff petticoat and waistcoat in summer, and cloth in winter, a little garden where we could live on the fruit and herbs it yields. . . ."

Little Catherine died in convulsions ten months after her birth.

Mary Beatrice was heartbroken for a long time; Mary did her best to comfort her and for a while James deserted his mistresses and became the devoted husband.

There would be other children, he assured her; she was so young.

The little girl was buried in the vault of Mary Queen of Scots in Westminster Abbey; and after a short period of mourning Mary Beatrice was obliged to take her part in Court functions.

The devotion of her husband and the company of her two stepdaughters did a great deal for her over this unhappy time.

Although Mary mourned her half-sister, life had become too exciting for brooding on what was past. There was the gaiety of the Court, the friendships with the girls, none of which rivaled that with Frances, but Mary had much affection for friends such as Anne Trelawny. Her sister was very dear to her, and although at times she would feign exasperation because of Anne's imitative ways and her refusal to change her mind once she had made it up, even when as in the case of the man in the park, she was confronted with the truth, the two sisters were inseparable.

Their stepmother was not in the least alarming. A little imperious, sometimes, a little pious often, but as she recovered from the death of her baby, ready to play a game of blindman's buff, hide-and-seek, or "I love my love with an A."

Then there was dancing, in which Mary was beginning to excel, and acting which was amusing. Sarah Jennings generally managed to infuse intrigue into the household which made it a lively one.

The years were slipping past and so absorbed was Mary by her own circle—and in particular Frances—that she forgot she was no longer a child: she had little interest in affairs outside her own domestic circle.

A crisis occurred when there was a question of a husband being found for Frances.

A husband! But they had no need of men in their Eden.

"No one could ever love you as I do," wrote Mary. "Marriage is not a happy state. How many faithful husbands are there at the Court, think you? They marry, tire of their wives in a month, and then they turn to others."

It was alarming to contemplate. It reminded her of what she had seen when she surprised Jemmy and Henrietta Wentworth; it reminded her of the stories she had heard about her father and her uncle.

Unpleasant thoughts which it was best to avoid, but how could she avoid them when there was talk of Aurelia's marrying!

For some months her anxiety persisted; and then the matter seemed to have been forgotten and the serene state of affairs continued: meetings with Frances on Sundays and holy days; and always those letters which must be smuggled out to the Apsley home. Her dancing master Mr. Gorley, the Gibsons, and very often Sarah Jennings and Anne Trelawny acted as go-betweens. It was a pleasant intrigue, for it must be carried on without the knowledge of Lady Frances Villiers who did not entirely approve of the correspondence.

So life went on merrily until Mary was nearly fifteen.

It was the day of the Lord Mayor's feast and the King was dining at the Guildhall. This was one of the greatest occasions in the City of London and when Charles had told James that he thought Mary and Anne should be present James guessed that his daughters would soon be called upon to play their part in state affairs.

Anne's favorite form of entertainment was attending banquets; as for Mary she enjoyed the pageantry. Both their uncle and father watched how the crowd cheered the girls; and how charmingly they responded. James was not surprised therefore when, on the day following the banquet, Charles sent for his brother, in order, said Charles, to discuss some small projects concerning the Lady Mary.

"James," said Charles, "how old is Mary?"

"Fifteen."

"Old enough, most would say."

"For marriage, you mean?"

"What else? My dear brother, don't look downcast. You must have realized that before long it would be necessary to find a husband for her."

"She seems but a child to me."

"Still, you would wish a brilliant *parti* for her?"

"I suppose it will be necessary."

"Then the sooner the better."

"She seems such a child."

"It matters not what she seems but what she is. She is fifteen. Time she was betrothed. Have you a husband in mind for her?"

James hesitated. "There is Louis's son," he said at length. "I should like to see Mary Queen of France—and France is not so very far away."

Charles grimaced, and James went on hotly: "Our own cousin, Charles. Why not?"

"Our little Mary is an important person. We must not forget that, as matters stand now, she could follow us to the throne. If you had a son, James, Mary's marriage would not have been a matter of such deep concern."

"Where could she make a better marriage than with France? The Queen of France. That is a position I should like to see her hold."

"Alliance with a Catholic monarch, James?"

"With one of the greatest powers . . ."

"The people want a Protestant marriage, and I have thought of a likely husband for Mary."

"And who is this?"

"Our nephew, William. William of Orange."

THE THREE CROWNS

*T*wenty-seven years before *Charles* decided to marry his nephew to his niece, William of Orange was born into a house of mourning. Eight days before his birth his father had died suddenly and his mother had ordered that her lying-in chamber should be hung with black crêpe; and even the cradle was black.

"A dismal welcome for a child," mused the midwife, and she shook her head for she believed it to be an evil omen.

If the child were a boy, he would be the Prince of Orange; his father was lamentably dead, it was true; but she believed that the entry of a child into the world should be a matter for rejoicing.

The Princess of Orange was English. She was considered one of the most fortunate members of the unlucky Stuart family in those days of exile which had followed the execution of Charles I. She had helped her brothers, Charles and James, by giving them refuge in Holland; she had been devoted to them both and one of her most cherished hopes was to see Charles restored to the throne of England.

And now she had to face her own tragedy. The death of her William, Stadtholder of Holland, only a short time before she hoped to give him a son.

The child must be a son, she was thinking, as she lay in her darkened room. The child must be strong; he would be born ruler of his country. Never, it seemed to Mary of Orange, had a birth been so important; never would one take place in more tragic circumstances.

Mrs. Tanner, the midwife, bustled about the chamber giving orders. The Princess of Orange lay on her bed waiting.

In the anteroom Mrs. Tanner found several of the Princess's women, and paused, for she could never resist a gossip.

"The mourning should be taken away," she said. "It is not good. A little one coming into the world to black crêpe! What a welcome!"

"But he has no father, Mrs. Tanner," said one of the women.

"Well, there's no need to greet the baby with that knowledge. 'Tis something the little mite should come to know in time. And don't call the child '*he*' before you know the sex. That's another bad omen."

"The Princess is praying for a boy."

"That's tempting fate. Show as you'll be pleased with what you get, and like as not you'll get what you want."

The women looked with respect at Mrs. Tanner, for she had attended so many births that they felt she knew what she was talking about.

"Then 'tis to be hoped the Princess gets what she wants—for if this little one's a boy he'll be the Stadtholder. They'll call him William after his father and . . ."

"Hush I say. Hush. The air is full of omens tonight. I sense them."

The women looked at each other in awe; and Mrs. Tanner left them. "For," she said, "the child will be with us soon. I know it."

She was right. Almost immediately the Princess's pains had begun.

The welcome cry of a child! How often was that waited for in the palaces of kings? The words: "It is a boy." How welcome and how rarely they came! It seemed that boys could be born in humble cottages but royal palaces were less favored. This was one of those occasions when wishes were granted.

William Henry, Prince of Orange, was born.

Mrs. Tanner, gossiping afterward to the women, assured them that it was no ordinary birth. Her little William—he was already hers—was destined for a great future. This day was one which was going to be remembered in the history of Orange.

"She was crying out in her anguish, our poor sad Princess; and I knew that the birth was near. Poor soul, she had forgotten the tragedy of her loss; there was nothing for her but the pain and the agony. And then . . . there he was . . . the blessed boy. And at that moment all the candles went out. So he came into a world of darkness. Poor blessed royal mite! He yelled; and I took him in my arms and shouted for light. I said: 'This is a boy.' And they all took up the cry and I had to remind them that I must have light. And then . . . while I was waiting for the lights to be brought . . . I saw it clearly. The darkness helped; and afterward I asked myself did the lights go out that I could see the symbol?"

"What symbol, Mrs. Tanner?"

Mrs. Tanner's eyes were narrowed. "Three haloes of light . . . right about the baby's head."

"Does it mean he is going to be a monk and holy man, Mrs. Tanner?"

"Monk and holy man indeed! They were *crowns*. He'll have three crowns, that blessed infant. I saw, I tell you."

For a few days everyone talked about Mrs. Tanner's vision. Then it was forgotten. After all, Mrs. Tanner was a romancer, several of them believed, for all that she posed as being such a wise woman. And of course this was an important little boy. He was the heir of Holland; more than that, the tragic death of his father made his birth the more joyous event. The Princess of Orange had a reason for living. The people of Holland had their new Stadtholder.

YOUNG WILLIAM

To young William the Palace in the Wood was home. This was a very beautiful house which his grandmother had had built within a mile or so of the state palace. Here he lived with Lady Stanhope, the governess chosen for him by his English mother—a serious little boy whom none were very sure of because he prided himself on keeping his opinions to himself. The fact that he was not strong was a great anxiety to his mother and those whose duty it was to care for him. William in his grave and serious way decided to make the utmost advantage of everything; therefore his weakness seemed an asset rather than a fact to be deplored. Because he was inclined to be asthmatical, his governess was in perpetual terror on his account. He was delicate and because his father was dead and there could be no other of the same line, he was very precious indeed.

William was aware of this, but in his cool judicial manner he knew exactly the reason why. He was small of stature and this hurt his pride; he could not compete with boys of his own age in sport; for one reason he had not the physique, for another his governors and governesses were always in fear of his overtaxing his strength.

"Oh," he would say, "they will not allow me to do this or that. . . . It is because I have no father and am the Prince of Orange."

That was well enough to say to others; but he accepted the true state of affairs. He had been born a Prince but of such weak body that he could not enjoy rough games. One could not have everything in life; therefore he would try to make up for physical imperfections by cultivating wisdom.

He was alert and missed little; he had heard an account of what Mrs. Tanner had seen at his birth. Three crowns! That sounded wonderful; when he stood beside tall strong boys he reminded himself of what Mrs. Tanner had seen at his birth. He would be ready to take the crowns when they came to him as he was sure they would. It would not matter then that he was not very tall and that he sometimes found breathing difficult.

He quickly learned that a country was not happy when its hereditary ruler was a minor. He was descended from great William the Silent who had won the gratitude of the Dutch because of what he had done for them in their struggle against Spain and the Inquisition, but his father was dead, he himself was a child, and de Witte with his Republicans was ruling Holland at this time. The office of Stadtholder had been abolished by the de Witte government soon after young William was born; and although he was the Prince of Orange and the son of rulers, while de Witte was supreme he could not be regarded as the future ruler.

His mother was a Princess of England; but alas, what help could be expected from a country which had executed its King and was now ruled by a commonwealth under a man such as Oliver Cromwell?

William was serious; William was determined; he realized at a very early age all that was expected of him, all that would be required of him. He had to win back the Stadtholder and make the House of Orange supreme again.

This he was certain he would do.

He was never driven to work at his lessons because it was feared that too much study might be bad for his health. He worked when he thought he would; and this was not infrequently. His mother's maids of honor would often play games with him which were always sedate.

He would never forget the day when he was summoned to his mother's apartments and told to expect an important visitor.

"Your cousin," she told him, "is coming to stay with you for a while. I trust you will like her. She is Elizabeth Charlotte, and I want you to make her welcome."

He expressed his willingness to do so, and wanted to hear more of this cousin.

"Her great-grandfather was James I of England and he was, as you know, also your great-grandfather, so you are cousins. She is a very gay little girl and I am sure you will enjoy her company. Sometimes, my dear boy, I think you are a little too serious."

"Should I try to be more gay then, Mother?"

"Oh no, no, William. You must not over-excite yourself. But I think the company of Elizabeth Charlotte will be good for you."

William was inclined to distrust that which was supposed to be good for him and was already thinking of his cousin with suspicion.

When she arrived, however, he could not help but be excited by her. She was a tomboy; she was pretty and she was determined on mischief.

"Of course," she told him, when they were alone together, "you know why I am here?"

It was because they believed he should have a companion who would be "good" for him, he answered.

Elizabeth Charlotte laughed aloud and gave him a push which made him stagger. "They are planning to marry us. Depend upon it."

"But they have said nothing to me."

Elizabeth Charlotte put her hands on her hips. "And tell me, do you expect them to? No, we are children. We do as we're told. And now they are putting us together that we may become accustomed to each other. Sooner or later it will be announced. The betrothal between William Prince of Orange, and his cousin Elizabeth Charlotte."

"How can you know this?"

The little girl put her fingers to the tips of each ear, which she pulled out as far as it would go. "Oh," she said lightly, "I use these. It's what they're meant for, Cousin William."

William studied her intently, asking himself whether he wanted her for a wife. It would depend, of course, on what she had to bring him; but he supposed his mother would have thought of that.

"Have you seen my mother?" he asked.

She shook her head. "*I* am only a child, cousin. I am not presented to the Princess of Orange. I am in the care of my aunt Sophia who must do as she is told. She has brought me here to present me to the Princess of Orange."

"Why must your aunt do as she is told?"

"William, how little you know! I can see I shall have a great deal to do if I am going to prepare you to be *my* husband. Aunt Sophia married for love—which it seems is a very silly thing to do. They have little money or position—her husband being one of the *young* princes of the House of Hanover. Poor Aunt Sophia! She is poor, and grandmamma, who is Queen of Bohemia, tells her what she must do. This is her latest duty to bring me here and to present me to the Princess of Orange."

"And to see that you and I become good friends."

"*That* is not important. Whether we are friends or not, they will marry us . . . unless you or I get a better offer before we reach the right age. But in case we do have to marry, we may as well get to *like* each other, do you not agree? After all, no harm will be done. We can always be good friends and then if I am somebody else's Queen and you are Prince of Holland, we can help each other. Send men and arms to help fight our enemies. Do you not think that is an *excellent* idea, William?"

He said slowly that he had heard one could not have too many friends.

"Then we will begin . . . without delay . . . being friends."

This was his first meeting with his cousin Elizabeth Charlotte.

He found her entertaining, but he doubted whether she would make a good wife. She would wish to have everything done as she wanted it; and when he married he would want to be the master. That was one thing of which he was absolutely certain. It was all the more necessary because he was slight and delicate. He must show everybody that bodily weakness was more than made up for by mental ability and strength.

Elizabeth Charlotte was an amusing companion but she would not, he believed, make a good wife for a man such as he was.

She had an imperious habit of instructing him.

"Now, William," she would say, "you must be more gallant. You must look pleased even when you do not win a game. You should really be pleased that I have won because after all if I am to be your wife, you will have to love me beyond all else . . . even beyond yourself—so you may as well start getting used to it."

"And what of you? Will you not be obliged to love *me* better than anything else . . ."

But Elizabeth Charlotte had already dismissed that subject and was thinking of something else.

"I am to be presented to the Princess of Orange," she said. "Aunt Sophia has warned me that I have to be very careful and remember to speak only when spoken to."

"That," said William, "will put a great tax on your memory."

She agreed that it would.

"Well, I do not see why it should be such an ordeal. After all she is my own kinswoman. Perhaps she will be as pleased to see me as I'm supposed to be to see her. She is English they tell me."

"I am too, because she is my mother."

"But you are half Dutch, William. You are the Prince of Orange, which is why of course they want you to marry me."

She was incorrigible and it was impossible to suppress her.

Sophia, who had herself been suppressed since her marriage to a minor prince, despaired of instilling the necessary good manners into the child.

"Elizabeth Charlotte," she said severely, "I am depending on you not to disgrace me."

Elizabeth Charlotte threw her arms about the aunt for whom she was sorry.

"I never will," she declared.

"You must behave very discreetly when you pay your homage to the Princess of Orange. Remember that she is not only the Princess of Orange but the daughter of a King of England."

"Oh, him," said Elizabeth Charlotte. "They chopped off his head."

"Hush, my child. Where do you learn such things?"

"Well, you see, Aunt Sophia, it's history and you know how they are always telling me I must learn my history. Those are the things I can learn best."

"Elizabeth Charlotte, you must try to be more serene. You should be more like William."

"Like William! And not be able to breathe properly. And I don't think, Aunt Sophia, that he stands up very straight. I shall be taller than he is, I am sure; and that is not a very good thing for a wife to be. Should I stoop? Should I wheeze to be a little more like William?"

"You are deliberately mischievous. I implore you not to be. You must be William's good friend. If you are and come to love him while you are young, it will be so much easier when you are grown up. But who has told you you are to marry him?"

"Something in here . . ." She tapped her heart with a dramatic gesture. "Something in here tells me."

"You imagine too much, my dear. And you have imagined this. You should be thinking of how you will conduct yourself before the Princess of Orange instead of dreaming of marriage plans which exist only in your imagination."

"I am pleased. I do not think I want to marry William. I want to have a love match like yours. I think they are the best really."

"Hush, child, hush. Go now to your room; your maids will prepare you. Remember all I have said."

"I will remember, dear Aunt Sophia."

From the Palace in the Wood to The Hague. Elizabeth Charlotte riding beside Aunt Sophia and her grandmother the Queen of Bohemia.

Elizabeth Charlotte sat upright. This was a very solemn occasion because of the presence of her grandmother—the Queen of Bohemia—who had once been so beautiful and was the sister of that poor King Charles I who had had his head chopped off.

Dreamily watching her, Elizabeth Charlotte was thinking of that King: and how the wicked Oliver Cromwell had not only killed him but driven his family out of their country. They were wandering about on the Continent, she had heard, being entertained by any Court that would have them. She imagined them as gypsies—barefooted, dark-skinned, singing a song or two and for their trouble being given the scraps that were left after the banquet.

"You must curtsy deeply to the Princess of Orange when you are presented," Aunt Sophia was reminding her.

"Yes, dear Aunt."

"And when the Queen of Bohemia leaves the Palace you must be ready to leave with her. Do not go off and hide with William, who will be there."

"No, dear Aunt."

Grandmother, Queen of Bohemia, nodded at her absently, and Elizabeth Charlotte imagined she was thinking of her poor brother having his head cut off.

When they arrived at the Palace she saw William and immediately called to him. The Queen of Bohemia and her daughter Sophia smiled at each other with gratification; it pleased them to see the friendship between the children.

"William wishes to show me the gardens," said Elizabeth Charlotte. "May I go with him?"

When the children went off together William said: "But I did not wish to show you the gardens."

"William," chided Elizabeth Charlotte, "you will have to be sharper when you are my husband. I wanted to get away. Do you not see?"

"I see," said William, a little sullenly, "that you wish everyone to dance to your tune."

Elizabeth Charlotte pretended to play a pipe and called: "Dance, William, dance."

He was annoyed and went into the palace; she followed him.

"Now," she said, "we will play hide-and-seek. I shall hide and you shall seek."

"You have come here to pay homage to the Princess of Orange. Have you forgotten?"

Elizabeth Charlotte clapped her fingers over her mouth.

"No. But they did give us permission . . ."

"Only to look at the gardens. Come along. I will take you to the reception chamber."

Elizabeth Charlotte followed him. The reception chamber was an exciting place. The decorations were magnificent and there were so many people, and one woman with a very long nose who fascinated her. She tried not to stare but could not prevent herself.

That must be one of the longest noses in the world, she told herself. I wonder whose it is? I must know.

"Who is that woman?" she whispered to a man who was standing nearby. He did not seem to have heard for he took no notice.

Then she saw William, who had moved some little distance away from her.

"William," she whispered. "Come here, William."

William regarded her stonily and kept his distance.

"William," she said a little louder. "I want to speak to you."

This was not the manner in which to speak to the Prince of Orange. When they were alone he endured a good deal; but he would not in public.

"William," she cried in a loud voice, "I want to ask you something."

Still he ignored her.

"William," she screamed, "who is that woman with the long nose?"

There was a hushed silence all about her. The long-nosed woman did not appear to have heard the interruption.

Elizabeth Charlotte felt her arm gently but firmly taken by a plump young woman and she was led out of the hall.

In the anteroom Elizabeth Charlotte tried to struggle free. "Who are you?" she demanded.

"Her Highness's lady in waiting, Anne Hyde," was the answer.

"Then how dare you lay hands on me? How dare you force me where I do not want to go?"

William had come into the apartment; as soon as he entered he smiled, which was strange for it was not a habit with him.

"William . . ." began Elizabeth Charlotte imperiously.

But William interrupted her. "You asked me a question in there. I'll answer you now. Who is the long-nosed woman? You wanted to know. Well, she is my mother, the Princess of Orange."

The Princess of Orange had sent for her son and as he stood before her she studied him intently. She wished that he could add a few inches to his stature. It would later be such a handicap for him if he remained small. She wished too that he could throw off that wheeziness of his, which really alarmed her. He must learn to stand up straight, for his stoop was growing more pronounced each week.

William guessed what she was thinking; it made him resentful—not against her, but against life which had given him the title of Prince and withheld all that was outwardly princely.

One day, he thought, I will show them that it is not necessary to be tall to be a king. Small men can be as brave—or braver—than big ones. He would show them . . . one day.

The Princess had no idea that her son read her thoughts; she said: "Pray be seated, William. I wish to speak to you about very important matters."

He thought that she was going to reproach him for the behavior of Elizabeth Charlotte, not realizing that when events of such magnitude were happening in her family, the lack of decorum of a child was of small importance to his mother.

"Your uncle has returned to his kingdom."

William said in his correct manner which was more suited to a diplomat than a boy of nine: "Your Highness refers to King Charles II?"

The Princess smiled, thinking of her brother—so tall and charming, so graciously expressing his gratitude for what she had been able to do for him. As if she would not have given all she had to help him! Fleetingly she wished William was a little more like his uncle Charles . . . not that she wished William to grow into a libertine; but she would have liked to have passed a little of the Stuart charm to William. Poor William! That was what he had so missed. Charm? That naughty little playmate of his had more than he had. Not that she would have wished her son to have so disgraced himself as Elizabeth Charlotte had. She must speak to the Queen of Bohemia about the child. But it was no great concern of hers, for now that Charles was back on the throne she saw marriage possibilities for her son which did not include Elizabeth Charlotte.

"Certainly I am referring to your Uncle Charles," she said. "I hear the people gave him such a welcome as has rarely been given to a King before. They were tired of puritan rule in England. And now . . . your uncle is back where he belongs."

"That is good, Your Highness."

She wanted to shout at him: Oh, you little Dutchman. Smile. Do not be so reserved . . . at least with your mother.

She wondered whether she might take him to the English Court. It would do him good to learn a little grace. But she would not want him to adopt the manners of his uncle. One forgave Charles his lechery; but one naturally did not want a son to be the same. No, all William needed was to be less serious, more charming.

"It is very good; and I am going to England as his guest. While I am away I wish you to behave . . . as though I were here."

She paused. He would naturally be well behaved. When had he ever been otherwise?

She said quickly: "But of course you will, William. I am merely telling you what a matter for rejoicing this is in the family. It was that villain Cromwell who insisted on your exclusion from the Stadtholderate. One of your uncle's first acts was to repeal that. Do you see what this means? While your uncle is firmly on the English throne . . . we have a strong ally against our enemies."

"Let us pray that he remains on his throne," said William solemnly, "and that his father's fate never overtakes him."

The Princess smiled. "Oh, William," she said, "you behave as though you are indeed the Stadtholder. You will be, in due course. I know that your uncle will look after your affairs as though he were your father. He has the kindest heart, and if I ask it as a special favor to me he will look to your interests."

"I thank Your Highness."

"The King will marry now and doubtless have children. If he does not . . ."

William waited, and she went on quickly: "Well, my son, you are in the line of succession to the English throne, though some way back. James's children come before you, but one can never be sure what is going to happen. When you marry it must be a match which will bring you every possible advantage."

William was watching her eagerly. Perhaps, she thought, I am saying too much; but he is so serious that he makes me forget he is little more than a child.

"Well," she said briskly, "I shall be praying for you while I am away. And you must pray for me, William. Remember that what is happening in England is a good augury for the future."

"I will remember, Mother."

"I shall speak of you to your uncle. I doubt not we shall discuss your future."

William bowed his head. My marriage? he thought. Whom would they choose for him? He knew that his uncle, James, Duke of York, had two girls—Mary and Anne. Would it be one of these? He hoped that his bride would be tall. She must be to make up for his being so small. She must be the most beautiful woman in the world; she must be witty and clever; but there was one quality above all others which she must possess: Meekness. Having all the virtues, being clever, she must yet realize that there was one whom she must obey. She must be a docile wife ready to adore her husband.

His mother embraced him. "When I return from England we shall have a talk. I shall tell you what it is like to live at the English Court. Now you may go. And I beg of you do not follow the manners of your cousin. Elizabeth Charlotte is a most undisciplined child."

"I agree with Your Highness."

The Princess smiled a little wistfully. She was thinking that if a little of Elizabeth Charlotte's mischief could be transferred to William it might not be a bad thing.

Elizabeth Charlotte was waiting for him.

"What did the Princess want?" she demanded.

"To discuss affairs."

Elizabeth Charlotte turned a hasty somersault and William stared at a swirl of petticoats in shocked silence. Her round saucy face, red with exertion, was mocking yet curious.

"You do give yourself airs, William," she said. "To discuss affairs!" She imitated him. "What affairs? Come on. Tell me."

"You would not understand."

"Now, William, if I am going to marry you you will have to learn to treat me with respect."

"But why?"

"Because I shall be your wife. I shall be the Princess of Orange."

"You will never be that."

"And why not? Why am I here as your constant companion if it is not to prepare me to accept you?"

William drew himself up to make himself as tall as possible. Mischievously Elizabeth Charlotte came to stand beside him to show that she was taller.

He knew in that moment that he would never marry her.

"Do not be too sure that *I* shall accept you," he said. "You have not the qualities which I shall expect to find in my wife."

"Oh, William, you talk like Grandmamma of Bohemia or your mother or some of her old ministers. If they say we have to marry we shall, and you'll have to accept me as I shall you."

"My wife," said William, "will be very tall, very beautiful ... and ..." His voice was suddenly so firm that the grin on Elizabeth Charlotte's face momentarily disappeared, "She will do exactly as I say."

William knew that he would never forget that morning in early January and that it would stand out as one of the momentous occasions of his life. He awoke as usual in his apartments in the Palace in the Wood, rising early, doing the exercises which he never failed to perform because he believed that they would make him grow and develop his muscles. Every night and morning he prayed that he might grow tall and strong so that he would be a worthy war leader. He never forgot that his first ambition was to regain the office of Stadtholder which had been his father's and which the de Wittes and their party had taken from him. The duty of the Stadtholder was to lead Holland against her enemies; it had been the prerogative of the Princes of Orange and he was determined to regain it. Therefore he must discipline himself every day for the task and learn to excel in the art of war. Holland was a small country which had suffered persecution because it was vulnerable and he was determined to make it great.

His zeal was beginning to show results. He could manage a horse with any man; and because of his somewhat short legs he looked bigger on a horse than when standing. That again endeared him to horses. In the saddle he forgot to be concerned with his lack of inches.

He left the Palace for the stables on that morning; his horse was waiting for him and he rode out, galloping with growing excitement. His mother was away at the Court of England making plans for his future. His Uncle Charles was on the throne of England. The de Wittes and their friends had better be wary because he, William, now had some very good and powerful friends who would not be content to see him deprived of offices which were his by right of inheritance.

When he came back to the stables the groom ran out to take his sweating horse and began to stammer words which the Prince could not understand.

William waited coldly for the man to overcome his excitement.

"Your Highness . . . a visitor to the Palace . . . They came to the stables searching for you. I told them you had gone out with your horse."

"Well? And who wished to see me?"

"A very great personage, Your Highness. Mynheer de Witte."

William did not show that his heart had begun to beat faster. He leaped to the ground and when the groom took his horse left the stables and without hurrying walked into the palace.

A page who was evidently on the lookout for him saw him approaching and ran out to him.

"Your Highness," he stammered.

"I know," said William, subconsciously measuring the height of the page—about his own, he reckoned, and the boy younger. "I have a visitor. Take me to him."

The man who was waiting for the young Prince stood, hands behind his back looking out of the window across the gardens. He turned as William entered the room.

William caught his breath and for a few seconds his habitual calm left him. The man who stood before him was the most talked of, the most influential in Holland; John de Witte, the Grand Pensionary, who more than any had been responsible for the abolition of the Stadtholdership.

John de Witte and his brother Cornelius were names which the Prince had learned to abhor. These two men, brilliant and humane, believed that they could best serve their country by freeing it from hereditary rule; and because the Prince of Holland had died before his son was born they had seen their opportunity to abolish the Stadtholdership which set up one man, the Stadtholder, as supreme ruler. They had affected this because there was no one to defend the title.

Now John de Witte and the deprived Prince of Orange were face to face.

"Your Highness," said de Witte, coming forward and bowing, "I have tragic news to impart to you, so I have come to do this in person and to convey my deep sympathies. There has been an outbreak of smallpox at the English Court and . . ."

William, who had been staring at this man, thinking of him as the great enemy, now tried to grasp the importance of what he was trying to tell him. It came to him before the Grand Pensionary could tell him. There was one reason which would bring de Witte to the Palace in the Wood. Smallpox! And his mother at the English Court.

John de Witte's expression was one of compassion as he went on gently: "Your Highness, it is with sorrow that I have to tell you. Your mother died of the smallpox on the twenty-fourth day of December."

William did not speak. He stood, a small pathetic figure, trying to realize what this would mean. His father had died before his birth, and his death was merely something that he had heard talked of. True, it meant to him the loss of the Stadtholderate, but this was different. This was the loss of his mother whom he would never see again.

A great sense of loneliness came over him in that moment. It stayed with him for a very long time.

That was indeed a turning point. William was ten years old when his mother died; he had lost his greatest ally, but he had others in his uncles across the sea, for the King of England and the Duke of York let him know that they did not forget him. The Stuarts were a united family; and although he was a Dutchman, he was also English on his mother's side; he was half-Stuart and the Stuarts' days of obscurity were over; they were back in favor and they would not forget their own.

He became more reserved than ever; his life seemed governed by one purpose. He was going to regain the Stadtholderate and show the world that a great spirit could burn within a meager frame. He realized quickly that those about him were uncertain of him and that this worked to his advantage. He was no ordinary boy; it was not that his tutors found him brilliant; apart from a natural aptitude for languages he did not excel in the schoolroom. His great strength was in his ability to hide what he was feeling; that almost unnatural calm which appeared to hide a deep profundity of thought. He was not interested in sports; he considered them a waste of time apart from hunting, which was, he believed, necessary to his manhood, and in this he showed that especial equestrian skill in which even he could not hide his pleasure. On a horse he was more, so his attendants said, like a human man than at any other time.

De Witte selected his tutors and watched his progress uneasily, realizing that the people would never forget the magic name of Orange. William the Silent would always be one of their greatest national heroes; and this young Prince bore the same name and was of the same heroic branch.

Throughout Holland the people talked of the young Prince and all they heard of him was to his advantage. When he was seen—on horseback—they cheered him, and as he passed into adolescence he became so popular that de Witte realized that sooner or later something would have to be done for him.

Meanwhile William became more and more reserved with the years, keeping his own counsel, never forgetting for a moment his intention to show the world that diminutive William of Orange was one of the greatest figures of the time.

He had his eyes on his uncles across the water! Charles, the King, who would help him one day when he was of an age to fight for his rights, and Uncle James, the great Admiral.

When William was sixteen a plot was made to restore him to the Stadtholderate. William could not be blamed for taking part in it but John de Witte, seeing the direction in which public opinion was turning, decided it was wise to admit him to the Council of State.

In his quiet manner William distinguished himself, and his popularity was growing.

William was nineteen years of age when his uncle invited him to pay a visit to the English Court.

The English Court. What a scene of vice! Sodom and Gomorrah! thought William.

The manner in which the women painted their faces and exposed their bosoms appalled him; the men he considered to be even worse. Their satins and silks, their laces and scents, their conversation, their boasting of their conquests, their descriptions of their amatory adventures, were all very shocking to a young man who drank little wine, rose early and retired early, rarely laughed, and whose only indulgence was a love of the chase.

And this was the English Court from which he hoped for so much. The King sporting with his mistresses—not one but several; the Duke of

York notoriously unfaithful to his wife—she who had shocked his mother so much during that visit which had resulted in her death.

He had come to talk seriously to the King about his prospects, and although Charles greeted him kindly and did not appear to think the less of him because he was so small and his back was not quite straight, he did not appear to wish for serious conversation with his nephew. William began to believe that they had invited him merely to take a look at him; and that because he was not like them—which God forbid—they despised him.

One day Charles invited him to walk with him in the park of St. James's. William felt a disadvantage walking beside his uncle, who was some six feet tall and in his feathered hat seemed a giant. Charles was kindly though; he seemed to understand William's feeling for when they had walked a little distance he said, "We will sit a while, nephew. There we can talk at our ease."

He asked William questions about life at The Hague and talked with affection and humor of the days when he had been an exile there. Occasionally he would ask a shrewd question and William realized that while Charles was discovering what he wanted to know, he, William, had little chance of asking the questions he had had in his mind.

But William was not one to be put off. When his uncle stopped speaking for a while, he began to tell him of the difficulties of his position and how he feared he would never regain his rights while the de Wittes were in power. William believed his uncle would understand the advantages to England of a Holland ruled solely by his own nephew who would be forever grateful for the help he received.

"We are a grateful family, we Stuarts," said Charles, smiling warmly. "We stand together, which shows that as well as being a united family we are a wise one. Why look, there is Buckingham. Buckingham! Come and amuse the Prince of Orange."

George Villiers, Duke of Buckingham, came languidly to the seat on which the King and his nephew sat. The King signed to him to be seated and he placed himself on the other side of the Prince of Orange.

Between these two William felt immediately at a disadvantage. Buckingham was decidedly handsome; he was arrogant, and not inclined to hide the fact even from the King who seemed to delight in his company and to show no resentment at being treated as an equal. How could the King make a favorite of a man of such a reputation? William asked himself. The scandals concerning this man had reached Holland and William knew that the Earl of Shrewsbury had challenged him to a duel because of his guilty intrigue with his, Shrewsbury's, wife. Shrewsbury had been wounded and two months later had died; and afterward Buckingham had lived openly with the Countess. And all this the lazy good-natured King had known and shrugged aside. Men must settle their own affairs, was his verdict.

It was no way to rule.

William's thin lips were drawn up into an expression of disdain as Buckingham took his seat; and both the Duke and the King were aware of this. William did not see the glances which flashed between them. Buckingham's said: Watch. We'll have some sport with the Dutch boy.

"Ah, Your Highness," he said, "and how is The Hague? I remember The Hague. Never shall I forget it. Surely the neatest trimmest town in the world. And the neatest trimmest people. I always felt a little more wicked in The Hague than I did anywhere else. The comparison, you see, Your Highness."

"Comparisons are odorous," murmured the King.

"Not in Holland, Sire. In Holland all is scrubbed free of odor. I believe that to be why there is such an abundance of canals?"

"You are mistaken," began William.

Charles laid his hand on the young man's arm. "Buckingham intends to joke. It's a poor joke, my lord. You should try to do better."

"I stand reproved in the sight of Your Majesty and Your Highness. And I fear my stupidity may spoil my chances of having a favor granted."

"Well, let us hear what favor you ask before you lose heart," suggested Charles.

"It was an invitation from some friends for His Highness. A little supper party—which we would try to make worthy of the Prince."

"I do not attend supper parties . . ." began William.

But Charles intervened, by tightening his grasp on his nephew's arm and smiling benignly. "Oh, come, nephew. You must not decline the hand of friendship. Join the revels. You must get to know us. We are friends, are we not? Then we must understand each other's customs."

It seemed to William that there was a promise in that.

He turned to Buckingham. "I thank you. I accept your invitation. And . . . thank you."

Buckingham inclined his head and as he lifted it, his eyes met those of the King. Charles's were sardonic. Some little joke was being planned. It would be a good one, since it was Buckingham's idea. He looked forward to hearing what happened to William at the Duke's supper party.

William entered the small chamber which seemed to be full of extravagantly clad men, laughing gaily and drinking. He looked about him anxiously and saw with relief that there were no women present. He did not know what to expect, but knowing the morals of this court greatly feared he might have been invited to an orgy for the sexes. The thought of this had filled him with terror; and yet at the same time had awakened thoughts in him of which he would not have believed himself capable. He had begun to ask himself whether if he had not such a destiny to fulfill he might not have enjoyed a little dalliance with women. And might it not be part of a great soldier's life to indulge in amatory adventures? Women to admire him, to tell him that he was the most attractive man in the world, that men such as his uncle were tolerated for their rank while he . . .

But what was happening to him since he had come to the English Court? Did he not despise these men with their effeminate lacy garments, and to whom the whole meaning of life seemed to be the seduction of women?

Buckingham was greeting him with more reverence than he had shown in the garden and in the presence of the King.

"Your Highness, our little gathering is honored indeed."

Others were crowding round him, and he recognized them as some of the biggest rakes and libertines of his uncle's court: Rochester, Dorset, Charles Sedley, and Henry Savile. His nose twitched in disdain as he remembered some of the almost incredible stories he had heard of their exploits. Nothing, it seemed, was too wild for them. Theirs was no company in which the Prince of Orange should find himself. He should never have accepted Buckingham's invitation.

"We are greatly favored," murmured Rochester.

"My lords," replied Sedley, "we must have such sport this night as we have not had since those days when His Majesty first returned to his kingdom."

"I am not much given to sport," said William dourly.

"We have heard reports of Your Highness's decorum," Savile murmured. "A lesson to us all."

"We shall all be better men from this night onward," declared Buckingham, "for it is our great desire to learn from you how a gentleman can restrain his fancies."

"I do not understand," began William.

"Will Your Highness be seated and allow us to sit with you?"

"Certainly."

William sat down and Buckingham cried, "Wine...wine for His Highness."

"Not wine for me. I drink little and then only when thirsty. Perhaps a little ale?"

"Or Hollands Gin?" suggested Buckingham. "A right goodly drink, I'll swear. Shall we drink to the future prosperity of the House of Orange in Hollands Gin?"

"His Highness must certainly drink to the friendship between our two countries," said Sedley. "And it is the custom here that if we drink in his country's drink, he drinks in ours."

"I have told you that I take little drink."

"For a custom, Your Highness."

William felt uneasy; he looked into that circle of faces aware that all eyes were on him. He fancied they were laughing at him, at his lack of worldliness, at his inability to drink as they and most certainly at his meager body—they who apparently worshipped their bodies, decking them out in silks and satins, indulging their appetites.

"For a custom then," he said rashly.

"Done!" cried Buckingham.

They stood and raised their glasses. "Hurrah for Orange, Stadtholder of Holland!"

"Hurrah for Orange!"

There was a slight flush in William's face; they were all smiling at him as though they were in truth his friends. They would help him to regain his rights. This was what he had dreamed of. Was it not for this that he had come to England?

The Duke of Buckingham was calling for more wine. Sparkling wine! Now they would drink to the friendship between their two countries.

"It is our custom, Your Highness, to drain the glass. To leave a little in the bottom is an insult." He rose to his feet. "My friends, we are greatly honored tonight. Come, the toast! Our Sovereign Lord the King and his nephew the Prince of Orange—friends and kinsmen. May they never forget the bond between our two countries."

William drained his glass. He felt a little light-headed, but Buckingham was at his side.

"Your Highness, this is a happy night for us all . . ."

Sedley had leaned forward and filled the Prince's glass. "I see Your Highness is a man who knows how to hold his drink. Now I propose the toast. Victory for His Highness of Orange in all that he endeavors."

William drained the glass.

He was beginning to feel pleasantly at ease. A warm glow had settled on him; he no longer believed that his companions were laughing at him. Far from it. He felt six feet tall, a man among men; they were his friends, his kind respectful friends. They wanted to please him, Buckingham was telling him. In fact it was the object of this party—in honor of the Prince, to please the Prince.

No one in Holland had ever accorded him such respect; and never had he felt quite as he did on this day.

He was lolling back in his chair. Buckingham was telling him how he had fought a duel with Shrewsbury. It seemed very funny, although William had, only that day when he had been regretting that he had accepted Buckingham's invitation, recalled that incident with distaste.

Buckingham was talking of his mistresses—familiarly and again amusingly; and he spoke as though William were as knowledgeable in these matters as he was.

Sedley and Rochester joined in, capping each other's stories. Every now and then one of them would stand and lift his glass, mention a woman's name and they would all drink. The more William drank of the wine, the more he liked it; and the less sleepy he became. He heard someone laughing uproariously and to his amazement discovered that it was himself.

"His Highness is cleverer than any of us," said Buckingham.

He liked that. The sense of power was with him. He was cleverer than any of them. He needed to be.

"So solemn. So serious. Ah, but what is he like in my lady's bedchamber?"

William joined in the laughter.

"Oh, His Highness admits it among his friends." Buckingham sighed. "Would that I had had the wit to hide my weakness. What a lot of trouble I should have been saved."

"His Highness could teach us much."

"Oh, depend upon it."

"Did you see that pretty maid of honor. The new one. A ripe young virgin, I'll swear. Not more than sixteen. Ha, I see His Highness is listening intently. I'll warrant he has already marked her for his own?"

"Seen her, smiled on her! Then what is the betting she is a virgin no more?"

"I'll take you up there, Sedley."

"One hundred."

"Make it two."

"But how test the truth?"

"I'll warrant His Highness will tell us how."

Buckingham bent closer to William. "Your Highness," he said, "we promised you good sport tonight."

"Lead me to it," said William in slurred voice.

The others exchanged glances. The plot was a wild success. Charles was going to laugh at this; and there was nothing that he liked so much as to be amused by the wild adventures of his roystering courtiers. And this one was going to please him more than most. He had said that William was like a eunuch and he often wondered whether those clever de Wittes hadn't made him one just to make sure of the end of the House of Orange.

Buckingham had countered. "Would Your Majesty wager on the matter?"

"Right gladly," the King had replied. "And to have it proved that my nephew was indeed a man would give me such pleasure that I'd be willing to be the loser."

"All in good time. I can see Your Highness is a man who does not like to wait when the urge is on him," Buckingham was telling William.

All the others were laughing; so was William. They knew him better than he knew himself. They were sure he was a success with women. He thought of Elizabeth Charlotte who had quite clearly wanted the marriage between them far more than he had. His dear friends knew more about him than he knew himself. He would be the greatest ruler in Europe—wise, shrewd, successful in all campaigns—yes, every one he undertook, on the battle-field or in the bedchamber.

"As His Highness is in no mood for waiting, let us be gone," suggested Sedley.

Buckingham rose and put his fingers to his lips. The others did the same. Then William stood up and he too put his fingers to his lips.

The room reminded him of the ship on which he had crossed to England, so unsteady was the floor. He laughed aloud. He was so happy to be in England because the English understood him as no one in Holland ever had.

Buckingham took one of his arms, Rochester the other, and with exaggerated caution they left the apartment.

"They will be in bed now," whispered Sedley.

"All the better," retorted Rochester.

"All locked up securely for the night, chastity belts securely fastened, but His Highness the Prince of Orange will know the password. He will have the key."

Such laughter—all the more hilarious because it must be suppressed. Buckingham put his fingers to his lips and they all did the same.

William felt the cool air on his face and this was the only intimation he had that he was out of doors. The fresh air revived him a little, made him feel as strong and brave as a lion.

He stood with the group looking at the row of lighted windows.

"How do we get in?" asked Rochester. "My Prince, pray tell us."

"Yes, Your Highness," said Buckingham. "Could it be through the windows?"

"Yes," said William and his voice sounded muffled. "Through the windows."

Sedley pressed a stone into his hands. "You will lead your men, Sire," he said.

William had never felt so happy. He forgot that he was smaller than most men, that he suffered from that humiliating asthmatical wheeze, that his clothes had to be cut in a special way to hide his deformities.

He was a leader of men—and not in battles. These rakes of his uncle's Court, who were noted for their brilliant wit and fascination were looking to him to lead them.

He threw the stone. Laughing triumphantly he scrambled up the wall to the broken window.

There were cries of alarm from within and faces appeared at the windows.

Buckingham's voice came from a long way off: "His Highness of Orange . . . a little merry. Looking for the ladies."

William had seen the girls' faces and they seemed very fair and inviting. He was irresistible. Buckingham and his friends had said so.

"I'll not disappoint them," he cried. "I'm going in."

The girls began to scream. There were the sounds of shouting and a lantern appeared among the revelers below. Then Buckingham seized the Prince's legs and pulled him to the ground.

"Your Highness, you are waking the Palace."

"I will not disappoint them. The maids are waiting for me. I will not disappoint them."

"Your Highness, we know of your reputation, but you are waking the Palace."

"I will share the bed of the fairest this night . . ."

Sedley and Rochester took his legs, Buckingham and Savile his arms, and he was lifted off the ground.

Now he was angry. He no longer cared for these men. They had promised him good sport and now they were standing in his way of getting it. He wanted to seduce a maid of honor. He knew now that he did not find women as uninteresting as he had believed; tonight had been an education and he wanted to complete it.

The governess of the maids of honor had put her head out of the window.

"Disgraceful!" she cried. "Her Majesty the Queen shall hear of this!"

"Madam," answered Buckingham, "we have done all we can to restrain His Highness. We fear he is a desperate fellow where the ladies are concerned."

"Then take him away from here," was the answer. "Rest assured he will have to answer to Her Majesty."

The laughing courtiers, the shouting governess, and the struggling Prince of Orange made, declared all those who saw it, as goodly a sight as they had seen outside the playhouse. But what was most amusing was that the solemn prudish young Dutchman should be at the center of it.

The King smiled sardonically at his nephew. A chastened William this, who understood that the previous night he had, for the first time in his life, become intoxicated and shown himself to be what no one—including himself—had suspected he might be: a budding libertine.

"Sire," said William, "I cannot express my sorrow . . ."

"Then do not attempt to achieve the impossible, nephew. It is a waste of good time. But let me assure you, this is not a matter which causes me great sorrow—so nor should it you. A broken window is a small price to pay for experience; and last night you learned that nature has not denied you the normal instincts of a man. Would that the old lady had not awakened; then you might have enjoyed the fruit of your labors. I am sure you have made a good impression on the maids and doubtless one—at least—will find some means of assuring you that it is not necessary to break more windows."

"I fear, Sire, that my reputation is ruined."

"On the contrary, it is enhanced. A little light-heartedness is a blessing on all occasions."

"Your Majesty, I believe it is time that I had a wife."

"You are young yet. Why not enjoy the advantages of marriage and none of its disadvantages for a while?"

"I shall not shirk the responsibilities of marriage, Sire," answered William primly. "An alliance with my mother's country would I believe be advantageous to both hers and mine."

"I'll warrant you are thinking of your cousin Mary. Yes, of a surety, Mary! God's fish, man, you would have to wait too long for the child. Do you know she is as yet eight years old?"

"I would be prepared to wait."

Charles pretended to consider. What would his nephew say if he knew that he was on the point of signing an agreement with Holland's greatest enemy, Louis XIV of France, one clause of which was that together they should declare war on the Dutch?

"I can see you are a very patient young man."

William was excited. The King did not refuse him Mary. His thoughts ran on; he had to have an ambitious goal to help wash out last night's disgrace. He was after all in the line of succession and marriage with Mary would put him several jumps ahead.

Ever since he had come to England he had become obsessed by a desire to rule the country. He would sweep clean the Court of all its vice. England was a great country, with advantages denied to Holland, and he could be King of England, Scotland, and Ireland if he married Mary.

And the King was not dismissing the idea.

"Your Majesty, could I see my cousin?"

Charles nodded. "I see no reason why you should not. She is at Richmond with her family. When you see her you will realize how young she is. Oh, William, do you want to wait some six or seven years for marriage?"

"A good match is worth waiting for, Your Majesty."

"I see that you are a very wise young man; and judging by your nocturnal adventures you will know how to amuse yourself during the waiting."

Charles began to laugh and William allowed the corners of his own mouth to turn up. He had secretly decided never to come under the influence of wine again; but he was not displeased to be thought something of a gay gallant.

When the King was riding with the Prince of Orange they found themselves near to Richmond, so it was natural that they should stop there.

A pleasant family party was being enjoyed. The Duke of York, who had been indisposed, was spending most of his time at Richmond with his Duchess, who was clearly very ill, and their children were with them there.

Charles strode into the Palace and there was the immediate bustle which was an essential part of a King's arrival.

But this, said Charles, was an informal occasion; he wanted no ceremony.

He embraced his brother and his sister-in-law.

"And where are the children?" he wanted to know.

"They had all been playing a game together," James explained, and sent one of the attendants to bring the little girls to His Majesty. Edgar had a slight fever and was in bed.

William watched her as she came forward; a pretty girl, with dark ringlets and almond-shaped eyes, she was not in the least shy and appeared to be very sure of an affectionate welcome from her uncle.

She kissed the King's hand, at which he drew her to him. It was clear to William which one of the girls was the King's favorite, although he was obviously fond of both of them.

"Mistress Anne, you grow plumper every time I see you," said Charles. "Tell me, what do you do when you are not eating?"

Anne tried to think. "I wonder what I shall have for dinner, Sire," she said at length, which made them all laugh.

"And now I'll warrant you're wondering who is this handsome young man whom I have brought to see you."

"He is not very handsome," said Anne.

"You are not old enough to appreciate his charms, my dear niece." Charles was smiling at Mary who had seen the tightening of the young man's lips; she knew what was expected of her.

"Anne is a child," she said. "She and I never agree."

The King's hands gripped her shoulder and his dark face gleamed with pleasure.

"Mary," he said, "one day you shall have a seat on my Council. I knew that you and your cousin of Orange would be good friends. Take him to sit over yonder and talk to him. He would like to talk to you, and I must perforce speak to Mistress Anne and endeavor to persuade her that honey flavors words as pleasantly as sweetmeats."

As Mary smiled up at her cousin she heard Anne protesting: "But, uncle, we should always tell the truth, you know."

And Charles's reply: "The truth is a slippery eel, Anne. When we use it toward others we call it honesty; when they use it toward us we call it bad manners."

Mary said: "You are my cousin from Holland. I knew that you were here."

"I am glad to meet you."

"I hope that you will stay long with us."

He liked her. She was tall, but as yet not as tall as he was—being only eight. She was physically attractive with her long almond eyes; a certain gaiety mingled with her gravity which he found pleasant.

He wondered if she had heard about the escapade with the maids of honor, decided that she had not, and liked her better than ever.

Her little brother was in bed with a fever; he had heard that he was a sickly child. The duchess was very ill, and looked to have death at her elbow; as for the King, he had been married ten years and had no child— although he had plenty of illegitimate sons and daughters.

England was a powerful country; he was in the line of succession, but not so close as this girl.

As he talked to Mary he made up his mind that, in due course, he might be very pleased to do her the honor of making her his wife. There was only one thing that caused him a little uneasiness. She was rather sure of herself. The manner in which she spoke to the King and her father betrayed that. Of course she had been indulged. Would she be a meek and docile wife, for he would accept no other.

Yes, he believed he could mold her. Mary would, when she was of age, please him well as a wife.

THE ORANGE

BRIDEGROOM

*D*uring *the two years since his return from* England William had remained on good terms with his uncles; but he had learned to be wary. His great enemy was Louis of France whom he knew wished to make Holland into a protectorate under France, which was something William would never accept. Spain was now an ally but not a reliable one, and William's great hope was in England.

There was one friend with whom he could talk without restraint; this was William Bentinck who resembled him in some ways; they had been drawn together when they had first met and William had found Bentinck serious, intelligent, in fact so much like himself that he might have been his brother. Bentinck, however, was less brusque than William; he was able to couch a demand diplomatically in a manner which William found impossible. He supplied a quality which William lacked and William was beginning to rely on him and kept him at his side.

It was Bentinck who was with the Prince on that fateful day in the year 1672, two years after William's visit to England.

The two friends had been talking uneasily for England and France had become allies and were threatening Holland; there was a smoldering anger in William's eyes as he faced his friend.

"Traitors," he said. "My own uncles! I believe that they had no intention of being my friends."

"They would if it was to their advantage."

"But they are ready to make senseless war."

"Not senseless from their point of view if they subdue us. I have always suspected that Charles was secretly trafficking with Louis."

"I hate Louis. I should hate Charles, but he is my uncle and when I am with him I find it impossible to do anything but like him."

"It is an effect he has on many, I believe. Therefore we should be especially wary."

William clenched his fists together and said: "Bentinck, what will happen now? I will never let Holland be conquered. If they would make me their Stadtholder . . ."

"The de Wittes will never allow it. They cling to their power. They are determined as ever that the Stadtholderate shall not return to Holland."

"The Dutch Republic needs a leader. It needs me as once it needed my great-grandfather."

"I believe the people know it."

"But what use when they are ruled by the de Wittes. Who are these de Wittes? Why should they rule our country? What tradition have they? It should be Orange for the Dutch . . . as it used to be. And now, Bentinck, this war! I shall lead my men to victory. And then . . . come back to be ruled by . . . the de Wittes. Would to God I could be rid of that pair of brothers."

"They are too strong . . . as yet."

They heard sounds of arrival from below and Bentinck went to the window to see who had come to Dort.

They were not left long in doubt. A messenger had arrived with a letter for William.

He dismissed the messenger, read it slowly; then looked at his friend.

"From de Witte," he said. "It seems that the people are growing angry. They are threatening him and Cornelius. They're blaming them for the war. Louis has five times our forces and they are blaming the de Wittes . . . who are afraid, Bentinck, because in the streets of The Hague the people are crying for Orange."

"Your moment has come."

William nodded his head. "They need me now. When disaster threatens they call for Orange. This is strange, Bentinck. The de Wittes are calling for Orange."

"How so?"

William looked at the paper in his hands. "The people are gathering about their house. They are waiting for them to come out. The people of Holland are not easily aroused, Bentinck, but when they believe justice should be done they do it. The de Witte brothers are afraid. They are hinting great promises, Bentinck. If I go to The Hague I shall have this and that. If I go to The Hague . . . show myself to the people I will calm them, so they think. It's true, Bentinck. I could go into those streets and disperse the crowds. Are they not calling for Orange?"

"Then you will make haste to go?"

William shook his head slowly.

"Not yet, my friend," he said. "Not yet."

The mob had lashed itself to a frenzy of hatred. Groups of angry people shouted together. "This," they cried, "is what happens when two men seek to rule us. Who are these de Wittes? They have robbed us of our Prince and they have taken the titles themselves—only they do not use them. They assume all that goes with them though."

"Hurrah for Orange. Where is our Prince? Our Prince will lead us to victory. He will save Holland. He is William . . . like that other William. William of Orange. God bless the Prince."

And the more they shouted for William, the more angry they grew with those men who had robbed him of his position among them. Men felt for daggers at their sides; some carried cudgels. The de Wittes could not remain within the house forever. And if they did it was not impossible to force an entry. But let them come out. Let them see what a crowd of angry people had in store for them.

They waited and grew impatient. But the de Wittes were not cowards. When it became clear that the Prince of Orange had no intention of coming to The Hague, they knew what they would have to do.

John and his younger brother Cornelius understood what was in the other's mind. They had done what they had done for the sake of Holland; they were two men who had loved their country and believed that she needed to be free of a ruler who was such because his father was before him.

"Are you ready, Cornelius?" asked John.

"I am ready, brother," was the answer.

Calmly they walked into the street. A shout went up as they were recognized.

"It is. It is!"

"The brothers de Witte!"

"Come, you brave men, what are you waiting for?"

The crowd fell upon them.

William came to The Hague with high excitement in his heart. This was the dream of a lifetime achieved.

Holland was his to command; and the first thing was to wage war against her enemies. He was Stadtholder now, General of his armies and

Admiral of his navy. That which he believed was his by right of his inheritance was returned to him; and all because two men—two good men he would admit, but two mistaken men—had been viciously murdered in the streets of The Hague.

Bentinck said: "This is the turning point."

"At least," answered William, "now I shall have a country to rule."

"It may be said in some quarters that you could have saved the de Wittes."

"My presence in The Hague might have done that. On the other hand the people hated them. They wanted me, Bentinck. The people love a Prince. They want no old men who have taken their place because of their shrewdness. They want a Prince and I am their Prince. It was a horrible murder and I suppose one should regret it, but to you I will confess that this deed has much relieved me."

"I trust you will not be so frank with others."

"Nay, when have I ever been over-frank? When have I talked when silence should be maintained? They called my great-grandfather The Silent. I think mayhap that is another virtue I have inherited from him."

Later he addressed his people while they shouted themselves hoarse for Orange.

The times were stark, he told them. He had no soft words for them. Weary battles lay ahead of them. They had had false friends but at least now they knew who their enemies were, and they could trust him to lead them.

"I will fight for Holland," he told them, "and if necessary I shall die in the last dyke."

The country was wild with joy. They could not fail. William of Orange would lead them to victory; they could put their trust in him as their ancestors had in that other William.

The people of Holland were not disappointed in their new leader. William showed himself to be a man of single purpose; and that purpose now was to free Holland from her enemies and to keep her free. He was a man who was determined to lead them; now was his opportunity to show the world that inches are not necessary to greatness.

After a few months of battle England was not averse to peace. Both Charles and James had come to understand that the young man who had been led to storm the apartments of the maids of honor with such determination could show the same enthusiasm for more worthy causes. William of Orange had become a man to be respected.

In spite of the peace with England, William was still engaged with his Spanish allies in a war against France, and Charles in England, ally of Louis, sought to make a general peace. Under Orange, Holland was a formidable little country and Louis was tired of that particular war, but clearly could not make this known; therefore Charles would help him to gain what he needed.

Charles's idea was to offer Orange the Princess Mary as his wife. When Orange had come to England some three years previously he had clearly had such a union in mind. At that time it had not seemed politic. Now Orange was the Dutch leader; he was a Prince with more than a title who had shown himself to be astute, and he was Charles's own nephew. But none of these was the main reason which prompted the King. Since his marriage James, Duke of York, was becoming more and more unpopular. Wherever he appeared there were continual cries of "No popery." James was a fool, thought Charles; but he was his brother and for that reason it was necessary to protect the fool from the results of his folly.

Now if James's daughter married a Protestant the people's growing resentment would be halted. They would say to themselves, Since he is prepared to give his daughter to Protestant Orange can he be such an ardent Catholic?

James would oppose the match, of course, having set his heart on a French marriage for Mary. A French marriage! A Catholic marriage! When the people hated the French and were determined to have no Catholics on the throne of England.

Charles, leaning toward the Catholic faith did so secretly. Secretly! That was the point. Poor James, he was half idealist, half sensualist; the one was continually getting in the way of the other.

Orange for Mary then! Let it be done!

William laughed aloud when he received the news that the King of England was desirous of making a match between his niece and his nephew.

He called to his dear friend Bentinck and told him what had happened.

"Marriage with England. My friend, when I was at my uncle's Court I intimated that such a marriage would be acceptable to me. I saw the Princess Mary. She is comely, but without reticence; she seemed over familiar with the King and her father; and they have brought her up to speak without thinking first of the effect of her words; they have allowed her to excel at dancing and playacting."

"She could be Queen of England, Highness."

"There is that in her favor." He gave that faint twist of the lips which could scarcely be called a smile. "As yet," he said, "I am not ready for marriage. Nor shall I allow my uncles to think I am waiting on their words to give them back my friendship. Do not forget Bentinck that they made war on us—for I do not forget it."

He wrote to the King of England: "My fortunes are not in a condition for me to think of taking a wife."

He was inwardly exultant, guessing what effect those words would have on his uncles.

Charles laughed. "Our little nephew plays the great man. Well, perhaps we must accept the fact that he is half as important as he thinks himself. All in good time. We'll marry him to Mary yet."

The Duke of York was furious. The little upstart, to refuse his lovely daughter! To flout England, for that was what he had done since Mary could one day bring him England.

"I hate the fellow," said James. "I shall never forgive him for insulting my daughter."

Charles shrugged his shoulders. He displayed no passion but all the same he was determined that the marriage should take place at some future time.

These were good days for William. The Dutch nation adored him. His solemnity endeared him to them; they would not have wished for a monarch like the King of England. They shouted for the Prince of Orange wherever he went, and were certain that he would lead them to victory.

William lived for Holland; he was full of plans for defeating her enemies; he had determined to bring peace and prosperity to his people; it should be his life's ambition. He knew that he had been born to rule. He wanted no wife; he wanted no pleasure; he wanted his people to know that another William the Silent had come to lead them.

He was proving himself to be a leader, a brilliant soldier, a man of few words and great solemnity. He was a hero.

Then the disturbing news was circulating throughout the land. Orange was sick of deadly malady.

When the first sign of the sickness had come to him he had not believed it could be; but when his doctors had seen him they withdrew in horror.

Bentinck came to his bedside.

"My friend," said the Prince, "you should not come near me. You know what ails me?"

"I have been told you have the smallpox."

"The disease," said the Prince, "which killed my mother."

He was exhausted, Bentinck saw; he had taken the disease badly, and his chances of survival would therefore be slight.

Moreover, it was inconceivable that such a man would not have enemies. How easy to prevent his recovery!

Bentinck knelt down by the bed.

The Prince looked at him as though seeing him vaguely through half closed eyes.

"Go away," he murmured.

"I will never leave you while you need me," said Bentinck.

William's brow puckered; he was rapidly becoming too ill to understand.

Bentinck called the doctors into an anteroom.

"It is His Highness's wish that I remain."

"You have had the pox?"

Bentinck shook his head.

"You run grave risks."

"We all must run grave risks for Holland."

"You can do him no good, and yourself much harm."

"It is the Prince's wish that I remain."

"He would not wish that for his worst enemy."

"But perhaps he would," said Bentinck wryly, "for his best friend."

Hourly the Prince's death was expected. In the streets of the cities people said: "He came like a promise that is not to be fulfilled. What will become of us? What of Holland now? We shall be under the French before we know where we are. Louis doesn't strike now because he is waiting to hear that the Prince is dead. He wouldn't dare while he still lived."

"Let us pray for him. What is Holland without Orange."

In the country the people ran out of their houses every time they heard the sound of travelers on the road.

"Any news . . . any news of the Prince?"

In the sickroom Bentinck sat by the Prince's bed, determined that none but himself should look after the invalid. William lay as though dead but Bentinck believed he knew his friend was near and took comfort from the fact.

Bentinck would talk to William even though there was no answer.

"You must fight death, my Prince. All Holland depends on you." That was the theme of his conversation and there were times when he believed the Prince understood him, for after sixteen days of uncertainty William showed the first signs of improvement. When the doctors expressed their astonishment that he, who had suffered such a violent attack, had a hope of recovery, Bentinck cried: "He is determined to live and when this Prince determines he succeeds."

Now was the time to prepare the Prince good nourishing food—food which should come to him only through Bentinck's hand.

William looked at Bentinck.

"You were with me all the time," he said.

"Yes, Highness. But you were too sick to know it."

"I sensed your presence here, Bentinck. It gave me great comfort. It is good to have a friend; and I believe you to be my friend, Bentinck."

"Your Highness has many friends."

"Friends to the Prince of Holland," answered William. "Those who support him because they know he will bring good to them. Only one Bentinck. I believe one should be grateful for one such. Bentinck, I shall never forget you."

That was all he said, for he was always one to avoid expressing emotion. But the bond was there between them.

Bentinck had risked his life for his Prince. It was something one never forgot as long as one lived.

William began to recover rapidly. Bentinck prepared all his food himself; they talked together of their future, which was Holland's.

The people were ready to adore their Prince. Not only could he conquer their enemies but the most dreaded sickness, and they believed they could look with confidence to their deliverer.

One morning Bentinck came to his master and told him that he was exhausted and needed a little rest; had he the Prince's permission to retire to the country for a while? The permission was readily given.

Within the next few days William heard that Bentinck was suffering from the smallpox.

William was more moved when he heard of Bentinck's sickness than he had ever been before in his life. He sent his own doctors; he genuinely deplored the fact that he could not go himself and do for his friend what Bentinck had done for him, but the nation's affairs occupied him and he must concern himself with his duty. Continually he thought of Bentinck; he missed him; there was so much he wanted to discuss with him, and if Bentinck died, he believed it would be one of the greatest tragedies of his life.

But Bentinck did not die. The best doctors, the greatest care in nursing, the constant messages from the Prince, and the great will to survive were on his side. And as William had, eventually he began to recover.

It was a day of great joy when the two friends were together again.

William looked at Bentinck and said, "It pleases me to see you well again. I have need of you."

That was all; but Bentinck was aware of the deep feeling beneath the words. Their friendship was sealed; it would last for the rest of their lives. William was aware of this too; but being the man he was he expressed his pleasure in a few brusque words.

The months of anxiety followed. Holland was a small country and her enemies were strong. All the bravery in the world could not stand out against the might of arms and men many times greater than those possessed by Holland. During these months William's natural characteristics became stronger and unshakable. He believed that he had been chosen to rule—not only Holland. He was predestined to be a King. He had never forgotten Mrs. Tanner's vision. Always it seemed there must be on this earth a conflict between Catholic and Protestant, and he, a stern Calvinist, was ideally fitted to lead the Protestant Cause. He saw himself as the Protestant leader of Europe, perhaps the world. He must defeat Catholicism; and he believed that it did not matter how he did so as long as he was successful.

His ability to remain calm, to give no hint of anger was one of his great gifts, he realized; he must cultivate it. He would hide his thoughts from all; so that when he said one thing he might well mean another. If necessary he would lie for the Cause.

Mrs. Tanner had prophesied three crowns. Could these be England, Scotland, and Ireland? His eyes were on England, for neither the King nor the Duke of York seemed now to be able to beget heirs. Mary of York would very probably succeed her father if he did not have a son; and if William married Mary, because of his claim through his Stuart mother, he could become King of England.

When he had been offered Mary he had said that his fortunes were not such as to enable him to think of a wife, but times had changed. Without support it might well be that Holland would become a protectorate of France; but if he married Mary, England would be obliged to stand by Holland. Had he been rash to make such a reply when Mary had been offered him? He did not think so. His reply while it had angered James had made others respect him. It was as well for them to believe themselves to be more anxious for the match than he was. But when Mary was offered again . . . and it was certain that she would be, his reply would be lukewarm instead of cold.

William was brave; he had proved himself to be a shrewd and subtle leader, but the forces against him were too strong, and his ministers suggested that the peace terms which were being offered from France should be accepted.

Now he showed himself in all his strength. He had declared he would fight to the last dyke, he told them, and he meant it. If Holland were not to fall under the French domination she must not give way.

"There is not a man in Holland who does not desire peace," he was told.

"There is one," he retorted. "I know him well, for he is the Prince of Orange."

They admired him; they respected him; they looked up to him, and remembered his noble ancestor. And when he stood before them, his expression cold and stern, they could believe that if there was one man who could achieve the impossible, that man was William of Orange.

"I saw an old man this morning," he told his ministers. "He was rowing his little boat against the eddy of a sluice on the canal. Every time he was about to reach his destination the eddy carried him back. I watched him repeat this four times. Every time it happened he took up his oars again. Do you see what I mean, my friends? I am like that old man in the boat and I shall never be beaten as long as I can return to my oars."

So in spite of efforts for peace, the war continued.

There were victories and defeats; neither side was the victor. Louis was tired of the conflict and Charles attempted to negotiate a peace.

William received Louis's envoys, prepared, he said, at least to listen to what terms he had to offer.

When he heard that Louis wanted to suggest a French marriage for the Prince, William considered this.

Who was the lady? he asked.

Louis's own daughter, was the reply. She was very beautiful and her mother was Louise de la Vallière. The King delighted in her and it showed the extent of his esteem for the Prince that he should offer him this favorite girl.

William was furious. "She is a bastard," he said coldly. "You should return to the King of France without delay and tell him that the Princes of Orange do not wed kings' bastards."

This refusal and the terms in which it was made, infuriated Louis when he heard it. He vowed that it was an insult he could never forget and consequently would never forgive the insolent Orange.

William was now more than ever eager for the English marriage. He could not forget the insult Louis had given him by suggesting that he might accept his illegitimate daughter, and only marriage with a Princess of very high rank and with dazzling prospects could give balm to his wounded vanity. He was thinking more frequently of the Princess Mary, eldest daughter of the Duke of York. He was as eager for that marriage as he had been several years before when he had gone to England and been involved in the disgraceful scene outside the chambers of the maids of honor.

He decided to send for Sir William Temple who was in Holland at this time for the Congress of Nimeguen. Sir William had shown himself a friend to Holland and it seemed to William that he was the man to be trusted with this matter.

Sir William was a cautious man who rarely took any action without making sure that it was absolutely safe to do so, and although he was a reliable ally he was an unimaginative one. William felt a bond between them and it was for this reason that he decided to call him at this stage.

Sir William was known to favor Dutch interests, an attitude in which he persisted even though it resulted in a loss of popularity in England, so the Prince was certain that he would be in favor of a marriage between him and Mary.

When Sir William arrived at the Palace of Hounslaerdyck whither the Prince had summoned him, William came straight to the point.

"Marriage," began the Prince, "is a state which a man in my position must consider at some time, and it would seem to me that time has come. I have had proposals from various sources. One from the King of France." He paused and glanced sideways at Sir William. Would he have discovered that Louis had offered him a bastard? Sir William gave no sign and the Prince enlightened him no further. "In spite of this," he went on, "if I decided to marry it would be to England that I should look."

"I am glad to hear it, Your Highness."

"Oh, I have not brought you here as a diplomat. I wish to speak to you of this matter as one friend to another."

Sir William intimated that he was very willing to be a friend to the Prince of Orange.

"I should want a wife who did not give me trouble at home, for I shall be much engaged abroad. Before I married there are certain facts I should want to know about my wife's character and education. My wife must be a woman who would live well with me and I might not be easy to live with. In fact, certainly those women who live at the various courts today might find it difficult to live with me; the tendencies which displease me are prevalent in the Court of the King of England and that gives me pause for thought."

"I believe, Your Highness, that the best marriage you could make would be with England."

"Such a union would please me, but I should need to know those facts I mentioned about my wife."

"My own wife is a great friend of Lady Frances Villiers who is in charge of the Princess's household."

"Then I would ask you as a friend to command her to give me an account of the Princess Mary. If it pleases me well then I should not be averse to this match."

Sir William said he would dispatch a message to his wife without delay; and he doubted not that she would do her utmost to give the Prince of Orange a true picture of the Princess Mary.

Lady Temple sent glowing accounts of the Princess Mary. She was a charming girl, more beautiful than her sister, skilled in dancing, of good temper, and would almost certainly prove a docile wife; moreover she was young for her fifteen years and could doubtless be molded.

William liked that description. He sent for his good friend Bentinck.

"There is no one else whom I would trust with this mission," he told him. "I wish you to set out with all speed to London. There it will be necessary to negotiate with the Lord Treasurer, Lord Danby. He is the man.

I doubt not that your mission will be successful for I know that you always work tirelessly for my good. I want this marriage with England."

They discussed each point in favor of such a marriage while they considered the disadvantages.

"Providing the Duke and Duchess of York do not have a son, this could be a most brilliant marriage for Your Highness," said Bentinck.

"It is a chance we have to take," was William's answer. "They have tried and failed before."

Bentinck agreed that apart from the brilliant prospects of William's ascending the English throne through his wife, the marriage would still be a good one.

"Holland is fighting a desperate battle for survival," said William. "The bravery of the Dutch cannot stand out against the power of Louis. Our Spanish allies are unreliable. Bentinck, we need England. The crown . . . that is a matter for later." His eyes glowed. "It will come. In the meantime England, standing with us—as the King will do if his niece is Princess of Orange—can save us."

Bentinck, who knew his friend very well, understood that William had no doubt that one day the English crown would be his. He was a man who believed in predestination and he was certain that he was born to rule not only Holland but England, Scotland, and Ireland.

To be with him was to feel that certainty. Bentinck set off for England with high hopes of success.

Shortly afterward William of Orange received an invitation from Charles to visit England.

THE RELUCTANT BRIDE

The King was smiling across the table at Lord Danby. Poor Danby! he thought lightly. His position is not a happy one.

"In the circumstances, Your Majesty," Danby was saying, "the Dutch marriage is greatly desirable."

Charles agreed. "The people hate the war with Holland and marriages are the best guarantees of peace."

The eyes of the King and his Lord Treasurer met. There were so many secrets which they shared and which it would be advisable, both knew, should never leak out. Danby had helped in those transactions with France which some might consider shameful and which would certainly shock the King's subjects if they were aware of them; Charles's secret leanings toward Catholicism, his monstrous promise to Louis, could lose him his throne if they were known. They had much to hide, these two. But the King was nonchalant; he had an infinite belief in his ability to extricate himself from the difficult situations into which he could not resist falling in his continual attempts to provide himself with money which his Parliament would not—and indeed could not—grant him.

Danby, on the other hand, trying hard to appear calm, could not hide his disquiet. His fall could be imminent. In the streets they were singing lampoons about him. He was the most hated man in England. He had not sinned so deeply as his master; but he would be blamed. Charles had only to flash his famous smile—which was merry and sardonic at the same time—on his subjects and they would forgive him his lechery, and his treachery. Such was not the case with Danby. He could not charm them with his unromantic appearance—his lean figure, his pale face, and his obvious ill health. Moreover, he knew that if Charles's secret dealings with the King of France ever came to light, it would be Danby who would be blamed for them, not Charles.

And now the people were restive largely because they hated war. Charles would show them that he was prepared to put an end to the war and that he was no friend of the King of France because Louis would be furious at a match between Holland and England. Perhaps of late his subjects had begun to suspect Charles favored Catholicism.

"Very well," said the King. "We will send for Orange. We will show the people that we are anxious for peace with Holland, for can we want to be at war with the husband of our own Princess Mary?"

"Your Majesty," said Danby, "the Duke of York will not consent to this marriage."

"You must make him understand the importance of it, Danby."

"Your Majesty, the Duke of York has not your understanding of affairs. I feel sure he will remind us that you once promised not to dispose of his daughters without his consent."

Charles was thoughtful. "It is true I made such a promise. But God's fish, he must consent."

Danby bowed his head. Consent or not, he thought, the marriage should take place. He, Danby, was rushing headlong to his ruin, as Clarendon had some years before. It was not easy to serve a King such as Charles II, a clever man who was in constant need of money and not too scrupulous as to how he acquired it, a man who was ready to conduct his own foreign policy in such a manner that his Parliament knew nothing about it.

For them both the marriage was a necessity.

Charles's shrewd eyes met those of his statesman. He knew what Danby was thinking.

"You see the need as I do, Danby," he said. "So, it shall be done. Tomorrow I leave for Newmarket. . . ."

James, furious, stormed into his brother's apartments.

"I see you are speechless," said Charles, "so I must help you out of your difficulty as I have so many times before by speaking for you. You have doubtless seen Danby."

"This marriage . . ."

"Is most desirable."

"With that Dutchman!"

"A dour young lover I will admit, but our nephew, brother. Forget not that."

"I will never give my consent to this marriage, and I am her father."

Charles raised his eyebrows and gazed sadly at his brother.

"Without my knowledge Danby has dared . . ."

"Poor Danby. He has his faults, I doubt it not . . . and many of them. All the more sad that he should be expected to carry those of others."

"You promised that my daughters should never be given in marriage without my consent."

"And, as ever, it grieves me to break a promise."

"Then Your Majesty must be constantly grieved."

"I fear so, James. I fear so. My dear brother, do try to be reasonable.

This marriage must take place. It is more necessary to you than to any of us."

"To me! You know I dislike that Dutchman."

"He is of our flesh and blood, James, and we loved his mother. Families should live in amity together. He is a dull fellow, I'll be ready to swear, but he did once try to get at the maids of honor."

James shrugged impatiently.

"And you, James," went on Charles, "are far from popular. This ostentatious popery of yours is a constant irritant."

"And what of yourself?"

"I said ostentatious popery. You should learn to show proper respect to words, James, if not to your King. Now listen to me. If Mary marries our Calvinist the people will say: How can the Duke of York be such a papist if he allows this Protestant marriage! *You* need this Protestant marriage more than any of us."

"Your Majesty has always been for tolerance."

"I am more tolerant than my subjects are prepared to be. You have always known that."

"And Charles, is it not your dealings with the French which make you so eager for this marriage?"

Charles smiled wryly. "As I have said before, I have no wish to be like a grand signor with mutes about him and a bag of bowstrings to strangle men if I have a mind to it. At the same time I could not feel myself to be a King while a company of fellows are looking into all I do and examining my accounts. There, James. That is your brother and King. Tolerance, yes. Let every man worship as he pleases and let the next fellow do likewise. Thus if I wish to be a papist I'd say I'll be one and that is my affair. And if I make agreements with foreign kings because by so doing I can get what my Parliament denies me—well then, that is my affair too."

"And because of this my daughter must marry the Dutchman?"

"Because of this, James—my follies, your follies, and the follies of those who want to go to war when they could live so much happier in peace. You'll give your consent, James. Then . . . we must see that we get the better of our little Dutchman."

When William arrived at Newmarket the King greeted him cordially.

"It is long since we met, nephew, too long. And now you come as a hasty lover."

"I would wish first to have a sight of the Princess Mary," replied William cautiously.

Charles laughed. "Do you think that we would ask you to make an offer for what you have not seen? Not a bit of it. You shall see her and I will tell you this: there is not a more charming young girl at this Court, nor in the length and breadth of England I'll dare swear—perhaps not in Holland!"

William did not smile. He knew that they would attempt to make fun of him as they had before; he had always suspected that Charles had played a part in the maids of honor episode.

"I shall be delighted to meet her."

"And in the meantime, my dear nephew, we will discuss less agreeable matters. We will save the tasty tidbit until the last which I believe is a very good habit. There are the peace terms which I suppose we should consider of the utmost importance. We will go into council here at Newmarket, and then it may be that there will be two great events to be celebrated."

William's lips were tight as he said: "Your Majesty, I could only discuss the terms of peace after the Princess Mary was affianced to me."

"Oh come, nephew—business before pleasure you know."

"I can do no more than explain to Your Majesty my intentions."

Charles showed no sign of annoyance.

"What did I say," he appealed to his friends. "Here we see the eager lover."

The Lady Frances Villiers sent for the Princess Mary. She was fond of the Princess and yet relieved that very soon she would not be in charge of her. Mary had always been eager to please and gave little trouble; her passionate friendship with Frances Apsley was the only real anxiety she had felt on her behalf; and now there would be no need to worry about that.

"My lady," said Lady Frances, "your cousin, the Prince of Orange, has come to Court and His Majesty is anxious for you and your sister to be presented to him."

"I heard that he was in England," replied Mary lightly. She was wondering whether Sarah Jennings would show her a new seal she had. It would be amusing to use it for her letter to Frances.

"Tomorrow you and your sister will be presented. The King and your father wish him to find you agreeable."

Mary wrinkled her brows. "I have heard that he himself is not always considered so."

"Who said this to you?"

Mary lifted her shoulders; she would be careful not to betray the offender. Lady Frances, who knew her well, was also aware that Mary had no realization of the reason behind her cousin's visit.

Poor child, thought Lady Frances. She will have a great shock, I fear.

Mary was pleasant enough to look at, thought Lady Frances. She was trying to see the child with the eyes of a stranger and a would-be lover at that. She would most surely please him. Her complexion was unusually good; her nose well proportioned and her almond-shaped eyes really beautiful. She scarcely looked marriageable; but she had always seemed young for her years—and in any case she was only fifteen.

While Lady Frances scrutinized her charge Mary was looking anxiously at her governess.

"You are pale, Lady Frances," she said. "Have you one of your headaches?"

Lady Frances put a hand to her brow and confessed that she had been feeling unwell for the last few days.

"You must go and lie down."

Lady Frances shook her head. "And you must tell the Princess Anne of the appointment for tomorrow."

"Oh, yes," replied Mary, "I shall not forget."

Face to face with William she thought that the stories she had heard about him might well be true. He looked as though he rarely smiled.

"Welcome to England, cousin," she said; for the King and her father seemed to wish that she be the one to talk to him.

He inclined his head and she asked him how he liked England.

He liked it well enough, he answered.

What a dour creature he was. She would remember this conversation and report it all in her next letter to Frances. Better still keep it until they met. She smiled as she visualized that meeting.

"Very different, I'll swear, from your Court at The Hague."

"Two Courts could hardly be expected to be the same."

She was thinking: But, Frances, it was so difficult to talk to him. He makes no attempt to carry on the conversation at all . . . and it simply dies out. I had to keep thinking of fresh subjects.

"Do you . . . dance much at The Hague?"

"Very little."

"I love to dance. I love playacting too. Jemmy . . . the Duke of Monmouth, excels at it all . . . dancing, playacting . . ."

"Is that all he excels at?"

Flushing, suddenly remembering Jemmy with Henrietta Wentworth and Eleanor Needham, she did not answer the question but said, "Pray tell me about Holland."

That forced him to talk and he did so briefly. It sounded a dull place to Mary; she was watching Anne, who was with their father, out of the corner of her eye, while she longed to be rescued from William who was so dull.

She was pleased when it was over and she could escape.

William was pleased too. She had perhaps been brought up to be too frivolous, but that was something he would soon remedy.

She was not without beauty; she was young, very young, and he believed that he could mold her into the wife he wanted.

James and Charles were well aware of the impression Mary had made on her cousin. William was eager for the marriage, and Charles delivered his ultimatum: Peace terms agreed on first and after that the marriage should be discussed.

William had betrayed his desire for the marriage and his uncles might use his eagerness to their own good and the detriment of Holland. That must never be. The marriage contract must be settled first so that he might not be forced into accepting disadvantageous terms in order to secure it.

William now stood firm. The contract must be completed *before* the peace terms were discussed.

James was angry; Danby was terrified; and Charles lifted his shoulders in a significant gesture. Orange was not the most charming of men; tact was a quality which had not been bestowed upon him; but, God's fish, the marriage was important. Charles was never a man to cling to his dignity when he found it expedient to dispense with it.

"Our lover shall have his bride," he declared. "It shall be as he wishes. Wedding first; business after." He turned to his brother and momentarily his eyes were sad. "Now, James," he went on, "there can be no further delay in breaking the news to Mary. You're the man to do that."

Mary started at her father. She could not believe she was hearing him correctly.

Marriage! But she did not want marriage. All she wanted was to go on as she was now. Marriage was something she had never considered seriously because she found the subject distasteful. Married people were rarely happy. She knew how her uncle the King deceived the Queen again and again and she was aware of the Queen's unhappiness. She remembered the quarrels between her father and her mother; and even now that he was married to the beautiful Mary Beatrice he was not faithful to her. Mary Beatrice wept often because she was so hurt by his infidelities.

And now it was her turn! And the husband they had chosen for her was that little man, her cousin William, who looked as though he had never learned how to laugh. If she had to marry he was the last husband she would want.

"So you see, my dearest," James was saying, "you are no longer a child and it is time you married."

"I do not wish to marry."

"That is often the case, but when you are married you will be content."

"I never shall. I never shall."

"Now, Mary."

She turned away from him for the tears were already on her cheeks.

"Please, Mary, you must be sensible. This is difficult I know. You have had such a happy time and perhaps some would say have been a little spoilt . . . but now you must realize your duty. You see, my dear, you are in a position of great importance . . ."

She was not listening. Marry Orange. Go to bed with Orange. It was shocking. It was distasteful. She hated it.

Then another thought struck her. He did not live in England. He had a kingdom over the seas. So she would not only have to endure him, but she would leave home. Leave her dearest Frances . . . Frances, her true husband! She would leave Anne, her sister, from whom she had never been separated in the whole of her life. How could she be happy without Anne to scold, to laugh at, to play with. She could not endure it; she *would* not endure it.

She flung herself at her father and began to sob wildly.

"Father, do not make me leave home. Do not make me marry. Let me stay at home. I cannot bear to go away."

James stroked her hair and tried to comfort her.

"Oh, my dearest, alas that this should be."

The Princess Mary was inconsolable.

The Queen came to her to try to comfort her, but Mary would not be comforted.

"It happens to us all, my dear," said Catherine. "I came to England to marry the King."

"The King is not like Orange."

Catherine had to admit that. Charles was the most charming man in the world and she loved him dearly; in spite of his constant infidelities she considered him a good husband for he never spoke an unkind word to her and all she had to suffer was his neglect and the pain which his preference for other women gave her.

"You will feel better later," Catherine assured her. "It is the first shock."

Her stepmother, heavily pregnant, also tried to reassure her.

"When I came here I was your age. I hated your father and now I love him dearly."

"But this is Orange," persisted Mary. "He is not like my father."

"Yet you will come to love him. You must because he will be your husband."

They could not understand. It was not only that they had given her this most unattractive man; it was the contemplation of marriage itself.

Her sister Anne was moved out of her usual placidity.

She came running to her sister, her face puckered in distress.

"Mary, they are saying that you will go away."

The sisters clung together.

"But you cannot, you cannot. How can we be parted?"

"They will send me to Holland . . . with William, Anne."

"It will never be the same again."

"They say that nothing ever stays the same forever."

"But you are my sister and we have always been together . . . we always should be."

They could only cling together, weeping in their despair.

That day Mary wrote to Frances. She must find some means of coming to her, for she was so desolate that she thought her heart was breaking. She must talk of her trouble, for the most distressing calamity was about to fall upon her.

The King sent for his niece. Lady Frances Villiers was anxious because Mary was in no condition for such an occasion; hours of weeping had made her eyes red and swollen.

She was dazed as she was helped to dress. Elizabeth Villiers watched her in silence. What a child she was! thought Elizabeth. Hadn't she considered that a girl in her position would be forced into marriage at an early age, and that all these matters were arranged for such as she was. Those like Elizabeth had to look out for themselves. How different she would have felt if a brilliant marriage were being arranged for her! Mary had always been a simpleton.

"My dear lady Mary," mourned Lady Frances, "you look so wretched."

Mary's lower lip trembled and for a moment it seemed as though she would burst into further tears. "I am . . . wretched," she stammered.

"You must not look like that or the King will be displeased."

"I don't think he will. I think *he* will understand."

"Come," said Lady Frances catching at a stool to steady herself, for her limbs felt as though they did not belong to her today. "You must not keep His Majesty waiting."

Listlessly, Mary allowed herself to be conducted through the corridors of Whitehall to the royal closet. Those who accompanied her, Elizabeth Villiers among them, waited outside.

When Charles came into the closet his smile was kind.

"Why," he said, "this is an important occasion for my little niece. But I no longer regard you as my niece, Mary my dear. From now on you are my daughter."

Mary knew that she should have expressed gratitude for these gracious sentiments but when she opened her mouth to speak, her sobs prevented her.

Charles patted her shoulder, as the door of the closet was thrown open and William was brought in.

"Ah, nephew, you are indeed welcome," said the King. "Now it is not good for man to live alone, so the Scriptures tell us, and even kings should not argue with them. Therefore I have a helpmate for you."

The Princess Mary was brought forward and stood before her cousin, her eyes downcast, her mouth sullen.

William looked at her in astonishment. This was not the same girl who had talked animatedly to him at their last meeting. She was scarcely recognizable. Her lovely eyes were almost hidden by her swollen lids; her expression was forlorn, even sullen. He could not understand what had brought about the change.

"You two will be well matched, I doubt not," said the King. "And remember this, nephew, love and war do not agree well together."

The King turned to his brother. "The Duke wishes to give his consent to the marriage." He nodded to James who murmured that he was willing to give his daughter into the care of the Prince of Orange.

"Then all is well," said the King. "I doubt not that our lovers will wish to be together. They will have much to say to one another."

He signed to Lady Frances to stay with them and all the others left the closet.

William's puzzled gaze was on his bride-to-be.

He said: "Something has displeased you?"

"Yes."

"There is something you want and cannot have?"

"Yes."

"And you have been weeping because of this?"

She nodded and turned her head away.

"You were different at our last meeting."

"I did not know then that I should be forced to marry you."

He drew back as though her words were a lash which had cut into his flesh. He could not believe that he had heard her correctly.

There was a short silence; then the Lady Frances began to remonstrate with the Princess.

"You should remember to whom you speak, my lady."

"I do not forget. I do not want to marry."

The Prince was looking haughtily at Lady Frances, who said hastily: "Your Highness, you must understand that the Princess is very young. She had no notion that she was to be married and the idea has shocked her a little, but she will recover from the shock and realize her good fortune."

"*Good* fortune!" cried Mary bitterly.

Lady Frances looked imploringly at the Prince. "Have I your permission to take the Princess to her apartments?"

The Prince inclined his head; and Lady Frances, greatly relieved, took Mary by the arm and led her away.

William looked after them; his cold expression was in contrast to the fierce anger which was burning in him. How dared she! Those red eyes, those sullen looks were there because she was to marry him! When he had last seen her, she had had no notion that she was to be betrothed to him, and therefore she had been gay and clearly happy. Then she had been told of her—as he believed—good fortune; and she had promptly wailed and moaned and, being completely undisciplined, had made it clear to all that she had no wish for the marriage.

What insolence! What childish tantrums! And this was the one they had given him for his wife!

He had an impulse to go at once to the King, to tell him that he had decided to return to Holland a bachelor. He wanted no reluctant bride.

Then he thought of those three crowns. To be King of Britain—well, was it not worth a little sacrifice.

Besides, she was a child; he would soon teach her the kind of conduct he expected in a wife. He must not jeopardize his future in a moment of pique over a spoilt child—especially as, after the marriage, he would have the whip hand.

No, he would marry this foolish child; and he would teach her who was master.

All the same his pride was hurt. She had made him see himself as he must appear to her—a man undersized, who stood awkwardly because his back had grown crooked, and wheezed a little because it was not always easy to breathe. Since the death of the de Wittes he had forgotten that image of himself. He had become a great leader, a man whom the King of

England wished to please; he had ceased to think of himself as that pale young man who found it always necessary to assert himself.

She had brought back that image—that spoilt child!

He would show her.

Angrily he strode from the room and as he did so he almost collided with a young woman. He was brought up sharp and looked full into her face. She flushed and lowered her eyes, which he noticed were unusual; one seemed larger than the other and there was a cast in them. In his present mood the slight abnormality seemed to him attractive.

"I beg Your Highness's gracious pardon," she said.

The sound of her voice, humble, a little alarmed, soothed him.

"It is given," he answered.

She lifted those strange eyes to his face and her look was one of recognizable adulation.

His lips moved slightly; it was not quite a smile, but then, he rarely smiled.

She passed on in one direction, he in another; then on impulse—strange with him—he turned to look after her at the very moment when she turned; for a second they gazed at each other; then she hurried away.

He found the memory of the girl with the unusual eyes coming between him and his anger with Mary. That girl had by a look and a few words restored a little of his lost pride. He wondered who she was; presumably she belonged to Mary's suite; if so, he would see her again. He hoped so, for she had made quite an impression on him.

The Prince had made an impression on Elizabeth Villiers.

She knew what had taken place in the closet. How foolish Mary was! But Mary's folly might well prove to the advantage of Elizabeth Villiers. She had been anxious. It was hardly likely that the Princess Mary would select her when she was in a position to choose her own household. Elizabeth Villiers would be no favored friend. But if not the friend of the Princess, why not the friend of the Prince?

Was she arriving at false conclusions, was she seeing life working out a certain way because that was what she wanted?

Well, that was a necessity which often occurred to an ambitious woman.

Mary, in her apartment, wept steadily throughout the day. Anne sat at her feet leaning her head against her sister's knees crying with her.

Nothing could comfort either of them.

Elizabeth Villiers had been unexpectedly sympathetic to Mary; she did not attempt to persuade her to try to control her dislike of the marriage.

She was with her when, red-eyed, her body shaken by an occasional sob, Mary received the King's Council and listened in silence to the congratulatory speeches.

The Prince of Orange was often present and although he gave no sign, he was very much aware of Elizabeth. In fact if she were not there he would have felt very angry but, by the very contrast to his betrothed, she made him feel less slighted by the insults Mary was giving him.

It was gratifying that through the country the news of the marriage was received with wild enthusiasm. The sky glowed with the reflection of hundreds of bonfires; although Mary Beatrice was pregnant and expected to give birth any day, not much hope was given to her producing a son and Mary was looked upon as the heiress to the throne. It was well, therefore, the people of England believed, that she was making a Protestant marriage.

The King was delighted with the people's enthusiasm for the marriage. He told James that he should be, too.

"This is particularly important to you, James," he reminded his brother. "You will see that people will not hate you quite so heartily when your daughter has married a Protestant. We'll get this marriage made and consummated here on English soil before our bride and groom leave for Holland. You look ill-pleased."

"I was thinking of Mary."

Charles was momentarily downcast. "Poor Mary!" he said. "But peace, James . . . peace abroad and at home. Mary must do what is necessary for the sake of that."

James was silent, thinking of his daughter's unhappiness and the Prince of Orange whom he would never happily accept as a son-in-law.

The last day of freedom. A dull dreary day. Mist and cold outside the Palace of St. James; inside, dark foreboding.

Anne spent much of that day with her. Poor Anne, she was almost as wretched as her sister; and Mary tried to comfort her.

"We shall see each other often," she told her.

"How?" asked Anne.

"You will come to Holland and I shall come to London."

"Yes," cried Anne. "We must. I could not bear it if we did not see each other very, very often."

When they clung together Mary thought Anne seemed a little feverish. She mentioned this and Anne said: "It is because I am so unhappy at your leaving us, dear sister. And what shall I do while I am waiting to go to Holland and for you to come to England?"

"You will be at home," Mary replied. "Think of me, far away in a strange land with a strange husband."

And the thought of that calamity set the tears falling again.

Nine o'clock in the evening in the Palace of St. James. The hour of doom. In the bedchamber of the Princess Mary those who would participate in the ceremony had assembled. There was the bridegroom, pale and stern, gazing with distaste at the red eyes and swollen face of his bride. Henry Compton, the Bishop of London, had come to perform the ceremony and the Duke and Duchess of York had now entered with the King.

James's eyes went at once to his daughter and he came to her side and embraced her.

"My dearest Mary," he whispered, "my little one."

"Father . . . ?" she murmured and there was an appeal in her eyes.

"My dearest, if I could . . . I would."

Mary saw that her stepmother, who was as round as a ball expecting as she was to end her pregnancy at any moment now, was trying not to weep.

"I shall miss you so much," she whispered.

The King was approaching, and seeing the tears of the bride and her stepmother, the sullen looks of his brother, and the grim ones of the bridegroom, he was determined to make as merry an occasion of the wedding as was possible in the circumstances.

"Come now, Compton," he said, "we are all impatient to be done with the necessary business."

Charles laid a hand on Mary's shoulder and pressed it affectionately. Poor child! he thought. But she would soon recover; she was a Stuart at heart and the Stuarts were gay by nature. Moreover, she was pretty enough to find herself someone who would please her as it was certain dour William would not.

He was sorry for her but he had long learned to feel emotions lightly, and while he was outwardly tender and kind to his sad little niece he was less concerned with her misery than anyone else at the melancholy wedding.

He looked slyly at William who, he knew, was hoping through this marriage to have the throne in time. An ambitious man, the bridegroom. Strange how big dreams often filled the hearts of little men.

"Come, Compton," cried Charles, "make you haste or my dear sister the Duchess may give birth to a son before the ceremony is over and so disappoint the marriage!"

William's expressions scarcely changed. He was becoming accustomed to his uncle's sly witticisms.

William had placed a handful of gold and silver coins on the book as he promised to endow his bride with all his worldly goods. "Take it and put it into your pocket, niece," whispered Charles, "for it is all clear gain." The bridegroom had put the little ruby ring on her finger. The ceremony was over.

Mary stood shivering beside the man who was her husband. She was becoming more and more fearful, for the worst was yet to come.

The crowded room had been stifling hot in spite of the cold November air outside. Mary was bemused by the congratulations, the hot wine had gone to her head and she felt dizzy.

Queen Catherine, her stepmother and the Duchess of Monmouth were with her now; they had come to prepare her for bed.

They were kind, all of them, infinitely sorry for the fifteen-year-old child who was being forced into marriage. They tried to comfort her, but they could only do so by their gentleness; no words could help.

They led her to the bed. They had taken away her clothes; she and William were together and the King was there smiling at them. He had insisted that he would be the one to pull the bed curtains.

And now that moment had come.

He did not look at Mary; he could not face her pleading eyes. So he laughed and shouted: "Now, nephew, to your work. Hey! St. George for England!" as with a flourish he drew the bed curtains.

Alone in the darkness—alone with the grim dour man who was her husband.

Mary felt him grasp her shuddering body; and shutting her eyes tightly, although it was dark enclosed by the curtains, she gave herself up to . . . horror.

William had left her and Mary was being dressed by her attendants. She was dazed by the experiences of the previous night. Intimacy had not endeared William to her nor her to him. Her shuddering distaste had been an affront to his pride which he was going to find it hard to forgive. He was determined to subdue her to absolute obedience. As for Mary, she could only contemplate that the last night was but a prelude to her future life, that it would go on and on like that for as long as she would live; nor, very soon, would she wake to the familiar surroundings of St. James's and Whitehall. She would be in a land of foreigners, with a strange dour Dutchman as her master.

"There is someone at the door," said Sarah Jennings; and she gave the permission for whoever was there to come in, which it was not her right to do, but Sarah Jennings constantly assumed rights which were not hers, and Mary was too miserable to care about such trivialities now.

The arrival was Bentinck—the right-hand man of the Prince of Orange; he came, he said, with a gift from the Prince to the Princess of Orange.

The women were clustering around him, their eyes eager with anticipation. What had the Prince sent to his bride? He had not appeared to be the most generous of men. They could scarcely wait to see.

Bentinck came forward, bowed and put a box in Mary's hands.

"Please thank the Prince," she said listlessly.

Bentinck bowed and retired; and as soon as he had left, the girls implored Mary to relieve their curiosity and open the box. When she did so Mary drew out a row of pearls from among the ruby and diamond ornaments.

"They are magnificent," said Elizabeth Villiers, her eyes sparkling with sudden excitement.

"I doubt not it is the Dutch custom to present these very jewels to each bride of Orange after her wedding night," replied Mary.

"A pleasant morrowing gift," said Anne Trelawny, holding a ruby emerald against Mary's throat.

"Worth a fortune," declared practical Sarah Jennings. "I'd say somewhere in the region of ... thirty or forty thousand pounds. Just look at those pearls!"

Mary looked at them. I would rather have my freedom, she thought, than all the jewels in the world.

It was inevitable that there should be festivities to celebrate the wedding since it was the wish of the King. There must be a ballet, dancing, and revelry. The palaces were a little shabby, because the King was always in need of money and in no mood to forego other extravagant pleasures for the sake of refurbishing them. But his courtiers could be relied on to provide a witty entertainment.

The King liked to amuse himself, surrounded by the fair ladies whom he favored at the time; as he was far too kindhearted—and too lazy—to dismiss those who no longer excited him, there were always a gathering of beauties about the throne. Monmouth could be relied on to enliven the company.

Besides the banquets and balls which celebrated the Protestant marriage, there were revelries in the streets. This was a defeat for popery, said the people. God save the King and the Princess Mary!

But while the bridegroom glowered and made it clear that he was heartily sick of England, his perfidious uncle, his sullen father-in-law, and his constantly weeping bride, and while the bride could not restrain her distaste for her marriage and her repulsion for her bridegroom, the revelries went on.

The Duke of York was cool to the bridegroom and it was clear that he was longing to shatter his hopes by becoming the father of a son in the next few days. Mary Beatrice, hourly expecting, had yet time to feel sorry for her little stepdaughter who had been more like a sister to her.

And in her apartments the bride's only comfort was in weeping, which she did so frequently that it was quite impossible to hide the fact, and when she was receiving ambassadors or other state officials who had come to congratulate her, the tears would start to flow.

Two or three days after the wedding William came to her apartments when she was alone. She started up when he entered, her hand to her throat. He frightened her because he always looked so contemptuous and severe.

"Weeping again?" he said, in his cold voice.

She did not answer and he went on: "It would seem *I* have cause for grief. You have a stepbrother."

Mary stood up, her fear forgotten. "So . . . it has happened."

"Your stepmother has given birth to a son and your father is jubilant."

He was looking at her with disdain, and she knew what he meant. It was as her uncle had suggested it might be: the marriage was disappointed. Now that she had a stepbrother she had lost her place in the succession, and William was thinking that the marriage was no longer the desirable union it had been a few days ago. He was saddled with a foolish child who spent most of her time in tears, who was quite insensible of the honor he had done her, and had no longer a crown to bring him which would have compensated for all these failings.

"We depart for Holland at the earliest possible moment," he said sharply, and left her.

There followed days of ceremony and waiting for inevitable doom during which the son of the Duke and Duchess of York was christened Charles after his uncle, and the King himself, with the Prince of Orange in attendance, acted as the boy's sponsor, while Lady Frances Villiers stood as proxy for his fifteen-month-old sister Isabella.

Three days after the christening Mary was in her apartments being prepared for yet another ball when Sarah Jennings—always first with any news—burst in with her usual lack of ceremony.

"My lady," she cried, "Lady Frances is very ill. There is great consternation throughout the palace because they are saying it is smallpox."

Mary stood up, startled out of her grief. "You must not go to her, naturally," said Sarah practically.

"But I must be assured that she is well looked after."

"That is being taken care of. We are not to go near the sickroom. Those are firm orders."

Mary stared at her reflection. The curls bunched on either side of her head gave a look of coquetry which was incongruous with that sad little face.

Lady Frances ill of the smallpox! Her secure and happy world was disintegrating. What next? she asked herself.

There was the unexpected joy of a visit from Frances Apsley. They embraced fervently.

"Oh, Frances, what shall I do? How can I endure this?"

"My dearest Mary-Clorine, you *must* endure it. It is cruel, but it had to be. You must write to me every day. We must comfort each other with our letters."

"And not to see each other . . . ever!"

"We may be able to arrange meetings."

"Oh, Frances, dearest husband, you say that to comfort me. Have you seen . . . *him*?"

"Yes, my dearest."

"Then you know."

"He looks stern. He looks as if he could be cruel. But you must remember you are a Princess, and he gains much by this marriage, a fact which you must not let him forget."

"He terrifies me, Frances."

"He is only a man, beloved—and not very old."

"He is years older than I."

"You think that because you are so young. You must not show your fear."

"How can I hide it, dearest husband? How can I? Oh, Aurelia, beloved, it is you with whom I should be leaving the Court. Do you remember my dream of a cottage in the country?"

"I remember, my love, but it was a dream which we knew could never be a reality."

"Aurelia, you will remember me always. You will never forget your poor Clorine who loves you more than she can express. You must never forget that only your letters will assure me of your fidelity. You must write to me . . . every day . . . *every* day . . ."

They could only assure each other of their undying love. They met and made their vows; but they knew that there could not be many more meetings.

Lady Frances Villiers was dying and the Princess Anne had taken the smallpox.

Mary was in desperation. She had been fond of Lady Frances and to contemplate her death made her very sad; but the fact that Anne was in danger, terrified her. Her distasteful marriage no longer filled her mind; if Anne could be well again she would be ready to accept anything, she told herself.

She wanted to go to her sister, to nurse her herself, but she must not even see Anne—and this when there was so little time left to them!

William came into her apartments and told her that she was to prepare at once to leave St. James's Palace for Whitehall.

"Although I cannot visit my sister yet I wish to be close to her," she answered.

"Do you not understand anything?" he asked coldly.

"I certainly do not understand what you mean," she retorted.

"There is smallpox in this place and it is possible that you may catch it."

"I wish to remain near my sister," she said stubbornly.

"It is obvious that you have no conception of what this means—I begin to think you have little conception of anything!"

"I know that the smallpox is deadly. It is killing Lady Frances." The tears came to her eyes again, and William turned away impatiently muttering: "Tears. Tears. Can she offer me nothing but tears?"

"She was my guardian . . . she was like a mother to me. And now that my darling Anne . . ." Her voice broke.

William said impatiently, "Prepare at once to leave for Whitehall."

"No," she retorted firmly.

He gave her a look which contained more than contempt. It might have been hatred; then he left her.

That she should openly defy him was something he found very hard to forgive. If they had been in Holland, he assured himself, he would have enforced obedience; it was not so easy here where she was surrounded by her family and friends. So she stayed at St. James's—the little fool. What if she succumbed to the smallpox? She might die—as he almost had, and would have, but for his dear friend Bentinck. She might be disfigured; how could she hope to please him then? With her pretty delicate complexion and almond-shaped eyes she *had* pleased him—before she had known he was to be her husband, then her reluctance to accept him, her actual repugnance had so wounded him where he was most vulnerable, that he intended to make her very sorry for her actions. If she were disfigured by smallpox, if she failed to bring him the crown of England—of what use was she?

Had he been a more passionate man he would have hated her; as it was he merely disliked her.

But because she had humiliated him, he was determined to humiliate her.

Everyone noticed that at the ball which Charles had insisted should be given in spite of the smallpox being in St. James's Palace, Mary's husband ignored her completely; he would not dance with her nor sit with her if he could avoid it; but when he had to do so he showed his indifference by not addressing a single remark to her.

His conduct was noted.

What a sullen clown the Prince of Orange is! was the general comment, and many felt sorry then for the Princess Mary.

The Princess Anne was in a state of high fever.

"I must stay in England until my sister is better," declared Mary.

"We shall sail as arranged," William told her.

She looked at him pleadingly, but he pretended not to see her. She had refused to leave St. James's for Whitehall when it was known that he had commanded her to; and he had in fact gone to Whitehall and left her at St. James's—and everyone had noted that the bride and groom already had separate lodgings. He had shrugged aside her recalcitrance. Let her wait till she was without her family to support her. Then she would see who was the master and she would be forced to obey him.

They were to sail on the sixteenth of November and as the fifteenth was Queen Catherine's birthday the King had said there should be a ball which would celebrate his wife's birthday and at the same time be a farewell to the Prince and Princess of Orange. Since the newly married pair would be leaving on the next day, they should retire early and say good-bye to all their friends at the ball.

Mary was dressed in the jewels which he had given her, but their luster only called attention to her wretched appearance. So much crying had made her eyes swollen and she could not disguise her misery.

Anne was desperately ill; Mary did not know when she would see Frances Apsley again; and the next day she would say good-bye to her family and leave with William.

If only Anne or Frances could have accompanied her she felt she could have borne her wretchedness more easily. Frances could not come because her father was ill; and who should be her attendants had been settled by the King and her father. The Villiers were well represented. Barbara Castlemaine had seen to that; so Elizabeth and her sister Anne were to be in the suite in addition to a cousin of theirs—Margaret Boyle, who was Lady Inchiquin. Lady Inchiquin, being married and more mature than the others, had been given the post of head of the maids; she it was who would keep them in order and pay their salaries. Mary was delighted that her friend, Anne Trelawny, was coming with her and that her nurse, Mrs. Langford, would be there too. She believed she could have been almost happy if she could have substituted Frances Apsley and her sister Anne for Elizabeth Villiers.

But here she was on what would very likely be the very last night she would spend with her family; and instead of throwing herself on to her bed and giving vent to her misery, she must go down, receive congratulations, and try to smile while she accepted good wishes.

She would not have believed a few months ago that life could change so much.

In the ballroom a glittering company was assembled.

The King smiled kindly at his niece and led her in the dance.

"Would I were King of the winds, Mary," he said, "instead of merely of these Islands. Do you know what I would do? Send forth my commands and there would be such a gale that no one—not even the Prince of Orange—would dare set sail."

"If that were possible," she sighed.

He pressed her hand. "Troubles come and go," he said. "There was a time when I thought I should never return to England . . . but I did."

"Your Majesty was a King . . . and a man. I, alas, am only a woman."

"Do not say 'only,' my dear niece. In my opinion women are the most delightful of God's creations. I cannot command that wind, Mary, but I might pray for it. Though perhaps the prayers of sinners are never answered. What think you? Or is one more likely to receive blessings because one rarely asks for them?"

He was trying to amuse her; she loved him; but her sad smile told him there was only one way of relieving her misery and that was to free her from this marriage.

When the dance was over the King took her to her father who smiled at her with pride and told her that she looked beautiful.

"Such jewels," he said. "They become you well."

She shook her head and he, fearing that the tears would start again, said quickly: "The Duchess and I will visit you in Holland. Dear child, you are not going to the other end of the world."

"Anne . . ." she began.

Anne. He thought of his beloved daughter who lay desperately ill and his expression darkened. To lose one daughter to Orange and the other to death would be unbearable.

"Anne shall come with us," he said. "You will see, Mary, that we shall take the first opportunity."

She nodded. "I shall wait for that day," she assured him.

"And your stepmother sends her love to you. She wishes that she might be with you . . . to comfort you. She says that she knows how unhappy you are. And she calls you her dear little Lemon—because you are paired with an Orange."

Mary smiled. "Pray tell her I love her . . . and the little boy."

"The little boy is frail, Mary, but we believe he will live."

"I shall pray for him," said Mary.

"Daughter, we shall pray for each other. We shall all remember, shall we not, that we are of one family. Although we are apart, that is something we shall remember till we die."

Mary nodded. "And my dearest Anne . . ."

"She does not know that you are leaving England. We fear the news would make her very unhappy and she needs all her strength."

"Oh, Father, how sad life can be!"

"Mary, I beg of you, do not weep here. You are watched, and tears do not please your husband."

"There seem to be so many things about me that do not please him."

James's face hardened. "If he should be unkind to you, Mary . . . let me know."

"Of what use?" she asked.

"I would find a way of saving you."

"Would that you had thought of it before the marriage."

"Oh, Mary, my dear, dear daughter, circumstances were too strong for us."

She remembered those words later. Circumstances were too strong. She reflected then that it was a phrase used by those who wished to excuse their weakness.

The hands of the clocks were approaching eight—that hour when she must leave the ball, take off her satin gown and her jewels, and prepare herself for the journey.

All those who would accompany her were in her apartment, many of them chattering with eagerness, for the journey to Holland was for them an adventure. Even Anne Trelawny could not keep the excitement out of her eyes. The Duke of York had taken her aside and asked her (because he knew that of all her ladies his daughter loved her best) to take care of Mary and let him know if aught went wrong with her. Anne Trelawny believed she had a special mission. Lady Inchiquin could not hide the pleasure she found in her new authority. Jane Wroth, a pretty girl, was frankly looking forward to the adventure. Anne Villiers was heartbroken on account of the serious illness of her mother, but nevertheless glad to be going to new surroundings; then there was Elizabeth, subdued and different, so that Mary wondered whether she was capable of deeper feelings than she had imagined. Elizabeth had changed very much of late and Mary, who was always ready to forgive, now accepted the fact that their childish quarrels must be forgotten.

They took off her jewels and carefully put them away; they helped her change her dress.

Then the party set off for Gravesend.

There was after all a respite. Mary remembered the King's words and wondered whether his prayers had been answered, for such a gale arose that it was impossible to sail and the party were forced to return to Whitehall where, said the King, they might have to reconcile themselves to a long stay.

As he said this he smiled at Mary and she thought then that her uncle would be one of those whom she would most sadly miss.

William was angry. His great desire now was to be back in his own country. He stood glowering at the windows watching the river and listening to the howling wind. The King said they should occupy themselves with a little amusement while they waited. There should be dancing or cards. What did his nephew think?

Neither, said William, were diversions which appealed to him. He preferred to watch and wait for a change in the wind.

It was two days and nights before there was a change; then William gave rapid orders. They were to set out at once before the wind changed again; the King smiled tolerantly and took barge with the Queen and Duke and Duchess of York, the Duke and Duchess of Monmouth, and the bride and groom.

Mary looked back at her home as they sailed along the river and exerted all her control that she might not distress and exasperate with further tears. But she was unable to restrain them. How could she sail along this beloved river without asking herself when she should see it again? How could she look back at St. James's Palace without thinking of dearest Anne whom she might never see again, of Frances, the true husband to whom she had not even been able to say good-bye.

Queen Catherine was beside her. "My dear Mary," she said in her quaint accent, "you will make yourself ill with so much crying. This is no worse than what happens to us all. Why, when I came to England I could not speak English and I had never even seen my husband."

"Madam, you came into England," replied Mary sadly. "I am going out of England."

Those who heard those words knew there was nothing to be done to comfort her.

The Prince heard them and his expression was grim.

Good-bye! Good-bye!

The words seemed to go on repeating themselves in her brain. They had started on their journey at last, for although William had been told that it was unwise to set sail, he would not listen. He would wait no longer, and was determined to reach Holland without further delays.

He stood on deck, watching the louring clouds being harried across the sky.

"Your Highness." The captain was at his elbow. "We should not go on. We must put into Sheerness, and wait there until the storm blows itself out."

He was furious; but the expression on his pale face did not change.

"Very well," he said, "to Sheerness."

And he thought: Nothing will induce me to go back to Whitehall. I'll have no more tearful farewells. I never knew a woman could shed so many tears. But when we are in Holland it will be different.

Wistfully he looked across the stormy sea. How he longed to shake the dust of England off his shoes forever . . . No, not forever. But until that time when he could come back—not as a Prince, but the King. For if this child did not live . . . and it was a sickly child . . . well, then, this humiliating ordeal, these tears of his silly little wife, would have been well worth the enduring.

The wind had dropped suddenly and the ship was becalmed; there was nothing to be done but to go ashore at Sheerness. Mary felt a faint relief because as yet she was still in her own country.

Sheerness had little hospitality to offer royal guests, so the Prince, his Princess, and some of their suite, took coach to Canterbury where they put up as ordinary travelers.

William was quick to sense the mood of the people and their approval of the Protestant marriage was obvious. They would have preferred the child which had been born recently to the Duke and Duchess of York not to have been a boy because it was very probable that he would be brought up as a Catholic; and if he came to the throne, which if he reached manhood he certainly would, there would be a Catholic monarch. Their attitude delighted William; it seemed to him that the birth was not quite the calamity he had thought it to be. He was anxious to ingratiate himself with the people and finding himself short of money with which to pay for the stay at the inn he asked the Corporation for a loan, letting it be thought that he had been reduced to this state by the meanness of his uncles. Although the Corporation would do nothing, Dr. Tillotson, the Dean of Canterbury, brought money and gold plate to the inn and begged the Prince to accept it.

William did so with expressions of gratitude which delighted Tillotson who was certain that if—and this was not exactly unlikely—the Princess Mary were ever Queen of England and William, her consort, King, they would remember the Dean of Canterbury.

The news of the royal party's state spread through the neighborhood with the result that good things were constantly brought to the inn for the royal table.

The fact that messages were arriving on behalf of the King and the Duke of York, inviting the Prince and Princess to return to Whitehall, was not known to the people; and William felt that, after all, those days of idleness at Canterbury were not wasted.

It was while they were at Canterbury that news of the death of Lady Frances Villiers reached them. Mary felt more desolate than ever, and thought sadly of the past when Lady Frances had ruled her life. But there was little time for brooding.

On Sunday the twenty-fifth of November William and Mary attended a service in the Cathedral; the next day, when the party prepared to embark at Margate, the rain pelted down and the wind began to howl; Charles sent a message to his nephew reminding him of his warnings about weather and once more suggesting a return to Whitehall until a more clement season.

Mary, hearing of this, was hopeful, but William soon put an end to that.

"I will not be delayed much longer, even by wind or weather," he declared.

A few days passed; then he decided. The wind would now be behind them, and would help to blow them across the sea.

They set out, carried along by the fierce wind; and all the ladies—with the exception of Mary—were seasick.

"As for me," said Mary, "I am only sick at heart."

The journey was not long, thanks to that violent wind, and on the morning of the twenty-ninth of November Mary had her first glimpse of her husband's country as the *Montague*, the ship which had carried them safely across, arrived at the fishing village of Terheyde—not a great distance from The Hague.

AT THE ORANGE COURT

*I*t was several months since Mary had left England; and the new life was strange no longer; there were even occasions when she ceased to mourn for England for a week at a time. Her sister had recovered and wrote now and then; regularly, loving letters came from Frances which brought her image clearly to Mary's mind, and Frances provided her greatest comfort.

She was changing; perhaps she was growing away from childhood. She did not understand her feelings for the reserved man who was her husband. One thing she had learned: he expected complete obedience and if he did not receive this he could make her wish that she had not defied him. He never harmed her physically; what she found so difficult to endure was his coldness, the manner in which, by a short sentence, or a disdainful look, he could convey utter contempt.

Should she care? Strangely enough she did. She tried not to think of him but he had a way of forcing himself into her thoughts. He was, after all, her husband; and she was at heart a romantic, longing for an ideal relationship; she wished that their marriage could have been an example to all young people, and would have been prepared to give the obedience he demanded for a little tenderness, a little outward display of affection which would have soothed her. Perhaps, she told herself, I grew up among those who showed their feelings too readily. When her father, her uncle, Jemmy, Frances, and Anne loved they made no secret of the fact; they considered it no shame to care deeply for another person. But could William ever care deeply for another person?

Lovemaking was almost like a state duty. It was desirable to have an heir; and that was the sole purpose of their embrace. It was true in a way and William was too honest to make any pretense. All the same, it would have been comforting and very pleasant if at times he could have behaved a little like a lover.

He often disapproved of her actions and when he did so never failed to point out her folly. She must cease to be such a child, he told her; she must learn better sense. These scoldings invariably produced the tears which irritated him but which she could not restrain. She cried too easily, just as she laughed too easily—or had in the old days.

A certain wistfulness was becoming apparent in her attitude toward William. She wanted him so much to be a beloved husband.

She understood that he had little time to be, because he was such an indefatigable worker. She noticed that while many people in Holland respected him, there were one or two, whose duty it was to live close to him, who loved him. There was no mistaking Bentinck's feelings, which were something near idolatry. A man who could inspire such devotion, Mary assured herself, must be worthy of it. If only he would be kinder to her! If only he did not always seem so contemptuous!

She saw very little of him during the day; they sometimes supped together, but he never discussed state matters with her, and when she timidly attempted to, he dismissed her questions with exasperation.

There were times when she wrote vehemently to Frances—"her dearest best beloved husband"—and told her how she longed to see her, how she would never forget their love and hoped Frances would not do the same. Sometimes she would weep because of the sadness of her thoughts; then she would try to curb her tears, remembering how he despised them.

There was enough to occupy her days; she wrote numerous letters, for she had always felt happy with a pen in her hand; she sewed, a talent at which she excelled and her needlework was very much admired by the Dutch; she had her collection of china and her plants; William was interested in plants too; he had helped to plan some of the palace gardens; she showed great interest in them but as yet he had received her congratulations coolly.

She had begun to realize that life was never completely wretched, just as she supposed it was never completely happy. From the day of her arrival she had sensed the approval of her husband's subjects. She was so much more friendly than William, and the people liked it, while at the same time she had a natural dignity and air of royalty which appealed to them. She walked beside her husband with a meekness which was apparent; and she was attractive; her dark hair and eyes being unusual in this land of the flaxen-haired; she danced exquisitely and played delightfully on the harpsichord, viol, and lute. The people clearly believed that their Prince had made a worthy match; and since she was the heiress to the English throne—for the little boy who had "disappointed the marriage" had died shortly after his birth—she was very welcome in Holland.

Mary sensed this and it helped her to settle down more happily.

The cleanliness of her new country delighted her, for after the shabbiness of St. James's and Whitehall the palaces were magnificent. There were three at The Hague. The Hague itself, the Old Court, and the Palace in the Wood. It was at this last that Mary had taken up residence and to her surprise she quickly grew to love the place which was situated about a mile from The Hague in one of the most beautiful settings Mary had ever seen, surrounded by oak trees and magnificent gardens.

To compare these palaces with those at home surprised her, because her husband's were so much more modern than those of her uncle. The murals were exquisite and the domed ceiling of the ballroom with its Vandycks was fascinating. In all the palaces there were pictures and some of these represented Mary's intimate relations. Her aunt, William's mother, was there; and there was one which delighted her of her martyred ancestor Charles I portrayed trampling on anarchy. There were portraits naturally of William the Silent, the Dutch hero; and when Mary heard stories of his greatness she thought he was very like her husband who bore the same name and could, as reasonably, have been given the title of Silent.

Her husband was a man of ideals. That she must accept. When she listened to stories of William the Silent she began to picture her husband as the hero of them. This pleased her; and she found that William was often in her thoughts—not so much the brusque indifferent husband of reality, but the hero, the idealist, who, because he was so concerned with righting the wrongs of his country, had little time to become a romantic lover.

The little group sat over their needlework, and they were all occupied with their own thoughts.

Mary was thinking of home and wondering what her sister was doing. Talking, she guessed, with Sarah Jennings. Perhaps writing to Frances, her dear Semandra. Mary was momentarily jealous. Lucky Anne to be so near the loved one.

She glanced away from her needlework, for her eyes often tired her and although she loved to do fine work she did feel the need to rest continually.

Elizabeth Villiers was smiling at the pattern of her tapestry as though she found it slightly amusing. She had changed since she had come to Holland. The death of her mother has made her more gentle, thought Mary.

Then there was Elizabeth's sister Anne, who had always been gentle—so different from Elizabeth—meek and kind. There was Jane Wroth and dear Anne Trelawny. Were they dreaming of home as they worked?

She would have been surprised if she could have read their thoughts, for Mary was inclined to endow others with her own innocence.

Anne Villiers was thinking of William Bentinck, who had begun to show that he was interested in her. *She* had been interested in him from the moment she had first seen him. Anne Trelawny was telling herself that the Princess was being badly treated by her boor of a husband. Caliban! Anne secretly called him, a name given him by Sarah Jennings before they left England. Anne loved Mary dearly; every time she saw the tears start to her eyes she felt furiously angry; and it occurred to her that someone ought to tell them at home how badly her husband behaved toward her.

Jane Wroth was dreaming of her lover William Henry Zuylestein who but a few weeks before had succeeded in seducing her. He had promised to marry her and she was wondering whether he would, because it was doubtful if here in Holland they would consider the daughter of Sir Henry Wroth, an English country gentleman, worthy to marry into the Dutch royal family—for Zuylestein was royal, although on the wrong side of the blanket, and the prince accepted him as his cousin and was in fact quite fond of him; he had loved the young man's father who had been an illegitimate son of his grandfather's, and his guardian until the de Wittes, disliking his influence on the Prince, had removed him in favor of their man. The elder Zuylestein had been suspected of being deeply involved in the murder of the de Witte brothers and when he had been almost hacked to pieces in battle many thought this was in retribution.

But he was dead and his son was a kinsman of the Prince—and the lover of Jane Wroth.

Jane could not think of the future beyond this night. They had an assignation. He was so dashing, handsome, and so persuasive that it was impossible to say no. How different from the Prince. Poor Princess of Orange, with a husband who was scarcely a man! She would have no conception of the ecstasy enjoyed by her maid of honor.

There was another in that little circle who was thinking of the Prince of Orange. Elizabeth Villiers felt certain of eventual victory, and it might be tonight. Perhaps tomorrow. The circumstances would have to be exactly right; but it was coming nearer. He was pretending that this was not so, which was natural enough, but she would know how to act when the moment came.

She was a sensual woman; and oddly enough his very coldness appealed to her. She would destroy that coldness which should be reserved for others, never for her. It would be a constant battle and that was what she wanted; she did not ask for an easy victory. After all, she had been patient enough.

Not yet to bed after all these months! she thought ruefully. And the first time we met . . . before the marriage . . . I knew it would come.

She had believed she had been foolish in alienating Mary when, in the days of her adolescence, she had been unable to curb her sharp tongue and had been so envious of the Princess. The King and the Duke had doted on her so and she was a silly little thing with her constant tears, her sentimental ideas, and her pretended relationship with Frances Apsley. Dear husband indeed! Her real husband's infidelity would be her just deserts. In any case she would never know how to manage William. She, Elizabeth Villiers, would know perfectly, and she would do so for as long as it interested her. Which might be for a very long time, because not only was he ruler of this little country but one day he could become King of England, for if Mary ever inherited the throne, it was certain that William would still be her master—and the one who ruled the sovereign was the true ruler.

Her unusual eyes with the slight cast in them were enigmatic, which was as she intended them to be. No one was going to guess what thoughts were going on in her mind.

Mary said suddenly: "My eyes are tired with this close work. Let us put it away and sing for a while. I have a fancy for the lute."

"Your Highness sings so sweetly to the lute," said Elizabeth Villiers gently.

How she has changed! thought Mary. She is growing older and wiser. I believe she begins to be a little fond of me; perhaps we all grow closer together when we are far from home.

Elizabeth brought the lute and watched Mary while she played and sang so prettily, and they all joined in the choruses.

It could well be tonight, thought Elizabeth. It must be tonight.

William was deeply concerned by matters of state and his personal life.

How could he trust his English allies? Charles was the most slippery friend with whom he had ever had to deal. How could he be sure what his uncle was planning with the French while he feigned friendship with Holland? And the Duke of York hated him. The fact that he was now his father-in-law had not altered that; it might even have increased his hatred. William knew that there were people at the Court of The Hague who made it their business to inform James that his daughter was not treated with the respect due to her. Her chaplains, Dr. Lloyd and Dr. Hooper, were not to be trusted. They suspected that he was trying to make a Calvinist of her. They were wrong. He was far more tolerant in his outlook than they were; he had always hated the thought of religious persecution; it was strong in one who was a true son of a land which had suffered more from bigotry than any other. William the Silent had fought against the Spanish Inquisition, its intolerance and religious persecution, and stern Calvinist that he was, William would like to see tolerance in Holland.

Yet those two prelates reported ill of him, although Mary would not say a word against him he was sure. She was reckoned to be beautiful and he supposed she was. She had never aroused great passion in him, but then he was not a passionate man; he did not believe that any woman was going to play a very important part in his life. To plan a battle was to him the most exciting adventure; the seduction of any female a mild diversion.

Was this entirely true? He thought of the woman who was never far from his thoughts. She was unlike all other women he had ever known;

those extraordinary eyes with the cast were fascinating; she was clever, he knew, and she read his thoughts. He pictured himself making love to her—not with any heat of passion, but as he thought of it—efficiently. His body had not been fashioned to make of him a great lover. He was no Charles or James of England, and well aware of the differences between himself and such men. All the better, he had told himself; he would never be diverted from important state matters through his desire for a woman.

Yet, secretly, he longed to be an ideal of manhood; and it was no use pretending the physical side of such an idea did not exist. The perfect man must be virile. What ideas were these! He was a man with a mission, the leader of a small country which could at any moment be in acute danger from her enemies. It was absurd to allow the thought of a woman to occupy his mind for a moment.

He had a wife who was a beautiful young girl, but he could never forget those eternal tears. He believed he would always dislike women who cried. She had been happy before she had known she was to marry him. What a different creature she had been! He had been quite excited at the prospect of marrying her; and then they had presented to him that red-eyed, sullen child. He could never forgive those who insulted him and Mary had insulted him in a manner he would never forget. He thought fleetingly of Elizabeth Charlotte, the companion of his childhood, whom many had thought enchanting. She was married now to Philippe, brother of Louis XIV. He had once thought she might be his bride, but he had no regrets there. She would have been impossible to subdue.

His thoughts went back to the fiasco of the wedding night: Mary's shuddering body; her repulsion. These could not inspire desire in a man who was never passionate. Because she had insulted him he took pleasure in humiliating her; even if he tried he could never show any warmth toward her. Yet now she was changing; she was ready to be friendly. Friendly indeed! He did not want her friendship.

And there was one thing which he longed for and yet dreaded. He had married her for the sake of the three crowns: England, Scotland, and Ireland. Those he was sure were the crowns Mrs. Tanner had seen about his head when he was born. And if Charles and James were dead and there was no male heir, it would be Mary who was acclaimed as Queen of England. And William? Her consort! He would never accept that. She should never be Queen to his consort. He wanted to talk to her, to make her sign a document in which she resigned all her rights to him. But that would not be possible. There would be the English to stand in the way of it. They had not liked him, many of them; and they did like Mary. Of course they liked her; she was meek, she did as she was told.

"By my ancestors," he swore, "she shall do as she is told . . . as I tell her."

As he went toward his own apartments, he had an idea that he would meet Elizabeth on the way. She would have arranged the encounter for she was eager to become his mistress. He had read that in those amazing eyes; and he was eager too . . . in his mild way. He liked her eagerness; she was clever; she hid her feelings from others while she showed them to him. He was convinced that she was no ordinary woman.

When he saw her he paused and said it had been a pleasant day.

She curtsied charmingly, he thought, and there was a faint flush in her cheeks. He suddenly wanted to touch those cheeks and he put out a thin white finger and did so.

She caught his hand and kissed it. He had never felt so excited by a woman.

She had thrown herself against him and lifted her eyes to his face.

"Let me not wait longer, my lord."

The choice of words exhilarated him. She was in deep need of him, and she was merely putting in words what she had told him in looks and gestures before.

His heart was beating a little faster. This was how he felt when he achieved a victory on the battlefield—a great man, a man whom the world looked up to and forgot his lack of inches.

He put out a hand and touched her. She put her lips on his and he was caught for a moment in her passion.

"I beg of you . . . tonight . . . my lord."

He said in a cool voice. "I will see that I am alone at . . . midnight."

She gave a little sigh which in itself made him feel like a conqueror.

That night Elizabeth Villiers became the mistress of the Prince of Orange. He was astonished and greatly bewildered. He knew that he had missed something in his life before, without being aware of it. He wondered how he was going to do without Elizabeth Villiers.

Elizabeth did not wonder, for she was determined that he never should.

Mary was pregnant. At first she told no one because she wanted to be absolutely sure; she imagined William's pleasure which would be restrained but nonetheless deep for all that; she could also imagine his contempt if she had made a mistake.

How wonderful to have a child of her own! It was difficult, keeping the secret; she wished her sister Anne were here so that they could whisper together about this enchanting prospect. Anne would immediately want to have a child. Had she not always wanted to imitate her sister?

If Frances were here, how she would enjoy confiding in her! But Frances was her "dear husband" and how incongruous it was to have to tell one's husband that one was about to have another man's child!

Frances, of course, must be the first one to know. It was long since she had written to her dearest one, but before she had believed herself to be pregnant she had suffered from the ague which had attacked her since her stay in Holland. Anne Trelawny said that the climate did not suit her; and Anne was very grave when she said this, meaning more by the climate than the weather.

Dear Anne, she loved Mary so much that she was ready to be angry with anyone who did not share her tender devotion. It was useless to explain to her that William was a man whose mind was occupied with noble ideals so that the follies of his wife seemed trivial and at times he showed his contempt for them. There! She was doing what she did so often. Making excuses for William's neglect and even cruelty to her.

It is because I am beginning to understand him, she told herself.

All the same, what fun it would have been if Frances were in truth her husband and they were to have this child. How different indeed! Gentle, loving Frances instead of harsh, stern William. Was it because women were able to give more to love; men such as her husband had their careers to occupy the greater part of their minds; their loves were diversions. Even her Uncle Charles—reckoned to be one of the greatest lovers of his day— was never entirely involved with a woman.

The cottage in the wood; the little piece of land to be cultivated; the dogs they might have had. The world would have passed them by and she would have cared for the comforts of her dear husband who would have been capable of giving her all the love and protection she needed in another little house in the wood.

But that was not the way of the world. The love of two women was frowned on, because it was unproductive. Poor Lady Frances Villiers had deplored the writing of those passionate letters. Yet it seemed to Mary that there could be a closer bond between two of the same sex. Herself and Frances, William and Bentinck. In Frances's company she was happier and more relaxed than she could ever be in any man's; and William, she was sure, had more respect for Bentinck than any other person.

But the first one to know that she believed she was to have a child must be her beloved Frances, so she went to her closet and taking up her quill began to write. She wanted Frances to know that she was the first to hear the news and that she had not even told her stepmother who had begged her "dear Lemon" to give her such news as soon as she believed it possible.

"I would hardly give myself leave to think on it and nobody leave to speak of it so much as to myself. I have not yet given the Duchess word though she has always charged me to do it. But seeing it is to my husband I may, though have reason to fear because the sea parts us and you may believe it is a bastard . . ."

She paused and smiled thinking of Frances reading that.

"...If you have any care for your wife's reputation you ought to keep this secret since if it should be known you might get a pair of horns..."

Those ever ready tears came into her eyes. It was a game of make-believe. William would call it the utmost folly. Was it?

Was she growing older? Was she beginning to stretch out for reality and was there a desire to escape from fantasy? How could she and Frances ever share a cottage in a wood? How could they live in comfort and peace? What child's letters were these she was writing, what silly pretense! She would have been happiest living with Frances; but she was William's wife; she was pregnant by him. That was the reality of life and she should accept it. One must stop craving for that old relationship; she must accept the reality and banish the shadow. But how could she when he was so cool, so disdainful and for her there must always be the ideal.

Perhaps when she held his child in her arms it would be different. Perhaps she would grow up then. As yet she wanted the comfort Frances could give her. She could not release her hold on one dream until she could take hold of another.

She took up her pen and wrote:

"Dearest Aurelia, you may be very well assured though I have played the whore a little, I love you of all things in the world. And though I have spoken to you in jest, for God's sake don't tell it because I would not have it known yet since it cannot be above six or seven weeks at most, and when you hear of it by other people never say that I said anything of it to you."

She laid down her pen.

She pictured Frances reading the letter. It would make her smile; perhaps it would make her long for the companionship of her little "wife."

It may be, thought Mary, that I shall never see her again.

When William heard of the pregnancy he was more pleased with Mary than he had been since the wedding; his smile was restrained but nevertheless it betrayed his pleasure.

"I trust," he said, "that you will take every precaution for the sake of the child. I insist that you do. There must be no more dancing . . ." His lip curled distastefully. "No more games of hide-and-seek in the woods. It may well be that now you are to become a mother—and a mother of my heir—you will agree that it is beneath your dignity as Princess of Orange to indulge in such pastimes."

Mary replied: "I wish you could have seen my father—who was a great Admiral—sitting on the floor playing 'I love my love with an A'."

"I consider myself fortunate to have been spared such a sight."

Mary flushed and wished she had not spoken. He looked at her coldly and she was terrified that the tears would come to her eyes. The fact was that because she so fiercely tried to suppress them they came even more readily.

With others she could be the dignified Princess; with him she was the foolish child who wept when scolded or disappointed or afraid.

When the child is born, she promised herself, it will be different.

She wanted it to be different. She longed for him to smile at her, just once, in approval.

Mary was sitting with her women, painting a miniature while the others took it in turns to read aloud to her.

She was happier than she had been since she had heard she was to marry. When she had taken her exercise in the gardens that morning William had joined her; he had walked beside her, and her ladies had fallen into step behind them. He had said very little but then, of course, he never did; but he had looked at her not unkindly, a little anxiously, watching she guessed for some outward sign of pregnancy.

She had laughed aloud. "Oh, William, it is not noticeable yet."

His mouth had tightened. He was shocked by open reference to a delicate matter. She knew he was asking himself what he could expect of one who had been brought up so close to the licentious English Court.

"I trust you are taking good care."

"The greatest," she answered fervently.

He glanced sideways at her and there was something in the look which pleased her. She knew that she was beautiful; her dark hair was abundant and she wore it after the fashion which was prevalent at Versailles—drawn away from her face with a thick dark curl hanging over her shoulder. It suited her; and her almond-shaped eyes were softer because they were myopic; her shortsightedness gave her a look of helplessness which was appealingly feminine. She was growing plump and her white shoulders were rounded. She had changed a good deal from the young girl he had brought to Holland.

But she seemed to displease him and she wondered why. She did not know that he could never forget her rejection of him in the beginning, that he was constantly wondering what would happen if she attained the throne, and whether she and the English would refuse to let him take precedence. That was very important to him. There was one other matter which disturbed him. As a husband he was deceiving her. He had taken a mistress from among her very maids of honor, and this troubled his Calvinistic soul; but he could not give up Elizabeth Villiers. He had believed it would be a brief affair—to be quickly forgotten; but this was not so. Elizabeth was no ordinary woman; she fascinated him completely. He talked to her of his ambitions and she listened; not only did she listen but she talked intelligently. She made it her affair to study that which was important to him. She was edging her way into his life so that he felt as strongly for her as he did for Bentinck. For the friend who had saved his life he had a passionate devotion; the strength of his feelings for the young man had on occasions alarmed him; that was another blessing Elizabeth had brought to him. She had shown him that while he was not a man who greatly needed women, he was a normal man.

He could not do without Elizabeth and every time he saw his wife he wished fervently that Elizabeth Villiers had been the heiress of England and the sentimental over-emotional young girl her maid of honor.

But now that his wife had conceived he need not often share her bed; and since she was clearly trying to please him he was disliking her less.

Once she had given him a son—a William of Orange like himself—there would be a bond between them and he would forgive her her childishness.

Yet his conscience disturbed him and for that reason he felt more critical of her; he was constantly looking for reasons why he should have taken a mistress. He had to justify himself not only to those who might guess his secret, but to himself.

But that morning in the gardens they had seemed to come a little closer.

She asked him to show her the part he had planned and he did so with a mild pleasure. She was ecstatic in her praise—too fulsome. He waved it aside and she said pleadingly: "William, after the child is born, may I plan a garden?"

"I see no harm in it," was his gruff reply; but he was rather pleased to show her the crystal rose he had planted himself; and then he took her to the music tree.

The ladies exchanged glances.

"Caliban is a little more gracious today," whispered Anne Trelawny.

"Caliban could never be gracious," replied Lady Betty Selbourne. "He could only be a little less harsh."

"My darling Princess. How does she endure it!" sighed Anne.

Elizabeth was aware of them and she was a little uneasy. When she became a mother Mary would inevitably become more adult; she *was* beautiful, something which Elizabeth never could be. But she was a little fool— an over-emotional, sentimental little fool, and Elizabeth Villiers assured herself she need never worry unduly about her.

Both Mary and Elizabeth were thinking of that morning in the gardens and neither were listening to the book.

Mary put a hand to her forehead and said suddenly: "This puts too big a tax on my eyes. Have done. I will walk in the gardens for a while."

Anne Trelawny shut the book; Lady Betty took the miniature from her mistress and laid it on a table; and the Princess went to the window to look out on the garden, so green and promising on that bright April day.

But as she stood at the window she gave a sudden cry and doubled up with pain.

Anne Trelawny was at her side at once. "My lady . . ."

"I know not what is happening to me . . ." said Mary piteously, and she would have fallen to the floor had not Anne caught her.

She lay in bed, pale and exhausted. Throughout the Palace they were saying that she might die.

She had lost the child but she did not know this yet. No one could account for the tragedy, except that some perversity of fate often decreed it to be difficult for royal people who needed heirs to get them.

Her ladies waited on her, each wondering what the future held. Elizabeth Villiers could not stay in Holland if her mistress died. But could she? Was her position strong enough? She did not believe the Prince would lightly give her up. Jane Wroth was wondering what she would do if parted from Zuylestein; Anne Villiers was thinking of William Bentinck.

Only Anne Trelawny was wholeheartedly concerned with her mistress.

It is his fault, Anne told herself. He has never treated her well. He has neglected her and been cruel to her.

She went to Dr. Hooper, the Princess's chaplain, and together they discussed the Prince's cruel treatment of the Princess.

"It is his harshness which has made her ill," insisted Anne. "Every day he makes her cry over something."

"It is no way to treat a Stuart Princess," agreed Dr. Hooper. "I doubt her father would allow this to go unremarked, if he knew."

When Mary recovered a little the Prince came to see her. She looked at him apologetically from her pillows. His expression was cold and it was clear that he blamed her.

She had behaved with some lack of propriety; *she* had not taken enough care of this precious infant.

When he had gone Mary wept silently into her pillows.

William showed the letter he had received to Bentinck; and there was a cold anger in his eyes.

Bentinck read: "I was very sorry to find by the letters of this day from Holland that my daughter has miscarried; pray let her be carefuller of herself another time; I will write to her to the same purpose."

Bentinck looked up at his friend. "His Grace of York?"

"Suggesting that I do not take care of his precious daughter. He is insolent. He never liked me. He was always against the marriage. A foolish man."

"I am in agreement," added Bentinck.

William's eyes narrowed. "He grows more and more unpopular in England as he reveals himself as a papist."

"The people of England will never accept a Catholic monarch."

"Never," said William. "Bentinck, what do you think will happen when Charles dies?"

"If the people of England will not accept James . . ."

"A papist! They won't have a papist!"

"He is the rightful heir . . . the next in succession. The people of England want no papist . . . at least the majority do not . . . but they have a great feeling for law and order."

William nodded. "Ah, well, we shall see. But in the meantime I do not care to receive instructions from my fool of a father-in-law."

"Your Highness should ignore him. There is no need to do aught else."

William nodded. He slipped his arm through that of Bentinck and gave one of his rare smiles. Bentinck was a comfort to him, a friend on whom he could rely completely.

Bentinck and Elizabeth, they were his real friends. And although neither of them spoke of this—it being too dangerous a subject—yet each was thinking that one day William would be the ruler not only of Holland, but of England too.

Mary recovered slowly from her illness; but no sooner had she returned to her normal life than she became pregnant again. This delighted her. She was determined this time to show the Prince that she could give him his heir. She was very careful; she never danced, although she loved dancing; she did not ride; she sat with her women and all her conversation was of the child.

Her father wrote warningly from England.

He hoped that she would go her full time. She must be careful of herself; he had heard that she stood too long which was bad for a young woman in her condition. He would have her remember it.

She smiled, recalling those days when she had sat on his knee and he had delighted in her. He had been a good father to her, never showing her the least unkindness. *He* had never been stern or harsh. . . .

She flushed. She was thinking hard thoughts of her husband, which was wrong.

William came to her apartment—a thing he rarely did since her pregnancy. She often reminded herself that he believed the sexual act should be performed for one reason only—the procreation of children.

He is right, she thought; he was often right. It was because he lived by a righteous code that others believed him to be harsh; and if he was harsh with others he was also harsh with himself.

"I have news from your father," he said.

"Oh!" she clasped her hands together delightedly. He wished that she did not betray her feelings so readily—joy or sorrow, it was always the same.

"I have a notion he thinks we ill-treat you here."

"Oh . . . no. I have said nothing."

He raised his eyebrows. "Nor could you in truth."

"No . . . no. Assuredly I could not."

He was eyeing her sternly.

"He is sending over two people to . . . inspect us, I believe."

"To . . . inspect us."

"Pray do not repeat everything I say. It is both foolish and monotonous."

"I . . . I'm sorry, William."

"And try not to stammer when you speak to me."

"N . . . no, William."

His cold eyes took pleasure in her embarrassment. At least she was in awe of him.

Now he was going to watch the transports of joy.

"You have not asked who these . . . spies are to be."

"Oh, not spies, William. How could they be!"

He said: "Your sister and your stepmother are coming to Holland incognito . . . *very* incognito, as your father says."

It came as he expected. The flush to the cheeks, the tears to the eyes. She was half laughing, half crying. When would she grow up?

"Oh, William . . . I'm so happy."

"You had better prepare to receive them," he said.

There was Anne, plump and pink; there was Mary Beatrice, dark and lovely. Mary could not take her eyes from them. She could only embrace first one then the other and kiss them and cry and laugh over them.

"My dear, dear Lemon," said Mary Beatrice. "You must control yourself or the Orange will be displeased with us for over-exciting you."

"How can I help being over-excited when you are here . . . my precious ones, my darlings. Besides, William has gone away."

"Does he often go away?" asked Anne.

"State affairs occupy him all the time," explained Mary.

"He should have been here." There was a hint of criticism in Anne's voice.

"Do not forget we came very incognito," her stepmother reminded her.

They were lodged near the Palace in the Wood and would only stay for a few days.

"You see, it is not a state visit," Mary Beatrice explained, "and how could we stay 'very incognito' for longer?"

There must be reunion with the maids of honor. The Princess Anne wanted to chat all the time about what was happening at the English Court. She embraced the Villiers sisters, Betty Selbourne, Jane Wroth, and Anne Trelawny.

"It has seemed years and *years* since I saw you," she declared.

She explained to Mary how desolate she had been when recovering from smallpox she had heard that her darling Mary had left for Holland. "What I did without you I cannot say," she said. "If it were not for Sarah I should be quite, quite desolate. Oh and sister, I have such news of Sarah! It is a secret as yet . . . Only I and my stepmother are supposed to know. But I must whisper it to my own dear Mary. Sarah is married!"

"Sarah! Married!" cried Mary delightedly. "Her husband must be a brave man."

"Oh, Sarah would only marry a brave man! She would never tolerate a coward."

"I meant, dearest Anne, that he will have to be brave to stand up to Sarah."

"He is, dearest sister, he is. I'll whisper his name. John Churchill. You remember John?"

"Arabella Churchill's brother," said Mary, and her happiness was slightly clouded. Her father's relationship with that woman was a matter which had bewildered her childhood and turned her to fanciful dreams because reality had seemed somehow unpleasant.

"Arabella found him his place in the army, some say, and Monmouth helped him too. But he is very handsome, Mary, and so charming, and so devoted to Sarah . . . and she to him, although she does not show it so much. But she is determined to make a great man of him and you know Sarah *always* has her way." Anne laughed. "He was very, very gay . . . and then he fell in love with Sarah and now they are married there will be no more philandering. But it is very, very secret."

"Why should it be secret?"

"Because the Churchills will be *quite* furious. Sarah is so fascinating and clever and attractive but she is very, *very* poor and the foolish Churchills think she is not good enough for John. Sarah will show them."

"Sarah will, I doubt not."

"But our friendship will never, never change . . . even though she is married. We have sworn it."

"And Frances?"

"Dear, *dear* Frances. She sends loving messages. She will never, never forget you. I have letters for you."

Oh, what a happy time this was!

Her stepmother told her how at home they talked constantly of their dear Lemon. The King said he wished they had not married her into a foreign land because he missed her. As for her father, he was more melancholy than any.

"I shall think of you thinking of me when you have gone," Mary told them sadly.

Anne wanted to examine her sister's wardrobe; she chattered about the latest fashions in England.

Those were the happiest days Mary had experienced since she had arrived in Holland; and when William came to the Palace in the Wood and was gracious to the ladies she was delighted.

Alas, the stay had only been intended for a short one and very soon the ladies took their departure.

Anne embraced her weeping sister.

"At least, dearest Mary," she said, "we have proved that we are not so far apart as we thought; I shall come again, very incognito, to see my darling sister, for I cannot be happy for long away from her."

Mary Beatrice fondly embraced her dear Lemon; and they left Holland for England where they were able to tell the Duke of York that they had found his daughter happy.

Shortly after they had left Mary had her second miscarriage. There was no reason for it.

She was desolate. Sadly she missed her visitors. If they had been here they could have comforted her. She could not understand what had happened this time. Had she not taken every care?

William would blame her. She was young and foolish; and she could not even do what any peasant could: produce a healthy child.

"Oh William, William," she cried into her pillows, "it seems I am doomed to disappoint you."

Mary had finished supper when William came to her apartments. Although his expression betrayed nothing, she guessed he had some reason for coming at this hour; she had seen less of him since the second miscarriage and she had begun to wonder whether he believed her incapable of bearing a child and therefore saw no reason why he should not neglect her.

She felt her heart begin to beat faster as with a cold peremptory gesture he waved a hand and dismissed her women.

When they had gone he strolled to a table and picked up a book there, frowned at it and muttered: "I suppose Dr. Hooper persuades you to read these books."

"Well . . . he . . . he gave me that one."

William gave the book a contemptuous push. "I expected it." He studied her and still she could not guess what was behind the look. "The man is as much a bigot as your father," he said at length.

Mary flinched; she hated any criticism of her father and she knew that her husband was continually critical of him, disliking James as heartily as James disliked him. What she would have given to bring them together and make them friends.

"He is as fanatically against Calvinism as he is against popery." He gave that half smile which was more like a sneer. "If ever I have anything to do with England Dr. Hooper will never be a Bishop."

This was almost as wounding for Mary was very fond of both Dr. Hooper and his wife and she was afraid that the visit meant William was contemplating sending them back to England.

But this was not the case . . . not yet at any rate.

William did not look at her as he said: "Your father is on his way to Holland."

"My father!"

She stopped in time. Her habit of repeating everything irritated him. Oddly enough she only did it with him.

"He is paying a visit to his daughter. He is so anxious for her welfare that he will come and see for himself. That is what he tells me. In actual fact he is coming to Holland because they will no longer tolerate him in England."

"No longer tolerate my father!" she was stung to protest. "But England is his home. He is the heir to the throne."

"He is a papist. That's the root of the trouble. The English will not have a papist on their throne. That is why your father is being sent into exile."

"But they will *have* to have him . . ."

"The English are not a people to be told they have to have what they do not want, I believe."

Mary's eyes were wide with horror. "But it cannot be as bad as that. They can't be turning him out?"

"You, I suppose, will be fully aware of what is going on in England—even though you have been out of it for so long."

It was cold sarcasm and her cheeks burned, but because her father was being attacked she lost her fear of her husband in the need to defend him.

"I know this: my father is a man who has served his country well. When he returned from his victories at sea the people treated him like a hero."

"And now they treat him like an exile."

"It is not true."

William raised astonished eyebrows.

"I do not believe it," she said, and there was no trace of tears now; her voice was firm, her color high; and she looked very beautiful. She said in a voice which matched his for coldness: "When may I expect my father?"

William felt temporarily defeated. "In a few days, I dare swear. As soon as the favorable wind carries him here . . ."

"Then I must prepare to give a good welcome to the heir of England."

As she moved away from him, William felt alarmed. She was growing up, and this interview had given him a glimpse of a different woman. This was not the docile wife. Her father had a great influence on her. That was bad. He would have to be very watchful. Not that he feared James would make her change her religion; she was a firm Protestant. But he was her father and a deeply sentimental and emotional woman would doubtless have her head stuffed with notions of filial duty.

He must never forget that when James died—or was turned from the throne—it was Mary who was next in succession. He would never submit to playing the part of consort. Mary must therefore be conditioned to accept her husband as supreme in all things; and if that meant turning her against her father then that must be done.

THE UNFAITHFUL

HUSBAND

In spite of his dislike of his father-in-law William received him with respect. He met the royal party on their arrival and conducted them, surrounded by a guard of three thousand, to the Palace at The Hague.

As soon as the formal greeting was over James asked after his daughter, making many inquiries as to her state of health and expressing his concern.

"Your climate here is not good," he said. "It is damp and cold."

"I believe it to be very little different from that of England," retorted William.

"There's a world of difference. Ours is far more clement. Has not Mary suffered from ill health since she has been here? The ague! Those two miscarriages! She rarely had a day's illness before she came to Holland."

As James was the most tactless of men and William never made any concessions to flattery, there was certain to be friction.

William conveyed the fact that he was well aware why James was in Holland; and he strongly hinted that that reason would not endear him to a nation which was firmly Protestant and still remembered the miseries of the Spanish Inquisition.

Before they reached The Hague both knew that the visit was going to be an uneasy one.

When James and his wife were alone with Mary they embraced her tenderly. James held her at arms' length and studied her; then they wept together. It was a great joy to Mary to be able to weep in comfort.

Mary Beatrice said: "Our only happiness at this time is to be with our dear Lemon."

"Is it true," asked Mary anxiously, "that you have been turned out of England?"

"I fear so, Mary," James confessed. "I have many enemies and do you know who is foremost among them? Monmouth."

"Oh, no." Mary shook her head. She would always be especially fond of Jemmy and although she knew he behaved shamefully now and then she had always tried to make excuses for him. She would never forget how he had come to Richmond and been so kind to her, teaching her to dance. She believed that the reason she danced so well—and dancing was one of her greatest pleasures—was due to Jemmy's tuition.

"He goes about the country calling himself the *Protestant* Duke. He is always urging Charles to legitimize him and you know what that means."

"The King loves him dearly."

"The King can be foolish when he loves—as we have seen with Castlemaine and Portsmouth."

"Most men can be foolish over their mistresses," said Mary, glancing at her father.

"Monmouth has made everything so much more difficult. I have always had my enemies and they have prevailed upon my brother to send me out of England. It is a polite kind of exile."

"The King was deeply moved when we left," Mary Beatrice reminded him.

"Oh, yes, he did not want us to go. But he had to accept it. My only comfort during these days is in my family . . . my dear wife—my dear daughters, you, Mary, dear Anne, and little Isabella."

Mary thought: And your mistresses—unless you have very much changed, which I greatly doubt.

And she wondered why she felt her sympathy for her father touched by criticism. Was she beginning to think a little like her husband?

"Father," she said, "all your troubles are due to your religious beliefs."

"Well, I shall not be the first to be victimized for that reason. Mary, while I am here I want to talk to you about religion."

She stiffened. "I do not think it would be any use," she said quickly. "I respect your views, father, but I have mine; and they are far removed from Rome."

"Oh, you are becoming a little like your husband. Do not, I pray you, become a Calvinist."

"I belong to the Church of England, Father, as I was taught from a child. It is a faith which suits me well and in which I believe."

"Hooper has been instructing you, I'll be bound. Here is a sad state of affairs—a father who is not allowed to have charge of his own daughters." James shook his head and looked melancholy. "You were taken away from me when you were beginning to grow up. They were afraid I would influence you, I . . . your own father. Anne wanted to come with us, in fact was coming . . . but the people did not wish it. They feared that I . . . her father . . . might influence her, might turn her into a Catholic. That is the state your father is reduced to, Mary. Here you see him . . . an exile from his country."

"It is very sad," said Mary; and she thought: But if you were not a papist none of it would have happened. She was beginning to see through William's eyes.

William could not hide his distaste for his father-in-law and James, aware of it, found his position becoming more and more uncomfortable. He was turned away from his home because he was not wanted there, and however much Charles expressed his regret he showed clearly that he was ready to accept the demands of his brother's enemies. And so he had become a guest at his son-in-law's Court—but not a welcome one.

One night he awoke in his apartments with griping pains, alarming Mary Beatrice as for some minutes he could do nothing but groan and press his hands against his stomach.

"What can it be?" cried Mary Beatrice fearfully. "I must call for help."

But James shook his head. "We are here in a strange country, an enemy's country. How do we know what that enemy plans against us?"

"James, you think William is trying to poison you!"

James groaned aloud. "My body tells me someone has."

She was hastily scrambling out of bed, but he detained her.

"Wait awhile. I fancy the pain grows less. Perhaps they have not succeeded this time."

"I cannot believe this of the Prince. Our dear Lemon would never allow it."

"Do you think Mary has any say in matters at this Court? Have you not seen the manner in which he treats her? My daughter will always be a good daughter to me—but how I distrust her husband!"

"You are a little better now, James?"

He nodded. "The pain is subsiding. For a moment I thought this was the end of me."

"My poor, poor James."

"Ah, you have been a good wife to me. You have given me our dear Isabella."

"And I shall give you sons one day, James."

"If that hope is to be realized," he said, smiling wryly, "I do not think we should spend another day at The Hague. If I am well enough we shall leave in the morning."

"We cannot go back to England, James. Where can we go?"

His lips twisted into a bitter smile. "Exiles!" he said. "Behold the heir of England who has no lodging but that which is grudged him. No, my dear wife, we cannot return to England and if we value our lives we cannot stay at The Hague. We will go to Brussels for a while and there await events."

In the morning the Duke of York was sufficiently recovered for a journey. With his wife and a few friends he set out for Brussels.

To be an exile! To know that in one's own country one was not wanted. It was enough to make the gayest of men melancholy; James was scarcely the gayest.

In Brussels he dreamed of home. Mary Beatrice did her best to console him—and herself, with the reminder that at least he was separated from some of his mistresses, but she was certain that it would not take him long to fill those vacancies. It was a pity he could not find men to support him as easily as he found women to share his bed.

Mary Beatrice loved him dearly and to her he was always tender. Like Anne Hyde she found him a good husband apart from this failing—which was, alas, the cardinal sin of marriage. He himself deplored it, but found temptation irresistible. Poor James! He could not help failing in everything he did.

Mary Beatrice longed for the company of her enchanting little daughter Isabella, the only child who had survived and had now lived three years.

Such an adorable creature, a delight not only in herself but because she was a symbol that Mary Beatrice could have healthy children, a promise that one day she would have a son.

If her stepdaughter Anne could have accompanied them she would have enjoyed those days in Brussels more; and of course she saw nothing now of dear Lemon; in any case she was worried about this stepdaughter, because William was not pleasant to James and it seemed that Mary was a little cowed by him.

A not very happy state of affairs for James—with Monmouth setting himself up in opposition to his uncle, ostentatiously calling himself the Protestant Duke, William of Orange an ungracious host, and all the enemies at home! Just when Mary Beatrice was beginning to be happy and to love England all these troubles were rising round her.

"If," she told her husband, "I could only have little Isabella with me, I could I think be more reconciled."

James clenched his fists and cried: "Why should we endure this? Why should we be cut off from home and family? I shall write to my brother without delay. I am going to tell him that since we are to stay here we must have our children with us."

"They may allow Isabella to come. But will they allow Anne?"

"I will promise not to contaminate my own daughter," retorted James bitterly.

He went to his table and wrote such an impassioned appeal to his brother that in a short time news came to them that the Princesses Anne and Isabella with suitable attendants were on their way to Brussels.

The Princess of Orange was suffering so acutely from the ague that her father was summoned to her bedside at The Hague.

James went at once and there was no doubt that his presence comforted

Mary. When she heard that Anne and Isabella were on their way she was delighted and her determination to get well quickly was so beneficial that in a short time she had left her bed.

But relations between the Prince of Orange and his father-in-law were as uneasy as before and James declared his intention of returning to Brussels. Mary said that when her sister and half-sister arrived they must be her guests and William made no objection.

There followed a few happy weeks. Anne had arrived with the adorable Isabella who took an immediate fancy to her half-sister Mary which was reciprocated. In Isabella Mary saw the child she had recently lost and could scarcely bear her out of her sight; and to have her dearest Anne with her, that she might hear all the gossip from England, filled her with delight. How was Frances? she wanted to know. She had only her letters to tell her and letters were inadequate. There was Sarah Jennings, now Sarah Churchill, full of vitality, governing all those about her, including her Colonel John who had accompanied the party. After a few days Mary felt she could have been very happy without the company of Sarah Churchill who seemed to have completely bewitched Anne, for she listened attentively to everything she said and appeared to take her advice on all matters.

Sarah, sensing the hostility of the Princess of Orange, was not in the least perturbed. She thought Mary a ninny who was considerably under the thumb of the man she had married. That was no way to live, in Sarah's opinion. And her John, who adored her more as the weeks passed and who rarely acted without taking her advice, was proving her right.

She had the Princess Anne in leading strings; she was determined to make a great career for John; so she was in no mood to allow the faint criticism of such a weakling as the Princess of Orange to disturb her ways.

Mary Beatrice awoke each day with desire to enjoy it which was almost fanatical. She wanted each day to be twice as long; for always at the back of her mind was a fear that it could not last; and in fact she knew it could not. When her mother arrived from Modena, she felt that this was the happiest time of her life—or would have been if she were not continually reminded of the exile and the memory of their enemies.

The Duke of York burst into his wife's apartment; an unusual color burned in his cheeks and his eyes were brilliant. He shut the door and made sure that they were alone before he told her what had excited him.

"A letter," he cried, "from Halifax! Charles is ill . . . unto death, they say. Essex joins with Halifax. They say a few days will see the end of my brother."

"Charles . . . dying!" Mary Beatrice was horrified, vividly picturing her brother-in-law with his dark, smiling face showing her such kindness and understanding on her arrival in England that he had made the future seem just tolerable.

James nodded. He, too, was fond of his brother, but this was no time to indulge in sentimentality.

"You see what this could mean! Charles, dying, and myself in exile. Just the chance Monmouth and his friends are waiting for. I have to go back to England . . . without delay."

"But, James, it is forbidden. If you were betrayed they could send you to the Tower."

He put his hands on her shoulders and smiled at her tenderly. "My dear," he said, "if this be the end of my brother, I shall be the one who decrees who and who shall not be sent to the Tower."

"So you are going to England?"

"I am."

"But James, Charles is not dead. You are not yet King."

"Have no fear. I shall be disguised and no one will recognize me."

Mary Beatrice clasped her hands in dismay. This was an end of peace. James was going into danger. And what would happen to them if her dear kind brother-in-law were no longer there to protect them?

She would be Queen of England and James King—but, she asked herself, what would become of them?

A party of five men were riding to the coast. At the head of them was the Duke of York and with him rode John Churchill, Lord Peterborough with Colonel Legge; his barber came on behind.

They spoke little as they rode; every one of them was aware of the need for speed; even now what could they know of what was happening in England? Delay could be disaster.

It took them two days to reach Calais; the first night they spent at Armentières and when they arrived at the coast James bought a black wig and with this hoped he would disguise himself. They found a French shallop and in this crossed to Dover; from there they rode with all speed to London, and went to the house of Sir Allen Apsley in St. James's Square, where Frances and her father welcomed the party warmly.

"The King still lives," said Sir Allen, "and indeed is much better. It is well that you have come, but I trust the Monmouth gang are unaware of your arrival."

"'Tis to be hoped so," said James, "for I must see my brother before my enemies know I am here."

Frances was longing to ask for news of Mary but this was not the appropriate time. The Duke's brother-in-law, Laurence Hyde and Sidney Godolphin, came at once when Sir Allen let them know that James had arrived. Both these men occupied high places in the government. Godolphin was now a widower having married Margaret Blagge, the gentle girl who had been reluctant to join the ballet and so upset when she had lost the borrowed jewel; Margaret had died three years after her marriage and Godolphin had never married again. Charles, one of whose favorite ministers he was, had said of him that he had the great quality of "never being in the way and never out of the way."

These two, being aware of the aspirations of Monmouth, were

determined to flout them and on their suggestion James left at once for Windsor to see the King.

Four days after he had left Brussels, James arrived at Windsor. It was nearly seven o'clock when he saw the towers of the castle and he made his way at once to his brother's apartments where Charles, miraculously recovered, was being shaved.

Charles looked at him, feigned astonishment—but in fact he was well aware that he had been sent for—and then embraced his brother with affection.

"It does me good to see you," he said. "We are brothers and good friends . . . nothing should be allowed to part us."

James expressed his emotion less gracefully but it was more genuine. He was fond of Charles and always would be; and he was sincerely delighted to see him well.

He knelt and begged Charles forgiveness for returning.

"You should be at my side at this time," said Charles seriously.

James was welcomed by the King's courtiers but it soon became clear that he would not be allowed to stay. There was a large section of the people who did not want him; the cries of: "The Duke is back. No popery!" were heard again. His enemies were too numerous.

Charles said: "You will have to go away, James. I sometimes fear that if you stay they'll send me off too."

"Return to Brussels!" cried James. "Have you an idea what my life is like there?"

"A very good idea. I was once an exile myself in Brussels."

"Then you will understand that I find it . . . unbearable."

"We bear what we must."

"Is it necessary?"

"For a while James, yes."

"Then I ask a favor . . . two favors. Let me go to Scotland where I have friends and where I can feel less of an outcast."

Charles considered. "It could be arranged," he said at length.

"And the other favor," began James.

"I had hoped you had forgotten it. But let us hear what it is."

"Should Monmouth stay in England while I am in exile?"

Charles looked at his brother wryly.

Reluctantly he agreed that he had a point there.

Monmouth would be sent abroad; and James would return to Brussels to collect his family and then go to Scotland.

Mary missed her family sadly and found it hard to settle down to life without them. William was as brusque as ever and she longed for him to show a little affection toward her. She excused him again and again to herself; he was noble, idealistic, she believed; naturally he had little time to fritter away with a wife when state affairs were such a concern to him. And she was a frivolous young woman who liked to dance, play cards, and playact.

He was unaware of her wistful glances but she began to build up a picture of him as a hero; he was the savior of his country; one day perhaps when she was older and wiser she would be able to share his counsels; that would be a goal to hope for.

There was something else which grieved her. Dr. Hooper and his wife, of whom she was very fond, returned to England. His stay had not been a comfortable one for William disliked him, mainly because he had persuaded Mary to remain faithful to the Church of England and not to join the Dutch Church.

It seemed to Mary when they left that not only had she lost the very dear members of her family but two good friends. In Dr. Hooper's place came Thomas Kenn, a fiery little man who never hesitated to say what he meant and right from the first he expressed displeasure with William's treatment of his wife. He was unkind and impolite, said Kenn. And that was no way in which to treat a Stuart Princess.

Mary wished that he would not call attention to William's attitude when she was just beginning to make herself believe that the unsatisfactory state of her marriage was due to her own inadequacy. She wanted to make a hero of William; it was the only way in which she could find life endurable. She had to love someone because it was her nature to do so. Dear Frances, the beloved husband of fantasy, was so far away; besides, she had a real husband; in her imagination she was building William up into the hero figure, and people like Kenn with their caustic criticism did their best to destroy the dream.

There was another newcomer to The Hague. This was Henry Sidney who replaced Sir William Temple as British envoy; he was a very handsome man, the same who had been over-friendly with Mary's mother and on account of this had been temporarily banished from the Court by James. Sidney was still unmarried, extraordinarily attractive, and in a very short time had become very friendly with William.

Mary had begun to suffer more alarming attacks of the ague and with the coming of winter these were more frequent, causing her to take to her bed.

During the cold weather she became so ill that she was not expected to live and there was consternation at The Hague. William saw his chances of the throne diminishing, for Anne and her children would stand in his way. In vain did he remind himself of Mrs. Tanner's vision of the three crowns. But if Mary died how could he achieve them?

He visited her and sometimes she was aware of him.

"You must get well," he said. "You must get well. What shall I do without you?"

Those words were like a refrain in her mind. Had she not always known that he was no ordinary man? He loved her; he needed her; because he had not been able to show his affection she had believed it did not exist.

It was a thought which sustained her through those days and nights of semi-delirium. Sometimes she thought she was floating down the Thames in a barge from Windsor to Whitehall; at others she was acting with Jemmy, and Margaret Blagge was there crying because she had lost a diamond; sometimes she was standing at the threshold of a room looking on at Jemmy and a woman . . . or her father and a woman; she cried out her protests and someone put cool ointment on her head and soothed her with gentle words. Then she was writing to Frances. "Dear husband . . ." And it was not Frances who was reading but William who said: "Did you not understand? I loved you all the time. I am not a man to talk of love. Would you have me as your father . . . as Jemmy . . . ready to make love to any woman anywhere?"

"No . . . no," she whispered. "I would have you as you are. I have been foolish. I did not understand. But I do now. I must get well. You said you needed me."

She did begin to recover. The fits were less frequent; the spring was coming and the apartments were filled with sunshine. Flowers were laid on her bed.

"The Prince of Orange sent them from his own gardens."

Her fingers caressed them. "They are wonderful," she said, and told herself: "I must get well. I have grown up now. I understand what I could not before. I shall no longer irritate him by my tears and childishness. I shall try to be wise, to talk with him of his plans, of his ideals. I shall listen at first while I learn . . . but I will let him know how willing I am to learn."

She saw a future in which they would sup together; and they would talk. He would tell her what he thought of certain ministers; perhaps there would be little conferences between them, with Bentinck sharing of course. She would have to accept Bentinck who rarely left his master's side.

So she began to get better.

Anne Trelawny and Elizabeth Villiers were quarreling.

"I trust you will be a little more careful now that the Princess is so much better."

"What I do is my affair," replied Elizabeth Villiers.

"It would be very much the Princess's affair if she knew you were sleeping with her husband."

"Do you propose to tell her?"

"You know your secret is safe with me . . . if it is a secret. She doesn't suspect. So innocent is she."

"One would have thought having been brought up in her uncle's Court she might have learned a little suspicion."

"He is so . . . so . . ."

"Yes?" mocked Elizabeth. "Pray proceed. What, you will not? Are you afraid I shall tell him?"

"How do I know what you say to him in bed at night?"

"Well, rest assured I shall not tell *you*."

"I beg of you do not tell the Princess either. That's one thing I would ask of you, Elizabeth Villiers. For God's sake don't let the Princess know you are the Prince's mistress."

"And one thing I would ask of you, Anne Trelawny, is look to your own affairs, and keep your nose out of mine."

Mary had meant to surprise them, to walk a little farther, to open the door quietly and say: "See how much better I am!"

She had paused by the door. She had heard them. Anne, loyal Anne, who had nursed her so devotedly, her best friend in Holland, and Elizabeth Villiers, the traitor.

She stood against the door, her hand on her heart which was beating irregularly and as though it would burst out of her body.

"Don't let the Princess know you are the Prince's mistress."

Elizabeth Villiers! who had been the jarring influence in the nursery. And William loved her!

If it had been anyone else, it would have been bearable. But would it?

She had fallen in love with her image of William during those hazy days of illness. She had fought off the listlessness which could have carried her to death; she had wanted to live; she had fought for life, because she had wanted to be loved by a husband whom she could love; she wanted a happy family, a man whom she could admire and adore, children made in his image.

"What shall I do without you?"

She had heard that? Or had she imagined it?

He had said it, she was sure, and then he had gone to bed with Elizabeth Villiers.

Elizabeth was so much older than she was, so much wiser. How long had it been going on? From the beginning? When she had so disappointed him, had Elizabeth been there to console him? She remembered hearing that Elizabeth had had a lover. Was it true? A lover before William? She would not have been a silly shrinking virgin, frightened by the touch of a stranger.

Elizabeth . . . and William!

She did not know what to do. If she sent for Elizabeth and accused her of being a harlot, what would William say? He would despise her more than ever.

Something had happened during that illness. She had fallen in love with an ideal husband who did not exist and she had fallen out of childhood.

She must remember that she was a woman now; she was royal. Princesses and Queens did not make scenes with their husband's mistresses unless of course they could banish them from Court, which she could not. She thought of poor little Mary Beatrice, who had been nothing more than a child when she had discovered that her husband still kept his mistresses. How she had wept and stormed! And what had James done? He had made vague promises which he had not kept; and he had avoided his wife because he hated scenes. William was different. She could picture the coldness with which he would receive her accusations.

She faced the truth. She was afraid of William—afraid of his coldness and anger. She had intended to melt that coldness with her own ardor; but Elizabeth Villiers had done that before her.

Strangely she did not weep.

She was grown up now; she had done with weeping; but she would keep herself under a rigid control; neither Anne Trelawny nor Elizabeth Villiers should know that she had overheard their words.

When Anne came into the apartment she found her mistress lying on the bed, her face pale but composed. Anne thought she looked exhausted and anxiously asked if she needed anything.

"To be left alone," said Mary. "I am so tired."

Mary was eighteen and when she finally rose from her sickbed she seemed older. The change in her was noticed; she, who had always seemed young for her years, had become a woman.

She was composed and dignified, quiet and gentle. She did not betray by a gesture or look that she knew Elizabeth Villiers to be her husband's mistress, even though Elizabeth was in constant attendance. William rarely visited her; she wondered whether he had come to the conclusion that she could not give him children or whether being Elizabeth's lover demanded all he had to give in that way—his physical disabilities would make it difficult for him to play the constant lover.

She did not complain; she waited, praying for strength to bear whatever she must; and because she had built up an image of William which she had forced herself to love, she continued to love that image and to tell herself that indeed it was the true William.

Had she been as eager to escape from him as she was in the early days of marriage her life would have been easier; but she could not do this now.

She wanted to please William; she longed for his approval; she continued to hope that one day he would turn from Elizabeth to her and the ideal relationship for which she craved would begin.

But there were times when she was very unhappy; then she would take up her pen and write to Frances.

It was long since they had corresponded and now she upbraided Frances for her long silence.

It was soothing to scold a dear husband. She could think of them as one—William and Frances. Dear husband . . . dear faithless husband!

"I daresay you are grown cruel," she wrote, "for it is long since you wrote to me. Oh, dearest, dearest husband, send me a letter. One kind word will give me ease. Have you forgotten me? Do you love someone else? I do not now mourn a dead lover but a false one. Daggers, darts, and poisoned arrows I could endure them all for one kind word from you. . . ."

Dear Frances, she said as she sealed the letter. Frances would understand. Perhaps she had heard. Rumors traveled quickly; and those in the center of a scandal were often the last to hear of it.

If she knew, Frances would understand that Mary had grown to love her stern William and had discovered that he was an unfaithful husband.

The cry of dear husband was not addressed to Frances . . . but to William.

THE ZUYLESTEIN

SCANDAL

While William was away on one of his various journeys Mary made another discovery. He had remained as aloof as ever and did not appear to have noticed the change in his wife. Others had, for when Mary rose from her sickbed although she still played cards and liked to dance, she was often serious and thoughtful. Only occasionally did she weep and that was always due to some harshness of William's. Those about her complained of his treatment of her, in particular Dr. Kenn; and Betty Selbourne declared that his behavior, not only to his wife but to everyone (with the exception of Elizabeth Villiers and her sister Anne who had now married Bentinck) was enough to make one scream. Much as they loved the Princess, they all thought longingly of the English Court where everything was more lively.

William was quite indifferent to the impression he made. He was deep in political schemes; he was cultivating Monmouth as one Protestant to another who was deeply concerned to see England tottering toward

Catholicism. The fact that Monmouth was illegitimate meant that he, William, had little to fear from him; William believed that if Charles died the people of England would not have James and would turn to Mary. He was anxious to show Mary that he was her master—and this fact, in conjunction with his guilty feelings about his *affaire* with Elizabeth Villiers, set up a barrier between them and made him avoid his wife's company.

He had visited England to try to discover exactly what was going on; but other urgent matters claimed his attention. He was trying to find allies in the German states for he was in great need of help against the greatest of his enemies, Louis XIV of France, and it was during one of these absences when Mary came across her maid of honor. Jane Wroth was in great pain. She collapsed while Mary was being dressed one morning and was hurried to her bed by some of the other girls. When Mary went to visit her she had a suspicion of what was wrong with Jane, for it now occurred to her that she had seen a thickening of her body recently.

As she sat by Jane's bed, the girl looked at her fearfully. "You had better tell me, Jane," said Mary.

"I cannot, Your Highness."

"You are with child are you not?"

"Yes, Your Highness."

"That should not make you collapse as you did. Jane, you have not been trying to bring about a miscarriage?"

Jane was silent.

"That," went on Mary, "is not only wicked, but foolish. You could kill both yourself and the child."

"Your Highness," retorted Jane bitterly, "that could prove a solution."

"There is another. You could marry the father of the child."

"It is impossible, Your Highness."

"Did this man want you to bring about a miscarriage, did he help you in this?"

"Y . . . yes, Your Highness."

"It is a wicked criminal act. He should be punished for it. Who is he?"

"Your Highness, I cannot tell."

"Now, Jane, that is foolish. How am I going to command him to marry you if I do not know his name?"

"You cannot command him, Your Highness. He's in too high a position."

For a moment Mary felt sick with fear. William! Not Elizabeth Villiers *and* Jane Wroth!

"Your Highness, I have been a fool."

"We all are when we are in love," said Mary. She steeled herself. "You must tell me the name of the man without delay. Come, I command you, Jane."

Jane said: "Your Highness, you can do nothing for me. It is better that you should not know."

"I demand to know."

Jane hesitated. Then she said: "It is William Zuylestein."

Mary hid her relief. She could laugh at the foolish thought which had come to her. William with two mistresses! Impossible. He would never have time for more than one, nor a lover's energy. Why, he had not time for a wife and a mistress—that was why he chose the mistress.

But almost immediately she was concerned. Zuylestein was a member of the House of Orange, although through an illegitimate connection. Jane was the daughter of an English country gentleman of no very grand background. Could the cousin of the Prince of Orange marry such a girl? In the circumstances, he must.

"He must marry you without delay," said Mary.

"He will not do so, Your Highness. He says his family would not allow it. I should not be considered a suitable match."

"He considered you suitable to get you with child."

"Oh, Your Highness, I see nothing but disgrace. I shall be sent back to my father and I cannot bear it. I sometimes say to myself anything... anything is better than that."

"Has Zuylestein spoken to the Prince?"

"Oh, no, Your Highness. He would not dare. The Prince has other ideas for him. He will arrange a grand marriage..."

"Not surely when he so clearly owes it to you to marry you. How could you have been so foolish as to submit to him, Jane?"

"I loved him, Your Highness."

"Ah!" said Mary.

"And in the beginning he promised to marry me."

"In that case I think he should be made to keep his promise."

"The Prince, he says, will never consent to the marriage."

"*I* believe that this marriage should take place. I would that you had come to me earlier, Jane."

"Oh, Your Highness, so do I. You are so good and kind . . . so understanding. You have not once upbraided me."

"Now Jane, I am not a child. I know what it means to love. I am sorry though that you should have let your feelings run away with you. But in these matters it is not for any of us to put blame on others."

Jane kissed her hands and began to cry quietly.

"You are quite overwrought which I am sure is bad for the child. Go to your room and leave this to me."

"Oh, Your Highness, how can I thank you."

"Save your thanks until I have married you to your seducer. It may not be easy, but rest assured I shall do my best."

Mary sat in her apartments brooding on the difficulties of life. Poor Jane Wroth! One imagined her going back to her father's house in the country to have her illegitimate child. The reproaches would very likely continue through her life, for it was improbable that she would find a husband since she was neither rich nor beautiful.

Years and years ago in Holland her mother had become pregnant and had believed that *her* seducer would not be allowed to marry her. She had heard the story many times and it had not pleased her; it was another of

those unpleasant circumstances which had made her turn to Frances Apsley because men made unpleasant complications in life. Oh, for that cottage
in the woods with Frances to care for and love for the rest of her days! No.
That would not satisfy her now. She knew that her love for Frances was an
escape from reality; she was not a natural lover of women. But she needed
love though; she needed an ideal relationship; she needed William to be
kind and loving.

But this was no time to think about her own complicated relationships. What of Jane?

Zuylestein had promised marriage and he should be made to keep
that promise.

She sent for Dr. Kenn and told him what had happened.

The little priest was indignant. An English girl in trouble and the
Dutchman who betrayed her now trying to shirk his responsibilities! It was
something that Kenn would do his utmost to put right.

"Zuylestein, according to Jane, says that the Prince would forbid him
to marry her, that he has other plans for him."

"Such plans must be set aside then," retorted the fiery Kenn. "His
duty comes before grand plans and I have no doubt where that duty lies.
Nor has Your Highness."

"But the Prince . . ."

"Your Highness is the Princess, not only of Holland for your title did
not come to you through your husband. You are the heiress to the throne
of England; I think you are inclined to forget this in your relationship with
your husband. In any case, while he is away it is for you to rule in his stead.
And your duty is to see this girl married."

"Against the Prince's will?"

"What is done will be done."

"You are right, Dr. Kenn. Send for Zuylestein."

Zuylestein stood before the Princess and her chaplain.

"Your Highness desired to see me?"

"To ask you what you intended to do about Jane Wroth," said Mary
promptly.

"Do?"

"You intend to marry her, of course," went on Mary, "and the marriage should take place without delay for she is far gone in pregnancy."

"Your Highness, I would marry Jane but the Prince would not agree to the marriage."

"I give my consent to it," said Mary.

"Your Highness is gracious, but the Prince . . ."

Dr. Kenn growled: "The baby will be born like as not before the return of the Prince. We cannot wait for his consent. The Princess gives it and that will suffice."

"Your Highness . . ." stammered Zuylestein.

"You have sinned," said Kenn, "and there is one way of expiating that sin. You must marry the girl unless you prefer to rot in hell."

"I will make reparations. I will see that she is well cared for."

"There is only one reparation acceptable in the eyes of Heaven," said Kenn. "You will make it."

Zuylestein looked appealingly at Mary who answered sternly: "I command you to marry Jane Wroth and be a good father to your child."

"I would, Your Highness, but . . ."

"I will leave you with Dr. Kenn," said Mary. "He will explain to you the consequences of your sin to your victim and yourself. You will listen to him and I command that you come to me and tell me before the day is out that you will repair the harm you have done, as best you can, by marriage."

She left him with Dr. Kenn.

Limp from the fiery denunciations of Dr. Kenn, with vivid pictures of hell fire in his mind, Zuylestein presented himself to Mary.

"Well?" she said.

"Your Highness, I have given my promise to Dr. Kenn."

"I rejoice to hear it. You will do what is right for Jane and I am sure you will be happier for it."

"Your Highness, the Prince is not going to be pleased with me . . . . or Dr. Kenn or . . ."

She held her head a little higher.

"I am sure we have nothing to fear for we have done what is right," she said.

She dismissed him and sent for Jane, whom she embraced and told her that the marriage would take place tomorrow, with Dr. Kenn officiating.

Jane could not believe it; she fell on her knees and kissed the hem of her mistress's gown.

"Get up," commanded Mary. "It is bad for you in your condition to crawl about the floor." Then she embraced her maid once more and told her how happy she was.

"A woman who is to bear a child should know nothing but joy," she said a little sadly.

"I cannot thank Your Highness enough. But the Prince will not be pleased when he returns."

"He will see that we have done what is right," answered Mary firmly, "and none should be displeased with that."

Kenn lost no time in marrying Zuylestein to Jane. The Court was astonished—not so much that Kenn had persuaded Zuylestein to keep his promise to the girl whom he had seduced, but that Mary, knowing that she would most certainly risk her husband's displeasure, had concurred in this.

When William returned to The Hague he quickly discovered what had happened and was, as everyone had expected he would be, furious. He had decided on a brilliant marriage for his cousin; the House of Orange needed influential alliances. That this chance had been lost was infuriating.

And who had been responsible? Kenn and Mary. That Kenn had done this was no surprise; he had summed up the nature of that little man; but Mary, his docile wife, to go against him! It was monstrous.

He was so startled that he sent for Kenn before upbraiding Mary.

The priest came to him unabashed.

"I understand," said William, "that you take it upon yourself to arrange my family's alliances while I am away."

"I only discharge my duty, Your Highness, by righting the wrongs done to a poor girl."

"I would have you, sir, mind your own affairs and keep your nose out of mine."

"I must contradict Your Highness and point out that that girl's soul is my affair."

"If she is a slut, that is no concern of the House of Orange."

"If a member of that noble house is responsible for her condition then that is, I fear, the concern of the House of Orange."

"You are impertinent."

"And if Your Highness will forgive me, you are unjust."

"I must ask you to return to England. Your services are no longer required here."

"I am prepared to go, Your Highness, but I must remind you that I am in the service of the Princess."

When William was most angry he remained silent. He waved a hand to dismiss Kenn and went to Mary.

"I am grieved and astonished," he told her.

"I am sorry that you should be so."

He shot a look at her; her expression was serious. She did not seem to have changed from the meek wife he had come to expect.

"You know to what I refer—this disastrous marriage of my cousin's."

"It was a most necessary marriage."

"With that I cannot agree."

"Jane was far gone in pregnancy."

"She should have been sent away to have the child quietly."

"Your Highness does not know that she had received a promise of marriage from your cousin."

"Then she was a fool to take it seriously."

"But she did take it seriously and as a result was with child. Your cousin behaved particularly badly because he induced her to procure a miscarriage which might have killed her and the child."

"And saved a great deal of trouble."

Mary's cheeks grew pink; he expected her now to burst into tears, to ask his forgiveness; but she did no such thing.

"I should have been most distressed to have lost my friend in such a way."

He was bewildered, realizing that he was more shocked by the change in her than by his cousin's unfortunate marriage.

"You knew that I would never have permitted this marriage to take place."

"To my mind it was very necessary that it should take place. Jane's life would have been ruined. She came to Holland with me, in my care . . ."

"You surely do not hold yourself responsible for the behavior of all your maids of honor?"

She met his gaze steadily. "Not all of them," she said and there was something in her voice which alarmed him. How much did she know? Had she guessed? Was this a reference to Elizabeth?

He wanted to get away, to ponder on this change in her.

He said coldly: "I am most displeased."

And turning, he left her.

Mary looked after him sadly. He had been away so long and he had no warm affection to offer her on his return. How foolish she was to dream of that ideal relationship!

William had shut himself into his own apartments, to be alone, to think. He did not want to discuss this even with Bentinck yet.

She had changed. Lately she had seemed older, wiser, more serious. She had remained a child for a long time and now she was growing up.

William was visualizing the future: Charles dead; James rejected by the British; Mary the Queen; and William——her consort? That woman who had stood so firmly over the Jane Wroth affair might well decide that since she was Queen of England she would rule her country. He had been counting on her docility; but if she could take a stand over one thing she could over another and much greater issue.

William was really worried. He saw himself the consort of the Queen of England, waiting on her decisions, obeying her commands.

It was no life for him. Mrs. Tanner had promised *him* the three crowns——not a seat beside a wife who wore them.

What did it mean? He must find out.

For the time being he avoided her. But he was very uneasy.

William did not insist on Kenn's dismissal. Instead he seemed a trifle more affable to him. Kenn was amused and made it clear that the Prince's opinion was of no great concern to him since he was in the service of the Princess.

He even remonstrated with William on the manner in which a Princess of England was treated in Holland; and then awaited William's fury.

It did not come.

William was considering how best to treat his wife. If he gave up Elizabeth Villiers he could pay more attention to her, but he could not give up Elizabeth. She completely fascinated him, although he was not a man to be very interested in women. Elizabeth was the one woman he needed in his life and he was determined to keep her.

But he could not make up his mind how to treat Mary. He was determined to make her realize he was the master; she must remain cowed as she had been in the past. The tears in her eyes when he expressed his displeasure had exasperated him, but it was disturbing that he rarely saw them now.

He believed that her father might try to wean her from him. Several unfortunate possibilities occurred to him. What if she died? Then Anne would inherit the throne.

He must keep Mary healthy, and at the same time he must make her his slave. He had thought he had achieved the last until the Zuylestein affair.

That was a warning.

Perhaps he should take her into his confidence a little, pretend to discuss state affairs with her, turn her against her father, make her understand the importance of preserving Protestantism in England.

That was his difficulty. He had to take her into his confidence over state affairs and at the same time never let her lose sight of the fact that he was the master. He was not sure how to do this.

That was why during that time he scarcely saw her and she, conscious of the widening rift between them, was very sad.

Mary waited for the letters from Frances. She wrote to her "beloved husband" as though she were writing to William. It was a fantasy she clung to.

Then one day there came a letter from Frances. She was to be married to Sir Benjamin Bathurst. It was a marriage desirable on all sides and as Frances was now twenty-nine it seemed to be time she married if she were ever going to.

Mary read and re-read that letter. It was long past the time when that dream of the cottage in the wood should have been forgotten. They would both be matrons now; how everyone would laugh if they knew they wrote to each other as dearest husband and beloved wife!

Frances wrote that she was very busy preparing for the wedding. She seemed very happy. Mary fervently hoped she would be and that they would be friends for the rest of their lives.

"I wish you nine months hence two boys," wrote Mary, "for one is too common a wish."

She was seeking ways of pleasing William now; when he talked to her she was delighted; he was building his new brick palace at Loo and if there was anything William could really grow excited about it was building and the construction of gardens. Over the Palace of Loo they grew more friendly. He showed her the plans of the suite of rooms which were to be allotted to her.

"I think," she said, "I should like flower beds here."

He considered this and replied: "Flower beds would be pleasant but I have decided you should have a fountain which you will find more agreeable."

He was delighted with her response. "Yes, of course a fountain would be better."

He would ask her opinion and then superimpose his own. But he was at least taking notice of her. He showed an interest in the poultry garden she had set up and explained to her that she could have aquatic species of fowls because the canals provided the necessary water.

Mary listened eagerly; William's anxiety decreased. He was certain that he would know how to keep his wife in order.

She still wrote to Frances but the passionate love was missing from the letters. She wanted to hear all the news from London. What was being worn at the Court? There were certain materials which she could not procure in Holland. Would Frances get them for her?

Frances was quickly pregnant.

"Lucky Frances!" she wrote. "How I envy you!"

And she knew that Frances was now almost entirely preoccupied with her family.

She was turning to William, waiting on those days when he honored her with his company, seeking to please him. He had now begun to talk to her of the unsatisfactory state of affairs in her own country. A great shadow overhung the land: the shadow of Catholicism.

Mary was very unhappy because her father was responsible. She kept remembering how affectionate he had always been and how when she had been a child he had made no secret of the fact that she was his favorite daughter. It was sad to have this conflict between her father and husband; but as a staunch supporter of the English Reformed Church she believed that it would be a disaster if the Catholic Church replaced that of England.

Gradually William was making her see through his eyes; and with each passing week her opinion of her father began to change. She had always been distressed by his infidelity both to her mother and stepmother; but it seemed that he was guilty of even greater indiscretions.

He was actually William's enemy—her William's.

Her William was a noble prince of high ideals who served his country loyally, who was a great ruler and had brought Holland away from the disaster which once had threatened her and if he was unfaithful to his wife with Elizabeth Villiers, were not all men unfaithful? And William was but a man.

She assured herself that she loved William. He was stern and seemed unloving, but that was his nature, the same as her nature was to be affectionate and demonstrative.

As she walked by the pond in the Loo gardens, she let herself dream that one day he would dismiss Elizabeth Villiers and remove that sinister barrier which, she told herself, stood between that ideal relationship for which she longed so fiercely that she must believe it was possible.

*E*ngland *seemed far away. This was her home:* The Hague, the Palace in the Wood, the Palace of Loo, and William was at the center of her life. To others he was unattractive; those who thought highly of extravagant manners, of the courtesies which were practised at her uncle's Court, considered William to be brusque and ungracious, harsh and stern. She had heard all those epithets in connection with him, but believed she had come to understand him, and understanding, to love. He was deeply religious; his concern for the future of England, she told herself, had nothing to do with his own hopes; he sincerely believed that for England to return to Rome would be a major tragedy. He suffered from ill health, which was a fact most people seemed not to understand. He was asthmatical and easily exhausted. Yet he ignored this and drove himself, so naturally he was impatient at times. She was beginning to see everything through his eyes.

There were times when she wanted to tell him that he need have no fear of her ever disobeying him because her greatest joy would be to show herself as his loving and obedient wife.

Her days were passed almost in seclusion; there were her needlework,

her flowers, her fowls, her miniatures; and occasionally those treasured interviews with William. She had heard that her sister Anne had been involved in
an unfortunate affair with Lord Mulgrave and for that reason it had been
decided that a husband should be found for her without delay. Anne was
now married to George of Denmark and wrote to Mary that she was very
happy. Mary would always love her sister; she did not forget how close they
had been; but even Anne seemed far away now. In her letters Mary caught
glimpses of the somewhat frivolous life her sister led. She was pregnant
and thrilled at the thought of becoming a mother; she wanted Mary to
send her stuff for a bedgown because she had a notion that just what
she wanted could be found in Holland; Anne was content with her dear
George and her dearest Sarah whom she would never allow to be very far
away from her.

Then life began to change with the arrival of the Duke of Monmouth
at The Hague.

Jemmy was still one of the most attractive men Mary had ever seen
and now that she was older, now that she knew that even William was
guilty of adultery, she viewed his peccadilloes less severely. Jemmy came
with his mistress Henrietta Wentworth and he seemed a different man
from that gay—and perhaps heartless youth—who had fascinated her a
little in the past.

For one thing his love for Henrietta was so deep; or perhaps it was
Henrietta herself who made something beautiful of that relationship. She,
a great heiress in her own right, had sacrificed all hopes of a conventional
and comfortable life for the sake of Monmouth. He was aware of this and
did his best to return her devotion. Henrietta was naturally beautiful and
her love for Monmouth transfigured her so that she could not enter a room

without everyone's being aware of her, but she herself was conscious only of her lover. Such a devotion could not but have its effect on Jemmy.

He was more serious; beneath his natural gaiety and great charm there burned a zeal. He wanted to mount the throne of England; he was the son of the King and because he could ensure the continuance of Protestantism in England he believed his cause was righteous.

William, whose great enemy was James, tentatively offered friendship to Monmouth, but he would only do this as long as Monmouth's bastardy was recognized.

It was a delicate situation.

Moreover Jemmy was in Holland because of the discovery of the Rye House plot—the object of which had been the murder of Charles the King and his brother the Duke of York.

William and Monmouth were closeted together and Monmouth passionately explained that he had had no part in the plan to murder his father; he swore that that intention had been kept from him.

"It was to be a revolt against the threat of Catholicism, to bring back the liberties which my father took away when he installed the Tory sheriffs and confiscated the city charters. My father has always wanted to rule without the Parliament . . . as our grandfather did. My father has been lucky. He has enjoyed great popularity. Because he is the man he is, they have never tried to chop off his head as they did our grandfather's. But the people of England do not want an absolute monarch. And this was the object of the plot."

William regarded his cousin steadily. "And because of this you are sent in exile?"

"I was in the first plot but not the second. By God, William, you know my feelings for my father. Those near him love him and I am his son. I have had great affection from him; the only thing he has ever denied me is my legitimacy and if it rested with him . . ."

William nodded. Charles did dote on this handsome son who was more than a little like himself. William thanked God that Charles's sense of rightness had prevented him from giving his beloved son his dearest wish.

"My father and uncle were to be waylaid coming from the Newmarket races . . . and murdered. It was kept from me. I swear it, William, you know I would never harm my father."

"I know it," answered William.

"Russell, Algernon Sidney, and Essex are dead—Sidney and Russell on the scaffold, Essex in his prison—some say by his own hand. They wanted me to give evidence against them and I could not. They were my friends, even though they had kept me in ignorance of the plot to murder my father and uncle. And it is due to my father that I did not share their lot, William. It is due to him that I am here."

"And what do you propose to do now?"

"What can I do? I cannot return to England."

"Do you claim that your mother was married to your father?"

Their eyes met and Monmouth flinched. "I make no such claim" he said, "for my father has denied it."

William's lips curled in a half smile.

"Then you can take refuge here. You will understand that I could not shelter one who put my wife's claim in jeopardy."

Monmouth bowed his head; he understood that he could rely on a refuge in Holland, but Mary must be recognized as the heir who would follow her father (or perhaps her uncle) to the throne.

William visited his wife in her apartments and at his approach her women, as always, promptly disappeared. Mary looked up eagerly and was dismayed to find herself comparing him with Monmouth. They were both her cousins—and how different they were! Monmouth, tall and dark with flashing eyes and gay smile. It was difficult to imagine William gay;

his great wig seemed too cumbersome for his frail body and one had the impression that he would not be able to maintain its balance; his hooked nose, slightly twisted, seemed the more enormous because he was so small; he sat hunching his narrow shoulders, his small frail hands resting on the table.

"You realize the significance of Monmouth's visit?" he asked coldly.

"Yes, William."

Her face was alight with pleasure. She was always delighted when he discussed political matters with her.

"I think we must be watchful in our treatment of this young man."

"You are as usual right, William."

He bowed his head in assent. He was pleased with her; he was molding her the way he wanted her to go. She was beautiful too; her short-sighted eyes were soft and gentle; her features strong and good. He had always wanted a beautiful wife, but of course docility had counted more than beauty. In her he had both—or almost. When she stood up she towered over him; he could never quite forget her horror when she had learned she was to marry him; he could never forget his shuddering bride. He knew that she did not always agree with him but when she did not she bowed her head in tacit acceptance that it was a wife's duty to obey her husband. On the other hand he must never forget the Zuylestein affair and that she was not the weak woman she sometimes gave the impression of being; on occasions she could be strong; and how could he ever be sure when one of those occasions would arise?

This made him cautious of her, and cold always.

"I have received a warning from Charles that I should not give him shelter here."

She was alarmed. "We should not offend my uncle . . ." Then he was pleased to see that she realized her temerity in daring to tell him what he should do. She amended it. "Or William, what would be the best thing to do?"

"Monmouth shall have refuge here and I do not think in giving it we are going to offend our uncle. I will tell you something. When I was last in England he showed me a seal. He must have expected trouble with

Monmouth—and indeed who would not? Your father is causing so much anxiety in England."

She looked worried for it was almost as though William blamed her for her father's misdeeds.

"He showed me this seal, and said: 'It may be that at times I shall have to write to you about Monmouth. But unless I seal my letter with this seal do not take seriously what I tell you.'"

Mary caught her breath in wonder. "He must have a high opinion of you, William. And it so well deserved."

He did not answer that, but added, "These instructions were *not* sealed with the King's special seal; therefore we need not take them seriously."

He half smiled; Mary laughed. She was so happy to share his confidences.

Mary was reading a letter from her father.

"It scandalizes all loyal people here to know how the Prince receives the Duke of Monmouth. Although you do not meddle in matters of state, in this affair you should talk to the Prince. The Prince may flatter himself as he pleases, the Duke of Monmouth will do his part to have a push with him for the crown, if he, the Duke of Monmouth, outlive the King and me. It will become you very well to speak to him of it."

When Mary read that letter she realized how deep was the bitterness between her husband and her father. She wept a little. She so wanted them to be friends. If only she could make James understand how noble her husband was; if only she could make William see that for all his faults and aptitude for falling into trouble, her father was at heart a good man.

She went with it to William who, when he had read it, regarded her sternly.

"I see," he said coldly, "that you are inclined to listen with credulity to your father."

"William, he is a very uneasy man."

"Let us hope he is. He should be, after his villainies."

"William, he never intends to behave badly. He sincerely believes . . ."

William interrupted her. "Am I to understand that you are making excuses for your father?"

"I would wish that you could understand him."

"I would wish that I had a wife of better sense."

"But William, of late . . ."

"Of late I have tried to take you into my confidence. I can see that I have been mistaken."

"No, William, you are never mistaken."

He looked at her sharply. Was that irony? No, her smile was deprecating; she was begging to be taken back in favor.

He relented very slightly. "Because this man is your father you are inclined to see him as he is not. You should write to him and say that you can do nothing, for the Prince is your husband and your master and you are therefore obliged to obey him."

"Yes, William," she said meekly.

"In all things," he added.

Monmouth was prepared to spend the winter at The Hague. James wrote furiously to his nephew; William ignored his letters; instead he gave orders to his wife.

"I wish you to entertain the Duke of Monmouth. There is no reason why we should not give a ball. Please see to it."

Mary was delighted. A ball! It would be like old times. "Yet how shall we know the latest dances?" she cried. "But Jemmy will know them. I must have a new gown."

William eyed her sardonically. She had not grown up as much as he had thought. Now she looked like that girl who had delighted him when he had first seen her—vivacious, gay, a typical Stuart, as he was not, perhaps because he was half Dutch. Mary was like her uncle Charles in some ways and to see her and Monmouth together made one realize the relationship between them.

They were two handsome people. Monmouth had always been startlingly attractive and so was Mary now that she was in good health and preparing to lead the kind of life she had enjoyed in England.

She was beginning to believe that this was one of the happiest times of her life. William was growing closer to her and allowing her to share confidences; she knew what was going on in England and every day there would be a conference between them. How she would have enjoyed these if her father's name was not constantly brought into the discussions and she was expected to despise him! But since she was beginning to believe the stories she heard of her father's follies, even that did not seem so bad.

Then there was Henrietta—what a dear friend she had become! Monmouth declared that she was his wife in the eyes of God and although Mary had loved the Duchess of Monmouth dearly, she had to accept Henrietta; for Henrietta was not the frivolous girl who had danced in Calista but was a serious woman with a deep purpose in life which was to give Monmouth all he desired and to live beside him for the rest of her life. Henrietta's feelings for Monmouth were like those Mary held for William. They were two women determined to support their men.

Then there was Jemmy himself. It was impossible not to be gay in Jemmy's company. Whatever great events were pending, Jemmy had always time to play. He could dance better than anyone else and he was very fond of his dear cousin, Mary.

She believed that he understood her feeling for William and that he was sorry for her. She did not resent pity from him because she was so fond of him, and because she felt so close to him that she could accept from him what she could not from almost anyone else.

There were times when his beauty and grace enchanted her; when she saw him and Henrietta together she found herself thinking that Henrietta must be the luckiest woman in the world. She looked forward to those evenings when Jemmy taught her the new dances.

"Do you remember Richmond?" she asked him.

And he smiled at her and said: "I shall never forget dancing with you at Richmond."

Again she caught herself comparing William with Monmouth; and she stopped that at once.

They are *so* different! she assured herself. Each admirable in his way.

Then more severely: William is the idealist. He would never have indulged in all the pranks Jemmy indulged in. Jemmy was wild in his youth as William would never be. Jemmy might be handsome and charming but it was William who was the great leader.

She thought of Jemmy's wild past, how again and again his father had stepped in to save him from disgrace and disaster. She remembered poor Eleanor Needham who had left court when she was seduced by him and about to bear his child. Now she had five of his children; the Duchess had six and Henrietta two. Thirteen children that she knew of and there were probably others—and she had not one. How could she possibly compare William and Jemmy!

There was Elizabeth Villiers. . . . She shut her mind to that affair. She saw Elizabeth frequently but she had convinced herself that that trouble was over. William had too much with which to occupy himself; he simply had not time for a mistress. It was over. It was to be forgotten.

She was dining in public nowadays which was something she had not done for a long time. William no longer wished her to live like a recluse, and he was always anxious that people should know that they were in accord.

One day while she sat at table a dish of sweetmeats was placed before her and as she looked at them idly she saw a small fat hand descend on the dish and pick up handfuls of the sweetmeats.

She gasped with surprise and a pair of blue eyes were lifted to her in fear. They belonged to a small boy who had seen the sweetmeats placed there and had found them irresistible.

"Your Highness, I pray you forgive him . . ." The boy's terrified nurse had seized him; she was trying to hold him and stay on her knees at the same time.

Mary smiled. "Come here, my child," she said.

The boy came.

"So you wanted the sweetmeats?"

He nodded. "They are very nice."

"How do you know until you have tried them? Come, sit here beside me and eat one now."

He looked a little suspicious until Mary signed to the nurse to rise. Then the boy sat down and ate one of the sweets.

"Is it good?" asked Mary.

"It's the sweetest sweetmeat I ever tasted."

"Well, won't you try another?"

He did, and Mary, watching the little round head with the flaxen hair, the golden lashes against a clear skin, felt a great emptiness in her life. If he were but my son! she thought.

She talked to the boy and he answered brightly while his nurse stood by marveling at the success of her charge; and when Mary reluctantly let him go she told him that whenever he wished for sweetmeats and saw them on her table he should present himself because she would prefer to give them to him than that he should attempt to steal them.

When she danced with Monmouth that evening, he having seen the incident with the child, said: "Mary, do not be too grieved that you have no children. You will . . . in time."

She flushed. "Sometimes I think not, Jemmy."

"But that is not the right attitude."

She could not tell him that William rarely gave her an opportunity of having a child and that she had begun to fear that he was incapable of begetting one which would live. Perhaps Jemmy understood that though, for he was very worldly wise.

She always tried to make light of her misfortunes and she was now afraid that her treatment of the little boy that day had made many understand the void in her life and feel sorry for her.

"You who have so many should know. But I believe, Jemmy, that you often had them when you had no great wish to."

"The perversity of life," he remarked. "But, Mary, do not grieve for the children you never had . . . to please me."

"There is little I would not do . . . to please you," she said.

He pressed her hand and it was love she saw in his eyes. Her own responded.

Jemmy was devoted to Henrietta and she to William; but there was love between them for all that.

Monmouth had changed the dour Court of The Hague; he had changed Mary's life. Often she wondered how she could ever go back to live as she had lived before—almost like a prisoner! Rising early, spending much time in prayer and with her chaplain, sewing or painting miniatures when her eyes permitted, being read to, and her greatest diversion of course—playing cards.

She wondered why William had allowed this change. Was it because he wanted to show the world that he allied himself with the Protestant cause? The troublous matter of the succession in England was in fact one of Catholic versus Protestant. Her father would never have been so unpopular if he had not shown himself to be a Catholic.

But whatever the reason, the change had come; and when in December Monmouth told her that he was returning to England for a secret visit to his father, she was melancholy.

"I will be back," he told her. "Needs must. I am still an exile."

So he and Henrietta returned to London that December; and Mary was melancholy, wondering when she would see them again.

It had been a bitterly cold January day and it looked as though it were going to be a hard winter. Mary had slipped back to the old routine, rising early and retiring early.

On this particular evening she had decided to retire early as she intended to be up at a very early hour that she might take communion. Anne Trelawny and Anne Villiers, who was now Anne Bentinck, were helping her to undress when a messenger came to the apartment.

The Princess is to come at once to the Prince's chamber, was the order.

Anne Trelawny said indignantly: "The Princess has already retired." Anne Trelawny, indignant because her mistress was not treated with the respect due to her, was often truculent to the Prince's servants.

The messenger went away and came shortly afterward. "The Prince's instructions. The Princess is to dress and go to his chamber at once."

Even Anne Trelawny had to pass on such a message to her mistress and when she heard it Mary immediately dressed.

When she presented herself at her husband's apartments she gave a cry of pleasure, for Monmouth was with him.

"You are back sooner than I had hoped," she cried.

Monmouth embraced her.

"And how do you find events in England?"

"Much as before," answered Monmouth. "Your father is determined to have my blood. My father is determined that he shan't."

"And so you are to stay with us for a while?"

"I throw myself on the hospitality of you and the Prince."

"You are welcome," put in William. He looked at his wife. "There should be a ball in honor of our guest," he added.

She smiled happily.

This was a return to all that she had begun to miss so much.

Observers were astonished by the behavior of the Prince of Orange, in particular the French Ambassador, the Comte d'Avaux, who reported to his master, the King of France, that he and Monmouth stood for Protestantism. He did not know what they were plotting together, but it might well be that should Charles die they would make an attempt to put Mary on the throne.

Mary, he reported, was sternly Protestant, adhering to the Church of England; she was a woman he did not understand; she seemed to form no fast friendships with anyone about her; she was completely the dupe of the Prince. And yet she was not a stupid woman; one would have thought she had a mind of her own. In fact over the *affaire* Zuylestein she had shown she had. He was following events closely, for William was throwing her constantly into the society of the Duke of Monmouth, who had not a very good reputation.

Orange was determined to fête Monmouth; he had given him free access to his private cabinet at any time—a privilege accorded only to one other person, his faithful friend Bentinck. It was a strange state of affairs and the French ambassador could only guess that he wanted the world to know he stood firmly for Protestantism.

Meanwhile Mary and Monmouth were constantly together.

A frenzied excitement seemed to possess them both. He was thinking that if they had married him to Mary he would have realized his ambition and become King of England. She was happy as she used to be in those long-ago days at Richmond. She loved to dance, laugh, and chatter without wondering whether what she said would be considered stupid. With her cousin she could be carelessly gay, she could talk with abandon; she could laugh and sing and dance.

"Dear God," she thought, "I am so happy."

"There should be theatricals," said Monmouth, "as there used to be in the old days."

"I should love that!" cried Mary, and then wondered what William would say.

But William made no objection. "Let there be theatricals," he said.

So they played together—she, Monmouth, and Henrietta. William was a spectator—aloof but coldly indulgent, sitting there close to the stage watching. She could not act freely when she thought of him there. But it was at his command.

Because of the hard frost there was skating, and Monmouth expressed his pleasure in the sport.

"The Princess should skate with you," William said.

"But, William, I have never skated."

"Then learn. I doubt not the Duke will teach you."

"It will be a pleasure," Monmouth told Mary.

And so it was, after the first misgivings. How she laughed as she leaned against him, iron pattens on her feet, her skirts tucked up above her knees. Many times she would have fallen, but Jemmy was always there to catch her.

The French Ambassador was horrified. A most undignified sight, he commented. The Princess of Orange would only have so demeaned herself at the command of her husband, he was sure.

"We can depend upon it," he wrote, "that this fawning on Monmouth can mean only one thing. Orange and Monmouth are planning an invasion of England and Orange wishes the world to know that the heiress to the throne is with them in this plot."

Everywhere Mary went there was Monmouth; there was no need, William implied, of a chaperone. He trusted his dear friend.

"What a gay life you lead here in Holland," said Monmouth one day.

"It has only been gay since you came," she told him.

He kissed her on the lips for he was deeply moved. She stood very still and said: "Jemmy, have you ever wanted a certain time of your life to go on and on . . . ?"

He answered, "I have always been one to believe that the best is yet to come."

"But Jemmy," she cried, "what could be better than this?"

He took her arm and they sped over the ice. It was firm and strong at the moment; but a little change in the weather and the change would set in. That was inevitable. He felt it was symbolic but he did not call her attention to this.

She was charming, his cousin. They should have married them. But he loved Henrietta, and Mary was bound to William; thus their emotions were continually checked and they were safe from disaster.

But they were so happy together . . . and life might have been very different for them both.

A feverish excitement caught them. That evening they rode on sleds to Honselaarsdijk where there was a ball in honor of Monmouth.

William insisted that Mary and Monmouth lead the dance; his asthma prevented his taking a part; but he sat, watching them; and he saw his wife's excitement and he thought: she has honored our guest but she must never forget who is her master.

Shortly after the Honselaarsdijk ball, came that day of mourning which Mary had always observed throughout her life. The thirtieth of January—the day of the execution of Charles the Martyr.

"There will be no dancing today," she told Anne Trelawny, as she dressed in her gown of mourning. "Today I will pray for the soul of my grandfather and we will pass the time in sewing for the poor."

"It will do you good to have a rest from all the gaiety," replied Anne, "although I must say you don't look as if you need it."

"I could dance every day of my life," replied Mary.

"The Duke has done you the world of good. It seems strange that . . ."

Anne dared not utter open criticism of William before Mary, who was well aware that her friend did not like her husband.

During the day William came to her apartment. She rose delighted to see him and as was their custom her maids hurried away and left them together. She was astonished to see that William was more gaily dressed than usual—not that his garb was ever anything but somber; but she thought he must have forgotten what the day was.

"I like not that gown," he said curtly.

"Oh, it is dull is it not, but fitting to the day, I believe."

"Change it at once. Put on a brightly colored gown and wear jewels."

She stared at him in astonishment. "William, have you forgotten what today is?"

"I have made a simple request and I expect it to be obeyed."

"William, it is the thirtieth of January."

"I am well aware of that."

"And yet you suggest I wear a bright color . . . and jewels!"

"I do not suggest, I command."

"I cannot do it, William. It is our grandfather's day."

"Enough of this folly. Put on a bright gown. You are dining in public today."

"But, William, I never do on this day. I spend it in seclusion."

"Do you mean that you will flout me?"

"William, anything else I will willingly do, but always this has been a day we observed."

"Let me hear no more of this nonsense. I shall expect to see you differently dressed and ready to dine with me in public."

He left her and when her women came back they found her silent and bewildered.

"What now?" whispered Anne Trelawny to Mrs. Langford. "What new tyranny is this?"

Mrs. Langford, the wife of a clergyman who had been one of Mary's devoted servants for a long time, shared Anne Trelawny's dislike of William.

"He wants to show who is master, that's all," she retorted.

"Your Highness," said Anne, "what has happened?"

"I wish to change my dress. Bring out a blue gown and my diamonds and sapphires."

"But this is the thirtieth of January, Your Highness."

"It is the Prince's wish that I dine in public with him and show no sign of grief for my grandfather."

Anne Trelawny and Mrs. Langford lifted their shoulders and looked at each other.

What a wretched meal that was! Mary could eat nothing. William watched her critically as the dishes were placed before her and taken away.

How could he? she was thinking. This was a deliberate insult to their grandfather—his as well as hers. Everyone knew she spent this as a day of mourning and although he had not mourned as she did, he had never before prevented her.

After the meal he told her that they were going to the theater together.

"You are going to the theater, William?" she asked.

"I said we were going together."

"But you dislike the theater."

"And you love it."

"Not on this day."

"We are going," he said.

This was significant. He was telling the world that she and he dissociated themselves from that policy of Divine Right, which had lost their grandfather his life, which his son Charles had followed and his brother James was threatening to do.

William wanted the people of England to know that he stood for a Protestant England and an England which was ruled by a Sovereign who worked with his Parliament.

Thus there was no need to feel regret for one who had done the opposite.

Anne Trelawny and Mrs. Langford were talking of the affair while the Prince and Princess were at the theater.

"I have never known a Princess so shamefully treated," said Anne.

"He wants to show her that he is master."

"Why she doesn't stand up to him *I* can't imagine."

"Oh, she's gentle. She wants him to be a perfect husband. I know my Princess. She pretends he is one—and that she feels is as near as she'll get."

"*Caliban!*" muttered Anne. "I often wonder what her father would say if he knew the way she was treated."

"She's being turned against *him*. It's unnatural, that's what it is."

"I wish there was something we could *do.*"

"Who knows, perhaps one day there will be."

Mary found it difficult to fall back into the old gaiety after the January day. How could William have behaved as he did? She had been so unhappy. She thought she would never forget the misery of that public meal and afterward going to the theater and sitting there, not listening to the actors, just thinking of her grandfather and all that he had suffered.

It was like dancing on a holy day.

Her father would hear of it. Her father! What had happened to their relationship? She knew that she must love and obey William but there were times when it was very hard.

Monmouth tried to cheer her.

"You take life too seriously," he told her.

"Don't you, Jemmy?"

"No, never."

"There are times when you seem serious now."

"Ah, I have a feeling that this is the turning point of my life."

He was looking at her ardently, and although she reminded herself that that was how Jemmy must have looked at so many women, still she was deeply moved.

She tried to smile when they danced a *bransle* together, but she could not raise herself from her melancholy. There was something unreal about the strange turn life had taken, she saw now, and it could not last.

"Jemmy," she said, "how long shall you stay in Holland?"

"As long as I am welcome, I suppose," he answered.

"You know how long that will be if *I* have any say."

"Tell me," he whispered.

"Forever," she answered; and turned away, afraid.

On *the evening* of the sixteenth of February 1685 Mary was in her apartments playing cards with some of her women when a message was brought to her that she must present herself without delay to the Prince in his cabinet.

She rose at once and as soon as she saw William she knew that he was excited, although his expression was calm as usual. But a nerve twitched in his cheek and when he spoke he found it difficult to control his breath.

"News," he said, "which should have been brought to us days ago. On account of the ice and snow it has been delayed. Charles, King of England, is dead and your father has now mounted the throne."

"Uncle Charles dead!" she muttered.

He looked at her forgetting to be exasperated by this habit of repeating his words.

"You realize," he went on, "the importance of this to . . . us?"

She did not answer. She was thinking of Charles, her kind dear uncle, with his charming careless smile . . . dead.

"I have sent for Monmouth," went on William. "He should be with us soon."

No one could doubt the genuine grief of Monmouth. What had he ever had but kindness from the hands of his father? And what would become of him now that his greatest enemy was King of England?

He remained closeted with the Prince of Orange for many hours; then he went back to the Palace of the Mauruitshuis, which William had lent him during his sojourn in Holland, and there gave way to sorrow.

Bevil Skelton, the new Envoy from England, asked for an audience with the Prince of Orange.

This William granted. He had received a cold, somewhat unfriendly letter from Whitehall which ran:

"I have only time to tell you that it has pleased God Almighty to take out of this world the King my brother. You will from others have an account of what distemper he died of; and that all the usual ceremonies were performed this day in proclaiming me King in the city and other parts. I must end, which I do, with assuring you, you shall find me as kind as you can expect."

As kind as you can expect. There was an ominous ring in those words.

Great events were about to break and rarely had William felt so excited in the whole of his life.

When Skelton was ushered in he came straight to the point. "His Majesty King James II wishes you to send the Duke of Monmouth back to England without delay."

William bowed his head. "I shall do as the King of England demands. And now if you will leave me I will have him informed that he is no longer my guest. Then, when that is done, you may make him your prisoner and conduct him to your master."

Skelton was delighted with his easy victory; but when he was alone William immediately sent a messenger to Monmouth with money, explaining that a plot was afoot to carry him back to England and his only hope was to leave Holland with all speed.

Thus when Skelton went to arrest Monmouth, he had fled.

Gone were the gay and happy days.

Mary sat with her women thinking of the dances and the skating, wondering what the future would hold.

All through the spring she waited to hear news of Jemmy. There was none.

He will never be able to return to England because my father hates him, she thought.

But in May of that year there was news. Monmouth had left for England.

The tension at The Hague had never been so great. Messengers were arriving at the Palace all day. William was shut up with Bentinck for hours at a time; he hardly seemed to be aware of Mary.

Monmouth was in Somerset. Taunton was greeting him. He had followers in the West of England who would go with him to death if need be for the sake of the Protestant cause.

To William's surprise there were many to support the King, and his army under Churchill and Feversham was a well-trained force. What chance had the rebels against it?

King Monmouth, they were calling the Duke. *King!* William gritted his teeth and prayed for the victory of his greatest enemy.

It came with Sedgemoor and debacle. Victory for King James. Defeat, utter and complete, for King Monmouth.

In The Hague William secretly rejoiced. Monmouth, you fool! he thought. You deserve to lose your head and you will, *King* Monmouth.

Oh, Jemmy, thought Mary, what will become of you? Why did you do this? Why could you not have stayed with us, dancing, skating. We were so happy. And now what will become of you?

She quickly learned. Before the end of July Jemmy was dead. He was taken to the scaffold from his prison in the Tower. He went to his death with dignity and he did not flinch when he laid his head on the block.

THE WIFE AND THE
MISTRESS

Those months stood out forever in Mary's memory; they were the turning point in her life. Jemmy was dead . . . killed, on her father's order.

"He was his uncle," she said stonily to Anne Trelawny.

"Monmouth was a traitor, Your Highness."

"I do not believe he meant to take the throne."

"Your Highness was always one to believe the best of your friends. He called himself King Monmouth. He could not have been more explicit."

"Others called him that."

She could not be comforted. She shut herself in her apartments and thought of him—dancing, laughing—making love with numerous women. He was no saint. He was not a noble honorable man such as her husband was. But he was so beautiful, so charming, and she had never been so happy as when in his company—except of course on those occasions when William showed his approval of her.

If he had never come to The Hague, she thought, I should not be mourning him so bitterly now.

The entire Court was talking of what was called the Bloody Assizes which had followed Monmouth's defeat at Sedgemoor. They spoke in shocked whispers of the terrible sentences which were passed on those who had rebelled against the new King of England. Death, slavery, whipping, imprisonment. It was a tale of horror.

And this, said Mary, is done in the name of my father.

𝒟𝓇. 𝒞𝑜𝓋𝑒𝓁𝓁, 𝓌𝒽𝑜 had succeeded Dr. Kenn as chaplain to the Princess of Orange was flattered to receive a call from Bevil Skelton the English Envoy at The Hague.

Skelton implied that he wished to speak to Covell alone and when he came into the chaplain's apartment there was an air of secrecy about him which delighted Covell. Covell, an old man, who lacked the courage and personality of Hooper and Kenn, his two predecessors, guessed that some highly confidential matter was about to be communicated to him.

He was right.

"Dr. Covell," began Skelton, "I know that I can rely on your discretion."

"Absolutely, my dear sir. Absolutely."

"That is well, because I am going to take you into my confidence regarding a very secret matter."

"You may have the utmost trust in me."

"I believe," said Skelton, "that you deplore the way in which the Prince treats our Princess."

"Scandalous, sir. Quite scandalous."

"And you are a faithful servant of King James II, our lawful sovereign."

"God save the King!"

"I must insist that you keep this absolutely to yourself."

"I give my word as a priest."

"Well, then, this Orange marriage is not satisfactory. Not only is it without fruit but the Princess is treated like a slave. His Majesty knows this; the Princess is his favorite daughter and he is deeply concerned. It is clear that she is unhappy. She must be unhappy. No wife could be otherwise, neglected as she is. The King wishes to have the marriage dissolved and it is my duty to find a way of doing it."

Covell was too astonished to speak and Skelton went on: "Oh, I know you are thinking this is impossible. On the contrary it is not so. There is ample reason why this marriage should be dissolved."

"You mean the Prince is incapable of getting a son?"

"I mean that he spends his nights with another woman."

"I understand."

"The Princess does not seem aware of this."

"The Princess is not always easy to understand. At times she seems almost childlike; at others her control is astonishing and one feels that she is very wise indeed."

"I believe that if she were made aware of what is going on behind her back her pride would be wounded. She is a proud woman. Remember she is a Princess. Our first step should be to make sure that she is aware that her husband has a mistress to whom he must be devoted considering she has occupied that position since she came into Holland."

"Do you wish me to tell the Princess?"

"We must be subtle. Have a word with her women—those you feel will be most likely to put the case to her . . . as it should be put. I should not ask either of the Villiers sisters to betray the elder one."

Covell nodded. Skelton was referring to Anne Bentinck and Katherine Villiers, who had married the Marquis de Puissars, and were both in Mary's service.

"I will have a word with Anne Trelawny," said Covell. "She loves her mistress dearly and I feel sure she hates the Prince almost as much as His Majesty does."

"I see you have the right idea," said Skelton. "Now . . . let us go into action without delay."

Covell, who enjoyed intrigue and liked to think he was not too old to indulge in it, immediately sought out Anne Trelawny and as Mrs. Langford was with her, and he knew that lady to be as fiercely against the Prince of Orange as the other, he decided to take them both into his confidence.

He explained the nature of the plot and there was at once no doubt that he would have the assistance of these two.

"I have always said it was monstrous!" declared Mrs. Langford. "My Princess ignored for Squinting Betty!"

"What he sees in her, I can't imagine," added Anne. "When I think of my beautiful Lady Mary . . ."

"See if you can bring what is happening to her notice," said Covell.

"It should not be difficult," said Mrs. Langford.

"Sometimes," added Anne, "I wonder whether she knows and pretends it is not so. That would be like her. I am sure she is too clever not to have discovered it. After all it's been going on long enough."

"I don't know, Squint-eye is clever. Have you noticed since we have been in Holland and she's been playing the whore how retiring she's been. She's never given the Princess any cause to complain about her. Whereas before . . ."

"Never mind," said Anne, "the Princess is going to know now."

Anne was dressing Mary's hair and Mary said: "You are preoccupied, Anne. Is anything wrong?"

Anne stood still biting her lip. In apprehension Mary glanced at her body, remembering the case of Jane Wroth. Not Anne, surely!

Anne said: "I . . . cannot speak of it."

"Nonsense. Not tell me! Come! Out with it."

"Oh, I get so angry. It is Elizabeth Villiers. How dare she . . . deceive Your Highness so . . . and glory in it. There, I've said it. It's been on the tip of my tongue these last six years. Six years! It's no wonder . . ."

Mary had turned pale. That which she had forced herself to ignore and refuse to accept was now being thrust at her; and it was a hateful realization that she could not ignore it any longer.

"What are you saying, Anne?"

"What I should have said before. Your Highness does not know. They are so sly. But I hate . . . hate . . . *hate* to see it, and I can't keep silent any longer."

"Anne, you are becoming hysterical."

"I *feel* hysterical. I have to stand by and see your life ruined. You might have dear little children by now. But how can you? He is never with you . . . or hardly ever. Something will have to be done."

Mary called Mrs. Langford. She said: "Help Anne to her bed. I fear she is not well."

Mrs. Langford came to Mary.

"Your Highness," she said sorrowfully, "Anne Trelawny has told me what she said and she is afraid you are angry with her. She said it only out of her love for you."

"I know."

"Oh, my lady, my dear little lady, it's true."

"I do not wish to hear the subject mentioned again."

"My lady, I've nursed you since you were little. I know you are a Princess but you will always be my baby." Mrs. Langford began to cry. "I cannot bear to see you treated in this way."

"There is no need for you to be sorry for me."

"You don't believe it, do you? You don't believe he goes to her bed . . . almost every night. You don't believe that when he tells you he has state matters to deal with he is there. *She* is his state matter, the sly squint-eyed whore."

"You forget yourself. . . ."

"Oh, my little love, forgive me. But I cannot endure much more of this. Something should be done."

Mary was silent. It was true. She had always known it. For years she had known it and pretended. No one had ever mentioned it and that had made it easy to live in a world of make-believe. But now they had drawn aside the veil of fantasy and there was the unpleasant and unavoidable truth to be faced.

"You don't believe it, do you, my Princess?" went on Mrs. Langford. "It wouldn't be so difficult to prove. They've got careless over the years. Over the years! Years of deceit. Think of it. And you longing for babies!"

Years of deceit! thought Mary.

She closed her eyes and saw the little boy who had come to her table to steal sweetmeats. Jemmy had noticed—so had others. They had been sorry for her; and many of them would have said: How she longs for a child; but she is barren. Some say the Prince is impotent. Others that he spends too much time with his squint-eyed mistress.

Hundreds of pictures from the past crowded into her mind. Elizabeth in the nursery—sly hurtful remarks . . . always making her uncomfortable . . . an enemy.

And now, William loved her. What was the use of hiding the truth.

What was the use of pretending that William was a noble hero when every-one knew he was committing adultery under the same roof as that which sheltered his wife.

Perhaps they were right. Perhaps it was time something was done.

She spent a sleepless night and in the morning she told herself that she must ignore these whispers. She must speak severely to Mrs. Langford and Anne Trelawny.

But it was not easy.

"You don't believe us," said Mrs. Langford sadly.

Anne, that dear friend whom she knew had always loved her since their childhood, was bolder. "Your Highness does not *want* to believe," she said, "and that is why you will not put us to the test."

"Put you to the test?"

"Yes. Make sure that we are speaking the truth."

"How?"

"He goes to her apartment almost every night. You could wait for him to leave it."

She shook her head.

But she went on thinking about William and Elizabeth. She pictured him, slyly mounting the stairs to the maid of honor's room, opening the door, Elizabeth waiting... the embrace. Sly Elizabeth! Cold William! What was this attraction between them? Were they laughing at her for being so simple that she had not discovered their deceit?

The card game was over. Mary said that she was tired and would retire to her room.

She smiled at the Prince, who although he did not play cards, had joined the assembly.

"You are looking tired," she told him. "Could you not desert your work for one night and retire early?"

He looked at her coldly and replied that urgent dispatches were awaiting his attention.

"You work too hard," she said, smiling fondly, and bade him goodnight.

Her ladies prepared her for bed and she dismissed them all except Anne Trelawny and Mrs. Langford. Then Anne brought a robe and wrapped it about her.

"It may well be that you will have to wait a long time at the foot of the privy stairs to the maids of honors' apartments," she said.

"I shall wait," said Mary firmly.

They made her comfortable there.

They knew that he was visiting Elizabeth Villiers that night because Mrs. Langford's son had been set to wait behind the hangings and he had seen him go to her.

Only Mary's anger saved her from tears.

They had successfully convinced her that she had allowed herself to become an object of pity since, it seemed, all knew of the adulterous intrigue except herself.

William looked down at Elizabeth who yawned sleepily as she smiled up at him. She implied that she was utterly contented.

He felt rejuvenated, as he always did after these occasions. She attracted him as no other woman ever could. He did not know exactly what it was;

she was knowledgeable, dignified, and without a trace of humility, which surprised him for he had always thought that docility was what he would ask in a woman, but she was so eager to be all that he wanted, he was deeply aware of that and it flattered him. She kept in step with him on state affairs and he guessed that must have been a great task; she was not afraid to offer an opinion. She was sensual but never over demanding; she seemed to be able to assess his strength to the smallest degree. She had made him her life, and she flattered him without seeming to do so. He would not have known what he wanted of a woman until he met Elizabeth and she had shown him.

He could never break with her, however much the intrigue worried his Calvinistic soul. He told himself that she was a necessity to him. She supplied the recreation he needed; with his frail body and active mind, he needed that relaxation and only she could give it. That was his excuse; and he would scheme and lie to keep her.

Sleek as a satisfied cat she watched him, delighted with the part she was called upon to play. The power behind the throne! She could not have asked for a more exciting role. She was no longer jealous of foolish sentimental Mary as she had been in the nursery days and she could always hug herself with delight to consider their positions now.

William shut the door gently and cautiously descended the privy stairs.

As he reached the last step a figure rose before him. He stared, unable to believe in those first seconds that it was his wife.

"Yes," she said. "It is I."

"What are you doing here?"

"Waiting for you to finish dealing with those . . . state papers. I did not know that you kept them in Elizabeth Villiers's bedchamber."

"This is most unseemly."

"I agree. The Prince of Orange tiptoeing from his mistress's bedroom!"

"I do not wish to hear another word about this."

"I do not suppose *you* do. But *I* wish to speak of it."

"You are behaving even more foolishly than usual."

"And, William, how are you behaving?"

"With great restraint, I assure you."

"William . . ."

He pushed aside her arm.

"Go back to your apartments. I am most displeased with you. I should have thought you would have had more dignity than to behave like a cottage shrew."

"And your behavior . . ." But her voice had faltered, he noticed, and he seized the advantage.

"I am more than displeased by your conduct," he said. "I am very angry. I do not wish to see you or speak to you until you are in a more controlled and reasonable state of mind."

With that he left her standing there, forlorn and tearful.

Anne Trelawny and Mrs. Langford, who had been listening, came out to take her to her bed.

They looked at each other in exasperation. One would have thought that she was the sinner. Oh, it was indeed time she had a kind and loving husband.

They got her to bed and she lay shivering and sleepless.

For some days William avoided her but he was very uneasy.

He sent for Bentinck as he did when he was perplexed, and told him what had happened.

"Someone must have advised her to do this. I suspect that girl Trelawny. I am going to find out, and if she is guilty she shall go back to England."

"It's a little harsh on the Princess," suggested Bentinck.

"I don't understand."

"Your Highness *was* visiting my sister-in-law. She *is* your mistress. The Princess would naturally be disturbed to discover this!"

"And you think it right and fitting for her servants to help her to spy on me?"

"I think it a very natural state of affairs," said Bentinck.

"There are times, my friend, when you exceed your duty."

"I had believed that Your Highness always wanted me to answer your questions truthfully."

"I do not want insolence . . . even from my friends."

"I would respectfully point out that there was no insolence in my reply."

"You are being insolent now. You may go, Bentinck. I no longer need your presence."

As Bentinck bowed and retired, William stared at the closed door in dismay. This was the first time he had ever quarreled with Bentinck; he could scarcely believe it had happened.

First to be discovered in that undignified way by a wife waiting at the bottom of a staircase! Then to be told he was in the wrong by one whose friendship he valued!

He was ashamed, and when he was ashamed he was angry.

Elizabeth opened very wide those eyes with the—to him— enchanting cast and said: "It is simple. Anne Trelawny and the Langford woman are at the bottom of this. They are always whispering together. Get rid of them and everything will be well."

"I should want to prove them guilty first."

"It should not be difficult. Others will be in it. Leave it to me. I'll find out."

He kissed her. He could trust her he knew, his clever Elizabeth.

In a few days she had the answer.

"It is more serious than we believed. James is behind this."

"James? But how?"

"His idea is to have your marriage annulled so that Mary can make a marriage more to his liking."

"A Catholic marriage!"

"That is exactly what he would like. Whether the people of England would accept that is another matter. In any case, James does not want *you* to remain his son-in-law. Covell is an old fool . . . fortunately. He cannot keep his mouth shut. He's delighted to be working with Skelton who has his orders straight from Whitehall. You see the nature of our little plot?"

"You're a clever girl, Elizabeth."

"Have you only just discovered it?"

"I always knew it."

"I am glad, for the more clever I am the greater service I can offer my Prince."

She took the frail little hand and kissed it. She expressed herself charmingly; her gestures were delightful.

I'll never give her up, he thought. I'll defy James and all England if necessary; and I'll keep Elizabeth . . . and Mary.

The Prince of Orange was out hunting but his thoughts were not on his quarry. They were back at the Palace where he had given instructions to a few trusted servants to keep watch for anyone leaving with letters.

These were to be stopped and searched, and any letters found on them were to be subjected to scrutiny.

The stratagem worked.

When he returned to the Palace several letters from Covell to Skelton and from Skelton to his master were laid before him.

In these it was quite clear that a plot was in progress to bring about the dissolution of the Orange marriage. The Princess was first to be made aware of her husband's infidelity with Elizabeth Villiers, then to be made to see she could not condone it. The names of Anne Trelawny and the Langfords were mentioned.

William, having read the letters, sent for Covell.

There was nothing brave about Covell, and William in a cold rage could be intimidating.

"Do you admit that you have been plotting against me?" demanded William.

Dr. Covell, seeing that he could not deny it considering William was holding his letter in his hand, confessed that this was so. He told him that he was acting on instructions from Skelton, who had received his orders from Whitehall.

"Get out," said William.

When he had gone he sent for Mary.

She came in fear. He studied her coldly for some seconds before speaking.

Then he said: "I can only believe that you are so stupid that you do not understand you have been the victim of a conspiracy."

"I . . . William?"

Now she was like the Mary he knew, meek and frightened of him.

"Yes, you. Your father has decided to marry you to a Papist."

She gasped in horror. "But I am married to you, William."

"He does not intend you to remain so."

"But how could I . . . ?"

He lifted a hand to silence her. "You have been very weak. You have listened to gossip and believed the worst of me. In so doing you have played into their hands. Your father is a ruthless man. Have you forgotten Monmouth and the Bloody Assizes? Your father is to blame for those tragedies, and now he wants to add another to their number."

"He has had to defend his crown, William."

"So you make excuses for him?"

"He *is* my father."

"I wonder you are not ashamed to call him so."

"I know that he is mistaken so often in what he does. But it is true, William, that Elizabeth Villiers is your mistress."

A quiver of alarm touched him. That vein of strength in her was apt to appear when he believed he had subdued her, to make him never quite sure of her.

He felt a stirring of panic and said quickly: "She is nothing to me."

"William!"

"But . . ."

He would not let her speak, lest she ask questions he could not parry. He had heard the note of joy in her voice. She wanted Elizabeth Villiers to be of no importance to him. She was willing to meet him halfway.

"Why," he said, "have you forgotten that *you* are my wife?"

"I feared you had forgotten it, William."

"It is something I could never forget." That was true enough. Was she not the heir to the three crowns he coveted? "So let us be sensible, Mary."

"Yes, William."

"This affair . . . it was nothing. It meant little to me."

"And it is over?"

"I will never forget that you are my wife. Our marriage is important . . . to us . . . to Holland . . . to England. We have our duty. Let us never forget that."

"No, William."

· He put his hands on her shoulders and gave her his wintry smile. He saw the tears in her eyes and knew that he had won.

When she had gone he sent for Covell, Anne Trelawny, and the Langfords.

"You should begin your preparations," he said. "You leave for England tomorrow."

Then he sat down and wrote to Laurence Hyde—the King's brother-in-law—and asked that Skelton be recalled and another envoy sent to Holland in his place.

Mary was saddened by the loss of her dear friends. She had particularly loved Anne Trelawny and when she remembered how they had been allies in the days of Elizabeth Villiers's ascendancy in the nursery she felt her departure the more.

For it was useless to pretend Elizabeth was not William's mistress. William had said that the affair was of little importance, but he continued it. Elizabeth Villiers seemed slyer and more smug than ever; and now that Mary had been forced to face the truth she could not get it out of her mind.

Why should she endure this? When William was absent she felt very bold; it was only when he was with her that she told herself she must reconcile herself to her fate.

William had left The Hague for a short visit inland on official business—actually so this time, for Elizabeth Villiers remained in the palace.

Why should I stand aside while they conduct this intrigue under the very same roof? Mary asked herself. They think that I acted as I did because Anne Trelawny and Mrs. Langford advised me to. They think I have no will of my own.

They were wrong. Although she longed for ideal relationships, for peace between her father and her husband, she was not afraid to assert her will when she thought it necessary to do so; she would show them this.

She sent for Elizabeth Villiers.

Elizabeth stood before her—sly, always sly, and alert, wondering with what she was about to be confronted.

"I want a very special and important message to be delivered," said Mary, and her regal manner alarmed Elizabeth.

"Yes, Your Highness."

"Knowing your discretion and intelligence I am giving you the task of delivering it."

"Your Highness can be assured that I shall obey you to the best of my ability."

"I am sure you will do well what you must."

Mary went to her table and picked up a letter which was sealed with her royal seal. A great deal of thought had gone into writing that letter.

"You should leave at once," she said; and as she turned to look at her enemy a fierce jealousy struck at her. What had Elizabeth to offer him? She was clever; no one doubted that. But as far as beauty was concerned she was not to be compared with Mary who had been called one of the most beautiful women in Europe, and although royalty was always given more credit for beauty than it deserved, that opinion was not all flattery. It was true that she had put on too much weight but her hair was still abundant, her dark shortsighted eyes, although they were giving her a great deal of trouble, were still attractive.

And there was Elizabeth with that extraordinary cast; perhaps that was attractive, that, and her wit and her boldness.

"To whom is the message to be delivered, Your Highness?" asked Elizabeth.

"To my father."

It gave Mary pleasure to see the start of amazement quickly followed by panic.

"I beg Your Highness's pardon but . . . did I understand . . ."

"You understood very well," said Mary. "You surely do not imagine that I would ask *you* to deliver an ordinary message . . . like a page?"

"No, but . . ."

"I wish you to leave within the hour. You will be taken to the coast where a ship will be found for you. I trust you will have an easy crossing."

Mary was sure that never in her life had Elizabeth Villiers been so bewildered. Quite clearly she did not know what to say. William was away from The Hague therefore she could not appeal to him, and in his absence, Mary's orders must be obeyed without question.

Two of Mary's male servants came into the room as they had obviously been commanded to.

"Everything is ready," Mary told them. "You will leave immediately."

Nonplussed, Elizabeth could do nothing but follow them; Mary stood at her window watching the departure.

Now all she had to do was await the return of William.

William was back at The Hague for two days before he discovered Elizabeth's absence.

It was Bentinck who told him. The quarrel between them had been mended, and although William had not apologized—that would have been asking too much—he had implied he was no longer displeased, while at the same time he wanted his friend to know that while he respected his advice on matters of state he wanted no interference with his domestic affairs.

"My sister-in-law has left for England," Bentinck said.

For a moment William was so taken off his guard that he expressed bewilderment.

"She went on orders of the Princess."

William still did not speak, and Bentinck waited for the storm.

It did not come.

"I wish you to peruse these letters from Celle and give me your opinion."

Bentinck bowed his head. His master's control was admirable, but he wondered what he would do now, and he was sorry for the Princess, although he admired her action.

Anne Bentinck, advised by her husband to do so, warned Mary that the Prince knew of Elizabeth's dismissal. Mary waited for his reaction, but there was no sign that he was in the least affected. William might not have been the slightest bit interested in Elizabeth Villiers.

But inwardly he was deeply disturbed, because he realized that he did not know his wife. When he believed that he had subdued her, she would act in such a way as to confound him. He had been congratulating himself on the manner in which he had handled her discovery of his intrigue. She had seemed meek enough, ready to see it as he wished her to; and then, when he absented himself, she cleverly got rid of Elizabeth. He could imagine what would happen to Elizabeth when she reached England. Mary was clever enough to have arranged that. She was carrying a letter to James. He could picture what was in that letter.

How could Elizabeth have been so foolish? She should never have gone to England. She should have escaped to him and told him what had happened.

But Mary had planned well; Elizabeth had left the Palace in the company of Mary's servants—who were for that occasion Elizabeth's guards. Who would have believed it possible that while Mary was playing the docile wife she was making a careful plan to send Elizabeth out of Holland?

The thought which was never far from his mind came back to torment him. When Mary was Queen of England, with powerful ministers to back her—Englishmen who would work for her—what would her attitude be toward her husband? What would she make him: King or consort?

It was the burning question which was always between them; it was one he dared not ask her because he was afraid of the answer. He had tried to make her completely subservient to his will and he so frequently believed he had succeeded; then—usually choosing one of his absences—she would show that she could have her own way.

Their relationship would never be a comfortable one until this question was answered. He could never show her that he was an affectionate husband until she said to him: "When and if the crown of Britain comes to me, you shall still be my master." That was what he wanted from her; if she would give it, he would be prepared to treat her with respect and affection (although he would never give up Elizabeth). Until then, he would be cold to her, because he was uncertain of her.

He was miserable. Mary baffled him; and Elizabeth, the balm of whose company he needed, was gone.

But he told no one this; he asked no questions of anyone concerning her.

Nor did he mention to Mary that her action had angered him.

It is true, she thought. Elizabeth Villiers was not important to him.

Once she was safely on the boat which was to carry her to Harwich, Elizabeth's captors relaxed their vigil, while she sat huddled against the wind and cursed her bad luck. What was she, who had made herself so comfortable in Holland, doing on a boat which was carrying her to England?

What would William say when he returned and found her gone? She knew William well. He would deplore her loss but he would do nothing about it. What could he do? He was not a man to rant and rave about something that could not be altered.

Who would have believed Mary capable of such a plan! But Mary was often deceptive. She had been in the old nursery days. But for the fact that she was so sentimental and, strangely enough, over-modest, she would have got far more of her own way. Mary was a dreamer who wanted others to dream with her.

But why waste time thinking of Mary now! Her plan had succeeded, Elizabeth had left Holland, and that was an end of that. What Elizabeth had to think of now was how to get back to Holland.

She touched the letter which was in her pocket. A letter to the King. She could imagine what was in it. "Keep this woman in England and do not let her return to Holland." That was almost certain to be the gist.

And was she going to be so foolish as to present that letter to the King and meekly accept a lodging, possibly in the Tower?

When they reached England her captors were at her side.

She said: "I have to await an answer from my request to the King. I propose to have a message sent to him telling him I come from the Princess. In the meantime I shall lodge at my father's house."

This seemed reasonable and her guards accompanied her to the house of her father, Colonel Villiers, in Richmond. There her father welcomed her warmly for he knew of her position at The Hague and that of all his children she was, through her connection with William, the most influential.

As soon as she was alone with him she told him what had happened.

He listened gravely and said: "If James reads that letter you will never return to Holland."

"So I believe."

"You know what is happening here? There is trouble . . . Each week there are further complaints of the King's rule. What the people dread is that James will have a son who will be brought up as a Catholic and thus we should have Catholicism back in England. They will never endure it. If the Queen has a son there will be big trouble."

"You think that they will ask James to abdicate and set Mary in his place."

"They might ask it, but James would not go. He is a fanatic, I do assure you. But that is for the future. More immediately, what of *your* future, my dear?

"I want to return to The Hague as soon as possible."

"Before delivering that letter?"

"I should not be such a fool as to deliver that letter to the King."

"Where is it?"

She brought it out and showed him.

"Her Highness's seal," said the Colonel. "Well, we must break it in a good cause."

They did so and read the letter which was, as Elizabeth had suspected, an account of how the bearer, Elizabeth Villiers, was the mistress of the Prince of Orange and the Princess asked her father not to allow her to return to Holland.

"Well?" said the Colonel.

"There is only one thing to be done with such a document," answered Elizabeth briskly, leaning forward and holding it in the flame of the candle.

Her father watched her with amusement. "And now?"

"I will rest, for I am tired. While I sleep you must prepare an account of everything you know is happening here. At dawn I rise and ride for Harwich. With a good wind I shall soon be back in The Hague."

Anne Bentinck presented herself to Mary.

"Your Highness, my sister Elizabeth is in the Palace and asking to be received."

Mary said: "I do not wish to receive her."

"But Your Highness, her place . . ."

"Your sister has no place in my service."

Anne Bentinck retired to tell Elizabeth that she would have to leave the Palace at once; for Anne's husband had forbidden her to shelter her sister and as Anne was as docile a wife as Mary often was, she dared not disobey him.

When she was alone Mary asked herself why her father had failed her. Surely he would not, as he was trying to break her marriage with William. But of course Elizabeth had not given him the letter. She had guessed its contents, or read them.

In any case she was not going to have her back as a maid of honor. William might attempt to insist but she would stand out even against William.

Elizabeth was waiting for William in a small anteroom of the palace.

They embraced and she told him how Mary had planned to be rid of her.

William nodded. "She astonishes me."

"And me. Will you command her to take me back?"

"No," said William. "Not yet. I think she would stand against it."

"And you will allow her to?"

"For the time, I can do nothing else."

Elizabeth was surprised but too clever to show her surprise. He was, then, afraid of Mary. Well, he had to remember that if ever the crown of Britain came to him it would be through Mary, for Anne and her children would stand between his inheriting it in his own right.

Elizabeth accepted this. She had much to tell him. There was above all the information she had collected from her father in England.

"I made him sit up all night that he might write a clear account of what was happening there. I thought you would find it useful."

William pressed her hand.

"For the time," he said, "go to your sister Katherine. I will visit you at their house. And later . . ."

She kissed his hand.

"Later," he went on, "you shall come back to Court."

William Bentinck had a commission to carry out for his master.

Bentinck guessed for whom the Prince was buying the necklace, and was sorry for the Princess, for a few months after Elizabeth's return she was back in the Palace wearing a diamond necklace.

Mary did not know her strength; or perhaps she did not want to know it. She could have dismissed Elizabeth; she could have made her husband understand that she demanded to be treated, not as a meek consort, but as a Princess in her own right.

But she did not seem sure of the way she wanted to go. Thus there were these spurts of independence followed by subservience.

What would happen? wondered Bentinck, if she came to the throne of Britain? He knew that it was a question which disturbed his master.

THE VITAL QUESTION

Mary was twenty-four years old and would have been very beautiful indeed had she not grown so fat. The people of Holland delighted in her; for whenever she went among them her manner, while gracious and charming, was undoubtedly friendly. She was a contrast to her taciturn husband; she had a measure of that Stuart charm which Monmouth had possessed to a great degree and Charles overwhelmingly, and which usually meant that, whatever their faults, there would always be some to forgive them.

Mary, it seemed to those about her, had few faults. Perhaps she would have been understood better if she had had. She loved card playing, but that could not be called a fault; and although she was friendly in general, after the departure of Anne Trelawny she did not make a close friend of anyone.

They did not entirely understand her, so they remained aloof; her docility to her husband was interrupted now and then by those outbursts of firmness which showed themselves in the part she had played in the

Zuylestein marriage and in sending Elizabeth Villiers to England. She was meant to be gay and vivacious as she had been in the days of childhood; but life with William had subdued that. She had become devoutly religious, devoted to the Church of England—and to her husband. Those about her believed that no one could love a man like William as she professed to do, and that her obvious devotion was like a religion to her. She had chosen it as the right way of life and determined to pursue it. Those who remembered how gay she had been during the visit of the Duke of Monmouth were certain of this. Mary, because of some strange bent in her nature, was determined to subdue her natural impulses and become the sort of person she felt it her duty to be.

She knew that Elizabeth Villiers continued to be William's mistress. For some time she had visited William at the Palace and now was installed in her old position, yet Mary preferred to ignore it. Neither Elizabeth nor William ever mentioned to her that trip to England; it was as though it had never been.

Her women said that they could not understand a woman in her position accepting what Mary did; and Mary was an enigma.

She was to William also. If he could have been sure of how she would act in the event of ascending the throne of England, his entire attitude toward her would have changed. He could have talked to her more freely of his plans; but this stood between them; and he could not bring himself to talk openly of the position she would expect him to hold. Although to all outward appearances he had subdued her, yet he was afraid of her; and although she was the meek wife, seeming always to bend to his will, yet it was in her power to exclude him from the brilliant future which had been his goal ever since he had contemplated marrying her.

This was the state of affairs when Gilbert Burnet arrived at the Court of The Hague.

Gilbert Burnet was in his forties when he came to Holland. He had been a favored chaplain of Charles II but he had quickly fallen foul of James, for he deplored the threat of papacy. It became clear to Burnet that while his position was precarious under Charles, for his friends Essex and Russell had been involved in the Rye House Plot, it would be untenable under James. After that plot he had left England for France where he was warmly received.

One of the first things he did on returning was to preach a sermon against popery which was received with wild enthusiasm by an anti-Catholic congregation; and when Burnet thundered out: "Save me from the lion's mouth; thou hast heard me from the horn of the unicorn . . ." the applause rang out in the church, for the lion and unicorn were the royal arms and this could only mean that Burnet when denouncing popery was denouncing James.

After that there was only one thing for Burnet to do—leave the country. He had been writing busily for the last few years and had produced his *History of the Rights of Princes in the Disposing of Ecclesiastical Benefices and Church Lands* among other works. He was a man whom James could not afford to keep in England.

Burnet went to Paris where he remained until the repercussions of the Monmouth rebellion had subsided; then on to Italy and Geneva and eventually, receiving an invitation from the Prince and Princess of Orange, he arrived at The Hague.

William received him coolly. He was not sure that he trusted him completely for in his opinion the man was apt to talk too much. Burnet was without fear, there was no doubt of that, but the fearlessness made him indiscreet; and William always mistrusted indiscretion. With Mary, Burnet was on happier terms. She was interested in what he had to tell her of England and his travels, and would ask him to sit with her and while he sat she knotted fringe, for she had had to give up doing the fine needlework on which she had enjoyed working, since her eyes had given her so much trouble.

This was a pleasant domestic scene and sometimes William would join them and listen to the conversation.

Burnet believed that James could bring no good to England and for this reason William became gradually drawn toward him; and, since the coming of Burnet, was more frequently in his wife's company than he had been before.

Mary began to look forward to those hours as the most rewarding of her days. There she would sit working at the fringe close to the candles, to get the utmost light; Burnet would answer the questions she put to him and gradually a picture of the English Court would evolve. William would sit a little apart listening, now and then firing a question of his own, his head, looking enormous in its periwig drooping over his narrow shoulders and slightly hunched back, throwing a grotesque shadow on the wall.

It was the nearest to domesticity that Mary had ever reached; and she wanted to go on like this, for she believed that William was changing toward her since Burnet had come. While he was in her company he was neglecting Elizabeth. Perhaps he was finding that his wife could be of greater help to him in his political schemes than his mistress ever could be. So as she talked to Burnet she was deeply conscious of William; and she asked those questions which she thought would best please her husband.

As she talked William began to understand Mary more than ever before. She was not the foolish girl he had sometimes believed her to be, but a woman of intelligence and above all tolerance. William himself wanted tolerance . . . up to a point; and he appreciated this quality in his wife.

He listened to them discussing the preacher Jurieu who had written scurrilously of Mary Queen of Scots.

Mary offered the comment: "If what he had said was true, then he was not to blame. If Princes do ill things, they must expect that the world will take revenge on their memory since they cannot reach their persons."

An unusual sentiment for a Princess to express, thought William. Yes, she was an unusual woman, this wife of his.

He watched her, stately, plump, her dark head bent slightly forward over the fringe. She was beautiful; and she was not without wisdom. He began to think that he had been rather fortunate in his marriage.

Never would he be able to explain to her his need of Elizabeth. Mary lacked that sexual appeal which he found in his mistress. He knew of that passionate friendship with Frances Apsley—not a physical passion that, yet it was an indication of Mary's character. She could be firm and so very meek. She could love devotedly and at the same time had not that to offer which could make a perfect union between a man and woman.

Yet William himself was no virile man. He did not ask for great sexual passion. Mary's docility, her willingness to find in him an ideal husband could have made him very contented with his marriage. There were only two things which stood between them: his absolute need of Elizabeth Villiers and his ignorance of what attitude she would take toward him if the throne of England were hers.

Burnet, watching them, decided that his future lay with them, guessed what plans were forming in the mind of the Prince of Orange, was aware of this gulf between them, and sought to discover what it was and if it could be bridged.

The friendship between these three grew.

For Mary it was delightful to see her husband sitting by the fire listening gravely to her and Gilbert as they talked and occasionally throwing in a remark. Not since Monmouth had gone had she felt so contented. The skirt of her dark velvet gown caressed the black and white tiles and the candlelight touched the red velvet of hangings, high windows, and painted ceiling with a light which made them more beautiful than by day. Every now and then she would close her eyes to rest them a little, or glance up from her fringe to one or other of the two men—to William so fragile under his enormous periwig, his hands as delicate as a girl's; and Gilbert Burnet in great contrast in the black and white robes of the Church—a heavy man with coarse features illuminated by the light of a shrewd and clever mind.

The two men were bound by a common desire. They wanted James deposed and William and Mary reigning in his place, and were asking themselves, How can this be brought about without delay?

Mary talked of England too and of the days when there would be a new ruler; but the man these two wished so ruthlessly to depose was her father and it did not occur to her that when England was discussed, the future they talked of could be before her father's death.

As the pleasant sessions continued, spies carried accounts of them to England.

James wrote to William: It was unseemly, he declared, that his enemy should be treated as a close friend of the Prince and Princess of Orange.

William sent for Mary when he received this letter.

"Your father believes he can dictate our conduct to us, it appears," he said coldly.

Mary sighed. She hated trouble between her father and her husband, and always sought to put their differences right.

"I can understand his feelings. Dr. Burnet did preach against him."

"For which one can only admire Dr. Burnet."

"He is a brave man, certainly, and firm in his beliefs. I understand Dr. Burnet, William, but I also understand my father."

"You understand his desire to bring Catholicism back to England? You understand the cruel treatment of Monmouth?"

Mary winced; she could never think of that tragedy without a deep and searing pain; and in spite of her sense of justice and her natural tolerance she felt a sudden hatred for a father who had destroyed one whom she had loved.

William went on. "And not only Monmouth which is perhaps understandable. Those others, those men who fought for him because of their convictions—what do you think of the justice they received at your father's hands?"

"I think Judge Jeffries was to blame and that my father had no real knowledge of what was going on."

William gave one of his rare laughs. It was not pleasant.

"I doubt whether you understand what it is like to be a slave on a

Jamaican plantation. Transported from England to that hell. Yet that was the fate of many of your father's subjects . . . for what reason? Simply because they hated popery."

Mary said: "It was wrong to be so severe. But we must not forget, William, that Monmouth called himself the King."

"It might have been that others called him that. But if you wish to excuse your father, do so. I have no wish to listen."

"William, I do not excuse him. I . . ."

"Then," said William curtly, "it may be that you begin to understand him?"

He left her and she thought of Jemmy, dancing with her, teaching her to skate, teaching her so much more than she could ever speak of; and she wept afresh for Jemmy.

Jemmy dead, bending to the block; and the cruel executioner lifting that once lovely head and crying: "Here is a traitor!"

"A traitor," she said vehemently, "to a tyrant!"

And she knew then that she was beginning to feel toward her father as William wished her to. She was beginning to see him through William's eyes—libertine, ineffectual ruler, the King who, while he did not declare himself openly a papist, was trying to thrust popery on a country, the majority of whose people rejected it—all that *and* the murderer of Jemmy!

Gilbert Burnet came to her in some haste.

"Your Highness," he said, "something must be done. The Prince is in danger."

Mary grew pale and cried: "Tell me more. What do you mean?"

"I have spoken to His Highness and he shrugs it aside. You know that the King of France regards your husband as an enemy."

"I know all these things. Tell me quickly."

"I have discovered a plot to kidnap the Prince when he drives unattended along the Scheveling sands. The idea is to get him out of Holland into France."

"And you have told the Prince this?"

"I have warned him and he says he will know how to take good care of himself."

"And he will take no guard with him?"

"I fear not. He said that what is to be will be and if it is destined that he shall meet such a fate then so be it."

"I must go to him at once," said Mary. "Pray come with me, good Dr. Burnet."

Together they went to the Prince's apartment. William raised his eyebrows when he saw them together; but Burnet detected the faint pleasure which showed in his face when he beheld Mary's agitation.

"William, you must take a guard with you when you go on to the sands."

"So, you have heard this warning?"

Dr. Burnet put in: "Your Highness, I am convinced there is a a plot and that you are ill-advised to ignore it."

Mary clasped her hands together. "You *must* not ignore it, William. It would be disastrous if you were forced into France."

William looked impatient, but Mary went closer to him and looked imploringly into his face.

"William, I beg of you, to *please* me . . ."

William shrugged his shoulders.

"Very well," he said, "I shall take the guard."

Mary paced her apartments in agitation. She would not rest until William returned.

She sent for Dr. Burnet and asked him to pray with her.

When they rose from their knees William had still not returned.

"Dr. Burnet, do you think the plot could have succeeded in spite of the precaution he took?"

"No, Your Highness. The Prince will soon be back in the Palace."

"I shall know no peace until he is."

Burnet looked at the Princess intently. He was a man who had little restraint and the intimate friendship he had enjoyed with these two had put him into a position he believed where he could speak his mind.

"Your Highness," he said, "your devotion to the Prince is obvious. Yet I do not think there is always accord between you."

Mary looked startled and was about to show her displeasure when Burnet said quickly: "If I speak rashly it is because I have your happiness and that of the Prince at heart."

"I know this," she said, and moved to the window. Burnet saw that the subject was closed.

But he did not intend to let it rest if he could help it.

Mary said she would pray once more, for the longer the Prince's absence the greater became her anxiety.

They were on their knees when the sounds below them told them that the Prince was returning to the Palace.

Mary ran to the window. There he was riding at the head of the guards. On horseback it was scarcely visible that he stooped distressingly and that he was so slight.

Mary turned to Burnet. "How can I thank you?" she said.

"By letting me help Your Highness in every way possible," was the answer.

Burnet was in higher favor than ever, particularly with the Princess, and, when they were alone together, with habitual temerity he broached the subject of her marriage once more.

This time Mary did not feel she could rebuff the man who had saved her husband from being kidnapped, possibly murdered, so she allowed him to speak.

"I believe the Prince has a great regard for you, but there is something which holds him back from expressing his affection."

Mary said frankly: "The Prince has never expressed great affection. I do not believe it is in his nature to do so."

To Elizabeth Villiers? Burnet asked himself, wondering whether to mention that lady and then deciding not to.

"I believe," said Burnet, "that the Prince is always aware that the crown of Britain would come to you and that in the event you would be the Queen and he merely the Queen's consort."

Mary opened her eyes wide. "Surely the Prince knows that I would never put him into a humiliating position."

Burnet was secretly delighted; he believed that he was going to bring about a deeper understanding between the Prince and Princess of Orange which would be a great advantage when, as he hoped, they came to England to depose James.

"Your Highness," said Burnet to the Prince, "in the event of James dying or . . . some other contingency . . . and the Princess being acclaimed Queen, has Your Highness considered your own position?"

Even William was unable to hide the depth of his emotion.

This is the secret, thought Burnet; this is at the very heart of the matter.

"You can rest assured," said William sharply, "that nothing would induce me to act as valet to my wife."

"Nothing would induce me to believe that she would expect Your Highness to."

"When greatness comes one cannot always assess the effect it will have."

"But the Princess . . ."

William waved a hand. "The Princess has been a docile wife . . . almost always, and only rarely has she opposed my wishes."

"Almost." "Rarely." Those were the significant words.

So William was unsure of his wife, and it was a barrier between them. He could not bring himself to ask her what position, if she were Queen of England, she would assign to him; and the ministers of England would accept *her* as their sovereign; they would obey *her*, and if she said William was to be her consort merely, that was all he could hope for. The decision lay with Mary; and he did not fully understand Mary.

It was clear to Burnet that this was a question which burned continually in his mind. He was working toward a goal; he had married Mary in order to reach this goal; and now he did not know whether this meek obliging wife would, in one of her sudden moods of firmness, withhold from him that which had come to be the very meaning of his existence.

"Your Highness, I could put the question to the Princess . . . with your permission. I could discover what is in her mind."

William's pale eyes seemed to take on new life. He gripped Burnet's arm. "Do that," he said.

So once more Burnet sought Mary.

"Your Highness," he said, "I have just left the Prince and there is a matter which perplexes him greatly and which I believe is constantly in his mind. Have I your permission to right this matter between Your Highnesses?"

Mary, looking puzzled, implored him to go on.

"It is simply this, Your Highness: should you succeed your father to the Crown, what position do you intend the Prince to hold?"

"I do not understand you. What comes to me, comes to my husband, does it not?"

"That is not so. You will remember that when Mary Tudor came to the throne her husband Philip of Spain was not King of England. Your Highness, I do assure you that a titular kingship is no acceptable thing to a man—particularly when that is his only as long as his wife shall live."

"What remedy do you propose?" asked Mary.

"Ah, Your Highness, if you would be content to be a wife only and promise to give him the real authority as soon as it comes into your hands, I believe that the differences which are now between you and the Prince would be removed."

The differences? He would no longer keep a mistress? He would be the perfect husband she had tried to deceive herself into thinking he was? This had been between them, then, this knowledge that she could one day be a Queen and he only assume the title of King if it were her wish? Mary was excited. She knew William and his pride. That was the answer then. He had avoided her because her position could be so much higher than his. He could not endure to be merely a consort to a Queen; his pride was too great; just as it was too great for him to ask her what she intended to do. It had been between them all those years. She, too blind to see it; he, too proud to ask.

And so he had turned to Elizabeth Villiers who to him was merely a woman whom he could love—not a Princess who could one day be a Queen and hold his future in her hands.

Mary, sentimental, idealistic, believed that wrongs could be righted in a moment of illumination.

She turned to Burnet, her expression radiant.

"I pray you bring the Prince to me. I will tell him myself."

When Burnet brought him to her, assuring him that she wished to tell him herself the answer to the question, she went to William and taking his hands kissed them.

"I did not know," she said, "that the laws of England were so contrary to the laws of God. I did not think that the husband was ever to be obedient to the wife."

William's heart leaped in exultation, but his expression remained cold. He wanted a definite statement before he committed himself.

"You shall always bear rule, William," she told him.

Then he smiled slowly.

She added with a joyous laugh: "There is only one thing I would add. You will obey the command: 'Husbands, love your wives' as I shall do that of 'Wives, be obedient to your husbands in all things'."

"So," answered William slowly, "if you should attain the crown, you will be Queen of England and I shall be the King?"

"I would never allow it to be otherwise," she told him lovingly.

"If you once declare your mind," Burnet reminded Mary, "you must never think of retreating again."

"I never would."

"Then," said Burnet smiling from one to another like a fairy godmother, "this little matter is settled. When James goes, there will be a King *and* Queen of England."

"And the Queen will be a woman whose one desire will be to obey her husband," added Mary.

Those were happy days.

He shared confidences with her; theirs was a happy trinity—Burnet, Mary, and William; and they talked of England as though in a week or so they would all be there. The King and his Queen, who would always see through his eyes and obey him in every way; and Burnet, who would become a Bishop and remain their friend and adviser.

There was only one question that Mary could not bring herself to put to her husband: "Is it finished between you and Elizabeth Villiers?"

It would not have been difficult to find out. She could have had her spies who would soon discover the truth; she could have waited in the early hours of the morning to catch him as she had before. But she would do none of these things; she would only believe that she had attained the perfect marriage for which she had always longed.

William stood in his mistress's bedchamber looking down at her lying on her bed.

She grew more attractive with the years, he thought; her wits sharpened and her beauty did not fade, for it was more than skin deep. It was in the strangeness of her eyes, in her sensuous movements, in her low laughter, so indulgent for him.

"She will obey me in all things," he told her. "She has said I shall always bear the rule. It is what I have waited to ask her for years and now, thanks to Burnet, she has told me herself."

"And she asks no conditions?"

"She mentions none."

"I thought there might have been one."

Elizabeth looked at him passionately for a moment; then she rose and gracefully put herself into his arms.

"To abandon me?" she whispered.

"It is one condition to which I should never agree," he told her.

THE CONFLICT OF
LOYALTIES

There was consternation at The Hague. Mary Beatrice was pregnant. If she bore a son then he would be heir to the throne and if he lived that would be the end of Mary's hopes of being Queen of England.

William was in a black mood.

To have come so far and now be frustrated! It was more than he could endure. The three crowns, which Mrs. Tanner had prophesied would be his, had such a short while before seemed almost within his grasp; and now there was this alarming news.

If James had a son, that son would be brought up as a Catholic. How could it be otherwise, when he had a Catholic mother and father? The return of Catholicism to England would be assured.

It should not be allowed to happen.

William secretly believed that the people of England would never allow it to be.

The Princess Anne wrote from England, for she too was horrified by the news, so horrified that she simply refused to believe it.

"The *grossesse* of the King's wife is very suspicious," she wrote. "It is true that she is very big, but she *looks* better than she has ever done which is not usual in the case of women as far gone as she *pretends* to be . . ."

William read the letter with growing excitement. Envoys were arriving from England with secret messages for him and Mary. There was a rumor being spread through England that there was no truth in the Queen's pregnancy; that she flaunted it, was over-big and behaved in an exaggerated manner as a pregnant woman as though she was eager to call attention to her state every moment of the day. She was certain that it would be a son. Over-certain some said, as though it had been previously arranged.

The people in the streets were murmuring against the King and Queen. They did not want a Catholic heir and they were determined to prove there was no true one on the way.

As the summer wore on the tension increased. The Princess Anne, unknown to her father and stepmother, was at the head of those who were determined to cast doubts on the Queen's true pregnancy. Anne, staunchly Protestant, had grown to hate her father, although she had never shown him that she had. She was looking ahead to the day when she would have the throne. Sarah Churchill was certain that she would, and then ultimate power would be hers—or Sarah's. Anne was fond of her pleasant weak husband, but it was Sarah to whom she listened, Sarah on whom she doted.

Mary had no children so after Mary it would be the turn of Queen Anne; and now there was this child—or this supposed child—to oust them from their place.

Angrily Anne wrote to Mary. "I have every reason to believe that the Queen's great belly is a false one. Her being so positive it will be a son, and the principles of that religion being such as they will stick at nothing, be it never so wicked if it will promote their interest, makes it clear some foul play is intended."

Mary took the letter to William. They pondered on it; he dourly, she anxious because of his disappointment. If she could no longer bring him the throne he craved, she feared she would no longer have the same value in his eyes and she knew that that value had been enhanced when she had promised that he should rule her as well as England.

"William," she said, "why should my father pretend that the Queen is with child?"

"Because," replied William sourly, "they care for nothing so long as they can bring England back to popery. They will thrust a spurious child on the people—and that child will be a Catholic."

"Oh, William . . . my father would not be so wicked."

"Mary, it is time you looked at truth. It is unpleasant, but no good can come of looking away for that reason. Your father is an evil man. Accept that truth and you will suffer less."

She turned away from him and there were tears in her eyes.

"He was so good to me when I was a child. He loved me, William."

"You are a fool," said William brusquely and left her.

She wept a little.

It was so sad when there were quarrels in families but she must not forget that it was her father who had murdered Jemmy the man she . . . the man for whom she had had such regard.

Her father was a Catholic. He was trying to foist a child, not his son, on the people of England for the sole purpose of thrusting them back to Rome.

That was wicked. That was evil.

It was something no one should forget or forgive.

James's flair for projecting himself into trouble had not left him. While the country was listening to the stories put about by his enemies that his wife was pretending to be pregnant he brought forward his second Declaration of Indulgence which he ordered should be read in church on two Sundays. Seven Bishops petitioned him against the declaration, which James declared was rebellion against the King. These Bishops were sent to the Tower.

There was murmuring throughout the country. In Cornwall, since one of the Bishops was Jonathan Trelawny, the brother of Anne who had been sent out of Holland by the Prince of Orange, they were singing

> *And shall Trelawny die*
> *Then twenty thousand Cornishmen will know the reason why.*

And all over England there was equal resentment against the King. How much easier it was to believe of a King that he was preparing to foist a child on the nation in order to secure Catholic rule, when he imprisoned his Bishops because they disagreed with him on what should be done in the churches.

While the Bishops were in prison the child was born.

A boy! The son for which the King, Queen, and their supporters had been praying!

There was deep despair among the King's enemies which could only be tolerated by disbelief.

William preserved his calm. The birth of this child was the most bitter blow which could have come to him but he gave no sign of this. He sent Zuylestein to England to congratulate the King and Queen.

But before Zuylestein left he was alone with William who said: "You know what I desire of you?"

"To discover the true feelings of the people, Your Highness."

"Find out what they are saying of the King and the Queen . . . and the Princess of Orange . . . and myself. Find out what they think about the opportune birth of this child."

William waited impatiently for Zuylestein's return.

The Princess Anne wrote jubilantly.

"The Prince of Wales has been ill these three or four days and if he has been so bad as some people say, I believe it will not be long before he is an angel in Heaven."

When Mary showed the letter to William, he said: "Let them pray for the Prince of Wales in the churches."

Mary bowed her head. "How good you are, William," she said.

And she prayed fervently for the health of the child, for secretly in her heart she wanted him to live. These last weeks had made her look fearfully into a future which filled her with dread.

What was happening in England? Were the people in truth turning against her father? If the child died would they deprive him of his throne and if they did . . .?

She did not want to be Queen of England through her father's misfortunes. William desired the crown, she knew that; and she wanted to please William. But not through her father's misery.

She wanted her father to reform his ways and live in peace with his subjects. And she and William could continue in Holland, which was so much more pleasant since she had told him that she would always want him to rule. That had made him more pleased with her than he had ever been before—and all because she had told him that if ever she were Queen of England he should be the King.

But how could she be happy being Queen of England, even if she could give William his supreme wish and make him King, when it meant that she could only do so through the death or disgrace of her father?

And William, she admitted in her secret thoughts, was still the lover of Elizabeth Villiers.

When Zuylestein returned from England, he was triumphant.

"Your Highness, the Prince still lives and his health is improving, but there are many who believe him not to be the true son of the King. They are saying that the birth was mysterious, that just before the baby was said to be born the Queen asked to have the bedcurtains drawn about her; that the baby was brought into the bed by means of a warming pan. The temper of the people is high."

William sent for Mary. He told her that he was certain the King and Queen had deceived the nation. The child they were claiming was the Prince of Wales, was almost certain to be spurious.

Mary wept bitterly, contemplating the wickedness of her father, and William made a rough attempt to soothe her.

"What is," he said, "must be faced."

"William," she cried, "I can bear whatever has to be faced, if we face it together."

He bent toward her and put a cold kiss on her cheek.

It was as though a bargain had been sealed.

The rumors from London persisted; there was scarcely a day when a messenger did not arrive at The Hague with a fresh tale. Each day James grew more and more unpopular. The Bishops had been acquitted but their untimely incarceration had increased James's enemies by the thousand.

There came that day when William sent for his wife. There was a faint glow of triumph on that usually cold face.

The moment had come.

He said: "They have sent me an invitation."

Mary waited and he who rarely felt an inclination to smile now found one curling his lips. "Danby, Devonshire, Lumley, Shrewsbury, Sidney, Russell, and the Bishop of London. You might say the seven most important men in England at this time. They tell me they will collect forces for an invasion. They are inviting me to go over there . . . now."

"To go there, William? But what can you do? My father is the King . . ."

"I believe that he will not be so much longer."

She could not look at the triumph in his face. She thought: I am not worthy to be a Queen. I am only a woman.

And she saw her father setting her on his knee and telling those who came to see him how clever she was. She heard voices from the past: "The lady Mary is his favorite daughter." And his voice: "My dearest child, we will always love each other."

And now she was one of those who were against him. He would know that. How would he bear it in the midst of all his troubles? Would he say: Once I dearly loved this ungrateful daughter?

She wanted to cry out: He is my father. I loved him once.

But William was looking at her coldly, and his eyes reminded her of her promise always to obey.

Mary Beatrice wrote to her stepdaughter.

"I shall never believe that you are to come over with your husband, dear Lemon, for I know you to be too good that I don't believe you could have such a thought against the worst of fathers, much less perform it against the best, that has always been kind to you and I believe has loved you best of all his children."

How could she read such words dry-eyed?

Oh, God, she prayed, let it be happily settled. Let my father realize the folly of his ways, let him confess his wickedness, . . . and let William have the crown when my father has left this life.

She must not answer Mary Beatrice because she must always consider her loyalty to William. And William was exultant these days although he was coughing a great deal, even spitting blood, and she worried on account of his health.

Sad days! Oh for that happy time when dear Jemmy had danced and skated here at The Hague, and later when she had sat with Dr. Burnet and William and they had all talked pleasantly together. Dr. Burnet had now married a Dutch woman—very rich and comely—and he was happy; and was no doubt thinking of the time when William was King and she Queen and he would be recalled to his native land.

But her father haunted her dreams, his eyes appealing. "Have you forgotten, my favorite daughter, how I loved you?"

I must forget, she told herself, because I have a husband now.

She steeled herself to forget; she prayed continuously. There must be two idols in her life—her religion and her husband.

She must forget all else.

$\mathcal{B}ut$ it was not easy to forget when she read the letters her father sent her.

He did not believe she was in the plot to depose him; he could not accept that.

"I have had no letter from you and I can easily believe that you may be embarrassed how to write to me now that the unjust design of the Prince of Orange to invade me is so public. And though I know you are a good wife, and ought to be so, yet for the same reason I must believe you still to be as good a daughter to a father that has always loved you so tenderly and that has never done the least thing to make you doubt it. I shall say no more and believe you very uneasy all this time for the concern you must have for a husband and a father. You shall find me kind to you if you desire it . . ."

Mary broke down when she read that letter.

"I cannot bear it," she sobbed.

Why must there be this unhappiness for the sake of a crown. Three crowns—England, Scotland, Ireland. And so many to covet them!

She went to William, determined to fall on her knees and implore him to give up this design. But when she stood before him and saw the cold determination in his face, she knew that would be useless. As well ask him to give up his hope of the three crowns. As well ask him to give up Elizabeth Villiers.

And she had sworn always to obey; she *must* obey him. He was her husband and she had promised herself that hers should be an ideal marriage. It could only be so if she obeyed him absolutely.

She changed her plea. "William," she said, "promise me that if my father should become your captive, he shall be unharmed."

William had never been a violent man; it was easy to give that promise.

KING WILLIAM AND
QUEEN MARY

illiam was ready to leave for England. In spite of his ill health—that terrible cough which racked his body day and night and the ever-threatening asthma—he seemed to have grown younger during the last weeks. The dream was about to be realized; and he could scarcely wait for its fulfillment. Outwardly he was as calm as ever; but Mary sensed the inner excitement.

He looked at her intently and with more tenderness than he had ever shown her before. It might be that he understood her feelings, that he was appreciative of this immense loyalty to him which had forced her to turn her back on her father.

He had groomed her well and was pleased with her. Momentarily he thought of the shrinking girl who had been his bride. She was gone forever. She had turned into the docile wife and if he had the wish—or the potency—he could have made of her a passionate woman.

But such trivial dallyings were not for him. He had a destiny and he was about to grasp it in his frail, but nonetheless eager, hands.

"Mary," he said, taking her hands, "pray God to bless and direct us."

She bowed her head; this time the tears did not exasperate him.

"You have been a good wife to me. It is something I shall never forget."

"And shall always be, William, in the years to come."

"The years to come . . ." His expression darkened and he saw the fear leap into her eyes. Again he was satisfied.

"William, you frighten me."

"We must be prepared for all eventualities," he said. "I do not go in peace to your father's kingdom. You must prepare yourself for that. And if it should please God that you should never see me again, it will be necessary for you to marry again."

"Do not speak of it, William. Such words pierce me to the heart."

"Then you must steel your heart, for you will be a Queen, Mary, if all goes as it must go for the sake of England and our Faith. I need not tell you that if you marry again your husband must not be a papist."

He turned away as he spoke for the stricken expression in her eyes moved him as she had never been able to move him before.

"I give you pain by this plain speaking, I fear," he said quietly. "But I do it only because of my strong convictions. Protestantism must be preserved in England."

She nodded.

Then she went to him and clung to him; for some seconds he remained unresponsive then he put his arms about her and held her against him.

"I have never loved anyone but you, William," she declared tearfully; and even as she spoke she saw the reproachful dark eyes of Frances that "dearest husband" who had remained a dear friend; she saw the jaunty ones of Jemmy and for a few revealing seconds she seemed to glimpse a different life, a life of gaiety and adventure which might have been hers if she had married him. She shut out these images. Dreams. Fantasies. Her life with William was the reality.

"William, William," she cried, "all these years I have been married and have no child. If God does not see fit to bless me with children there would be no reason for my marrying again."

She delighted him. This failure to produce a child she took upon herself; she did not hint as so many did that William was the one who had failed in that respect. She was a wonderful wife. Only now that he was leaving her did he realize how wonderful.

"I shall pray to God that I do not survive you, William. And if it does not please God to grant me a child by you I would not wish to have one by an angel!"

She was overflowing with her emotions, which on this occasion was pleasant.

"Your devotion pleases me, my dear wife," said William; and Mary believed she saw a glint of tears in his eyes.

Again she clung to him and he did not resist. His kisses were warmer than they had ever been before.

"You must live, William," she cried. "You cannot leave me now."

"If it is God's will," he said, "victory will be mine. We will share the throne. God willing, there are good years ahead of us."

They left the Honselaarsdijk Palace together and Mary accompanied him to the brink of the river and watched him embark.

Throughout Holland the people fasted as they prayed for their Prince's victory. There was consternation when no sooner had he set out than a tempest rose which scattered his fleet and forced it to return to port.

Mary was frantic with anxiety; her doctors implored her to consider her health; but it was necessary to bleed her and it was a letter from her husband asking her to come to Brill which revived her more than any remedies.

There William spent two hours with her. He told her that there was no real disaster to the fleet and the rumors were being greatly exaggerated in England; he was going to set out immediately but he had wanted to see her once more before he left.

"Oh, William," she cried, "how happy I am that you should spare me this time . . . but it only makes the parting more bitter."

"As soon as I have succeeded in my task I shall send for you."

She shivered slightly. She saw herself going to England, but she could only go on the defeat of her father. Her exultation in William's response to her affection had temporarily driven everything else from her mind; but she dreaded returning to the land of her birth, for how would she ever be able to forget her childhood?

"It will not be long, I trust. And should it go against me, you will know what to do."

He kissed her tenderly once more; and left her.

She went to the top of a tower to see the last of the fleet. Tears blinded her eyes.

It does not matter now, she thought; I can weep my fill for he is not here to be offended by my tears.

"God Save William," she prayed. "Bring him success."

She went back to her apartments and shut herself in to pray; but as she prayed for her husband's success she kept seeing images of her father, and her stepmother; she kept hearing the latter's voice appealing to her "dear Lemon" to remember her father and all his goodness to her. And she thought too of the newly-born child.

She could settle to nothing. She was continually on her knees. On waking she went to her private chapel and was again there at midday; at five o'clock she was back, and again at half past seven she attended a service.

Her prayers were all for William.

"But," she cried to her chaplain, "what a severe and cruel necessity lies before me! I must forsake a father or forsake my husband, my country, character, and God himself. It is written Honor thy father.... But should not a wife cleave to her husband, forsaking all others?"

She wept. Never, she declared, was a woman confronted by such a cruel decision.

But her dreams came to her help. Why should not her father continue to wear the crown and William be set up as Regent? Thus her father would not be deposed; her husband would rule, and England be saved from popery.

This dream helped her through those dark days.

William had landed safely at Torbay, and the news filled James with alarm. In desperation he sought to win the approval of those whom he had offended. Catholics were not to stand for Parliament; he would support the Church of England; he would restore officials in Church and State who had lost their places due to their opposition of his will.

He appealed for support against the Dutch invasion.

But James was as ineffectual as he had ever been. It was too late to turn his coat now. There were many in the country who, while they deplored his Catholic leanings, did not approve of his son-in-law's actions. They were asking themselves why William of Orange should be the one to take the crown which, if James and the Prince of Wales were to be dismissed, rightly belonged to his daughter Mary. There were some who did not care to see a daughter working for her father's downfall, however much the actions of that father were to be deplored.

But James failed to see that he still had a chance.

He was concerned for the safety of his wife and the Prince of Wales; in his anxiety he was ungracious. He sent the young Prince to Portsmouth and kept his wife in London, and decided to march west and deliver a knockout blow to the forces assembled there.

His daughter Anne was popular, and he was sure he would have her support; and he would never believe that Mary, his best loved, would work against him. No, he decided, this was the work of his nephew Orange, whom he had always hated. He cursed the day he had ever agreed to that marriage in which he saw the seed of all his troubles.

He rode to Salisbury.

The shock of the invasion had been too much for him. Everyone else it seemed had been expecting it, except him. He had refused to believe the Dutch had set sail even when his trusted spies told him so; and when the fleet had been scattered he had assured himself that that was the end of the fine dreams of the Prince of Orange!

Now William was actually in England and he was marching to destroy him. At Salisbury James's nose suddenly began to bleed so violently that he was forced to rest there before joining the army under Churchill at Warminster.

Churchill and Grafton were reckoned to be two of the finest soldiers in England. The Orange would not be able to stand up long against them.

He should be at Warminster now, conferring with Churchill, but must lie on his bed while they tried to stem the bleeding. He could rely on Churchill, who had received great good through Anne, whose great friend was Churchill's wife, Sarah.

He had good generals; he had his dear daughters on whom he would rely, for nothing would convince him that Mary did not deplore what her husband was doing. It had been an unhappy marriage; Orange had deceived her with Elizabeth Villiers. My dear Mary, he thought, when Orange is my prisoner, when he is no longer in possession of his head, you shall tell your old father of your troubles and he will seek to make you happy.

A messenger to see the king. A messenger from Warminster!

"Show him in. Doubtless he comes from Churchill."

"Your Majesty, Churchill is no longer at Warminster. He has left with his men..."

"Left? For what destination?"

"Torbay, Your Majesty. He is joining Orange. Grafton is with him. They have gone over to the enemy."

James lay back on his pillows.

He saw defeat very near.

Churchill gone! Grafton gone! And there was one other. Prince George of Denmark, husband of the Princess Anne, had joined with Churchill and Grafton. They no longer served the King of England but had gone to Orange.

"There is a conspiracy in my army," said James.

"Sire," was the answer, "you no longer have an army."

He must return to London, he must see his daughter at once.

She would comfort him. His dear Anne! Her husband was a traitor, even as Mary's was; but George had always been a weak fellow, never much use.

In desperation he rode toward his capital. When he had seen Anne his faith would be restored. They would stand together; the people loved her; she was a Protestant as William was; they would prefer to see her on the throne rather than this foreigner who had no right to it while Mary and Anne lived.

But in London came the last defeat.

The Princess Anne had left hurriedly with Lady Churchill.
He knew what this meant; his daughter had deserted him.

So they are both against me, mourned James. My little girls. My
Mary! My Anne!

He could see them so vividly—one dark, one fair, and he could recall
his delight in them.

Charles had envied him his children and they had brought great joy to
his life . . . when they were children and afterward.

He was a family man; the happiest times of his life, he believed,
had not been when he was with his mistresses, but in the center of his
family.

My daughters, he mourned, whom I loved with all my heart—and
they have placed themselves among my enemies.

Mary Beatrice tried to comfort him.

"They cannot succeed," she cried. "They are so wrong, so cruel. You
are the King."

"They do not intend that I shall remain so."

"You think they will make William King? Never! He is not the heir.
Even if they will not accept the Prince of Wales, Mary comes before him.
She is your daughter. She would never agree to take your place."

"He will set himself up with Mary. It was for this reason he married
her. Would to God I had never allowed the marriage."

"I am sure Mary will never agree to force you from your throne."

"Mary is his creature . . . Anne is against me. I have lost both my daughters."

"You have your wife," she told him. "You have your son."

"I bless the day you came to England."

She closed her eyes and momentarily thought of it; the fear of this roué whom she had grown to love; the years of jealousy; and she was almost glad that he was brought so low for she was the one who could help him now; his mistresses could give him nothing but passing pleasure; she could give him unfaltering love and devotion.

"What should I do without you?" he asked.

"What should we do without each other?"

She saw that a slip of paper had been pushed under the door and withdrawing herself from his arms went to it.

It was a lampoon about the Prince of Wales having been brought to her bed in a warming pan.

She dropped it to the floor with a cry of distaste. James picked it up and read it.

"We are in danger," he said. "You and the boy must leave England without delay."

The Queen and the Prince of Wales had fled to France. Before the end of the year James had followed them. This was success beyond that for which they had dared hope. William was in London, and it would not be long before Mary must join him.

She was afraid.

There was no longer need to pray for William's safety, the revolution was over. The people had accepted William, although Mary was the Queen. William's position would depend on her, but he had no qualms; nor need he have. All that he desired should be his.

And now Mary must prepare herself for the great ordeal. What would she find on her arrival in England?

She did not want to think too much of it; yet she must make ready.

Elizabeth Villiers would make ready too. She had been calm and self-effacing during the difficult weeks, withdrawing herself from Mary's society as much as possible. She would of course leave for England when Mary went and both of them could not help wondering what her position would be when she was there.

Would William after the long absence have forgotten his mistress? Mary believed he would; his new responsibilities would be great; and she, Mary, would be the Queen, and he the King, to rule through her grace. He would not forget that; and surely he would not insult the Queen by continuing to keep a mistress?

No, thought Mary, this would be the end of Elizabeth's influence.

Elizabeth knew otherwise. While he lived, she was certain, he would never do without her.

She, far more than Mary, eagerly awaited the call.

Elizabeth and her sister Anne had not been on good terms since Bentinck had quarreled with William over his treatment of Mary; Anne had of course sided with her husband, which Elizabeth looked upon as treason in the family. They had tried to turn William away from her toward his own wife. She could not forgive that.

She envied Anne her children—there were five of them—and her happy married life; but of course she would not have exchanged her own lot for that of her sister, for although her position was precarious the adventure and ambition involved delighted her.

Anne had been ill for the past year; she had suffered great pain and one evening this so increased that all those about her knew she was near her end.

She asked for Mary who went to her at once and when Mary saw her friend's condition she was horrified.

She sank on her knees by the bed and took Anne's hand.

"My dearest friend," she cried, "let me pray with you."

Anne said: "If I could but see my husband . . ."

"Our husbands are together, Anne. I would I could bring yours to you, but he left Holland in the service of the Prince."

"They are in England now. Oh . . . do you remember . . . ?"

"I remember so much of England."

"I am going, Your Highness . . ."

"Let us pray together, Anne."

"Later. There is much I have to say. My children . . ."

"Do not fear for them. I will see that they are cared for."

"I thank you. I shall go in peace since you promise me that. Commend me to my husband and the Prince . . ."

Mary looked up and through her tears saw Elizabeth Villiers standing some distance from the bed.

She went to her and said: "Your sister is dying. Should you not make your peace with her before she goes?"

"I do not know if that is her wish."

Mary went back to the bed. "Elizabeth is here. She wishes to be friends. You must not die unreconciled."

"Elizabeth . . ." murmured Anne.

Mary beckoned Elizabeth to come to the bed, and she stood on one side, Mary on the other.

"Elizabeth," said Anne, "do you remember the days at Richmond?"

"I remember."

"Come closer, so that I may see you."

Elizabeth knelt by the bed.

"There is so much to remember . . . Richmond . . . Holland . . . I found great happiness in Holland. Elizabeth, you too, but you will not if . . ."

She was finding her breathing difficult and Mary whispered: "Rest, dear Anne. Do not disturb yourself. All is well between us all."

The eyes of Elizabeth and Mary met across the deathbed of Anne Bentinck. Mary's were appealing; Elizabeth's as enigmatic as ever.

But later, when they were still there and they knew that the end was very near, Mary saw the tears silently falling down Elizabeth's cheeks.

It was February—three months since she had said good-bye to William.

There was no excuse for a longer delay. Admiral Herbert had arrived with a yacht to take her to England. And this was good-bye to Holland; this was the end of one phase of her life. She was going to England to be a Queen and she was uneasy.

She had to take a Crown which, in truth, was her father's; it was only because it had been forcibly taken from him that it was hers.

What would she find in England? How would the people receive an ungrateful daughter?

I shall be with William again, she told herself. What greater joy could there be for me than that?

No sooner had she stepped aboard than a storm arose and it was necessary to stay in the Maas for the rest of the day; but at last they set sail and she stood on deck watching for the first glimpse of her native land.

With what emotion she saw those cliffs; she tried to tell herself that this was the utmost joy.

Then she was aware of Elizabeth Villiers; her eyes were fixed on the approaching land with a smile as though she too were asking herself what the new life would bring, and she was confident of her future.

Mary dressed with care, for the first meeting with William. She wore a purple gown with a low bodice about which muslin was draped; her petticoat was orange velvet; there were pearls at her throat and her dark hair was piled high above her head and its darkness accentuated by the orange ribbons she wore.

She was pleased with her appearance. She looked like a Queen returning to her Kingdom. There was no hint of sadness. There must not be, for that was something which would displease William.

They were sailing up the once familiar river and there was the great city spread out before them. At Whitehall stairs William would be waiting to greet her.

There was music coming from the banks, but she kept hearing the words of a lampoon which had reached her even in Holland and she asked herself how many of those people who had clustered on the banks to watch her arrival were singing it now.

Yet worse than cruel scornful Goneril, thou;
She took but what her monarch did allow
But thou, most impious, robbest thy father's brow.

"Father," she murmured, "it had to be. It was for William. You are to blame . . . you only. It need never have been. But now it is and I fear that even if William loves me as he seemed to promise—for have I not brought him what he most desired—I shall never forget what we have done to you."

Away melancholy thoughts!

How gay was the scene—the air bright with frost and gay with music. Cheers for the Queen who had come from Holland to rule them!

The new King was a mean-looking fellow—stooping, hooked-nosed, and small; he gave no sign of pleasure in his people; he did not care for shows and pomp; he had ridden into London for the first time in a closed carriage because it was raining. Not the man the English would have chosen for their King.

But here was the Queen—buxom and beautiful, smiling and seeming gay, orange ribbons shining in her coiled dark hair.

William had stepped forward to greet her. For the second time she saw the tears in his eyes. He embraced her, and the people looked on.

She thought: For William's sake, everything is worthwhile.

So amid the cheers and the music they left Whitehall stairs—Mary and William, and somewhere in the company, Elizabeth Villiers.

They had seen each other, Elizabeth and William; they had exchanged a glance, and Elizabeth was satisfied.

Mary was not thinking of Elizabeth as she went ashore. She was reunited with William. They were together until death parted them.

A great task confronted them which would draw them closer together.

She would cease to listen to refrains about ungrateful daughters; she would not concern herself with the presence of Elizabeth Villiers.

The bells were ringing out. The people were shouting: "Long live William and Mary."

A new reign had begun.

Bibliography

Aubrey, William Hickman Smith *History of England*

Bathurst, Lt.-Col. The Hon. Benjamin *Letters of Two Queens*

Bray, William, ed. *Diary of John Evelyn*

Bryant, Arthur *King Charles II*

Burnet, Bishop *History of His Own Time*, with notes by the Earls of
    Dartmouth and Hardwicke and Speaker Onslow, to which are
    added the cursory remarks of Swift Chapman, Hester W.
    Mary II, Queen of England

Dasent, Arthur Irwin *The Private Life of Charles II*

Loth, David *Royal Charles: Ruler and Rake*

Oman, Carola *Mary of Modena*

Pepys, Samuel *Diary and Correspondence* edited by Henry B. Wheatley

Sandars, Mary F. *Princess and Queen of England: Life of Mary II*

Sells, A. Lytton *The Memoirs of James II* (translated from the Bouillon
    manuscript, edited and collated with the Clarke Edition, with an
    introduction by Sir Arthur Bryant)

Senior, Dorothy *The Gay King*

Stephen, Sir Leslie, and Sir Sidney Lee, eds. *The Dictionary of National
    Biography*

Strickland, Agnes *Lives of the Queens of England*

Trevelyan, G. M. *England Under the Stuarts*

Trevelyan, G. M. *English Social History*

Trevelyan, G. M. *History of England*

Wade, John *British History*

Macauley, Lord, edited by Lady Trevelyan *The History of England* from
    the Accession of James II

ROYAL SISTERS

A HUSBAND FOR ANNE

The Princess Anne, walking slowly through the tapestry room in St. James's Palace—for it was a lifetime's habit never to hurry—smiled dreamily at the silken pictures representing the love of Venus and Mars which had been recently made for her uncle, the King. Tucked inside the bodice of her gown was a note; she had read it several times; and now she was taking it to her private apartments to read it again.

Venus and Mars! she thought, Goddess and God, and great lovers. But she was certain that there had never been lovers like Anne of York and John Sheffield, Earl of Mulgrave, Princess and Poet.

Her lips moved as she repeated the words he had written

Of all mankind I loved the best
A nymph so far above the rest
That we outshine the Blest above
In beauty she, as I in love.

No one could have written more beautifully of Venus than John Shef-field had written of her.

What had happened to Venus and Mars? she wondered idly. She had never paid attention to her lessons; it had been so easy to complain that her eyes hurt or she had a headache when she was expected to study. Mary—dear Mary!—had warned her that she would be sorry she was so lazy, but she had not been sorry yet, always preferring ignorance to effort; everyone had indulged her, far more than they had poor Mary who had been forced to marry that hateful Prince of Orange. Anne felt miserable remembering Mary's face swollen from so many tears. Dear sister Mary, who had always learned her lesssons and been the good girl; and what had been her reward? Banishment from her own country, sent away from her family, and married to that horrid little man, the Orange, as they called him—or more often Caliban, the Dutch Monster.

The exquisitely sculptured Tudor arch over the fireplace commemo-rated two more lovers whose entwined initials were H and A. Henry the VIII and Anne Boleyn had not remained constant lovers. That was indeed a gloomy thought and the Princess Anne made a habit of shrugging aside what was not pleasant.

She turned from the tapestry room and went to her own apartments. Delighted to find none of her women there, she sat in the window seat and took out the paper.

Soon, the whole Court would be reading the poem, but they would not know that those words were written for her. They would say: "Mul-grave writes a pretty verse." And only she would know.

But it was not always going to be so. Why should they hide their passion?

Her father had always been indulgent, and she preferred to believe he would continue so. Her uncle too, but state policy could come into this—as it had with Mary.

Anne was suddenly frightened, remembering that terrifying day when Mary had come to her, bewildered, like a sleepwalker. "Anne, they are forcing me to marry our cousin Orange."

Matters of state! A Princess's duty! Those words which meant that the free and easy life was over. An indulgent father and a kind uncle were yet Duke of York and King of England; and matters of state must take precedence over family feeling.

Anne refused to consider failure. It was a trait in her character which had often exasperated Mary. Anne believed what she wanted to believe, so now she believed she would be allowed to marry Mulgrave.

Reaching her apartment she went at once to the window and, as she had expected, she saw him in the courtyard below, where he had been walking backward and forward hoping for a glimpse of her.

They smiled at each other. He was not only the most handsome man in her uncle's Court, thought Anne, but in the world.

"Wait!" Her lips formed the words; he could not hear, of course, but with the extra sense of a lover, he understood.

She turned from the window, picked up a cloak, wrapped it round her, and pulled the hood over her head. It would help to conceal her identity. Unhurriedly she went down to the courtyard.

He ran to her and took both her hands.

"We must not stay here," she said.

"But we must talk."

She nodded and drew him to an alcove in the stone wall; here they could remain hidden from anyone crossing the courtyard.

"My poem . . ." he began.

"It was beautiful."

"Did you understand what the lines meant?"

"I think I understand," she said.

He quoted:

"And therefore They who could not bear
To be outdone by mortals here,
Among themselves have placed her now.
And left me wretched here below."

"It sounds as though she's dead," said Anne.

"It is symbolic. I daren't tell the truth. You *are* so far above me . . . a Princess. What hope have I . . ."

"You should always hope."

"You cannot mean . . ."

"I think they want me to be happy."

"And you would be happy?"

Anne never troubled to hide her feelings; she was always frankly herself.

"I want to marry you," she said.

Mulgrave caught his breath with joy, and surprise.

Marriage with the Princess Anne! That thought had entered his head, of course, but he scarcely dared hope. Why, if Charles had no legitimate child—and it seemed unlikely that he would—and James had no son, which also seemed a possibility, and Mary remained childless, well then it would be the Princess Anne's turn. The prospect was dazzling. Married to the Queen of England! She was not an arrogant woman; one only had to look into that fresh-colored face, those eyes which, owing to some opthalmic trouble which had been with her since childhood, gave her a helpless look, at that body which was already showing signs of indulgence at the table, to realize that her air of placidity was an absolute expression of her true nature. She would be easy going, lazy—a comfortable wife even though she were a Queen.

No wonder he was in love with Anne.

He shook his head. "They would never allow it."

She smiled at him fondly. "If I begged and pleaded . . ."

"You would do that?"

"For you," she told him.

He drew her toward him and kissed her almost wonderingly. She was delightful—gentle, yielding, frankly adoring, and a Princess! He, of course, was a very ambitious man, but this seemed too much good fortune. He must not let her delude him into the belief that it would be easy to marry her.

It was a pleasant state of affairs when ambition and pleasure were so admirably linked. Ever since he had become Gentleman of the Bedchamber to Anne's father he had observed the royal family at close quarters and consequently knew a great deal about their weaknesses. No one in the country could help being aware of James's position at this time for already his brother the King had thought it wise to send him into exile on more than one occasion and the Bill, the object of which was to exclude James from the succession, was being discussed not only in Parliament but in every town and village.

Mulgrave had served with the fleet against the Dutch and been appointed captain of a troop of horse. The Duke of York was inclined to favor him; but what would his reactions be when he knew he aspired to marry his daughter?

Looking into the eager face of seventeen-year-old Anne he believed she was too simple—or too determined to have her way—to see the enormous difficulties which lay before them.

He caught her hands. "We must be careful," he said.

"Oh, yes. We must be careful."

"This must be our secret . . . for a while."

She understood that.

"It would not do for His Majesty to know what is in our minds."

"He has always been so kind to me," she told him.

Kind, yes. Kindness was second nature to the King. He would smile at Anne, pat her hand, tell her he was delighted she had a lover; and immediately begin to arrange a marriage of state for her. In one respect Anne was a little like her uncle. There was a laziness in both natures which made them long for a peaceful existence and capable of doing almost anything to achieve it.

Charles was not very pleased with the Earl of Mulgrave at this time because he knew that Mulgrave had helped to increase the strife which existed between James and Charles's illegitimate son, the Duke of Monmouth. It had become difficult for Charles to banish his brother and not send Monmouth away also; so Monmouth had been exiled too. Charles had seen the necessity, but he remembered that Mulgrave had helped to exacerbate relations between the two Dukes and when he knew of this greatest ambition of all, he might decide he had been too lenient.

Mulgrave wondered how to impress on Anne the need to be very cautious while not letting her believe that marriage between them was quite out of the question. Gentle and yielding as she was to him, so would she be to others; and if it were pointed out to her that she must take a foreign Prince as a husband, would she placidly smile and accept her fate?

"But you understand, my Princess, that we must be very, very careful . . ."

He stopped and gave a little gasp, for someone had stepped into the alcove.

A rather shrill voice said: "Ah, Madam, I have searched and searched for you."

Mulgrave was horrified. Here he was, caught with the Princess Anne in his arms; but Anne merely laughed.

"It's only Sarah," she said. "My *dearest* Sarah how you frightened me!"

"Apologies; Madam. But I thought I should warn you. You are being somewhat indiscreet."

"We thought no one would see us here."

"*I* saw you."

"Oh, but Sarah, you are the one who sees all." Anne was smiling at her lover. "John," she went on, gently, "all is well. It is only my dearest friend who would never bring me anything but good. Sarah, you, who are happily married yourself, will understand."

"I understand, Madam, but at the same time I tremble."

"Tremble! You, Sarah! When did you ever tremble?"

"For myself, never. For you, Madam . . . often."

"You see, John, what a good friend she is to me? I am fortunate indeed

to have two such . . . friends. John has been telling me, Sarah, that we have
to be very careful not to betray ourselves. What say you?"

"I should say he is right," said Sarah. "And the best way, Madam, if
you will excuse my saying so, is *not* to embrace in the courtyards."

"We were well hidden from sight."

"H'm," said Sarah sharply. She peered up at Mulgrave. "You are silent,
my lord."

"My dear lady, you seem well equipped to keep the conversation alive."

Anne smiled fondly from one to the other. "You must know that I
want you two to be friends."

"Anyone who is Madam's friend is my friend," said Sarah.

Mulgrave put in: "That is a great relief."

"And now," went on Sarah, "I think, Madam, that I should conduct
you to your apartments. I will keep watch while you say your farewells."

With that she turned her back on them and for a moment they clung
to each other.

"John," whispered Anne, "what shall we do?"

"Nothing . . . as yet," he told her. "We must think of a way."

"Yes, John. You think of a way . . . but think quickly."

"I have only one desire in my life."

"And I."

Sarah said without turning her head: "I think I hear footsteps
approaching. It would be well to go now."

The lovers looked longingly at each other for a few more seconds;
then John dropped Anne's hand and she went to Sarah.

Mulgrave watched the two young women walk into the palace.

In the Princess's apartments Anne was telling Sarah about her love
for Mulgrave. Sarah was displeased; she had learned of this through her

own indefatigable efforts as she would always discover any intrigue; but it was disturbing that Anne had not confided in her, for it was unlike the Princess to exclude her from her secrets.

Although Sarah was lady-in-waiting to the Duchess of York, she was constantly in the company of the Princess Anne; and before Mulgrave had enchanted the Princess, Sarah had been more important to her than anyone. Sarah was piqued, but she did not show it. Arrogant and overbearing as she invariably was to others, she was careful in her approach to Anne.

Little fool! thought Sarah. Her sister Mary has a husband, and I have a husband; therefore *she* must have one. She always had to imitate, not having a mind of her own.

So she had chosen to fall in love with the Earl of Mulgrave—an ambitious young man, if ever Sarah saw one; and she was not going to tolerate ambitious people about the Princess, particularly those who would have more influence than Sarah Churchill.

She did not tell her this now; instead she pretended to be pleased.

Anne was explaining how she had loved him from the first moment she had seen him. "And the fact that his name was John . . . like your dear husband's . . . endeared him to me, Sarah."

"Ah, Madam, you always wish to do as I do."

"Mary used to say I imitated her. Alas, I can no longer imitate my dear sister."

"Nor should you wish to, Madam, seeing that the Princess of Orange spends a great deal of her time in tears."

"Poor, poor Mary, married to that hateful creature."

"Caliban!" said Sarah venomously.

"I pity Mary," said Anne, her lips trembling.

"Pity can do her no good, Madam. Let us hope that *you* never have to make a marriage of state."

"It will not be necessary," said Anne complacently. "Mary has done that. I believe I can persuade my father to let me marry for love."

"It will not rest with your father," Sarah reminded her grimly. "Remember the position he is in."

"Poor Papa!"

Poor Papa, indeed! thought Sarah. His future was not very certain. If this Bill succeeded and he was excluded from the throne, unless he had a son it would be the turn of Mary. And after that . . . Anne.

Sarah was a woman who had to make her way in the world by means of her own wits, and she constantly thanked God that they were sharp ones. She had to fight for herself and her John and she was going to find such a niche for them that would be the envy of the country. Both she and John had come to their present hopeful positions by great good luck; they must work hard to keep them.

John had been wise to choose her for his wife; and she had also chosen wisely. She would make him the greatest soldier in the world; yes, and have the world recognize him as such.

But that meant playing the game of life very carefully; knowing your luck for what it was and exploiting it.

Sarah had been a little shocked when she realized how far the Mulgrave affair had gone; not that she was alarmed; she was certain it could not go much farther. For one thing, she, Sarah Churchill, would not allow it.

"However," went on Sarah, "the King is kind to lovers."

"Oh, Sarah," laughed Anne, "how right you are! And so he should be."

"But," went on Sarah sternly, "for the time, you must be careful. This must go no farther than letters and an occasional meeting with another present."

"You, Sarah, of course."

"There is no one else you can trust."

"Oh, Sarah, how wonderful to have you to look after me! All will be well, I am sure. When you think they might have married me to that hateful George who, to my mind, was as bad—or almost—as poor Mary's Orange."

Prince George of Hanover! thought Sarah. She had been alarmed when that possibility had arisen. She had not liked the little German, who could not speak a word of English and gave the impression that he was not going to try. He was small of stature and uncouth in manners.

Ugh! shivered Sarah. And what place would there have been for John and Sarah Churchill at Hanover? She was glad *that* had come to nothing.

"A most distasteful man!" she muttered.

Then she remembered that Anne had been complacent enough. Of course Mulgrave had not appeared on the scene at that time; but Anne had shown no qualms, although the creature was so repulsive and would have carried her off to Hanover.

Anne was adaptable. That was why she was such an excellent mistress for an ambitious woman to serve. Serve! Proud Sarah was not one to serve. She wanted to guide her mistress into giving all that was best to Sarah Churchill, that Sarah might make use of it for John, and this clever couple become the most powerful people in the world.

She was not even in the service of Anne, but that of Mary of Modena, Duchess of York, so she would not have accompanied the Princess to Hanover. Nor had she had any intention of going—although with the Duke and Duchess so unpopular that they must periodically be banished from England, she could not see clearly ahead. If the Duke of York were King it would be good to be in the service of his wife; and to be in the service of Anne might mean that one were sent anywhere in the world if she made a foreign marriage—as the Princess Mary had been sent to Holland.

To play this game now was like walking a tightrope, but Sarah knew she was capable of coming safely across.

"Write your love letters," said Sarah. "I will see that they are delivered. Then . . . in time . . . we must think of a plan."

Anne threw herself into her friend's arms.

"I am thinking of all I owe you, Sarah," said Anne.

Sarah was thinking: She grows fatter than ever.

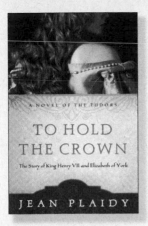

**Read all of the Tudor novels
in historical order published
by Three Rivers Press**

1

To Hold the Crown
The Story of King Henry VII
and Elizabeth of York
$14.95 PAPERBACK
978-0-307-34619-3

2

Katharine of Aragon
The Story of a Spanish Princess
and an English Queen
$16.00 PAPERBACK
978-0-609-81025-5

3

Murder Most Royal
The Story of Anne Boleyn
and Catherine Howard
$14.95 PAPERBACK
978-1-4000-8249-0

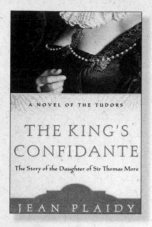

The King's Confidante
The Story of the Daughter
of Sir Thomas More
$13.95 PAPERBACK
978-0-307-34620-9
Previously published as
St. Thomas's Eve

4

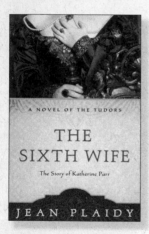

The Sixth Wife
The Story of Katherine Parr
$13.95 PAPERBACK
978-0-609-81026-2

5

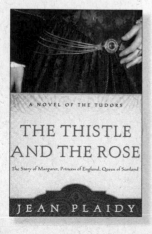

The Thistle and the Rose
The Story of Margaret, Princess
of England, Queen of Scotland
$13.95 PAPERBACK
978-0-609-81022-4

6

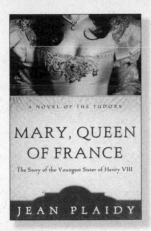

Mary, Queen of France
The Story of the Youngest Sister
of Henry VIII
$12.95 PAPERBACK
978-0-609-81021-7

7

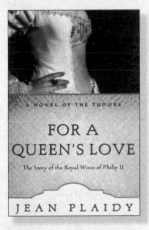

For a Queen's Love
The Story of the Royal Wives
of Philip II
$14.00 PAPERBACK
978-0-307-34622-3
previously published as
The Spanish Bridegroom

8

A Favorite of the Queen
The Story of Lord Robert Dudley
and Elizabeth I
$14.00 PAPERBACK
978-0-307-34623-0
previously published as
Gay Lord Robert

9

Read all of the Stuart novels
in historical order

www.threeriverspress.com

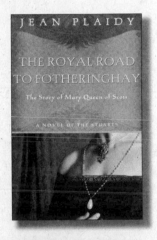

The Royal Road to Fotheringhay
The Story of Mary Queen of Scots
$15.00 PAPERBACK
978-0-609-81023-1

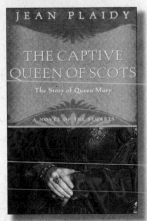

The Captive Queen of Scots
The Story of Queen Mary
$14.95 PAPERBACK
978-1-4000-8251-3

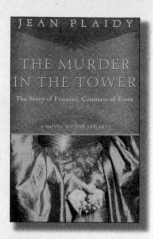

The Murder in the Tower
The Story of Frances,
Countess of Essex
$14.00 PAPERBACK
978-0-307-34621-6

3

The Loves of Charles II
The Stuart Saga
$16.00 PAPERBACK
978-1-4000-8248-3

Previously published as
three separate volumes:
The Wandering Prince
Health Unto His Majesty
Here Lies Our Sovereign Lord

4

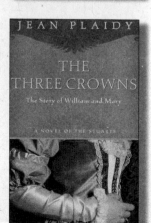

The Three Crowns
The Story of William and Mary
$14.00 PAPERBACK
978-0-307-34624-7

5

ROYAL
SISTERS

Royal Sisters
The Story of the
Daughters of James II
$15.00 PAPERBACK
978-0-307-71952-2

previously published
as *The Haunted Sisters*

COMING SPRING 2011!

6

COURTING
HER
HIGHNESS

Courting Her Highness
The Story of Queen Anne
$16.00 PAPERBACK
978-0-307-71951-5

Previously published as
The Queen's Favourites

COMING SUMMER 2011!

7